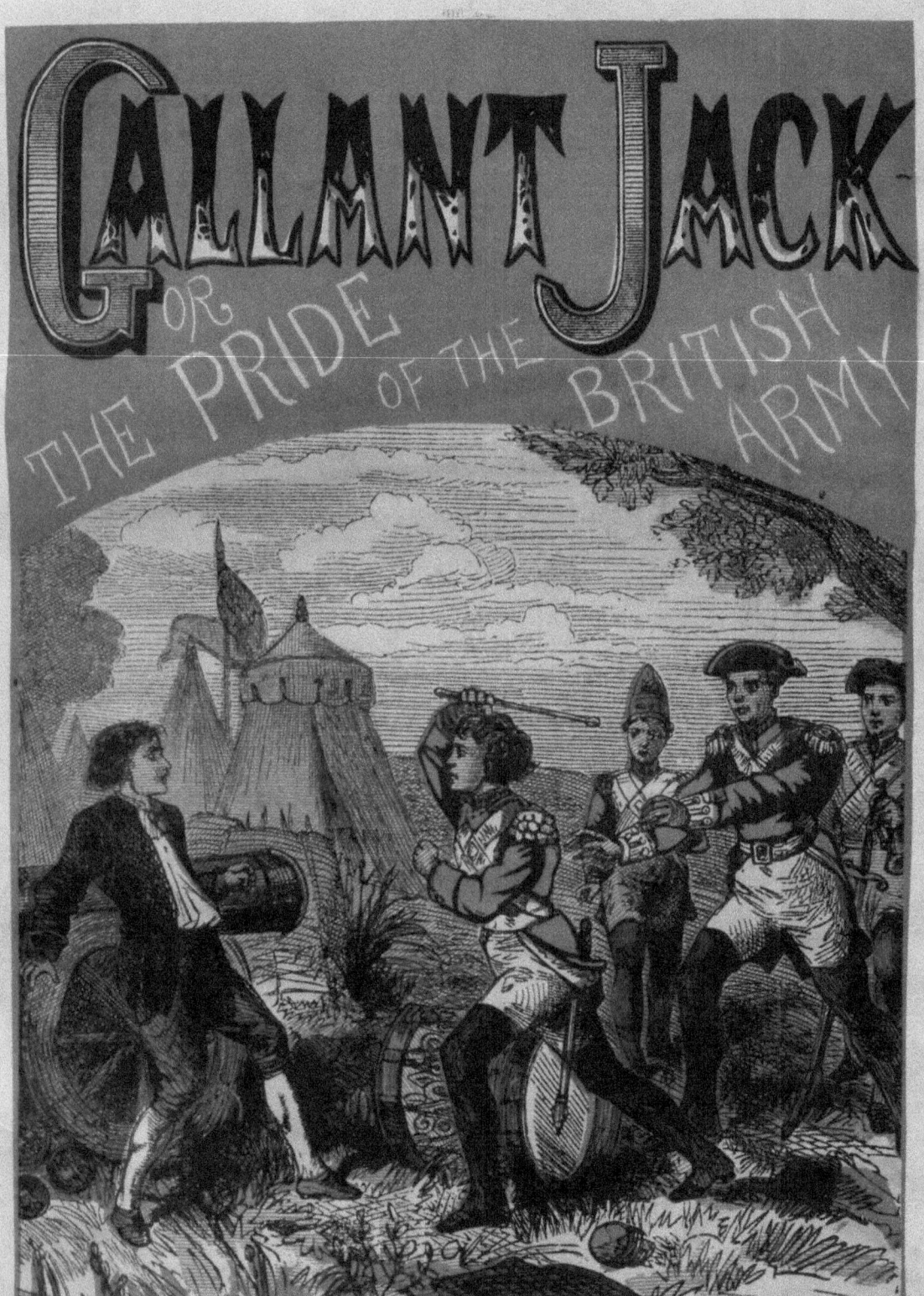

GALLANT JACK;

OR,

THE PRIDE OF THE BRITISH ARMY.

———•———

WITH NUMEROUS ILLUSTRATIONS.

COMPLETE IN ONE VOLUME.

———•———

LONDON :
PUBLISHED BY EDWIN J. BRETT,
173, FLEET STREET, E.C.

GALLANT JACK;

OR,

THE PRIDE OF THE BRITISH ARMY.

"BRING THE BOY HERE, SERGEANT," SAID THE GENERAL.

GALLANT JACK;

OR,

THE PRIDE OF THE BRITISH ARMY.

CHAPTER I.

ON THE EVE OF BATTLE.

IT was the 6th of July, in the year 1702.

The summer sun, which had shone in unclouded splendour during the day, had disappeared in a flood of crimson glory behind the western horizon.

Night was falling grey and chill, and the mists were slowly ascending the slope of the Hoendenberg, a frontier fortress of the Netherland town of Nimeguen, where the British army lay encamped.

War had been declared against France, and a portion of the English troops, having reached Nimeguen, awaited there the arrival of the remainder of their numbers.

The famous John Churchill, Earl of Marlborough—famous alike in war and peace—was with them—their general.

His name was like a tower of strength to the British arms.

As the day declined, the solitary wail of the bugle was heard floating through the evening mists.

The sentinels had been changed, the pickets placed, and the picket guards stationed at their posts. All was in order for the night.

The camp was perfectly quiet.

Probably many slumbered soundly.

But there was one who slept not.

This one was the Earl of Marlborough.

Wrapped in his cloak, with his night glass in his hand, he stood on the slope of the ascent, with his vigilant eyes turned in the direction from which he expected the reinforcements to arrive.

Near him was one attired in a long frieze coat, who stood silent and motionless at a short distance, leaning on his musket.

Presently the general spoke.

"The scouts should have returned ere this," he said.

"Yes, general," replied the other, in a respectful tone.

"From their delay, they will doubtless bring important intelligence "

"Doubtless, general. That our brave troops have landed, for instance, and are now advancing."

"Or that the French are on the march which is equally likely," returned the commander.

"Well, general, if they come, I dare say we shall know how to receive them," was the cheerful reply.

The general smiled as he answered—

"hey must not come yet, friend Benjamin. Let our reinforcements first arrive; then let them advance, if they dare."

"You know best, general," responded the soldier.

From this brief colloquy, it will be seen that there existed between the Earl of Marlborough and the man whom he addressed so familiarly an unusual degree of friendship.

Benjamin Crank had served in several of the earl's campaigns.

From being a drummer boy, he had risen to be a sergeant of infantry.

He had attracted the earl's notice from his unflinching courage.

On more than one occasion he had, at the hazard of his life, conveyed important dispatches through a raking fire of musketry from one wing of the army to the other.

No peril could deter the gallant sergeant from what he felt to be his duty.

It was enough for his general to say "Do this," and he did it.

Sergeant Crank had more than once been offered a commission, but had respectfully declined.

Presently the sound of a bugle was faintly heard in the distance.

"Hark!" exclaimed the commander, in a gratified tone, "there is news at hand."

A few moments later the bugle note was repeated.

The sound of a horse's hoofs became audible, and a dragoon dashed up the ascent at full speed.

Without dismounting from his reeking steed he saluted his superior, and said at once—

"The French are on the march, general."

"As I expected," returned Marlborough, with perfect calmness; "how near are they?"

"About four leagues off on the borders of a forest, which lies to the right of their route, where they will halt for the night."

"Too near, too near," murmured the general to himself.

He paused a moment, and then asked—

"You are sure they will halt?"

"Quite sure, general; I heard the orders given to the advanced guard."

"There may yet be time, then," said the earl to himself.

Hardly had he expressed this opinion when again a distant bugle was heard.

Twice the note was repeated, and then was heard the ring and rattle of hoofs.

The blue eyes of the general lighted up with something more than their usual fire, whilst Benjamin Crank stretched his neck several inches beyond his black leather stock, in his anxiety to catch a glimpse of the approaching horseman.

Onward he came rapidly, heedless of the steep slope or the darkness, till he reined in his steed before the earl.

"Your news, quick," cried the latter.

"Good news, general," exclaimed the scout, breathless with his headlong ride; "twenty thousand English troops have landed, and are rapidly advancing under cover of the darkness."

The earl made no reply.

He was considering his position.

At length he turned to the dragoon who had first arrived, and said, inquiringly—

"Know you the number of the French forces?"

"From what I could gather, general, they are estimated at more than sixty thousand," was the reply.

"Too many, too many," exclaimed the earl.

Then he beckoned to the sergeant.

With two mighty strides Benjamin Crank was at his commander's side.

"The reinforcements are advancing to join us," said the earl, in a low tone to him.

"So I heard, general," replied Crank.

"From the present position of the foe they cannot fail to be perceived as they march by, and such a *contretemps* at the present juncture might be fatal to our success."

"Certainly, general," assented the sergeant.

"It is absolutely necessary," the earl continued, "that they should pass without hazarding an engagement."

"Absolutely?"

"They must—mark me—must reach here by the morning, and there is only one plan by which this can be accomplished."

"What is that, general?"

"The attention of the enemy must be engaged by a *ruse de guerre*."

"I see, general," eagerly exclaimed Benjamin; "might I ask to be allowed to undertake this little job?"

"It is my intention to entrust you with it, for I know no one more dependable than yourself," replied the earl.

The sergeant's florid, good-natured face beamed with chivalrous enthusiasm.

"God bless your honour," he exclaimed, fervently; "if I don't carry out your wishes to the letter, I'll eat my three-cornered hat first, and swallow my bayonet afterwards."

"I have every confidence," said the general,

with a smile. "You know the position of the French?"

"Exactly, your grace; on the right of the wood."

"Under cover of the trees and the darkness you can easily harass them."

"Nothing easier, general; you may trust me to occupy the attention of the mounseers so thoroughly that they shall be able to look after nothing but number one till the reinforcements have passed."

"Do that, and all will be well," said the earl; "you will take with you a regiment of five hundred men, and, if possible, lose none of them."

"Not half a one, general, if I can help it."

No more words passed.

In less than a quarter of an hour Sergeant Crank and his troop were in rapid march towards the road.

CHAPTER II.

THE MURDER IN THE WOOD.

It was through the very wood on the borders of which the French were encamped, and towards which the English were advancing, four persons were threading their lonely way.

These were a man and a woman and two children.

By the light of the torch the first of these carried, it could be seen that the man was some three or four and thirty years of age.

Handsome, and of the English type of countenance, but now looking terribly haggard and careworn.

His companion, some years younger than himself, was exceedingly beautiful, with long dishevelled tresses of yellow hair hanging down her back.

One of the children was a little girl, whom she carried in her arms.

The other a pretty dark-eyed boy of about eight years old, who trudged along manfully by the side of his parents, although it was evident that his strength was well-nigh exhausted.

There was something in the general appearance of these travellers which seemed to suggest that they were fugitives.

They continued their journey, but not very rapidly.

At length, after proceeding some distance, the bearer of the torch came to a halt and looked scrutinisingly around him.

"I think we must be near the spot," he said, after a moment.

Just then the sound of bugles and the hum of voices reached them from the French camp.

The lady shuddered involuntarily and clasped her husband.

"Let us not remain here, dear Edward," she said, entreatingly; "let us go on."

"Nay, love, there is nothing to fear," replied her husband soothingly; "besides, I promised to meet my cousin Grimsby."

"Oh, I fear him," said his wife, shuddering again. "I'm sure he means you no good."

"My dearest Ruth, you wrong him. Would he have contrived my escape from a French prison, when he might have left me there to starve or die, if he wished me evil?"

"His motive, at least, was a mercenary one, since you are to pay him for his service," urged his wife.

"But since I agreed to certain terms, it is but honourable that I should adhere to them."

"I do not wish you to break your word," said Ruth; "far from it. But when we reach the English lines at Nimeguen, we shall be safe then, and you could send him the money from thence."

"What, in time of war, when the only acknowledgment of my payment might be a bullet in the heart of my messenger? No, Ruth; as I promised to meet him here, I intend to keep my word."

"Pray Heaven, my dear, confiding husband, you may not repent your confidence," Ruth replied; "but he who is renegade to his country is not a man to trust as a friend."

"I have no fear, love; but since you seem to dread my cousin so greatly, do you remain here till I have seen and spoken to him."

"I do not dread him while I am by your side," said Ruth; "and I will go with you."

"No, dearest; on second thoughts I would rather you should not. Wait for me here."

Embracing his wife and son affectionately, and imprinting a kiss upon the rosy cheek of his infant daughter, who slumbered in her mother's arms, Edward Barrington walked forward to the spot where he had appointed to meet his cousin, followed, unknown to him, by his little son.

He had scarcely reached the spot when the crackling of twigs was heard.

A light flashed through the surrounding gloom, and a dark, stern, sallow-looking man, in the uniform of a French cavalry officer, was seen advancing torch in hand.

He came forward in silence, with his brows knitted, and an evil expression in his face.

"Welcome, cousin," said Edward Barrington, in as cheerful a tone as he could assume; "I have to thank you that I am here."

Without returning his greeting, the other said, hastily—

"Spare your thanks. Have you brought the money?"

"Yes, and there is the five hundred pounds in notes."

As he spoke, he took a roll of notes from his pocket, and handed them to his cousin.

The latter, having hastily examined them, thrust them into his vest.

Then, peering around him, he said—

"Is your wife with you?"

"She is not far off," replied Edward, "and now, having kept faith with you, I will bid you farewell and rejoin her."

He was about to turn away, when the other cried—

"Stop, not so fast."

Edward Barrington turned and looked at him, surprised at his imperative tone.

He was still more surprised at the expression of deadly malignance on his face, and he said—

"I am at a loss to understand the meaning of your words and looks."

"I will explain," returned the other with a demoniac grin; "you forget you are an escaped prisoner."

"Set free by you in consideration of a sum which you have received."

His cousin uttered a sardonic laugh.

"Detected by me in the act of flight, you mean," he said, mockingly.

As he spoke, he called over his shoulder to someone behind.

"Quick, there! Advance, men, and arrest this traitor."

Several soldiers, already posted behind the trees, rushed forward and secured him.

In an instant, in spite of his struggles, he was a prisoner, with his arms and ankles pinioned with ropes.

"Gasper Grimsby, you are a villain!" cried his cousin, breathless with indignation.

"You are a fool, which is worse," returned Gasper, in a tone of contempt, "to suppose that I should connive at the escape of an enemy of France."

"False traitor, you turn against your own country, your own friend, your own kindred."

Gasper Grimsby took a step forward and looked him in the face with the withering scorn of a fiend.

"Friends, kindred," he re-echoed; "where are they? I have no friend but myself."

He lowered his voice, and continued in a subdued, hissing tone—

"I hate you, Edward Barrington, hate you with a deadly hatred, partly for your own sake and on account of your wife. I loved Ruth Stanmore; you snatched her from me, and for that I swore that nothing but your life should content me."

"Good Heaven! would you murder me?" exclaimed his listener.

"We do not call executing a runaway prisoner a murder; it is simply justice," was the cool reply.

Then turning to the men, he said—

"Soldiers, make ready."

The soldiers cocked their weapons.

"Have you no feeling of remorse?" cried the victim, desperately, as the certainty of his doom became apparent.

"None whatever."

Edward Barrington pleaded no more.

In that awful moment his courage did not forsake him.

Drawing himself up with dignity, he looked calmly upon the ghastly features of his enemy, and said to him solemnly—

"For this atrocious act of treachery you will one day have to answer."

Then glancing upwards, he added—

"Heaven forgive my sins, and have mercy on my poor wife and children."

"Present!" exclaimed Gasper, utterly unmoved.

The guns of the soldiers were pointed at the victim's breast.

"Fire!" shouted the traitor.

There was a discharge of musketry which drowned the shrill sound of a human voice.

When the smoke cleared away, the bleeding body of Edward Barrington lay stretched upon the ground, and over his lifeless corpse knelt his fatherless boy.

"Oh, father, poor father!" he wailed,

piteously, as he looked down in anguish upon the pallid features. "Look up, dear father."

Gasper started at the sight, and scowled at the little fellow.

Then he cried hastily to the men—

"Drive away that brat, and put the body under ground as quickly as possible."

One of the soldiers advanced and laid his hand roughly upon the child's shoulder.

But the latter shrank from his touch and clung to the body of his parent.

"You shan't take me away from my father," ne cried, wildly. "I love my father."

Gasper uttered a fierce oath, and called to him—

"If you're not gone in an instant, you young whelp, you shall be shot too."

The boy looked up, and fixed his dark, scared eyes upon the evil face of the murderer.

But there was more of indignation and abhorrence than fear in their glance, as he replied—

"Shoot me, if you like, coward ; I don't want to live now you've shot my father."

"I did not shoot your father," growled Gasper, turning pale in spite of himself at this.

"But you ordered him to be shot, and that's murder," was the bold retort.

Irritated at this bold accusation, the ruthless officer drew a pistol from his belt.

"Harkye," he said sternly to the poor boy ; "if you're not out of sight in less than a minute, I shall take you at your word and send you after your father."

As he spoke, he cocked his weapon.

"*Ma foi! capitaine*," remarked one of the French soldiers, "it's hardly worth taking the life of a poor little *coquin* like that."

The captain turned upon the man with a ferocious scowl.

"Mind your business, fellow !" he exclaimed, savagely.

Then, looking once more towards the fatherless boy, he said—

"Now, do you mean to go ?"

"No, I don't," was the brave answer. "I'll die, and be buried with my poor father."

With a muttered oath, Gasper Grimsby was about to raise the pistol, when suddenly a deafening shout rang through the wood, followed by a volley of musketry that sent a perfect hailstorm of bullets whizzing through the trees.

"*Sacré! Les Anglais*," cried the soldiers ; "*sauve qui peut!*"

Without waiting for further orders, the Frenchmen beat a hasty retreat, followed by the renegade, Gasper Grimsby, who forgot his murderous intentions in his anxiety to secure his own safety.

The shouts of the soldiers and the rattle of bullets still continued, but the brave boy stirred not. They had no terrors for him.

He still clung to the lifeless form of the father he loved so well.

CHAPTER III.

GALLANT JACK FINDS A FRIEND.

THE Duke of Burgundy, who was at the head of the French army, was a mere youth, of very little experience in the art of war.

He had retired to rest in perfect confidence expecting the arrival of Marshal Boufflers on the morrow, an officer of courage and activity, who would take upon himself the responsible post of acting general.

But the marshal was yet absent.

The young duke was not a little dismayed at being aroused from his first sleep with the intelligence that the English were close at hand.

The news quickly spread through the entire camp, and created almost a panic in the French ranks.

Sergeant Crank had acted with his usual promptitude and energy.

Having penetrated into the wood till he was almost opposite the camp of the enemy, he had ordered his followers to raise the ringing shouts and discharge the volleys that had struck terror to the hearts of the foe.

In a short time the French were all astir, but the discipline, owing to the want of experience in their leader, was utterly imperfect.

Everything was in confusion.

The sergeant, in the meantime, had posted his men on the borders of the wood, extending their line as far as possible.

From this shelter they poured forth a continual shower of bullets.

The darkness prevented the smallness of their numbers from being suspected, and the prevailing opinion in the French camp was that the entire English army was close upon them.

The loud and exultant shouts from the five hundred English throats confirmed this belief.

A few volleys were returned at random by the discomfited foe, which did no execution whatever, and then, the retreat being sounded, the whole of the French troops retired precipitately, halting not till they were far beyond the reach of the guns of their invisible adversaries.

The sergeant followed them up as far as he dared without exposing his men, and then waited patiently for the arrival of the scout.

It was almost two of the morning when the dragoon galloped up to the dark shadow of the wood.

"All's well," he cried. "The reinforcements are now passing, and are quite clear of the French lines."

"Good—very good !" exclaimed the sergeant, joyfully. "I look upon to-morrow's battle, then, as won. Take a drink, comrade."

As he spoke, he handed his brandy flask to the scout.

"For the queen and Marlborough," he cried, as he took a long draught, and returned the canteen.

"For Marlborough and the queen," cried Benjamin Crank, as he followed the good example.

The enterprise had been carried out with complete success, and the troop having been refreshed, the sergeant had no more to do but to lead them back to Nimeguen.

"Fall in !" he cried.

Instantly, with that splendid precision which characterizes English soldiers, the men formed into lines four abreast, and commenced their backward march through the forest.

The grey dawn was just struggling in through the tree tops as they came upon a strangely mournful sight.

The dead body of Edward Barrington, with his son stretched upon it.

"Halt ! Stand at ease," shouted the sergeant, and then approaching the prostrate forms, he knelt down and examined them.

Several of his comrades followed him.

"Poor fellow, poor fellow !" he murmured, pityingly, as his eyes fell upon the pale, rigid but still handsome features, and the bloodstained breast of the parent. "Nothing can be done for him ; he is dead."

"And is the boy dead too ?" asked a young drummer at his side, who, with his drum at his back, was looking wistfully on the melancholy spectacle.

"No, Ned," replied the sergeant, kindly ; "only asleep, I think. I'm sure I hope so."

As he uttered this benevolent wish, he gently turned the sleeper so that he could see his face. It was calm and tranquil.

Quite true it was that the poor boy, worn out with fatigue and grief, had fallen asleep.

But his cheeks were still moist with tears, and a deep sob quivered in his heaving breast, as though, even in slumber, he still felt his great sorrow.

The heart of Benjamin Crank was as tender as a woman's on such occasions as this, and so were the hearts of the brave men who stood round him, and down the sunburnt features of more than one sturdy grenadier, who would not have quailed before a host of foes, might have been seen trickling the drops of genuine sympathy.

At length the sergeant said, thoughtfully—

"I hardly know what to think of this ; but judging by the ropes round the dead man's limbs, it seems to me there's been foul play here."

His companions quite coincided in this opinion, and the sergeant continued—

"I should say there was no doubt from the likeness between these two unfortunates, that they are father and son."

"No doubt at all," echoed his comrades ; "they're as like as two peas."

"And what a pretty boy, isn't he ?" remarked the young drummer, who seemed to take a great interest in him.

"You're right, Ned ; he is," replied Sergeant Crank.

"And he sleeps as sound as a top."

"So he does," returned Benjamin ; "and I think it would be a pity to disturb the poor lad with questions just now."

"He seems quite tired out, that's certain."

"What's to be done with him, sergeant ? It won't do to leave him here."

"Certainly not ; we'll take him with us. One of you pick him up gently, and place him in the baggage waggon ; he'll snooze comfortably enough there, and I dare say he'll be able to tell us something of what's happened when he wakes."

In an instant a pair of strong arms raised the sleeping boy, and carried him to the rear of the detachment.

Here he was placed in the waggon, and covered up warmly.

Too thoroughly tired out to be conscious of his altered position, the young orphan slumbered on, neither his sorrows nor the jolting of the waggon causing him to wake.

"And now," said Sergeant Crank, "having provided for the youngster—at least, for the present—we have only one duty to perform to his parent."

"It's not much we can do for him, poor fellow," remarked a corporal.

"No," returned the sergeant, with a mournful shake of his head ; "the only thing we can give him is a grave, and that he shall have."

It took but a short time to remove a sufficient quantity of the moist soil with the points of the bayonets, and a cavity having been prepared, the body was lifted gently into its last resting place.

Then the soldiers gathered round bareheaded, with reverent and serious looks, and the sergeant, taking a little mould in his hand, said solemnly—

"We commit this stranger's body to the ground ; earth to earth, ashes to ashes, dust to dust. Heaven guard his remains, and have mercy on his soul."

"Amen," murmured the rest, fervently.

This simple, but none the less on that account, imposing ceremony, being performed, the grave was filled up, and a mark being set up to distinguish the spot where the dead rested, the signal to march was given, and the troop was once more in motion.

*   *   *   *   *

By the time the party reached Nimeguen the reinforcements had arrived.

All was life and activity in the camp.

The troops were refreshing themselves after their long march, but still the strictest order prevailed.

At the slightest signal the vast body of men would have been under arms in a few seconds, and every man at his post.

The occupant of the baggage waggon had awoke from his slumbers, roused by the roll of drums and the martial sound of the trumpets.

In great surprise he started up, and looked around him, as though at a loss to know what it all meant.

On every side he saw nothing but scarlet uniforms and files of glittering bayonets.

He rubbed his eyes as if to be sure he was not dreaming.

"Where am I ?" he exclaimed at length.

"You're all right enough, old chap," said young Ned Rattles, the young drummer, who was in the waggon with him, and had been watching him with much interest ; "don't fret yourself, my boy."

"Well, but how did I come here ?" returned the other in a bewildered tone. "When I fell asleep I was in the wood with—with——"

His voice faltered, he paused, and the tears filled his eyes as the terrible incident that had taken place there recurred to his memory.

Ned Rattles, divining his feelings, was silent for a moment.

Then he said kindly—

"We found you in the wood."

"Who found me?"

"Me and the soldiers."

"What soldiers?"

"The English soldiers; you're English, ain't you?"

"Yes; are you?"

"Rather."

There was a slight pause, and then the boy said, in a low, anxious tone—

"Where's father?"

"Was that your father by whose side you were lying in the wood?" asked the drummer.

"Yes."

"Did you know he was dead?"

"Ye-es," was the mournful reply, given with a long quivering sob; "I knew that, for I saw him die."

"Did you, though?" said Ned, with evident sympathy in his looks and tone.

"Yes; my poor father was murdered."

"Murdered!" exclaimed his companion, with a start; "by the French?"

"No; by an Englishman who wears a French uniform."

"The sneaking turncoat; and so this English Frenchman murdered your father, did he?"

"Yes."

"The vagabond," cried Ned Rattles, indignantly; "if ever I come across him, let him look out, that's all."

His companion looked at his flushed, honest face for an instant, and then asked—

"What have they done with poor father?"

"Buried him in a nice quiet grave under the trees," replied Ned, soothingly.

"In the wood?"

"Yes."

"And where's mother?"

"We saw nothing of her."

"Then she's in the wood still, waiting for—for father; I must go to her."

As the boy spoke this in a choked, husky tone, he rose, and would have sprung out of the waggon, but Ned prevented him.

"Don't stop me," cried the other, his eyes flashing excitedly; "I will go to mother. She doesn't know poor father is dead, and I must go and tell her."

Still the drummer boy held him fast.

"I can't let you go," he said; "I'm ordered not."

"Who ordered you?"

"Sergeant Crank."

"I don't know him."

"He's a kind-hearted man, and he'll be a friend to you," said Ned, earnestly; "so don't go. And besides, the French are coming, and if they were to catch hold of you, they'd kill you as well as your father."

"But what's to become of mother and my little sister Lyddy? They'll die all alone there in the wood."

"No, they won't, my little fellow," exclaimed the cheery voice of Sergeant Crank, who had been listening for some little time with much interest to the conversation. "I'll look after mother and little sister Lyddy."

There was something in the kindly expression of the sergeant's round, ruddy face, and the genial tone in which he spoke, that assured his *protégé*.

And he made no further attempt to depart.

"And now you've had your forty winks," continued Benjamin Crank, "come out of your nest, and I'll give you a look round."

With these words, he took the boy in his brawny arms and carried him along with him.

As he went, he encountered a handsome, noble-looking man in the prime of life, mounted on a charger, and surrounded by a brilliant staff of officers.

It was the great commander-in-chief, John Churchill, Earl of Marlborough.

Reining in his steed, he cried approvingly—

"You have executed your commission admirably, sergeant, and deserve to be made a captain.

"Thank your grace, all the same," returned Benjamin, saluting the earl with the utmost respect, "but I mean to live and die simple Sergeant Benjamin Crank, and your excellency's devoted servant."

Having said this, he whispered in the ear of his young charge—

"That's the Earl of Marlborough, the greatest general that ever was or ever will be. Look, look at him."

The boy opened his dark eyes, and gazed at the noble earl with a kind of wondering awe.

The general observed his glance, and said—

"Who is that you have there, sergeant?"

"A poor little orphan, your grace, that we found on our route."

"A marvellously pretty boy," murmured the earl to himself. "Bring him here," he said, after a moment.

The sergeant approached, and lifted him up in his arms.

The earl took him, and seated him before him in the saddle.

"And what is your name, my lad?" he asked, kindly.

"Jack," was the simple reply.

"Indeed," laughed the earl; "then we are namesakes, since my name is Jack."

The officers smiled one to the other.

"And how would you like to be a soldier?" asked the general.

"Very much, if I was big enough," Jack answered, his cheeks flushing slightly.

"Oh, we have warriors of all sizes here," laughed the earl, good-naturedly; "we must see what we can make of you."

With these words he consigned him once more to the sergeant.

"Look after him, Crank," he said; "it is possible that that boy may turn out to be the pride of the British army."

"Trust me, general; I'll look after the youngster," returned the delighted Benjamin. "I feel I love him already as if he was my own flesh and blood."

No more was said, for at this moment the booming sound of a cannon was heard, followed by the cry—

"The French are in sight."

In an instant all was motion.

Every eye flashed brighter, every heart beat quicker at the prospect of meeting the foe, but young Jack scarcely noticed this.

Young as he was, the words of the great general had been stamped upon his brain in the most vivid characters, and whilst all around him were longing for the coming strife, he heard only the earl's most flattering sentence—

"It is possible that that boy may turn out to be the pride of the British army."

Then a wild shout from the French, answered boldly by the English.

Boom! boom! went the cannon again.

A loud rattle of musketry.

The battle had begun in earnest.

CHAPTER IV.

OUR HERO GETS HIS FIRST GLIMPSE OF A BATTLE.

THE brave soldier Marlborough rode off at once with his officers.

Sergeant Crank beckoned Ned Rattles to him.

"Now, Ned, I entrust the boy to you," he said hastily, as he handed young Jack over to the drummer.

"Well, but, sergeant, I can't take care of him; I must go on duty myself," said the latter.

"I know that, but you must first see this youngster in a place of safety."

"Where am I to take him?"

"To the rear. Give him into the charge of Biddy O'Flinn, and tell her from me to look after him."

"I will, sergeant."

"But I don't want to go to Biddy O'Flinn. Can't I come and fight with you?" asked Jack, eagerly.

"You're a brave little bantam cock, but you must wait till your spurs are grown a little longer, before you try to tackle the mounseers," laughed the sergeant.

"Hark! there go the guns again. Away with him. Good-bye, my boy."

"Good-bye, sergeant; make haste back," cried Jack.

"Aye, aye! I'll be back, please God, when we've made the enemy run," called the sergeant, as he hurried away, musket in hand.

"Come on, old chap, and be quick," said Ned Rattles; "I shall be wanted with my drum. Be quick."

"Can't you get me a drum too?" asked Jack.

"What would be the use? You couldn't beat any of the calls."

"I could hammer away with the drum sticks, and make noise enough, at any rate," Jack replied.

"That wouldn't do," laughed Ned; "and, besides, I don't think you're quite old enough yet."

"Not old enough! Why, I'm nearly nine," exclaimed Jack.

"I'm fourteen," replied Ned, quietly.

"Fourteen," murmured Jack; "it will take me a long time to grow as old as that."

No more words were spoken just then, and they hurried along as quickly as possible, meeting files and files of infantry that marched past with fixed bayonets, colours flying, and the fifes and drums playing with martial din.

At length they reached the quarters of the camp sutler,* Biddy O'Flinn.

Biddy was a raw-boned, good-natured Irishwoman of middle age, whose roseate complexion spoke well for the excellent and wholesome properties of the liquors she vended to the soldiers.

She was attired somewhat quaintly.

Her head was adorned with a frilled nightcap, surmounted by a military cap.

The upper portion of her body was enveloped in a soldier's coat, whilst over her shoulders were slung several kegs containing various kinds of drinks.

She glanced at Ned and Jack as they came in, and said, without leaving off her work—

"Well, Masther Ned, is it a dhrink you're wantin' this mornin'?"

"No, thankee, Biddy. I'm one of Sergeant Crank's followers, a teetotaller."

Biddy screwed up her rubicund features in something like scorn at this declaration.

"Taytotaller," she muttered to herself. "The sergeant's a fine man enough, but he's ruinin' the risin' giniration, and my business into the barg'in, wid his taytotal notions."

"Well, Biddy, the sergeant sent me to you."

"What does he want?"

"He says you're to look after this boy till after the battle."

"Och thin!" exclaimed Biddy, "haven't I got enough to do sarvin' out dhrink to the thirsty sojers widout havin' a bit of a boy to mind?"

"But, Biddy, the sergeant knows you're a good-hearted soul, and that's why he sent young Jack to you," said Rattles, insinuatingly.

"It's thrue enough," said Biddy. "I've got a soft corner in my heart for little boys."

"This one has just lost his father," Ned whispered to her.

"Oh, the poor crathur, has he though?" exclaimed the good woman, pityingly. "Thin I'll look afther him as well as I can, and be father and mother to him, too."

"Thankee, Biddy, we were sure you would; and now I'm off. Good-bye, Jack, old fellow; I shall be wanted on the battle field."

"Good-bye, Ned. Shall you be long before you're back?"

"It all depends how long it is before the mounseers take to their heels; but I'll return as soon as the battle's over."

"Oh, don't get killed, pray don't," urged Jack, earnestly.

"I won't if I can help it, depend on it," replied Ned, with a laugh.

"Not he; he won't be killed," cried Biddy. "It's the dhrummers' duty to stir up the sojers to kill each other, not to be killed themselves."

"They are sometimes, though," remarked Ned, with a rueful grin, "by accident."

"You won't be. It's long life you've got written in your face, me honey. Away wid yez, an' don't come back till you've licked the French into smithereens."

"I won't," cried Ned, as he ran off with his drum at his back.

---

* One who attends an army to supply provisions and liquors to the troops.

Biddy looked after him for an instant, and then turned her attention to her new charge.

"He's an illegant boy, anyhow," she said to herself. "An' so yer name's Jack, is it?" she asked him, kindly.

"Yes," Jack answered.

"An' are you a taytotaller, like the rest ov 'em ?"

"I'm the same as Ned and the sergeant," replied our hero, simply.

"Umph!" assented Biddy ; "then maybe you'd like a cup of coffee and somethin' to ate ?"

Our hero, who was particularly hungry, said "Yes," and was not long in demolishing the meal Biddy placed before him.

"Have you had enough, me darlin'?" asked Biddy.

"Yes, thank you."

"Well, thin, now I must see what's to be done wid you. In the first place, I'll have to put you somewhere out of harm's way."

"Am I not safe here ?"

A tremendous report of musketry came rolling from the distance at this moment.

"Och, hubbaboo!" exclaimed Biddy, "it's hard to say where any mother's son's safe at prisint. Did yer hear that ?"

"Yes," said Jack ; "they're firing the guns now, ain't they ?"

"Shure, an' they are, too. The bullets'll be flyin' about like hailstones ; an' it's meself as'll be wanted amongst the brave boys, wid me cordials."

"I'll stop and take care of the place, while you're gone," volunteered our hero, cheerfully.

Biddy shook her head.

"No," she said ; "I'll have to pop you into one o' thim empty casks yondher ; and you'll have to lie snug, curled up there, till I come back."

"I'd rather stop where I am, please," said Jack ; "unless you'd let me go along with you."

Biddy O'Flinn looked at the boy admiringly.

His boldness pleased her.

"And so you'd like to go along wid me, eh ?"

"Very much."

"Thin, bedad, you shall," exclaimed the old Irishwoman. "It's sartin I can't stop here, and since I've got to look afther you, I can't do that betther than by keepin' you undher me own eyes."

"May I go, then ?"

"Sure, you may, me darlin'."

Biddy having loaded herself, and her tobacco pipe, slung a small keg of brandy over Jack's shoulder, and a bag of biscuits.

"There's your cargo," she said to him.

Then, having lighted her pipe, she said—

"Now then, off we go. Mind you stick to me as close as wax, and good luck to the pair of us."

"Hark!" cried Jack to the firing.

"Yes, me honey ; they are at it now."

As they stepped from the tent, another deafening roar of artillery burst like thunder upon their ears ; whilst a twenty-pound shot came whizzing through the air, over their heads.

Biddy was used to these little incidents, and swiftly glancing up at it as it passed, continued her course.

Jack walked along at her side, in quite a feverish state of excitement, at the prospect of seeing a real battle.

Every step they took brought them nearer and nearer to the scene of conflict.

The ground began to be strewn in all directions with the wounded, the dying, and the dead.

Biddy frequently stopped to apply her flask to the parched lips of some poor sufferer.

The sight of death made Jack think of his dead father.

From his father, his thoughts naturally reverted to his mother and sister.

It was just at this moment a troop of cavalry came galloping past, in a cloud of dust, and another terrible thundering discharge burst from the guns and muskets of the conflicting armies.

When the smoke and dust had a little subsided, our hero found that his companion was no longer at his side.

In vain he called her by her name.

What with the shouts of the soldiers, and the deafening sound of the cannon, he could not hear his own voice.

Was she dead, he wondered.

Ever and anon, a horse without its rider, scared, and wild with terror, came dashing with frantic speed across the plain.

He could see men, without any apparent cause, suddenly drop their weapons, throw up their hands in the air, and fall to the ground ; whilst over his head the fatal bullets sped with a sharp, whizzing sound.

He began to wish himself a little further off, and when an English grenadier, pierced to the brain by a bullet, fell dead at his feet, his musket ringing as it reached the ground, he came to a stand.

"I think I'd better get away as soon as I can," he said to himself, as he looked in dismay at the blood-sprinkled features of the lifeless soldier before him.

The musket with its fixed bayonet lay by the side of the dead grenadier.

"He'll never want it again, poor fellow," thought Jack, as he picked it up and shouldered it with some difficulty, for it was heavy.

Armed, or rather burdened with this addition, our hero struck out across the plain, and with the shouts of battle ringing in his ears, and the messengers of death whirling over his head, he hastened from the scene of conflict.

"I wish I could find mother and sister Lyddy," he said to himself, as he walked along ; "and oh! how I wish poor father was alive, or that I could meet the cruel man who killed him."

This thought imparted a sternness to his young face, and his dark eyes glittered as he clutched the musket, and muttered—

"I'd shoot him dead, as he shot my father."

CHAPTER V.
MOTHER AND SON.

RUTH BARRINGTON waited patiently for some time the return of her husband.

THE PRIDE OF THE BRITISH ARMY. 11

But when suddenly she discovered that her boy—whom she had believed to be sleeping at her side—was no longer with her, she became almost desperate.

With her infant daughter clasped to her breast, she hurried from tree to tree, calling her son by name.

But there was no answer.

It was not till broad daylight she found herself, almost worn out with fatigue, once more at the spot where she expected to find her husband awaiting her.

But he was not there.

Determined, if possible, to know the worst, she pressed onwards.

It was not long before she reached the spot where the tragedy of the past night had been enacted.

As she reached it, her eyes fell upon the long, narrow slip of newly-turned earth, with the rude wooden cross, placed by the friendly hands of the soldiers, at the head.

She paused, and her lips murmured ominously the words—

"That is a grave."

At a short distance from it lay a hat.

Ruth snatched it up.

It was her husband's.

This seemed to confirm her suspicions, and she repeated in a freezing tone of despair—

"That is a grave, and my poor Edward lies within it."

Hardly had she said these words when she heard footsteps.

Looking up, she saw approaching a burly, thick-set man.

He was clad in peasant garb; his complexion sallow to lividness, his thick hair and beard were coarse and black.

Altogether his appearance was repulsive in the extreme.

He drew near.

Ruth fixed her dark, tearless eyes (she was too full of despair to weep) upon him in silence.

At length the man spoke.

"Your name is Barrington, madame, is it not?" he asked, abruptly, speaking in indifferent English, with a foreign accent.

"It is," Ruth answered.

"You are waiting for your husband?"

"I am, I am!" exclaimed Ruth, roused to sudden earnestness by the question. "Know you aught of him?"

"I know you will wait long enough before he comes to you."

"What mean you?" demanded Ruth, desperately. "Where is my husband?"

"Dead!"

"Dead?"

"Yes. Shot last night as an escaped prisoner. He lies beneath the turf at your feet."

Although the hapless wife had divined this, still, when the intelligence was so decidedly confirmed, the shock was so great that she sank down prostrate on the grave.

When she recovered, the man was still waiting by her.

"So then my poor husband lies there," she said, in a cold, hard tone, "and my boy—did they murder him—does he rest with his father?"

The man shook his head.

"I know nothing about the boy," he said.

"I must find him, my poor darling," she murmured, and was about to hurry away.

"Stay, madame!"

She stopped and looked back.

"What would you?" she asked.

"The French and English are at war."

"I know it."

"This wood will soon be full of troops, and your life may be endangered."

"I have no fear."

"But your child."

"A mother can protect her child."

"Not from the chance bullets of skirmishers," remarked the man with an ugly smile.

"Heaven will watch over us."

Again Ruth was about to proceed.

Again the man called—

"I bring a message from Captain Gravellotte."

"I know no such person," Ruth replied.

As she spoke, a French officer, who had cautiously approached under cover of the trees, stepped forward.

"Ruth," he cried, "as your husband's friend, I offer you protection. Let me conduct you to the French lines; there you will be in safety."

The blood rushed into the pale features of the young widow, and her eyes flashed with indignation.

"So it is you, Gasper Grimsby, who dares to mock me with these words!" she cried, in a tone of withering contempt; "you renegade coward and murderer! you, who having sacrificed my noble husband to your base revenge, would now insult his wife with the offer of your protection. Wretch! I would rather seek it from the forest wolf than from you. Begone, assassin!"

She turned and walked rapidly away.

"Keep her in sight," said Gasper, "and when opportunity serves, you know what to do."

"*Parfaitement bien!*—perfectly well, monsieur," replied the man.

He was about to follow on her track, when suddenly the hurried tramp of soldiers and the rattle of arms was heard.

The next moment the uniforms of the English sharpshooters appeared between the trees in the distance.

With a celerity quite equal to the occasion, Gasper Grimsby beat a hasty retreat, whilst the peasant climbed as nimbly as a cat into the nearest tree.

Uncertain whether the approaching troops were English or French, Ruth Barrington crouched behind one of the giant trunks, whilst the men dashed on with eager haste and were soon out of sight.

The battle still raged.

But Ruth continued her sad journey through the wood, scared by the shouts, the roar of cannon, and the whistle of bullets.

She was thinking only of her lost boy, little dreaming that he was in the midst of it.

At a distance, like a vulture waiting for its prey, followed the bearded man, waiting for his opportunity to seize his victim.

When Ruth Barrington reached the confines

of the wood, she could see in the distance the long lines of troops, and the dense cloud of smoke that marked the scene of conflict.

Ruth looked wistfully towards the spot where her countrymen were posted.

But she dared not venture to approach.

Suddenly a figure on the plain before her attracted her attention.

Slight, wearing a dress, so far as she could judge from the distance, like that of her boy, and carrying on his shoulder a musket.

So impressed was she with the sight, that she could neither move nor utter a sound.

All she could do was to keep her eyes riveted on the small form.

Suddenly, as she looked, a flying squadron came tearing in wild disorder across the plain, raising the dust in clouds.

When it had passed, and the atmosphere had cleared again, the child-like figure with its weapon had disappeared.

"Could it have been Jack?" she asked herself. "It might have been. The darling boy has an adventurous spirit, and would dare, I think, even to venture into the peril of the strife. Oh, how can I be certain?"

For a moment she continued to gaze.

"That was the spot where I last saw him," she resumed, "and now he is there no longer."

She started up suddenly.

All her fatigue was gone as she cried—

"Oh, merciful Heaven! the soldiers cannot have trampled him beneath the hoofs of their steeds. I must go and see."

She was about to advance, when a heavy hand was laid upon her arm.

Ruth turned and found herself in the grasp of the burly peasant.

"You needn't be uneasy about your boy, madame," he said, with a kind of lurking grin.

"I believe I have seen him yonder," returned Ruth, hurriedly, "and if so, he is in danger, and I must go to him."

"He's in no danger, madame; he's safe in the French camp with Captain Gravellotte."

"Ha! how know you that?"

"Why, I saw him there with my own eyes; and if you return with me, you'll see him too."

The suspicions of the young mother were at once aroused, and she replied, quickly—

"You told me not long since that you knew nothing of my boy, yet now you say you have seen him in the French camp."

"It's quite true, madame."

"Quite false, you mean, fellow," returned Ruth, indignantly.

The man, thus baffled, grinned spitefully.

"Whether or not," he answered, shrugging his shoulders, "you'd better come back with me."

"No; I refuse," was the determined reply. "Release me."

The peasant did not obey, but continued—

"The captain admires you, madame. Why should you turn a friend into an enemy?"

"He is already my bitterest enemy, for he has murdered the husband I love better than my life."

And overcome by the recollection, she sank upon the ground.

"Oh, no; the captain did not murder monsieur your husband; on the contrary, he tried all he could to save his life," said the man, in a plausible tone.

But the fellow was not a little startled at hearing a boyish voice exclaim—

"Don't believe a word of it, mother."

At the same moment our young hero, who had made a slight circuit to avoid the hoofs of the dragoons' horses, sprang forward with his musket on his shoulder.

"Be off, fellow," said Jack, indignantly, as he presented his weapon in the most soldierly manner he could, considering its great weight.

The ruffian, finding an awfully sharp-looking bayonet within a few inches of his nose, released the arm he held, and recoiled a few paces.

"Sacrebleu!" he growled.

With a vivid cry of joy, Ruth at once recognised her son.

"Jack, darling!"

"Mother!"

The next moment the boy was clasped to her throbbing heart.

The peasant stood looking at them from under his thick brows.

After a moment Mrs. Barrington rose to her feet and turned towards him.

"Now, villain, your falsehood is exposed. Return to your master, and tell him I scorn him and his friendship."

"Yes, be off at once," cried Jack, fiercely; "or I'll shoot you with this gun."

"Ha, ha, mon brave!" laughed the man, eyeing the weapon narrowly which the young hero had brought again to a level with his breast; "so you will shoot me, will you?"

"Yes, I will; and your master, too, when I see him, for killing my father," returned Jack, determinately.

The peasant hesitated.

His gaze was intently fixed on the gun.

His eyes travelled down the barrel to the lock, and he could see that the hammer was not raised, and that, consequently, the weapon could not be discharged.

"Ha, ha! the young English cub thinks to frighten me, does he?" he chuckled to himself.

In an instant he had resolved what to do, and stepping quickly on one side, he sprang forward, and grasping the gun with his strong hands, wrested it from the boyish grasp that held it.

"Now then, my gallant English garçon," he said, with a vindictive gleam in his ogre-like eyes; "if you don't take care, I shall shoot you."

Poor Jack looked woefully chagrined at the loss of the weapon in which he had trusted.

His mother threw herself before him.

"Kill me, dastardly wretch, not my boy," she cried, excitedly.

"I don't want to kill either of you if you are quiet and come with me," grinned the ruffian, exultingly; "but if not, I shall kill you both."

"Don't go, mother," cried Jack.

"I will not, darling," she replied, hugging him closer to her.

"Bah! you must," growled the peasant. "Come on."

"I shall not stir," was Ruth's brave reply.

"*Diable!* you won't?"

"Not a step."

The eyes of the ruffian glared like those of an angry wolf.

"*Sacré!*" he hissed between his teeth, "you had better."

"No."

"No," echoed our young hero.

The man cocked the gun, and raising it to his shoulder, pointed it at Jack.

Then he cried to his mother—

"I give you one more chance—the last. Will you come?"

It was a terrible moment.

Ruth was about to yield to the ruffian's bidding, but Jack whispered to her.

She replied firmly—

"I will not."

"Then I shall fire."

"Fire away!" cried our hero. "You won't hit me."

The words had scarcely passed his lips ere the coward pulled the trigger.

The hammer fell with a sharp click.

The flint gave forth a few faint sparks, but there was no report.

"There," Jack exclaimed, triumphantly, "I told you you wouldn't hit me."

The man uttered a yell of rage.

"This cursed English fusil is worth nothing," he muttered; "it will not fire."

"Very few guns will when they're not loaded," retorted Jack, drily.

The baffled ruffian, furious at this taunt, dragged the bayonet off the barrel, and dashed the musket savagely to the ground.

"This will not miss!" he growled, as he brandished the glittering weapon over his head.

He was about to spring forward, when a sharp report rang through the air.

The peasant uttered a cry like the howl of a wild beast, as he dropped the bayonet, and wrung his hand in agony.

"*Sacré! mille diables!* I'm wounded!" he raved, as he howled with the pain.

At the same moment a French grenadier appeared, musket in hand, advancing from the shelter of the trees.

He was a young, handsome man, and came forward rapidly, reloading his weapon as he walked.

"*Coquin!*" cried the peasant to him, "you have wounded me—me, your countryman, your comrade."

"I disown you," returned the other, with intense scorn. "You are no true Frenchman. France does not make war against women and children. Go, wretch!"

The ruffian stood glaring at his compatriot for a moment.

Then, seeing he was in earnest, he skulked away, and was soon lost to sight in the shadow of the forest.

The French grenadier approached the spot where Ruth Barrington, pale with grief and anxiety, stood with her son and infant daughter.

"Fear nothing from me, madame," he said, courteously. "A true Frenchman knows how to respect the honour of a lady. Can I do anything else to serve you?"

"No, I thank you, monsieur," answered Ruth, gratefully. "You have done me all the service I require in ridding me of that ruffian."

She glanced as she spoke in the direction by which the peasant had disappeared.

"You must not regard that fellow as a type of France's soldiers," said the grenadier, with generous indignation in his tone.

"I do not, monsieur," returned Ruth, warmly, "for I know that beneath the French uniform beat many noble, patriotic hearts, full of the purest chivalry, and yours certainly is one of them."

The soldier bowed.

"Then I can be of no further assistance to you, madame?" he asked.

"I thank you, no, monsieur. With Heaven's help, I trust to be able to reach the English camp in safety."

"Adieu, then, madame. Heaven guard you and yours!"

With these words, the French grenadier politely saluted Ruth Barrington.

A body of his companions appearing through the trees at that moment, he joined them, and they retired together.

As soon as he was out of sight, Jack picked up his musket, and, having once more fixed the bayonet, he shouldered it.

Strutting with much complacency up to his parent, he said—

"And now, dear mother, that brave soldier has driven away the ugly fellow with the beard, let's march towards the camp, shall we? I'll take care of you."

"I am quite ready to make the attempt, darling, and with such a hero as you to guard us, we must be safe."

"Come on then," urged the boy, "and as we walk along, I'll tell you all about Sergeant Crank, and Ned Rattles, and Biddy O'Flinn, and the grand Earl of Marlborough."

"Have you seen the earl?" asked Ruth.

"Yes, that I have, mother; and he took me in his arms as he sat on his horse."

"Indeed?" said his mother, both surprised and pleased.

"Yes, and what do you think he said?"

"What?"

"Why, that I might one day be the 'Pride of the British Army.'"

As young Jack uttered these words, his fair cheeks flushed—his dark eyes sparkled like diamonds, and he took a firmer grip of the gun he was struggling under.

And he shouldered his heavy musket as though he no longer felt its weight.

Ruth Barrington could not repress a feeling of pride as she glanced at her boy, and felt a hope spring up in her heart that the earl's flattering prognostication might some day be realized.

As they proceeded, Jack gave his mother an account of all that had happened from the time when they were separated.

He had barely ended, when suddenly the dense mass of troops in the distance seemed to open.

Ringing shouts rent the air, followed by the roar of artillery, and the entire body of the enormous multitude seemed to be moving towards them.

At the same time, from behind, there burst forth a report, like the sound of a thousand thunders.

Turning to look, they beheld the French squadrons advancing in their rear.

Ruth shuddered.

It was a terrible position.

They were between two fires.

The air was dark with sulphureous smoke.

Hissing balls flew over their heads.

"Let's keep on, mother," said Jack, bravely, "don't be afraid. What a pity my gun isn't loaded, isn't it?"

Boom—boom—boom went the cannons.

It was evident two of the main bodies of the French and English armies were rapidly drawing nearer to each other.

The position of the travellers grew more and more critical every moment.

Grape shot now rattled past them.

The ground was torn up by shells and iron missiles.

"Oh! that we could find some place of shelter," cried Ruth in accents of terror.

"This way, mother," said our hero, as they turned aside, and hurried along to get as far as possible from the route of the approaching columns.

Suddenly they caught sight of a cottage that stood in a snug hollow.

"Hurrah!" cried Jack; "we can rest here till the battle's over."

They approached, intending to knock at the door, and beg for shelter.

But there was no need to knock.

The door stood wide open.

But not a soul was within.

The alarm of war had already driven away its peasant owner.

And the cottage was empty, silent, and deserted.

"Quick, Jack, let's enter; we may here be safe for a time," said Ruth.

"Yes, mother; but hark to the cries of the English and French soldiers, and the roar of the cannons! Oh, I hope Ned Rattles will not be killed."

CHAPTER VI.

THE DESERTED COTTAGE.

"QUICK, mother, let's enter here," repeated Jack, leading his mother to the cottage.

It was but a poor place, the walls being of plaster, broken away in some places, and showing the bricks beneath.

Of furniture there was but little.

A wooden settle was on one side of the door.

A large chest stood in the centre of the room, and a common daub of a picture, in a rough frame, hung from a nail near the window, the framework of which had been shattered; as if to show how, two spent cannon balls lay ominously on the floor side by side with the *débris* of bricks and mortar.

Jack placed his musket in a corner, as carefully as some old veteran

As he did so, he was reminded of the keg of brandy and bag of biscuits he carried across his shoulder, and which, in the excitement of his day's adventures, he had entirely forgotten.

In a moment, he had removed his burdens, and, quickly opening the bag, offered it to his mother.

"See, see, mother," he cried, eagerly. "Taste."

Ruth willingly complied with her son's invitation, for she was faint with long fasting.

Our hero then hurried away in search of water.

The back door led to a garden, and in this he found a well.

From it he filled a can with water.

As he was drawing up the bucket, his ear was attracted by a faint whine.

"That's a dog," thought Jack.

And he was right, for on looking round, he perceived a kennel, at the entrance of which was just visible a dark head.

On approaching, he found a young dog, fastened by a rope.

It had been left behind by its master in the hurry of flight, and being prevented by the rope from following, was almost dead with hunger and thirst.

"Poor fellow!" murmured Jack, pityingly; "but I'll soon set you to rights."

He quickly untied the dog, and filling an earthenware dish, which he found near the kennel, with water, brought it to him.

The poor animal struggled to its feet, and lapped the liquid greedily.

During this, Jack hurried inside with the can, and gave his mother a draught of the pure, cool element.

In a short time she sank down upon the ground exhausted, and fell asleep.

Jack, who had no sleep in his eyes, returned to the garden with some biscuit, and fed the dog.

In the meantime the battle was raging furiously without.

Bullets were whizzing through the air in all directions, whilst ever and anon a twenty-pound shot came sailing over the cottage, and fell crashing into the wood behind it.

The dog seemed affected by the unusual turmoil, and whined piteously, so when Jack returned to the interior, he took it with him.

The scared animal crouched in a corner, with his ears back, and his eyes fixed upon his preserver, starting and wincing nervously at every volley of musketry, and every "Hurrah!" of the soldiery.

There was quite enough, too, to induce nervousness, since there was a continuous clink and rattle of musket balls against the roof tiling, whilst occasionally a displaced brick would fall with a dull, heavy sound.

An hour passed, and then, as a tremendous burst of artillery rose on the air, Ruth started up as if under the impulse of some terrible alarm.

"Merciful Heaven preserve us!" she cried, excitedly, as she rushed towards her boy, and clasped him to her; "we are not safe in this place; let us leave it."

"I think we're as safe here, mother, as anywhere else just now," replied Jack.

Without replying, Ruth stepped up on to the chest, and looked from the window.

The air was heavy with the blue smoke of gunpowder, and she could see the forms of soldiers hurrying to and fro, like spectres shrouded in mist.

She descended, and seated herself on the chest, and looked down sadly at her infant daughter, who lay wrapped in a shawl asleep at her feet.

"Oh, what a terrible thing is war!" she murmured, sorrowfully.

"It's glory, isn't it, mother?" asked Jack.

"Some may call it so; but alas! how dearly purchased. How many homes does it destroy, how much happiness does it blight! Even the shouts of victory are but the knell of death and destruction."

"I wish I was a man," remarked our hero; "I'd go out then, and help the English."

"I'm very glad you are not then, darling," replied his mother.

"If I had a drum, I could do something."

"You are better where you are, my love."

"Oh, but there are lots of drummer boys very little bigger than me in the battle. Did you know that, mother?" Jack asked.

"Oh, yes; I know it," she answered, in a mournful tone. "Poor fellows! what must be their mother's feelings at this moment?"

"But mothers like their boys to be brave, don't they?"

"If they do, they tremble none the less for their safety."

Our young hero did not quite seem to appreciate the peril, and his cheek flushed, and his eyes kindled as he exclaimed—

"When I hear the guns and the shouts, I feel as if I should like to be in the midst of the fire and smoke."

"Where the first bullet might pierce your heart or your brain. Did you think of that?"

"No; soldiers don't think much about their hearts or their brains either," replied the boy, with a slight laugh.

"But they can all feel the agony of being wounded," said Ruth, seriously; "have you ever seen a wounded soldier?"

"Oh, yes, mother; while I was with Biddy O'Flinn, we passed a great many, and after I lost her, I saw some quite dead. It was from a dead grenadier I got that gun."

The smile had died away from Jack's face, and he now looked as serious as her whose anxious eyes were fixed upon him.

"I hope, my darling, I may never see you wounded," she said, earnestly; "I think it ——"

Her voice ceased as the sound of footsteps caught her ear.

They were evidently approaching, and almost immediately a heavy weight seemed pressed against the door.

Then followed a suppressed groan.

"Ouvrez, pour l'amour de Dieu!—open, for Heaven's sake!" cried a faint voice. "I am wounded."

"It is a Frenchman," said Jack, in a low voice, looking at his mother. "Shall I open the door?"

"Certainly," she replied.

Our hero quickly sprang forward, lowered the bar, and the door flew open.

A French grenadier, ghastly pale, staggered in, and sank down exhausted on the settle.

"Mille graces, madame—a thousand thanks, madam," he murmured, and then fell back fainting against the wall.

Both Mrs. Barrington and her son uttered an exclamation of pity and surprise.

It was the brave soldier who had not long before so befriended them.

In an instant Jack had brought the water can, and his mother held it to the parched lips of the wounded man.

The draught revived him, and then Jack poured some of the brandy from his keg into a cup and gave it to him.

He quickly recovered his consciousness, and remembered his benefactors.

"You have more than repaid me for the slight service I was able to render you," he said, gratefully.

"Not yet, monsieur," returned Ruth, "but we hope to be able to discharge our debt in full. We will if we can."

The grenadier had been wounded in the knee by a bullet, and was evidently suffering intense pain, which he bore with much patience.

Ruth tore a portion of her dress into strips, and bound them as tightly as she could round the wound.

The blood staunched, and the soldier began to recover himself.

It was just at this juncture that a tremendous crash was heard.

The roof parted asunder, and a shell fell through, and lay smoking in the very centre of the apartment.

For an instant there was an appalled silence.

"If that explodes, nous sommes perdus—we are lost," cried the grenadier, utterly unable to move.

"Are we?" exclaimed Jack, quickly. "Not if I can get rid of it."

And boldly springing forward, he raised the terrible missile in both his hands, and hurled it with all his strength from the window.

The next moment a tremendous explosion was heard without.

The contents of the shell were partly propelled against the cottage wall.

But those within were unharmed.

The presence of mind of our hero had saved all from certain destruction.

Ruth Barrington embraced her boy in silent emotion.

The wounded grenadier gazed at him admiringly, as he remarked—

"Your son is a brave boy for one so young, madame. He will make a good soldier one day."

"That's what I mean to be as soon as I can," said Jack, decidedly.

"There is time enough yet," said the grenadier.

"I would have gone out to-day to fight, if I could," continued the boy, with enthusiasm.

"What, to fight the French?"

"Yes, of course. They are our enemies you know."

"Ah, true. And do you hate the French?"

"Yes—n-o—ye-es," replied Jack, not quite certain whether he really hated them or not.

He blushed slightly as he added—

"Of course I'm obliged to say I hate the French; but I don't think I hate them all."

The grenadier smiled.

"There's one Frenchman I'm sure I don't hate, and never could," continued Jack, warmly.

"And who is he?"

"Yourself. I like you very much."

"And I like you very much," returned the grenadier, fervently.

"Oh, yes; I'm sure I should be very sorry to kill you," went on the boy, magnanimously.

"*Et moi aussi*—I should be sorry too."

"And I tell you what we'll do. We'll make a promise."

"What?"

"Why, that if ever we meet in battle—when I'm a man, I mean—that we won't shoot or kill one another."

"*Volontiers, mon cher garçon*—willingly, my dear boy," exclaimed the delighted Frenchman; "we will always be *chers amis*—dear friends."

But ere Jack could reply, another terrific crash of artillery thundered forth.

And then a ringing, triumphant cheer, as though the entire army had shouted with one voice—

"Hurrah!"

"England and the queen!"

"England and Marlborough!"

"Hurrah! they run, they run! hurrah, hurrah!"

Young Jack heard the cry, and, boy-like, was up at the window in an instant, joining in it with all the strength of his lungs.

"They run!" murmured the grenadier, moodily, half to himself; "who run? Is it the French?"

"Both French and English are running as hard as they can," called Jack to him, excitedly.

"Ha, both!"

"Yes; the French are first, and the English are running after them. Hurrah!"

In the midst of his cheer a bullet came crashing against one of the window-frames, shivering it to fragments.

But our hero did not stir.

In his enthusiasm he scarcely noticed it.

But Ruth did.

"Oh, pray come down, darling!" she cried, in terror.

"I'm all right, mother," was Jack's cheerful reply. "I like to see them all galloping past. There they go. Bang, bang, hurrah!"

Ruth, for a moment, glanced forth at the rushing, shouting, whirling mass as they dashed along. But that glance was fatal to her.

A second bullet sped on its deadly course through the window.

There was a crash.

The dog uttered a startled howl.

With a shriek Ruth sprang from the chest.

"Oh, Jack, I am shot!" she cried faintly, as she staggered a few paces and fell to the ground.

"Oh, mother—dear mother!" cried Jack, in a voice of anguish. "She is dying!"

"Heaven forbid!" said the French soldier, fervently.

"But see, see!" continued the boy, excitedly, "she is bleeding."

It was too true.

The vital stream trickled slowly along the floor, dyeing the fair hair of the victim with its crimson hue.

In spite of his own wound, the grenadier contrived to drag himself to the chest in front of which Ruth had fallen.

Raising her head, he sought to examine the extent of the injury.

It was soon found that the ball had pierced her shoulder.

"Is she dead?" asked Jack, tremblingly.

"No, my boy," answered the soldier, in as cheering a tone as possible. "See if you can find me something for a bandage."

Jack looked eagerly, and presently discovered a piece of linen cloth.

With this the soldier bound up the wounded limb.

Ruth sighed heavily, and stretched out her hand, as if feeling for her infant.

Jack placed his little sister in her mother's arms.

There she lay, motionless—speechless.

The Frenchman, with much pain and difficulty, returned to his seat.

Jack, full of grief and anxiety on his mother's account, seated himself on the chest, and sat watching her.

"She'll die if she's left there," he thought to himself. "What can I do?"

He reflected for a moment, and then exclaimed suddenly—

"I know what I'll do. I'll go and see if I can find Biddy or the sergeant. You'll watch my mother, won't you, monsieur, till I come back?"

"I will guard her with my life," replied the chivalrous Frenchman.

Jack was about to jump down.

Suddenly rapid footsteps were heard, and voices, approaching the cottage.

The next moment there came a loud hammering at the door.

The dog, with a sharp bark, sprang from its corner on to the chest by the side of his preserver, ready to protect him, if needs be.

The door flew from its hinges with a crash, and in came a party of English soldiers, headed by Sergeant Crank, with his musket slung over his shoulder, and Ned Rattles, with his drum at his back.

At the sight of our hero the sergeant stepped forward, and looking at Jack, said—

"Who do you belong to, my little man?"

The next moment the brave sergeant recognised our hero, and his three-cornered cocked hat almost sprang from his head with astonishment.

The scene at this moment was quite a picture.

The soldiers in their scarlet uniforms.

The wounded French grenadier.

The prostrate form of Ruth Barrington.

Our hero, seated ruefully on the chest, with his bare arm round the dog.

"' BE OFF, FELLOW,' SAID JACK, PRESENTING HIS WEAPON."

The sergeant, and Ned Rattles in front of him, and to fill up the background, the sallow, bearded face of the ruffian peasant peering cautiously through the window.

CHAPTER VII.
ALONE IN THE WORLD.

At length, the surprise having been got over, Sergeant Crank exclaimed, good-naturedly enough—

"Guns and trumpets! Who would have thought of finding you here, my little man?"

Jack shook his head.

"I'm sure I don't know," he answered, "but I'm very glad to see you."

"Not more than I am to see you, my boy," said the sergeant, warmly, "for Biddy told me she'd lost you."

"You thought that I'd been killed, I suppose?"

"That's just what I did think, my boy."

"You seem all right, too. You're not killed, sergeant, and you're all right, Ned, with your fine drum," remarked Jack.

"I believe you," joined in Ned Rattles, with a laugh. "I am as sound as my drum, my boy."

"Are you sure your drum is all right?"

"Quite; and able to make as much row as ever it was," grinned Ned.

"I'm so glad you're not shot," said Jack, warmly.

"Haven't got a scratch. The only shock I came across in the shape of a ball was this apple, and I kept it for you. Here."

As he spoke, he gave it to Jack.

Jack then called the sergeant's attention to the prostrate form of his mother.

"Look, sergeant, my mother!"

And Jack threw himself on his knees by her side.

"Your mother?" exclaimed the sergeant; "is she asleep?"

"She has been wounded," replied Jack, in a troubled tone; "and she lies so still, I'm afraid she's dead."

"Let me see," said Benjamin Crank.

Kneeling down, he raised the unconscious form gently, and examined the wound.

"She's not dead," he said, after a moment; "but she needs surgical care, and the sooner she has it the better. Ned, run for the doctor."

Ned Rattles, having divested himself of his drum, set off at once upon his mission.

As the sergeant turned towards the door, his eyes fell upon the grenadier who reclined in the settle in the corner.

"Hollo, mounseer, what are you doing here?" he asked.

"He's a friend of mine," said Jack.

"Friend," echoed the sergeant; "guns and trumpets! and a Frenchman too. He's a prisoner of war."

"He's badly wounded," pleaded Jack.

"Is he? Then that alters the case entirely," said Benjamin, generously. "A wounded foe becomes a friend, of course; but still he's my prisoner, none the less."

The grenadier's face became overcast, and he glanced sorrowfully at Jack.

Our hero's heart was touched, and he whispered to Sergeant Crank—

"Please don't take him prisoner; he's such a good brave man."

"He looks as if he was. But then there are lots of good brave men in the same pickle," the sergeant replied.

"But he saved my mother and me from a cruel wretch who would have killed us both if he hadn't driven him away," urged Jack.

"Did he though?"

"Yes, indeed," said our hero; "but for him, it's certain I should have been killed."

"Then, guns and trumpets! he deserves all the kindness we can show him," cried the sergeant, with enthusiasm, "and he shall have it too."

"Then you won't take him prisoner, will you?"

"Oh, no, no; I'll make that all right," whispered Benjamin Crank.

Then taking the grenadier by the hand, he said in a cheery voice—

"Keep up your spirits, mounseer; I'm only going to send you to the hospital to get healed of your wound; and as soon as you're in a condition to run away, I shall just shut my eyes, and you may bolt as soon as you like."

The Frenchman thanked him sincerely, and then calling Jack aside, he took from his pocket a small gold ring, and said to him, with considerable emotion—

"This ring was my mother's, and I give it to you, my brave boy. If in the time to come Victor Montsorel can ever do you a service, this ring sent to him will always ensure his sympathy and assistance."

With these words he placed the ring on our hero's finger.

Then pressing his hand fervently, he murmured—

"*Dieu vous bénisse*—God bless you. Remember my name."

At this juncture Ned came hurrying back.

"None of the doctors can leave, they are so busy," he said. "The wounded are to be sent forward."

"Umph!" grunted Benjamin; "very well."

He reflected an instant, and then ordering the men to form a litter of their muskets, he spread a great coat upon them, and on this the wounded grenadier was borne away.

"That's no common man, dash my cocked hat if it is," muttered the sergeant, as he watched his departure.

Then turning to Jack, he said—

"And now, my boy, let us come and find some means of conveyance for mother and little sister."

But he added to himself, as they went out—

"I'm afraid there's not much hope for either of them."

They hurried along, with the dog, which Jack had christened "Battle," running at their sides.

* * * * *

In less than half an hour they returned with a comfortable litter.

But Ruth and her infant were no longer there.

How they had been removed was a mystery not to be explained, unless the face of the ruffianly peasant at the window might account for it.

Jack uttered a cry of despair when he ascertained his loss.

"I've neither father, mother, nor sister now," he sobbed, bitterly.

Sergeant Crank tried to console him as well as he could.

"Poor boy! I'll be a father and mother to you," he whispered, soothingly.

"And I'll be a brother and sister rolled into one," whispered Ned Rattles.

Jack wiped his eyes, and tried to be cheerful, but he could not forget his mother.

He seemed now to be alone in the world, and felt quite heartbroken.

"Give me your hand, my boy. I will never forsake you. You shall be like my own son, and I will be a good father to you while I live. Come, my boy."

CHAPTER VIII.

JACK'S FIRST UNIFORM, AND HIS FIRST FOE.

SOME days had passed.

Sergeant Crank had instituted all possible inquiries respecting Mrs. Barrington and her child, but without success.

But no bodies had been found.

The sergeant augured favourably from this.

"I agree with the noble earl—God bless him!" he cried, "that a forlorn hope's better than none at all."

"So I say, sergeant," said Ned Rattles.

"Then you think my mother and sister Lyddy are alive?"

"Well, since there's no proof that they're dead, I think it's possible they may be."

"So do I," joined in Ned, heartily.

"If they are, then, I shall be almost sure to meet them again some day, shan't I?" said Jack.

"Of course."

"And now, Jack, my boy, do you think you'd like to be a soldier?"

"I'm sure I should, sergeant," replied Jack, with energy.

"That's hearty; you speak as if you meant it."

"I do mean it, in real earnest."

"Well, now, of course you must have a beginning."

"Oh, yes."

"You won't expect to be a commander-in-chief for a month or so," said Benjamin Crank, accompanying this remark with a sly wink.

"I should think not; nor for a year or two, either, you know that well enough," Jack replied.

"Ha, ha!" laughed the sergeant, "I see you understand me. Well, then, suppose you begin as a drummer boy."

"A drummer boy?" echoed Jack, his eyes sparkling.

"Yes; I began in that line. Will it suit you?"

"Oh, yes, yes. I should like that better than anything," cried our hero, eagerly, "but I shall want a uniform."

"You shall have it."

"And a drum."

"You shall have that too—you couldn't very

well be a drummer without a drum," laughed Benjamin.

"Why, I shall be exactly like you, shan't I?" said Jack, turning to Ned.

"Oh, you'll cut me out altogether, when you get on your military togs," said Ned.

"But it will be a long time before I shall be able to play the drum like you," returned Jack.

"Oh, no; you'll get on with the rat-tat-tat like a house on fire," said Ned.

This important matter being settled, the next day our hero was installed in a brand-new uniform, and supplied with a brand-new drum.

His dress fitted him admirably.

Sergeant Crank was in raptures at his appearance, and conducted him, drum and all, at once to the canteen.

Ned Rattles and several other drummers were assembled there.

"Here we are!" cried Ben, as he entered; "allow me to introduce to you Gallant Jack, the drummer of the 47th regiment of Grenadiers."

Our youthful hero stepped forward and saluted his comrades in military fashion.

"Bravo, capital!" cried Sergeant Crank.

"Bravo, capital!" echoed the rest.

"He's got the cut of a soldier already, hasn't he?" said Ned, to a drummer next him, whose name was Caleb Corder.

"Cut of a soldier! pooh!" muttered the latter, in a contemptuous tone; "more like an image of a twelfth cake."

"Well, you are a surly pig," retorted Ned.

Caleb scowled at his comrade, and looked as if he had half a mind to quarrel.

"He's a perfect model of a drummer-boy, isn't he, Biddy?" said Ben.

"Och, shure, he's that same," replied Biddy; "he looks like an angel in a sojer's coat dhropped from the clouds."

Caleb Corder was the only one who seemed to think differently.

But he was, as Ned Rattles had remarked, a surly lad.

Surly and vindictive.

Greedy of promotion, he had tried hard to curry favour with Sergeant Crank.

But it was by backbiting and telling tales of others.

He had failed signally in consequence.

"Never speak ill of a comrade behind his back," was one of the mottoes of the honest sergeant.

And instead of applauding Caleb Corder's sneaking ways, he despised them.

As Jack strutted up and down the canteen, he could not forbear sounding a rub-a-dub-dub to the best of his ability.

This, which raised a good-natured smile on the faces of most of his companions, excited only disgust in the mind of Caleb Corder.

"Ugh! you think a good deal of yourself, don't you?" he sneered, as Jack passed him, "you and your drum; and you can't even roll it."

"Not roll it?" echoed Jack; "I'm sure I can."

"Get out, you can't."

"You shall see."

With these words, he took the drum from off his shoulder and rolled it along the ground.

"Ha, ha, ha!" shouted Caleb Corder, "ho, ho, ho! call that rolling a drum; you're a pretty drummer, you are."

"What do you mean?" asked Jack.

"This is what I mean," Caleb answered, as he snatched up the instrument and beat the roll call.

"There, that's what I mean. That's the roll of the drum," said Caleb.

He was a good player, and looked round in the expectation of a little applause.

None came.

But the next moment a voice was heard exclaiming, in an unmistakable brogue—

"Brayvo, brayvo, brayvo! shure it's enough to charm the heart of a cabbage or a broomstick, sich playing as that."

There was a general laugh.

In the midst of which the round, good-natured face of Brian O'Flinn appeared at the door of the canteen.

Brian was Biddy's nephew—her own dear brother Pat's son and heir, as the old woman declared.

He was a young bugler in the army.

A good-natured, warm-hearted, rollicking son of Erin, full of fun and frolic.

Brave in war, friendly in peace.

Caleb set down the drum with a scowl.

Brian continued—

"That was a mighty pretty tune you played just now, honey, only it was all through alike. Couldn't you give it us ag'in wid variations?"

Caleb bit his lip, but said nothing.

"You're improving rapidly, me darling," went on Brian; "if you keep on at this rate, you'll be wanting a big drum wid two ends afore long; won't he, boys?"

Those around replied with a laugh.

"I don't want any of your chaff, Brian O'Flinn; go and play your bugle, that's enough for you," said Caleb.

"It's just what I'm going to do," grinned Brian. "I hope you'll like the tune."

And raising his horn to his lips, he bent down and blew such a ringing blast in the ears of the surly drummer that the latter was completely stunned.

Again the laugh was repeated.

And louder than before.

Caleb knew Brian O'Flinn could fight as well as he could joke, and he contented himself with waiting for some more favourable opportunity of avenging himself.

Brian O'Flinn turned towards Jack, who was contemplating his drum somewhat ruefully, with a drum-stick in each hand.

"Cheer up, me darlin'," he said to him in a hearty tone; "shure, it's a model drummer boy you are, ivery inch of you."

Just at this moment a burst of martial music from without reached their ears.

"What's that music?" asked Jack.

"It's the band of the commander-in-chief, my boy," said Brian.

"What! the Earl of Marlborough?"

"Yes, bedad, it's himself. He's got some as can play the dhrum in his regiment."

"I should like to be one of them," said Jack, in a longing tone.

"Well, who knows but what you may one of these days, honey?" replied Brian.

Just at this moment Sergeant Crank came hastily into the tent.

"Jack, Jack, my boy," he cried, "the general wants to see you directly. Come quickly this way."

The next moment Sergeant Crank had conducted him out, and he stood in the presence of the Earl of Marlborough and his staff, and a picked regiment of grenadiers.

CHAPTER IX.

BRIAN O'FLINN TELLS JACK A STORY.

"HERE he is, general," said the sergeant, proudly, as he pointed to his youthful *protégé*.

The earl looked down from his horse upon the miniature soldier, and a smile of satisfaction played upon his handsome features.

"Very good, very good, indeed," he ejaculated to himself.

Then turning to those around him, he addressed a few words to them.

During this, Caleb Corder had slung his drum on his back, and came from the canteen, and stood now with his head painfully erect, and his chest painfully inflated, and his eyes painfully right, grasping his drumsticks with painful rigidity.

"The earl must be struck with my soldier-like appearance," he thought.

But it unfortunately happened that the general took no notice of him whatever.

His entire attention, and the attention of his staff, was directed towards his youthful rival.

"I am extremely pleased with the appearance of my young namesake," said the earl at length to the sergeant; "see that you put him under tuition at once."

The sergeant touched his hat respectfully.

"By-the-bye, what is his surname?" the general inquired.

"Barrington, my lord," replied Benjamin Crank.

"Barrington? Very good; then take care that Jack Barrington turns out a good drummer, since I require him in the band of my own regiment."

"I have seen a face like his before, yet I cannot remember where," thought the earl.

He then waved his hand kindly to our hero, the trumpets sounded, and the troop marched on.

But never a glance did the general throw towards Caleb Corder, who stood there, stiff as a ramrod.

"It's all favour, and nothing else," growled the drummer to himself; "why should this bit of a baby be everything, whilst I——"

"Shure, it's becase you ain't good-looking enough, honey," whispered Brian O'Flinn, provokingly, in his ear; "but that isn't your fault, it's your misfortune."

Caleb muttered a little oath, and returned to the canteen.

The rest followed, Jack feeling himself several inches higher in consequence of the notice with which the earl had honoured him.

"You're a made man—I mean boy," exclaimed the sergeant to him, joyfully.

And then he called Caleb Corder.

"Now, Caleb," said Benjamin Crank, "you heard what the earl said?"

"Yes, I heard," replied Caleb, in a dogged, sulky tone.

"Very well; then you know his honour's wish respecting our young comrade here?"

"Oh, yes; he's to be made a good drummer."

"And you know why?"

"Yes; that he may belong to the band of the earl's regiment."

"Exactly; then now as you understand what's required, I shall hand him over to you to be instructed."

Caleb nodded his head, and his eyes flashed with an eager, vindictive light.

He liked the idea of being our hero's master.

"You'll find him an apt scholar," said the sergeant; "and mind you teach him all you know."

"All right," said Caleb, with a chuckle. "I'll teach him, but if he doesn't do as I tell him, I pity his knuckles, that's all."

But this last was thought, not spoken aloud.

Brian O'Flinn had kept his eyes on Caleb all the time that worthy was receiving his instructions, and reading his intention pretty accurately in the expression of his features, he took the earliest opportunity of calling Jack aside.

"So, me darlin', you're going to learn the dhrum, are ye?" he said to him.

"That I am," Jack replied, his eyes sparkling with animation, "and Caleb Corder's going to teach me."

"Oh, Caleb's going to teach ye, is he?"

"Yes; he says he'll make me a regular good player."

"Oh, yes, yes, no doubt. It puts me in mind of a story I once heard about dhrumming."

"A story?"

"Yes. I'll tell it you if you like; it may be of service to you."

"I should like to hear it," said Jack, eagerly.

"So you shall then, honey, an' mind yer pay partic'ler attention to it."

"I will."

"Well, then, once upon a time there was a nice little boy, named Jack——"

"Jack? Why, that's my name."

"What ov that? There's plenty ov Jacks in the world besides you. Well, this little boy wanted to be a soger, d'ye see?"

"Yes."

"An' so he enlisted; an' the sergeant ov the regiment put him under a drummer, ov the name of Caleb."

"Caleb? How strange."

"Yes, Caleb; wid orders that he should tache him to play the dhrum. Are you listening, darlin'?"

"With all my ears," replied Jack.

"Well, this Caleb was a thafe ov the world, an' had got a lot of bad blood in his heart agin the boy he was to tache."

"Why was that?"

"Why, because he was jealous of him, o' course. An' what d'ye think the bla'guard did?"

"What?"

"Well, you see, the dhrum isn't so asy to play as it seems."

"Isn't it? I thought anyone could play it."

"Anyone can make a noise on it. But that isn't playing it—as Jack soon found out."

"And Caleb taught him, I suppose?"

"Yes; an' this is how he taught him. When practise time came, he stood before his pupil wid his drumstick in his hand."

"Yes."

"An' ivery time he made a mistake, down came the stick on Jack's knuckles."

"That wasn't right."

"Devil a bit," cried Brian; "it was wrong entirely, especially for Jack's knuckles, which was puffed up, and swelled, and black an' blue."

"I wonder he could play at all," said our hero indignantly.

"He couldn't play at all, of course he couldn't," returned Brian, "wid his knuckles all bruised, and bleedin'; and so what d'ye think he did?"

"Threw down his drumsticks," said Jack.

"No; shure, he did something better than that."

"What?"

"Why, instead of throwin' down his drumsticks, he gave his bla'guard ov a teacher sich a whack on the sconce wid one of 'em, as knocked him down as dead as a door nail."

"Did it kill him?" inquired our hero, in amazement.

"Quite the conthrary, it did him a deal ov good, by tachin' him manners."

"Is that all?" asked our hero, with a smile.

"That's all," answered Brian, with a knowing wink. "Isn't it a nice story?"

"Capital."

"I thought it might be useful to yez, as you're goin' to learn the dhrum, so I tould yez."

"So it will," said Jack.

"If you should happen to have your knuckles rapped rayther more than what's good for 'em, you'll know what to do, won't yez?"

"Yes," replied our hero; "I shall know how to act."

CHAPTER X.

JACK DREAMS AND WAKES.

YOUNG Jack, at Sergeant Crank's suggestion, turned into bed early, as he was to have his first lesson on the drum at dawn on the following morning.

"Early to bed, and early to rise,
　Is the way to be healthy, wealthy, and wise,"

the sergeant declared, and a good drummer into the bargain.

Jack, perfectly happy at his prospects, and with the rat-a-tat ringing melodiously in his ears, laid his head on his pillow, and was soon sound asleep.

But he dreamt a good deal, and his dreams were strange.

He fancied he was haunted by a dark, shrouded figure.

A kind of mysterious human bogey, whose face and form he could not distinguish, but who followed him wherever he went.

This, though only a dream, pressed upon him heavily.

He thought he was walking in a long, narrow lane, with a high wall of thick hedge on each side.

All of a sudden, the shrouded figure sprang from the hedge right before his path.

"Stop!" it cried.

Jack stopped with a strange feeling of terror.

"Who are you?" he demanded, very excitedly.

"I am your evil genius," the figure replied, in a stern voice, that reminded him very much of Caleb Corder's.

"What do you want?"

"To ruin you," was the ominous reply.

"Why do you want to ruin me?" said Jack, feeling rather more indignant than alarmed.

"Because I hate you."

"I never did you any harm; why do you hate me?"

"Because everyone else likes you."

"That's not my fault."

"And I'll take care it's not my fault if I don't upset all your plans. Proud as you are of your new drum; clever as you think yourself, I mean to knock you over, smash you up, crush you!"

Jack looked at the figure in amazement as these fierce threats came hissing from beneath the dark shroud that enveloped it.

"You think," it continued, "because Sergeant Crank's taken you in hand, and because the Earl of Marlborough patted you on the head, you're going to be cock of the walk everywhere, don't you? Ha, ha! you young whelp, that for the sergeant—that for the earl. I don't care a fig for either of them."

Jack's indignation had been gradually increasing, and when he heard his best friends so scornfully spoken of, he could no longer restrain himself.

All his fear of the mysterious figure vanished, and springing forward (in his dream), he grasped the dark mantle that it wore, and with a desperate tug, dragged it away.

The figure stood revealed.

It was Caleb Corder.

The surprise burst the bonds of sleep.

Young Jack started up in his bed.

"It was only a dream, after all," he murmured, to himself.

But no.

What was that stealthy tread he heard almost close to his bed?

And that suppressed breathing?

"Someone's in the tent," he thought.

He remained quite still, listening.

Still he heard the muffled sounds.

It was evident he was not alone.

"Who's there?" he asked, after a moment.

There was no answer.

"Who can it be?" he thought.

Suddenly an idea flashed across his mind.

An idea, to him, more startling than knives, pistols, bayonets, or the whole array of deadly weapons.

His drum was in danger.

Some midnight intruder was there to steal it.

The thought was unendurable, and, with a quick bound, he sprang from his bed, and rushed towards the corner, where he had placed his instrument.

Joy! it was there safe enough.

He gave it a tap with one of the sticks, and it gave forth as sonorous a rub-a-dub as ever.

Jack breathed again.

"It must have been fancy," he said to himself. "The dream scared me, I suppose."

No more sounds were heard, and he got into bed again, but took the precaution to carry his drum to his bedside, and tie it by his handkerchief—passed through one of the cords—firmly to his wrist.

"Now, then," he argued, "if anyone takes my drum, they'll take me as well."

And with this thoroughly consoling reflection, he soon fell asleep again.

* * * * *

He was aroused by the gun firing at daybreak, and presently he heard the voice of Caleb Corder, calling gruffly outside—

"Five o'clock. Turn out, and look sharp."

Jack obeyed with the utmost readiness, and hurried to put on his new uniform.

But, to his astonishment and dismay, it had disappeared, and in its place there was a bundle of old clothes.

Our hero looked aghast at the miserable garments, the coarse serge coat and breeches, the blue worsted stockings, all over darns, and the high-low shoes cracked and brown with age, so utterly unsoldier-like, and so entirely different from anything he had ever worn before.

"I can't wear these horrid things. I won't," he exclaimed, quite in a passion.

His eye caught sight of a piece of paper, pinned to the coat, on which was written in capitals—

"For gallant Jack, *alias* Jack the bounce, *alias* the bantam cock and the duffing drummer."

These ironical epithets almost drove him mad, and tearing the paper into scraps, he shouted at the top of his voice—

"Thieves! thieves! thieves!"

"What are you making that confounded row about?" growled Caleb, looking into the tent.

"Some thief has stolen my uniform, and I can't come out."

"You must come out," returned Caleb, imperatively. "It's the sergeant's orders."

"But I've nothing to come out in," Jack cried, the tears almost in his eyes with despair.

"Tie a sheet round you."

"I shan't," shouted Jack, in a fury. "Bring me back my soldier's things."

"What do I know about your things?" said Caleb, scowling at him.

"I believe you do know something about them," Jack replied, fiercely.

"Curse your impudence."

"I believe you've taken my uniform away," Jack went on, "and if you don't bring it back, it'll be the worse for you."

"I know nothing about it, I tell you," growled his teacher. "Put on anything you can find."

"I won't put on these old rags," cried our hero; "that's flat."

"Oh, very well," returned Caleb, coolly, "then I can't give you your lesson, that's all; and when the sergeant hears of it, you'll be locked up for disobeying orders, and have your drum taken away."

Having uttered this as a warning, he withdrew a little.

Jack reflected.

The thought of displeasing Sergeant Crank was painful to him.

The idea of losing his drum was more awful still.

So after a moment he called out entreatingly—

"I say, Caleb; couldn't you give me my lesson inside the tent this morning?"

"No, I couldn't," was Caleb's surly reply.

"Only this once."

"No."

There being therefore no resource, Jack, very much against his will, put on the garments that lay at his feet.

They transformed him from a handsome soldier lad to a ragged peasant boy.

"I shall be laughed at by everyone that sees me," he exclaimed wistfully; "well, it isn't my fault."

And so slipping the strap of his drum over his shoulder, he emerged from the tent.

But he no longer held his head erect.

He felt crushed and humiliated.

To make the matter worse, Caleb, as soon as he saw him, burst into a violent fit of laughter.

"Ha, ha, ha! here's a member for the awkward squad. Ho, ho, ho! what a pretty drummer for the earl's band," he roared.

Jack Barrington bit his lips with vexation.

Caleb, having laughed till he was tired, exclaimed abruptly—

"Follow me."

CHAPTER XI.

JACK RECEIVES A LESSON AND GIVES ONE.

HAVING reached a quiet spot, they came to a halt under a tree, and the instruction commenced.

"Stand there," said Caleb sharply.

Jack went obediently where he was ordered.

Caleb had not neglected to bring one of his own drumsticks with him.

And as he stood before his pupil with frowning brows, and angry, bloodshot eyes, flourishing it ominously, Brian's story came vividly into our hero's memory.

It seemed quite like a repetition of it.

"Now then," cried Caleb; "attention! do you hear?"

"Yes, I am attending," said Jack.

"Don't make remarks, but notice me. Heads up, eyes right, elbows square; do you call that elbows square?"

"I don't know what you mean by elbows square," said our hero.

"Don't you? Then I'll show you," growled his teacher.

As he spoke, down came his drumstick sharply on Jack's elbow joint.

The blow was startling, and very painful.

"Oh, oh!" cried Jack, writhing under the pain, "oh!"

"Oh, you felt that, didn't you?" grinned his spiteful instructor.

"Yes, I did," returned Jack, looking up fiercely, "and I don't see why you need have hit me like that."

"Oh, you'll get no petting, I can tell you, my sweet suckling," returned Caleb, jeeringly; "you'll have lots of that sort of physic, if you come any of the obstinate dodge with me."

"I'm not obstinate," cried Jack, his face flushed with suppressed passion.

"Don't chatter, but do as I order you. Square your elbows?"

"How?"

"So."

As Caleb spoke, he, by several rough jerks, brought his pupil's arms into the required position.

"So, there," he cried.

"Is that right?"

"Yes. Mind you keep so; if not, look out for yourself. Now then, nurse your left stick this way."

"So?"

"Yes. Hold your right thus."

"Will this do?"

"Pretty well. Now then begin. Strike with right stick one rat, left stick one tat, and go on till I tell you to stop."

Jack commenced slowly and circumspectly.

Rat-tat, rat-tat, rat-tat, rat-tat.

Caleb Corder stood looking at him from under his brows with a very dissatisfied expression on his face.

His pupil was performing too well to please him.

"Double stroke," he shouted, suddenly.

Jack, not quite understanding, beat the drum quicker.

It was not what his master intended, and down came the drumstick savagely on the back of both his hands.

The blows were awfully painful and aggravating, and Jack felt strongly tempted to retaliate.

But he restrained himself, and Caleb then showed him what he wanted.

Rat-tat-tat!

Jack imitated very well, in spite of his bruised knuckles.

Then the strokes were changed again.

Rat-a-tat!

"There, beat that," said Caleb.

Rat-a-tat went Jack, quite correctly.

"Again," growled Caleb; "quicker, double quick."

Rat-a-tat!

"Confound him! he won't make a mistake," he muttered; "the young beggar does it on purpose."

Rat-a-tat! continued our hero.

"Stop!" roared the instructor, aiming a terribly vicious blow at his pupil's right knuckles.

But Jack was up to him this time, and popped his hands behind him.

JACK RAISED THE TERRIBLE MISSILE AND HURLED IT FROM THE WINDOW.

Caleb grew more savage than ever.

"What are you doing with your hands, you young humbug?" he bawled.

"Keeping them out of the way of your drumsticks," the young humbug replied.

"Don't give me any of your jaw," cried Caleb, "but bring your hands forward."

"I don't mean to have my knuckles smashed," returned Jack, doggedly.

"I'll smash your head as well as your knuckles, you young whelp. Take your hands from behind you, do you hear?"

"Will you promise not to hit me if I do?"

Caleb was about to make a fierce rejoinder, but a second thought crossed him, and restraining himself, he replied—

"Who wants to hit you, so long as you do as you re told?"

"I have done as I was told as well as I could, and you've hit me twice," Jack reminded him.

"Well, we shall go on better now; come, let me hear you play the rat-a-tat-a-tat again."

Jack, believing his teacher was in a little better humour, placed his sticks on his drum.

He had hardly commenced when Caleb Corder, whose improved temper was only assumed, brought down his stick once more with the most vindictive violence upon his unforfortunate pupil's knuckles.

"There, my artful, I owed you that."

Jack's patience was utterly exhausted.

His knuckles were all bruised and bleeding, just like Jack's knuckles in Brian O'Flinn's story.

Clenching his right drumstick firmly, he sprang forward and aimed a blow with all his strength at the head of his cowardly assailant.

From his not being tall, the blow fell a trifle short.

Instead of alighting upon Caleb's skull, the end of the drumstick landed with a tremendous whack on his nose.

The drummer uttered a terrific yell, and with his own drumstick made a blow at his pupil.

Jack had slipped out of his drum and put it on the ground, having previously thrown down his drumsticks.

"Ugh, you beast, you infernal young wretch," Caleb raved, as he made another rush forward. "I'll kill you!"

Jack staggered back against a gun, but in a moment recovered his balance and resolved to retaliate.

Which he did by an effective blow with his fist.

This was a settler for Caleb Corder, who lay howling in the grass.

When at length he was able to get up, he found our hero surrounded by a select party of his particular friends.

These being Sergeant Crank, Ned Rattles, and Brian O'Flinn, who had intended to stop the affair, but had not been quick enough.

"What's the meaning of this?" demanded the sergeant.

Jack looked towards Caleb and in a very straightforward manner said—

"He kept on hitting me, and at last I hit him."

"Nothing of the sort," groaned Caleb; "he's as obstinate as a pig and wouldn't do anything I told him, and when I tried all I could to show him, the young brute let fly at me with his drumstick."

"No, it was he struck me three times first," affirmed Jack; "look at my knuckles."

As he spoke, he held up the backs of his hands all puffed and bleeding, and black and blue.

"Look at my nose," wailed Caleb, as he pointed to that feature.

"Your nose," cried Sergeant Crank, indignantly; "serve you quite right; if it had been knocked off, it would have been no more than you deserved. I believe you have acted in a very brutal, unsoldier-like manner, and I shall order you under arrest. Tom and Brian, take him into custody."

"Wid all the pleasure in life," said Brian, as he collared his prisoner. "Hold him tight, Ned."

Ned Rattles seized him on the opposite side, and thus Caleb Corder was ignominiously marched off.

Half an hour afterwards he was seated in a cell handcuffed.

Doomed to a week's solitary confinement, and a mildly nutritious diet, peculiarly adapted to tame excitable and refractory spirits, bread and water.

Our hero was turned over to Ned Rattles, who had found Jack's regimental uniform, and under his friendly tuition our hero got on with the drum, as Ned predicted he would, "like a house on fire."

CHAPTER XII.

BRIAN O'FLINN DISCOVERS A PLOT.

A WEEK had passed away.

Inside the canteen were assembled Sergeant Crank, Jack Barrington, Ned Rattles, and Brian O'Flinn, with several of their comrades, smoking their pipes, and chatting over the prospects of the campaign.

"We make a move to-morrow, don't we, sergeant?" asked a grizzled, sturdy-looking grenadier.

"Can't say for certain," the sergeant replied, "but I think it's more than likely."

"The general isn't one to go to sleep on a success, like our last battle."

"Not he; God bless him!" exclaimed Crank fervently.

"Well, we licked the mounseers in the first engagement, anyhow."

"Aye, aye; that we did," chuckled the sergeant; "we've taken the fighting out of 'em for a bit."

"I 'spose they're laying up to get their wind, eh?"

"They'd better be quick about it, then; we shan't give 'em much breathing time."

"Is it known where they're encamped?"

"Not exactly. But there's a detachment gone off, to look after their movements."

"Ah! then we shall know before long."

"They're expected back to-night."

"Good!" exclaimed the grenadier.

Jack, who sat next to the sergeant, dropped in a word now.

"Are we going to-morrow?" he asked him with some eagerness. "I should like to march, now I can beat the rat-tat-tat on my drum."

"Ah, well, you won't be kept waiting long, my young hero," laughed the sergeant; "why, I heard from Ned Rattles you can play the morning call, or *réveillée*, as it's termed, as well as he can himself."

"That's a fact," cried Ned; "would you like to hear him?"

"Nothing I should like better," replied Sergeant Crank.

"Come along, then, old chap; on with your drum."

In a minute the instrument was slung over Jack's shoulder by his instructor, and the sticks placed in his hands.

"Now then, fire away, my honey!" exclaimed Brian O'Flinn, "an' don't spare the parchment."

Our hero had quite a flush on his handsome face, at the idea of playing before such a critical audience, but he threw out his chest, squared his elbows, and fired away in right earnest.

"Isn't he a picture of what a drummer boy ought to be?" whispered the sergeant admiringly, to his comrade next to him.

"A regler model from tip to toe," was the reply of the latter.

Rat-a-tat, rat-a-tat, went Jack's drum, to the great delight of all.

When he had done, he was greeted by a burst of applause.

"That's something like dhrumming," cried Brian. "By St. Patrick, if he don't bate that spalpeen, Caleb Corder, holler."

It was just at this juncture the door opened, and the identical personage last mentioned made his appearance.

His term of confinement having expired, he was again at liberty.

Bread and water for a week did not seem to have agreed with him.

His nose still bore traces of Jack's drumstick, and in its inflammatory condition, more resembled a ripe mulberry than the most interesting feature of the human face.

He was accompanied by a peculiar-looking individual, one Timothy Tootles, a fifer in the regiment to which he belonged.

He was tall for his age, and thin as a lath, with a pale face, a pair of pale, wandering eyes, and from much blowing at his fife he seemed to have blown whatever brains he might once have had out of his head, and all the flesh off his bones into the bargain, so that he was now little better than a shadow; in fact, he went by the nickname of "The Ghost."

He was too simple by nature to do any harm, and just the sort of individual to be made a tool of by others more reckless than himself.

He had a profound belief in his comrade, Caleb Corder.

On coming in, Caleb sneaked round as quietly as possible into a corner.

Timothy Tootles followed, and having ordered a foaming quart of beer and pipes to begin with, they sat smoking and speaking together in a low tone.

But Brian O'Flinn's quick eyes had caught sight of them, and he determined to give one of them, at least, very little rest.

"Hollo!" he cried suddenly. "Is it you, Masther Caleb? Yes, by jabers, so it is."

"Yes, it's me," returned Caleb, sullenly.

"I see it is, and Tootles alongside of yez."

"Yes, here I am," responded the fifer.

"You're not looking in first-rate condition, misther dhrummer," continued Brian, with mock sympathy; "why, I declare your own mother wouldn't know yez."

"No wonder, aither," said Timothy; "considering as he's been locked up and had nothing to eat for a week but bread and water."

Caleb scowled at him like a fiend, and as the only means of expressing his indignation, he gave his luckless comrade's toes such a crunch with his heel under the table that the latter uttered a piteous yell.

No one took any notice of this.

All inquired why Caleb had been locked up.

"Why," explained Brian; "for knocking a poor boy about, half his own size."

"Shame!" cried the listeners.

"And, dear me, what's the matter with his nose?" inquired a sarcastic old grenadier, as he pointed to Caleb's proboscis.

"Oh, shure he run it up agin a dhrumstick, and the dhrumstick proved too hard for it."

"No, he didn't," contradicted Timothy Tootles, nursing his toes as he spoke; "it was Jack Barrington, the new drummer, as hit him a whack on it; that's how it was done."

"Yes, that I did, and would do it again," cried Jack, "for he hit me many times first."

"Three groans for Caleb Corder," shouted Brian O'Flinn lustily.

The groans were given at once with the utmost heartiness.

The embittered drummer gnashed his teeth with impotent rage.

It would have been hard to say at that moment which he hated most.

Jack Barrington, who had struck the blow, or Timothy Tootles, for his lucid explanation of the way in which he had received it.

Caleb, after giving a scornful look, muttered—

"I'll yet be revenged upon Jack Barrington."

Timothy Tootles, seeing Caleb Corder was considerably perturbed in his mind, stood up.

Timothy had drunk some beer, and it had got into his head, and he felt himself unusually heroic.

"I don't see why you should all pitch upon my—hic—comrade, Ca—Caleb," he said, looking hard at the ceiling, instead of those he addressed.

"Shut up, Tootles," exclaimed Brian, in a soothing tone, "and don't be afther wasting your breath. Shure you'll be wanting all the wind in your poor body to blow your fife to-morrow."

"I've got plenty of—hic—wind," returned Tootles, rolling his eyes and seeming to look six ways at once; "I'm—hic—full of it."

"Ha, ha! only listen to the unhappy crathur," continued the bugler, with a pitying laugh; "and don't he look as if a puff from a bellows would blow him slap into the Bay of Biscay?"

"I'm a sight stronger than I looks," responded Timothy, swaying to and fro, like a poplar in a breeze.

"Ha, ha ! bravo, skeleton."

"Twig the Ghost," cried several voices.

"Ghost as I am, I've got a orful lot of sperrit in me, sperrit enough to stand—er—er—hic——"

Just at this juncture the fifer's brains, under the influence of beer, became greatly confused, and his comrade giving him a sharp side kick, his legs suddenly gave way and he disappeared under the table amidst a shout of laughter.

"Ugh ! you herring-gutted idiot," growled Caleb Corder, as he dived down after him and dragged him up by his neck; "if you say another word, I'll kill you."

This terrible threat brought Tootles to his senses, and before Brian O'Flinn could make any further remarks, some of the detachment who had just returned entered.

In the eager thirst for intelligence, Caleb and his ghostly comrade were forgotten.

"Where are the French?" was the excited answer.

"They've retreated to Brabant," answered one of the new comers.

"And the Duke of Burgundy, how's he going on?"

"Oh, he's had enough of it."

"What, was he wounded?"

"Not he. And lest he should get a bullet in his precious carcase, he has packed up his traps and gone back to Versailles."

"Ha, ha ! what a pretty general !" laughed the listeners, scornfully.

"And who takes the command now?" asked Sergeant Crank.

"Marshal Buffers, I think they call him."

"Marshal Boufflers," repeated the sergeant, correctively ; "a good general, too, though he is a Frenchman."

"But not equal to our own Marlborough?" cried several.

"Equal !" echoed Benjamin Crank, turning indignantly crimson at the idea. "Not to be mentioned in the same year with him. Three cheers for the noble earl."

The soldiers shouted three times three vociferously.

The tired and thirsty soldiers were in drinking mood, and throwing off their coats and cartridge boxes, they threw them on the ground in a heap, and began to be very convivial.

Caleb Corder sat moodily watching them from his corner.

Suddenly his eye rested upon a canister on which was plainly inscribed one word—

"Gunpowder."

That word was suggestive, and an idea had flashed across him. A terrible idea.

That tin case contained the means of inflicting ample vengeance upon all his enemies.

Without saying a word to his companion, who was nodding over his pipe, he rose from his seat and glided to the spot where the canister stood.

For a moment he waited to be sure no one was observing him, and seeing that the attention of all was fully engrossed, he snatched it quickly up and disappeared with it out of the room.

But with all his quickness he had not been unnoticed.

The quick eyes of Brian O'Flinn had caught sight of him, and noted his actions particularly, and as soon as he had gone out, he whispered to Ned—

"I say, honey, did you see that?"

"See what?"

"Why, what Caleb Cordher's just done.

"No. What was it?"

"He's just slipped out of the room, wid a canisther of gunpowdther in his fist."

"The deuce he has !" exclaimed Ned ; "what do you think he's up to?"

"Well, I should say he was after shootin' somebody."

"Seems like it ; but who?"

Ned Rattles considered a moment, and then repeated in a reflective tone—

"He hates young Jack and Sergeant Crank."

"That's sartin."

"He might be going to shoot one of them, or both."

"Och, murdher," muttered Brian, "the saints forbid."

"I don't think he's particularly fond of you, either, old fellow," Ned continued.

"Mayhap not."

"He doesn't like your chaff."

"Then you think, p'raps, he's going to give me an ounce of lead in exchange for my chaff, eh?"

"I think he wouldn't stand very nice about it, or about anything else that's bad," said Ned.

"Bad luck to the bla'guard !" exclaimed Brian ; "if I thought he meant shootin' me, or Jack the sergeant, or any ov us, by the powers I'd wring his neck, afore he could load his popper."

"P'raps it would be as well to tell the sergeant about this," Ned suggested.

"I don't know," replied Brian ; "I think it'd be as well first to slip out, and thry if we can find what the rapparee's intentions really are. Will you come?"

"Certainly."

"On we go then."

They were about to rise, when the door began to open very gently.

"Whist !" exclaimed Brian, in a low, hasty tone, as he laid his hand on his comrade, "don't stir."

They remained perfectly still.

The next moment the pale evil face of Caleb Corder appeared peeping through the partially-opened door.

"Talk of the divil," muttered Brian ; "it's himself. Let's pretend to be asleep."

CHAPTER XIII.
A GRAND BLOW-UP.

CALEB looked towards the assembled group for an instant.

Then feeling himself safe from notice, and little dreaming the pair of eyes were watching his movements, he stepped aside, and crept stealthily along till he reached the table, around which the soldiers were congregated, with their whole attention absorbed in the game of chess.

He then took a japanned case from beneath his frieze overcoat, which he had put on, and placed it under the chair on which the sergeant was seated with his arm round Jack, who was close to his side.

"That's the gunpowdther; och, the murtherous varmint," whispered Brian to Ned.

Caleb held in his hand what seemed to be a coil of white tape, one end of which communicated with the lower portion of the canister.

This he carried to the door, unrolling it, and placing it on the floor as he went, and throwing what remained on the outside.

Having accomplished this, he approached his comrade Timothy, who had just woke from a nap.

"I want you," he said to him in a low tone; "don't say a word, but step out quietly. I want to speak to you."

The weak-minded youth rubbed his eyes with his knuckles for an instant, and then did as he was told.

Caleb followed, and the door was closed.

As soon as they were gone, Brian quietly picked up the canister of gunpowder with the fuse attached.

"By all the saints," he muttered; "it ain't shooting—the divil's son—he manes, but blowing us all limb from limb."

An expression of indignant horror flashed into the faces of the young soldiers, as they comprehended the atrocious scheme, and Ned Rattles said—

"We'd better tell Sergeant Crank at once."

"No, me darlin'," rejoined Brian. "I think we've got brains enough in our heads and pluck enough in our bodies to upset the schemes of this unnat'ral varmint. Bedad, he bates Guy Faux holler."

"What do you mean to do?" asked Ned.

"Well, I don't quite know yet," answered Brian; "we must be guided by succumstances, but one thing I'm quite determined on."

"What's that?"

"Why, that neither me nor you nor any here shall be blowed to smithereens by Master Caleb, bad luck to him, and so come on."

"Where?"

"Outside."

Taking the canister in his hand, and dragging the connected fuse with it, Brian approached the door, and opening it very gently, listened.

"Do you hear anything?"

"Yes; the voice of Caleb; he's talkin' to his friend, the Ghost."

"Can you see them?"

"No. It's as dark as pitch."

"That's all the better."

"Ov course it is; they won't be able to see us. Now, then, get ready to slip out quickly. That's the sort."

Having got outside, the voice of the conspirator served to guide Brian and Ned Rattles to the spot where he stood, and they were soon standing close alongside him.

On the grass their footsteps made no sound, and shrouded in darkness, their presence was not in the least suspected.

They had only to listen.

The conference between Caleb and Timothy

Tootles commenced with a tremendous yawn from the latter, who then said to his comrade—

"What have you got to say to me?"

"This," returned Caleb; "I've been treated to-night very——"

"I haven't," interrupted Timothy; "not even to half a pint."

"Psha!" growled the drummer, "I didn't mean that sort of treating. I was going to say very badly treated. Do you understand me now?"

"Ye—es, I think so," returned Tim, rather vacantly.

"You think so? If you were not an idiot, you'd know I have."

"Well, I know you have, then; didn't I express my sentiments on that point?"

"They're all against me," continued Caleb, bitterly, "a regular dead set."

"Well, I consider it ain't by no means fair," said Timothy.

"Fair!" almost hissed Caleb; "it's infernal jobbery and corruption. There's old starchy Sergeant Crank and that Irish beggar, Brian O'Flinn——"

"I don't like him myself," interposed Timothy; "he said I'd got no wind."

"And Ned Rattles—all banded together against me. It's all on account of that sneaking young rat, Jack Barrington."

"The new drummer?"

"Yes; I'm determined not to stand it any longer," cried Caleb.

"I wouldn't, if I was you," said his comrade. "What are you going to do?"

"Wipe out the whole lot."

"Wh-wh-at d'yer mean by hic—wipin' of 'em out?" stammered the fifer, somewhat apprehensively.

"Why, blowin' 'em all to smash, of course," returned Caleb, in a tone of deadly determination.

"Oh, Lor'," murmured Timothy, "that would be wipin' of 'em out, with a vengeance."

"Well, and why not wipe them out? What good are they to me or to you?"

"Not much, as I knows on."

"Didn't that carrotty-headed Irishman turn you into ridicule, eh?"

"Yes, he certainly did call me a poor creetur, and said I'd got no wind."

"And all the time he knows you're the best fifer in the regiment."

Timothy cocked up his sharp nose in the dark, and felt decidedly flattered.

"I don't think there's many as could beat me," he replied, as he played an imaginary fife with his fingers.

"Well, then," returned Caleb, "give me your hand, and we will act together."

Timothy Tootles gave his hand readily.

"We'll put an end to all this," exclaimed Caleb.

"We!" echoed Tim; "how?"

"I'll tell you. I've put a three-pound canister of gunpowder under Sergeant Crank's chair, and the one end of the fuse I hold in my hand is connected with it—d'ye see?"

"I hear; well?"

"Well, you know the hollow tree yonder?"

"Yes, I knows it. There's a big hole up above, and a small hole underneath."

"Well, I carry the fuse up to the tree."

"Yes; and then?"

"Then all that has to be done is to light it."

"My I 'oo's goin' to do that?" asked Timothy.

"You are," answered Caleb, bluntly.

"Me?"

"Yes. I've done my share, and you must do yours."

Timothy hesitated and scratched his head.

"It's rayther a—a serious matter, b-b-blowin' up the 'ole lot, a-a-ain't it?" he stammered.

"Not at all," growled his evil counsellor.

"I—I don't quite like the idea of this," he said, after a moment.

"Psha!" hissed Caleb, between his teeth. "I thought you had some pluck in you."

"So I have," returned Timothy.

"Then show it now. Only get rid of this lot, and before a month's over, I shall be first drummer, and you first fifer in the earl's band."

"Shall I though?" exclaimed the simple-minded Tootles. "But s'pose I should be found out."

"It ain't very likely; we're safe enough."

"Very well; then I'll light it."

"That's brave—that's plucky," cried Caleb; "come on."

"Where are you going?"

"To the tree."

Walking carefully, and placing the fuse on the ground as he went, Caleb and his comrade approached the ruined trunk.

Very cautiously Brian O'Flinn and Ned Rattles followed.

Brian, carrying the canister of explosive material under his arm, and carefully carrying the coil of match with him.

They made a slight circuit, but reached the tree almost as soon as the conspirators.

"Now, then, where's the light?" asked Timothy.

"You shall have it as soon as I've climbed up into the hollow," Caleb answered.

"Are you going to get up there?"

"Yes, I want a good view of the explosion."

"Where's the fuse?"

"Here."

As Caleb spoke, he placed the end of the coil in his comrade's hand, and then at once got into the hollow of the trunk above, which was a few feet from the ground.

"Give us a match," called Timothy; "I feels all in a twitter like."

"Don't funk," returned his companion, "there's no danger."

With this assurance, Caleb took a small lantern from beneath his coat, and proceeded to light a piece of touchwood.

While this operation was performing, Brian O'Flinn quietly crept to the tree on his hands and knees, and placed the three-pound canister in the small hole at the bottom of the trunk, taking great care, however, not to disturb the fuse.

"Now thin," he whispered, as he crept back to Ned Rattles, "I think we've caught those murdtherous varmints in their own trap."

Caleb's voice was now heard.

"Here's the match," he said, as he leant down and handed the ignited touchwood to his agent.

"Now mind," he added, "as soon as you've lit the train, get up into the tree double quick time."

"Yer may be sure of that," returned Tim, as giving the touchwood a preliminary puff with his breath, he applied it carefully to the quick match.

With a sharp spiteful kind of a sound, like the hiss of a snake, the train began its journey.

Timothy Tootles scrambled into the hollow of the trunk, as he was directed, in double quick time.

"'Ere I am, all right," he said, as he joined his comrade very much out of breath.

They could distinctly trace the firing coil as it ran along the ground.

"Don't it fizz?" exclaimed the fifer.

Caleb Corder made no reply.

His eyes were riveted upon it in silence.

At length he turned upon his comrade, and exclaimed, with a furious burst that almost knocked him off his perch—

"What in the devil's name have you been doing to the fuse, eh?"

"I ain't been doin' nothink!" protested Timothy.

"It's a lie, you've been tampering with it," growled Caleb; "look at it. Look where it goes."

"So I am a-lookin'; it seems to me to be fizzin' proper."

"But is it going towards the canteen, idiot? Answer that," hissed the drummer, as he punched his luckless tool fiercely in his ribs.

"Oh, oh! No, I don't think it is," returned Timothy, in a wailing tone.

"I'm sure it isn't," cried Caleb wrathfully, "it's taking quite another direction."

"Lor' bless me, so it is," exclaimed Timothy suddenly; "why, I declare it seems to be winding round to the same point as it started from."

This was perfectly evident.

As Brian had cleverly arranged it, it was rapidly returning towards the tree.

Caleb little knew what was to be the result of this.

But in his wrath at the failure he uttered a bitter imprecation.

"You idiotic humbug, you bungling jack-ass," he cried, as he threw himself upon his brother conspirator, and grasped him by the throat; "you've disconnected the coil, and there'll be no explosion after all."

"I tell yer I ain't; leave go of my wind-pipe," gasped Timothy; "I can't get my breath."

"I'll choke the life out of your skeleton carcase," raved the furious Caleb, as he shook his unfortunate colleague savagely.

"Mur—mur—murder! help, help!"

"Ha!"

This exclamation was caused by a sudden and blinding flash of light.

Followed by a tremendous report.

The canister had exploded, shivering the trunk, and sending the two conspirators flying up in the air.

From which they descended with a tremendous thud to the ground again.

Aroused by the explosion, the party in the canteen came rushing out in a body.

The prevailing idea was that the French had attacked them.

But they saw nothing.

No signs of any enemy appeared.

The two victims of their own villany crawled away under cover of the darkness, with their hair singed off their heads, and every bone in their bodies bruised, scorched and blackened with gunpowder, and utterly baffled and dismayed.

"Bedad," chuckled Brian O' Flinn to his comrade, "it strikes me Master Caleb and the Ghost's had enough of gunpowder this time anyhow."

Brian spoke quite true, they had.

They had failed entirely in their atrocious plot, and only succeeded in blowing up themselves, nearly causing their own death.

CHAPTER XIV.
THE START FOR THE WOODS.

A FEW more days rolled by, and then the orders were issued to march.

Drums rolled, bugles sounded, tents were struck, and in a few hours the living mass was in motion.

Our hero, in full uniform, was, at his own urgent request, permitted to march by the side of Ned Rattles.

Caleb Corder and Timothy Tootles were also compelled to join the ranks, with aching joints, singed heads, and looking like a pair of half-washed sweeps, owing to the gunpowder with which their countenances were so thickly sprinkled.

Brian O'Flinn and Ned Rattles had kept their own counsel, and no one knew anything of the diabolical plot save the plotters and themselves.

The justly-punished conspirators had to account for the melancholy aspect they presented as best they could.

A powder flask had burst in their faces, they said, and this was believed readily enough.

But they found it awfully hard to perform their duties.

The French troops had marched on to Liege.

Thither the English followed, and came to a halt in sight of the town, where they waited for the word of command to attack the French.

It was the day after their arrival in Liege that two persons were together in a building which had been converted into a temporary guard-room. One was attired in the uniform of the French cuirassiers.

A man of sallow complexion, with dark hair and moustaches, who might have been called good-looking, but for the evil imprint which long-indulged licentious passions had left upon his features.

This was the renegade, Gasper Grimsby, who was known in the French army as Captain Gravellotte.

His companion wore a dragoon's uniform, and carried his right hand in a sling, but looked more like a military ogre than a soldier, being dark like his comrade, but—unlike him—bearded and hideously ugly.

He could be easily recognised, out of his disguise, as the ruffian peasant of the wood.

The captain was smoking a cigar.

After a few puffs he said to the dragoon, approvingly—

"You managed that business I entrusted to you very well, Jaques."

"I did ze best I could, captain," returned the other.

"And there is your reward."

As Gasper spoke, he held forth several gold pieces, which Jaques—whose surname was Sauvage—instantly took.

"And you have placed both mother and child in a place of security?" continued the captain, inquiringly.

"Oh, yes, monsieur ; I have put them under the care of Mother Barbel."

"They are safe with her, you think?"

"Certain. She'll look after them safe enough."

The dragoon grinned as he said this.

There was a slight pause.

Then Gasper said—

"The boy, it seems, slipped through your fingers."

"*Diable !* yes. The young wretch is as slippery as an eel."

"Jack Barrington has a good deal of his father in him, I suspect," muttered Gasper, to himself.

"*Ventrebleu !* the trouble the imp gave me !" continued Jaques. "I should have cut his throat or knocked his brains out, if that infernal bullet hadn't shattered my poor knuckles !"

As he spoke, the dragoon glanced down at his sling with a malignant scowl.

"I shouldn't have blamed you if you had," was his master's cool reply. "Still, on second thoughts, I'm not sorry you didn't."

"May I ask why, captain?"

"Well, I have my own private reasons," returned the other.

"Oh, yes, exactly," said Jaques.

"And you have reason to suppose that young Jack has been taken up by the English?" asked Captain Gravellotte.

"I saw him go away with a number of English soldiers."

Gasper looked up at the villanous countenance of the speaker, and said to him—

"The English army is encamped before the city?"

"Yes, monsieur."

"If by any possibility that boy, young Jack Barrington, could be seized upon—if you could lay hold of him, and bring him to me alive—mark you, alive !"

"Certainly—alive."

"I'll make the job worth your while."

"I'll see, captain. I dare say I can manage it."

"Do so, if you can."

"I will. *Au revoir, monsieur.*"

"*Au revoir.*"

Jaques Sauvage touched his cap and went out, pondering on the commission he had received.

"THE DRUMMER UTTERED A CRY, AND MAKE A BLOW AT HIS PUPIL."

"It will not pay me to waste my time and risk my life in looking after this young pup," he reflected. "I must employ a spy."

Having settled this point in his mind, he continued his walk.

Suddenly he espied, striding along a little ahead of him, a comrade—one Jules Gasconade, a corporal in the grenadiers.

"Hollo, *camarade!*" he cried to him.

"Ha, *mon ami*," called out the other in reply, as he halted and turned about.

The friends shook hands.

Jaques at once stated the service he required.

He could not have pitched upon a better man.

Jules Gasconade—surnamed the Great, from his bulk and the immense opinion he had of his own importance—was a perfect type of French egotism and self-conceit.

And under promise of a liberal remuneration he undertook to carry out the proposed plan.

"I shall do it, *mon ami*, I shall do it," he cried. "Not only shall I make inquiries about zis *petit garçon*, but I shall find him out. I shall bring him along viz me under my arm."

"I hope you will," Jaques replied.

"*Parbleu*, you shall see. What is his name?"

"Jack Barrington."

"Ah, yes, *ma foi*, let me put him down in my pocket book. So, Zhack Barreltone."

"No, Barrington."

"Ah, yes, Barrytone, zat is it."

Away went Jules, full of his enterprise, to a friend of his whom he had settled in his own mind should be his companion.

This was a baker named Pierre Pimpelot.

Pierre believed that he had mistaken his avocation.

Instead of baking bread, he was burning with military ardour.

Pierre was the tallest of tall and the sparest of spare individuals.

Jules was bulky and round as a tub.

Together they made a very capital pair of opposites.

"Ve shall start to-morrow at ze top of ze morning," cried Jules, who prided himself on his English.

And as they were going in search of an English lad, they both spoke the best English they knew.

"At ze top of ze morning to-morrow ve shall start," replied Pierre as they separated.

*   *   *   *   *

It was a beautiful day, and no immediate attack being contemplated, Ned Rattles proposed that he and young Jack should take a ramble in the beautiful country.

The sergeant was applied to for permission.

"Take care what you're about," he said. "Keep your eyes open and don't let the mounseers lay hold of you."

"We'll lay hold of them if they come near us," was young Jack's cheerful reply.

It took but little time to make preparations for the journey.

"We must take some prog with us," said Ned.

"What's prog?" asked Jack.

"How green you are," laughed his comrade. "I mean something to eat."

"Oh, yes," said Jack, laughing.

"And something to drink, too, in case we don't come upon any springs."

"Shall we take any guns with us?" asked Jack, with much gravity.

"Guns?" echoed Ned Rattles, with a lurking smile at the serious face our hero put on; "what sort, twenty-pounders?"

"Twenty-pounders, no," returned Jack. "I mean muskets with bayonets at the end."

Once more Ned Rattles burst into a hearty laugh.

"Why, you wouldn't be able to carry one of those heavy pieces a mile. And we're going farther than that, I hope."

"So do I. Into the woods I should like."

"Very well, then, we'll take our bayonets, and leave the muskets behind."

"But if we meet the French, what shall we do without guns?" asked Jack.

"Why, charge 'em with our bayonets, to be sure," cried Ned; "they can never stand English bayonets, they're so awfully ticklish."

"I think they are, especially at the point," laughed Jack.

At this moment, Jack's dog, which he had found and christened Lion, came running up, wagging his tail.

All being ready, Jack slipped on his drum, and clasped his drumsticks.

"You won't want that," said Ned Rattles.

"Yes, I shall," returned Jack.

"You'll be tired to death with the weight."

"Not I. I never feel tired when I'm beating the rat-a-tat-tat, but I wish Brian was coming."

"Niver mind, me darlin'," said Biddy O'Flinn, who was standing by; "I'll tell him to follow yez, as soon as I see him."

"Tell him," cried Ned Rattles, "we shall make for the wood."

"That's clear enough. But when ye get into the wood, what thin?" asked Biddy.

"Why, then we'll stick bits of paper on the brambles and trunks as we go along, and that'll be a guide to him."

"Bedad, and so it will," said Biddy. "Shure, it's a clever head you've got of your own, Ned, me honey."

By a singular coincidence, Caleb Corder and Timothy Tootles, having no duty to perform on this particular morning, had started off for a country ramble.

They had not asked permission, but taken French leave, and slipped away on the sly at an early hour, little dreaming what would befal them in the wood.

*   *   *   *

The sun had barely risen, when Jules Gasconade made his appearance, attired in his full uniform, with his musket on his shoulder.

As soon as he knocked at the door of his friend the baker, it was opened, and Pierre Pimpelot emerged, arrayed in his civic guard's attire, musket in hand, and a large basket containing very substantial provisions and sundry drinks for the day's consumption, not forgetting a long coil of new rope with a noose at the end, all ready prepared to encircle the arms of the youthful prisoner, when they caught him, and haul him back with them in triumph.

Had our hero known what active arrangements were on foot to capture him and place him in the hands of his deadly enemy, he would have preferred remaining under the protection of his kind friend, Sergeant Crank, of the British grenadiers.

Jules Gasconade and his comrade rejoiced as they went in search of our hero.

They smoked their pipes and sang martial songs till they were almost black in the face from their exertions.

"*Ma foi!* it is hot," exclaimed Jules Le Grand, as he stopped and mopped his face with his handkerchief.

"Ha, ha!" laughed the thin Pierre, "you are so fat, you shall melt all avay like a lump of vax, if you go on so."

"Ugh, miserable!" growled Jules, indignantly; "you have got no fat to melt, you are as dry as a broomstick."

In course of time they reached the confines of the wood.

"Ve must go through zis vood," said Jules; "from the ozair side ve shall get a good sight of ze Engleesh troops. *Marche!*"

And on they went through the wood.

"Suppose ve have a drop more Burgundee," suggested Pierre.

"*Avec plaisir*—with pleasure," replied Jules.

Again the bottle went to their lips.

"If ve succeed in zis surprise, and capture de English poy, it shall be a good sing for us," said Pierre, smacking his lips after drinking.

"If ve succeed?" echoed Jules, in a bombastic tone, as he wiped his moustaches; "ve are sure to succeed; ve shall get de little drummer in de rope. Vhen did I evair fail?"

"No, no, you are a clevair man; a very clevair man; but how shall ve know zis *garçon*—zis Zhack, a—vhat you call him?"

"Bag-a-stones; did I not tell you? What a memory you have got."

"Ah, yes; Bag-a-stones. How vill you know him?"

"By ze prescription I have got of him, of course," returned Jules, as he drew out his pocket-book and opened it. "Here it is. Young, *très juli*——"

"Very pretty—handsome."

"Dark hair and eyes, full of curls."

"Ha, ha! *Ma foi*, vot a funnee boy."

"Hold your tongues, and don't interrupt."

"Pardon; and his dress?"

"Short pantaloons, green serge shirt, arms and legs bare. Zere, is not zat varee clear?"

"Begar, yes," returned Pierre; "it is impossible to make a mistake."

"Certainlee it are; ve shall catch him as sure as—ch—vhat vas dat?"

"Vhat?"

"Did you not hear?"

"Vhat?"

"It sounds very mosh like somevone snoring through his nose," said Jules; "hush! zere it is again."

"I should say zere moss be a nose somevheres near," suggested his comrade.

"Let us look."

Grasping their muskets firmly, the two heroic adventurers glanced around them.

They were not long in discovering from whence the music they heard proceeded.

It was not from one nose alone.

There were two noses engaged in the concert, and these belonged to Caleb Corder and Timothy Tootles.

"*Diable!*" exclaimed Jules Gasconade, in a whisper, as he stood gazing at the slumberers; "who are zese?"

"Are zey *Anglais*—Engleesh?"

"It is ze Engleesh uniform what zey wears, *sans doute*," Jules replied, "but——"

He bent down to catch a glimpse of their faces.

They puzzled him extremely.

"*Ventrebleu!*" he ejaculated, after a moment, in a perplexed tone, "zey look like——"

"Like vhat?"

"*Ma foi!* it is impossible to say vhat zey look like."

Pierre then peeped.

"*Sacré!* zey are half black and half vhite!" he exclaimed, in profound astonishment; "vhat vill you do viz zem?"

"I sink," replied Jules Le Grand, after a long pause, curling his moustache, and throwing as much importance into his tone as he could; "ze best thing to do vill be to a—a—a—do nozing."

"Nozing?" echoed Pierre, opening his eyes with surprise. "How do you know vun of zese may not be ze *garçon*—ze boy you seek?"

"Vot, Zhack Barleycorns!" exclaimed Jules, contemptuously; "zey are not in ze least like him."

"Not mosh, dat is true," admitted Pierre; "but," he added, suggestively, "zey might be able to give you some news of him. Don't you see?"

Jules Gasconade raised his eyebrows quickly.

"Of course I see. I alvays see everysing," he replied, sharply. "You take ze words out of my mouse."

The question now was how the sleepers were to be roused.

Pierre was ready primed with another suggestion, which he proffered at once.

"Ve vill fire our muskets in zeir ears bang, bang!" he said, cheerfully.

"No, ve von't," snapped Jules; "zere is somesing to be done first."

"What is that?"

"Open your eyes, and you shall see," grunted the bulky corporal.

Having said this, he took the coil of rope which hung on his comrade's arm, and with a complacent look of superior wisdom on his features, he unrolled it.

Then kneeling down, he passed the noose over the right feet of the slumbering pair, and bound their ankles firmly together.

"There," he said, looking proudly at his companion, "zat is vhat vas to be done, and I have done it."

"Now zen ve can fire away," exclaimed Pierre, who was longing to hear the report of his own gun.

"Now, then — make ready — present — fire!"

Bang, bang! went the guns in the air.

With a startled yell of terror the sleepers burst from their repose.

"They're arter us for desertin'," shrieked Timothy Tootles, as he sprang up, and, checked by the rope, fell down again immediately on his comrade's body.

Caleb, with an angry oath, made a bound on to his feet, and for the same reason was as quickly on his back again.

Thinking it a favourable opportunity to approach, Jules Gasconade and his companion came forward with their muskets in their hands.

"Hallo!" they cried, fiercely, as they presented the weapons.

"'Ullo!" returned the prisoners, looking up at them in some bewilderment and dismay.

"It is no use trying to ron avay," exclaimed Jules.

"Who are you?" inquired Pierre.

"We are Engleesh soldiers," replied Caleb Corder, with some hesitation.

"Vat you vant here?"

"Nothing."

"Zat von't do; you must vont somesing."

"Yes, we wornts grub," said Timothy.

"Nevair hear of no such a person," answered Jules Gasconade, shaking his head.

"Summat to eat, I mean, mounseer," explained the fifer, rubbing his stomach, which was croaking lamentably.

"And to drink too," joined in Caleb; "we're regularly famished."

"Don't zey feed you Engleesh soldiers?" inquired the corporal.

"Yes, but we've been out since daybreak, and our provisions are all gone."

Jules eyed the speakers reflectively a moment, and then he said—

"What is ze mattair viz your *visages*—your faces?"

The spotted countenances of the parties addressed lengthened considerably at this question, and for a moment they made no reply.

At length Timothy answered in a very doleful tone—

"Me and my comrade's had a bad attack of the measles, that's what it is."

"De measel!" yelled Jules; "*ma foi*, it seem to me you have de black peppair in your face."

"It did give us pepper certainly. We was very nigh croakers with it," said the fifer.

"But we're all right again now, and are confoundedly hungry," said Caleb. "If you've got anything to eat in there, let's have a bit with you."

"Well," Jules replied, "I shall give you some food, if you will tell me first somesing I vant to know."

"Fire away, then, I'll answer," said Caleb.

"I vant to know if zere is a *jeune garçon*, a young boy among the Engleesh troops, what is call Zhack Barleycorns?"

"Ha, ha!" roared Pierre; "Barleycorn, ha, ha! *mon ami*, vhat a memory you've got."

Jules frowned heavily at this retort, whilst Caleb replied—

"There's a boy named Jack Barrington in the camp."

"Ah, *vraiment*, yes, zat is ze name. And he's there, is he?"

"Yes," growled Caleb; "what of him?"

"I vaut to see him," said Jules, somewhat impressively.

"Oh!"

"I have got a message to deliver to him from his mozair."

"His mother, eh?"

"Yes. Could you go and find him, and bring him here to me?"

"I dare say we could," answered Caleb, "if our legs were untied."

"I shall untie zem."

"And provided we had a feed before starting."

"Couldn't stir a single peg without havin' some grub fust," joined in Timothy.

"You shall have food, zen," said Jules. "Pierre, *mon ami*, undo the basket," and he himself unfastened the rope.

It was just at this moment, when they were congratulating themselves on a sumptuous meal, that the sound of a drum was heard in the distance.

They knew the sound perfectly.

Their absence had been discovered, and a party was coming to seek them as deserters, they thought, and the punishment of desertion was death.

Timothy Tootles looked at Caleb.

"They're arter us," whispered the fifer, apprehensively; "if we're found, we shall be shot."

"We must be off, that's certain."

"It's 'ard to leave all them lovely pies and bottles, ain't it?" he said, his mouth watering profusely.

"Can't we sneak one or two of them before we start?" Caleb whispered.

"I'm good to try."

"Come on, then."

Jules Gasconade's back was towards them. He was giving some special directions to his colleague.

Quick as thought the hungry soldier lads made a swoop upon the provisions.

One seized a pie, the other a bottle of wine, with which they hastily decamped.

When the Frenchmen turned to address their prisoners, no trace of them was to be seen.

"*Diable!* zey have gone," gasped the great Jules, his eyes almost starting out of his head.

"*Hélas!* yes," cried his comrade, despairingly, as he set his foot in a plate of cucumber; "and zey have run avay viz ze *pâté de foies gras*—ze Strasburg pie."

Jules Gasconade groaned audibly, whilst still the distant drum made its rat-a tat to be heard.

CHAPTER XV.
PRISONERS OF WAR.

THE Frenchmen were at first greatly chagrined at their loss.

"Vhy did you not keep your eyes open?" said Jules.

"Vhy didn't you?"

"*Sot!*"

"*Imbécile!*"

"Ha! my *honneur* is insulted. Ve moss fight," shouted Jules, crimson with fury.

"Fight ve moss," echoed Pierre, whose very hair stood erect with indignation.

The enraged comrades seized their muskets, bristling with their sharp bayonets, and stood with their points presented at each other's breasts.

"Ve shall fight to ze death."

"*Certainement, oui*, to ze death."

They glared at one another in an awfully ferocious manner for a moment.

Then Jules, giving a sidelong glance at the preparations for the repast, said solemnly—

"Stay! let us take a drink first."

"Vid pleasure," assented Pierre.

They laid down their weapons, and having pledged one another politely in bumpers of Burgundy, took them up again.

Once more they were about to advance, when again they paused.

"It is a pity to fight before dinnare," remarked Jules, regretfully.

"Vell, yes, it is," admitted Pierre, with a rueful shrug of his shoulders.

"I might kill you, and I should not like you to die before you have your dinner."

"Or I might kill you."

"Or ve might both kill von anozair."

"And zen zere vould be no vun to eat ze dinnare at all."

At this affecting prospect, tears came into the eyes of the belligerents.

"Suppose we put it off till after dinnare?" whispered Jules, after a moment.

"*Volontiers*—willingly, or after to-morrow, if you like," said Pierre.

"Or vat if ve do not fight at all?"

"I sink zat vould be bettair."

"Are ve not *amis*—friens?"

"Ah, yes; brozers."

"*Mon cher* Jules."

"*Mon cher* Pierre."

They dropped their muskets and embraced each other with effusion.

The next moment they were seated on the grass amicably, devouring the luxuries before them with intense satisfaction, and in a most harmonious and brotherly manner.

Leaving them to continue their repast, let us return to our hero and Ned Rattles.

*   *   *   *   *

The English excursionists wandered on under the shade of the wood pleasantly enough, leaving scraps of paper, as they promised, on the branches and brambles they passed, to be a guide to Brian O'Flinn if he should wish to follow them.

By noon, Ned Rattles, coming to a halt, said—

"I vote we sit down and feed."

"I'm quite ready," said Jack.

They threw themselves on the grass.

"Now then," said Ned, "where's the bag with the grub?"

"You've got it, haven't you?" Jack replied.

"No, that I haven't. I thought you had it."

"Not I."

"And the water keg?"

"Nor that, either."

The two excursionists looked ruefully at each other.

"Here's a pretty go," exclaimed Ned Rattles ruefully, after a moment; "not a bit of anything to eat, and not a drop of anything to drink."

"Oh, dear, dear; that is awkward."

"Awkward! I should rather think it was," said Ned. "I feel hungry enough to eat my boots."

"So do I."

"Well, as it can't be helped, we must make the best of a bad job."

"I tell you what I wish," said our hero.

"What?"

"Why, that there were such things as fairies in the world, as there used to be."

"Why?" laughed Ned.

"Because we might meet one here in this wood."

"And what if we did?"

"Why, if we asked her very civilly, she'd cause a beautiful dinner of all sorts of nice things to be spread out before us in less than a minute."

"Oh, don't," exclaimed Ned, clasping his stomach. "Ah! I don't think there's much chance of a banquet here."

"No. How quiet it is. I don't think there's anyone in it but ourselves."

"And the birds."

"Ah! they're singing merrily enough overhead."

"They've had their dinner, most likely," remarked Ned; "but when a chap's peckish, it takes all the singing out of him."

"Shall I give you a tune on the drum to enliven you?" asked Jack, jumping up.

"Oh, no, bother the drum," cried Ned; "unless you can knock a quartern loaf out of it."

"Perhaps I can," laughed our hero, as he took the stick and gave it a few taps.

At the third stroke a vehement burst of laughter echoed through the wood.

It came evidently only from a short distance, and was extremely hilarious.

"Hallo!" exclaimed Tom, "there's something up not far off. What's going on, I wonder?"

"A picnic party in the woods, perhaps," suggested Jack.

"Perhaps so," Ned replied. "Let's see if we can find out."

As they went along, the laughter continued, and presently a voice, with a decidedly foreign accent, began to carol forth a song.

It was the voice of Jules Gasconade.

This is what he sang—

"Ve is brave, ve soldiers of France,
    An' ve fights for our countree an' king;
Our foes, how ve make zem to dance,
    Vhilst ve songs of victoree sing.
Vive la France! La belle France! Vive la France!"

"Phew!" whistled Ned Rattles, coming to a halt, as the voice ceased; "do you know what that means?"

"No, what?"

"Why, it strikes me there's a troop of French soldiers yonder. We must mind what we're about."

"Why should we mind them?" exclaimed Jack, expanding his chest boldly. "**Haven't** we got bayonets?"

"Two wouldn't be much use against fifty or a hundred," remarked Ned, with a rueful laugh.

"But then there's the drum."

"That's no good at all. And mind you don't begin to rattle it now, or you'll bring the whole lot down upon us, and we shall be made prisoners."

"Prisoners!" echoed our hero, almost indignantly. "They wouldn't dare to take us prisoners."

"Wouldn't they? Only give them the chance and see."

"What, and the English army, and the Earl of Marlborough, and Sergeant Crank so near?"

"What would they care about them, if they're not on the spot?" said Ned. "I've no particular fancy for seeing the inside of a French prison, I can tell you."

"What shall we do, then; go back?"

"Well, no," returned Ned. "I think we might advance with caution."

"Ah, yes. I should like to see the troop," said Jack.

"If we can get near enough without being caught sight of, we may be able to hear what they're talking about, and get some news worth carrying back," continued Ned.

"Ah," cried Jack; "let's come on."

"Gently, old chap; you mustn't be rash," said Ned.

Keeping well under cover of the trees, and a sharp look-out, Ned Rattles and our hero advanced.

The frequent bursts of laughter from the convivial Frenchmen served to guide Jack and Ned.

"Why, there are only two, after all," whispered Jack to his companion.

"All the better," returned Ned; "let's get a little nearer."

Jules and Pierre had finished their repast, and were now smoking their pipes and quaffing Burgundy, with an occasional nip of cognac to fortify their stomachs and aid digestion.

Both were in the highest spirits.

Every trace of their recent squabble had disappeared, and they seemed now to be on the most affectionate terms with each other.

"I loaf you, Pierre, *mon ami!*" exclaimed Jules, gushingly, to his comrade; "you are a good man, you are brave, I drink to you."

"I loaf you too, *mon* Jules," returned Pierre, as he filled a bumper of brandy.

"Don't I wish I could get at that pie?" whispered Ned.

"Don't I?" echoed Jack.

Further conversation was prevented by the corporal continuing—

"Vhat a fine sing it is to have an enterprise—an enterprise of danger to perform. I'm fond of danger; ve vill get ze boy Zhack Barleystones, and den ve shall be rich."

Our hero started, and pricked up his ears at this.

"They mean me, I think," he said hastily, to his companion.

"Hush!" whispered Ned, "listen."

"But if zis boy is in ze camp," Pierre continued, "how are ve to get hold of him, eh?"

"Oh, I shall manage it," returned Jules, tapping his forehead and winking his eye with inebriate profundity. "I have got it all here in my brains."

"Vot shall you do? Tell me."

"*Parbleu!* I shall get hold of him, and I shall pop ze rope over his arms, tie him up all nice an' tight, an' drag him back viz us as a prisonare of var. Ha, ha!"

"Ha, ha! dat vill be capital. Ha, ha, ha!" shrieked Pierre.

Jack nudged his comrade.

"I say," he whispered, "wouldn't it be jolly if we could take those two fellows prisoners instead of their taking me?"

"Yes, it would, indeed; very jolly," returned Ned, thoughtfully; "and it would be jollier still if we could take the pie as well."

"And some of the grapes and nuts, too. Shall we try?"

"I'm thinking," Ned murmured, as his eyes roamed over the ground. "There are two muskets with fixed bayonets."

"And there's the rope they're going to tie me up with," said Jack; "if we could only tie them up instead."

"Perhaps we may," returned his comrade. "Keep quiet."

The two Frenchmen, in the meantime, had taken another glass of cognac, and were beginning to show evident signs of having had quite enough.

"They're getting as drunk as pigs," remarked Ned Rattles.

"Oh, how I wish Brian was here," exclaimed our hero.

He had hardly uttered this wish when a peculiar whistle attracked his notice.

Turning his head quickly, to his great joy he espied the Irish lad, couched snugly behind one of the trees only a few yards off.

"Whist!" he murmured, putting his finger on his lips to imply silence.

Then, gliding rapidly forward, in a few seconds Brian was at the side of his companions.

Messieurs Jules Gasconade and Pierre Pimpelot were at that moment embracing one another.

Consequently they had neither heard his whistle nor witnessed his approach.

The arrival of Brian restored Ned Rattles and young Jack to perfect confidence, and it was pretty certain now that the game was in their hands.

"Bedad!" chuckled the bugler, "we'll have a beautiful lark wid these two mounseers, anyhow, if we niver have another."

"First of all," said Brian, "it'll be as well to get hould ov them two muskets."

"I think so too," replied Ned, and suiting the action to the word, they crept forward and quietly removed the weapons, placing them behind the tree that concealed them.

Jack at the same time had secured the rope.

Brian and Ned then shouldered a musket apiece, and placing themselves behind two trees, one on the right and the other on the left, waited for their cue to appear.

All being ready, young Jack, who had withdrawn himself to some little distance, began to rattle his drum merrily.

Tat-tat, rat-a-tat-tat, rat-a-tat-tat, t-r-r-r-a.

The inebriate Frenchmen looked round to see where the sound came from.

"Zat is a—hic—drom, I sink," remarked Jules Gasconade, huskily.

"Yes ; a drom it is, no doubt," exclaimed his comrade.

"Vhere do it coam from ? Ah ! who is zis ?"

"It is a drummer Engleesh,' said Pierre ; "he come zis vay, an' he have two heads."

Jack advanced, beating his drum merrily till he was almost close to the Frenchmen.

"Hallo !" they shouted, at length.

"Hallo !" returned our hero, heartily, coming to a halt, and winding up his drum performance with an energetic rattle.

"Who are you, sare ?" demanded Jules Gasconade.

"*Je suis Anglais*—I'm an Englishman," exclaimed our hero, throwing out his chest, and flourishing his drumsticks.

"Engleesh, *ma foi*, and yet you speak French ?" spluttered Pierre.

"Yes."

"Ah, zat is goot. Have a glass of vine ?"

"No, thank you ; I'm a teetotaller."

"Vat does he say—he is a teetotum ?" hiccoughed Jules.

"No ; a teetotaller," said Jack.

"What is zat ?"

"I drink nothing but water."

"Ugh ! bah !" growled the corporal, in disgust, "you should have been a pumpkin. Vhat is your name ?"

"Jack Barrington," cried our hero, proudly, drawing himself up, and extending his right arm in the air.

At this unexpected piece of information the eyes of the Frenchmen rolled in their heads.

"Zhack Barrytone !" they re-echoed, in evident surprise.

"Yes. You've got a message for me, haven't you, from my mother ?"

If anything could have sobered the two convivialists, these words would have done so.

As it was, they were, although intoxicated, very much astonished.

"Message from your mozer ? Ah, yes—hic —so ve has," stammered Jules, after a moment.

"She vant to see you, Mastair Zhack, ver mosh," added Pierre.

"Where is she," asked our hero.

"She is somevheres vaitin' for you," Jules answered, "an' if you come viz us, ve shall— hic—take you to her."

"*Parbleu !* yes, ve—hic—shall," joined in Pierre.

Having said this, the two Frenchmen tried to get up.

The legs of Jules Gasconade gave way under him.

He fell on his back.

His comrade fell upon him.

"Ugh, *cochon*—pig !" growled the former, "you have smash ze bone of my rib. You are drunk."

Jules cried—

"Vill you have ze kindness to help me up on to my legs, Mistair Barrytones ?"

"I will presently," returned our hero. "I'm going to have something to eat first."

"Ah, *oui, oui*," muttered the corporal, as he fell back on the grass. "*Vive la*—hic— *France !*"

Our hero called to his comrades behind the trees—

"Come on ; dinner's waiting."

They came forward with the utmost readiness, and were soon hard at work upon the remains of the feast.

"This is jolly, isn't it ?" said Ned Rattles, with his mouth full.

"Bedad, you're right, me boy," returned Brian, with a grin. "These mounseers know how to make meat pies, anyhow."

"And fruit pies as well," joined in Jack.

The bugler poured himself out a glass of Burgundy.

"The queen an' Marlboro' !" he cried, "not forgettin' a little un in for Ould Ireland."

"Is it nice ?" asked our hero, seeing that Brian made rather a wry face after drinking.

"Divil a bit !" replied the latter. "Sure it's for all the world like vinegar, an' wants a dhrop of whisky in it to give it a flavour."

"I think we'll be able to get back to the camp in style now," Brian remarked.

"Yes, and take our prisoners with us," laughed Jack, as he pointed to the sleepers.

"Oh, ov course ; it'd niver do to lave them behind us. Tare an' 'ouns ! look at 'em."

"How are we to get them along ?" asked Jack.

"Whist, me darlin' ; hold hard a bit. I've a notion we'll be able to make 'em move fast enough."

"By what means ?"

"Well, first there's your dhrum."

"But suppose they won't wake, what then ?"

"Why, then we'll have to tickle 'em a little with the points ov the bayonets, honey," grinned Brian. "They're wondtherful ticklers, they are."

"Suppose they were only shamming all this time !"

"Shamming ! not they," returned Brian O'Flinn ; "but anyhow, to make sure ov 'em, we'll tie 'em together."

As the bugler spoke, he drew from his pocket a piece of stout cord.

With this he quickly fastened the right leg of the corporal to the left leg of his comrade.

This done, he uncoiled the rope and passed it round their bodies, drawing it moderately tight at their waists.

All being thus prepared, Brian said—

"Now thin, Jack, me boy, play up somethin' lively on yer dhrum, an' get as near the mounseers' ears as you convaniently can."

Our hero placed himself close to them, and commenced a very lively rat-a tat.

The sound quickly awoke the slumberers.

"Ha, ze enemy !" cried Jules Gascouade, in a startled tone. "*Aux armes*—to arms !"

"*Mon fusil !*—my gun !" exclaimed Pierre Pimpelot, nervously.

In a very straggling and bewildered manner they contrived to drag themselves up to a sitting posture.

There they sat blinking like a pair of sleepy owls at the picture that presented itself.

THE TWO CONSPIRATORS WENT FLYING IN THE AIR.

Jack Barrington with his drum stood before them.

At a little distance to the right was posted Brian O'Flinn, holding in one hand a musket, and in the other the end of the rope that encircled their bodies.

At a similar distance to the left stood Ned Rattles, also armed with a musket.

The sight was so perplexing that for a moment the Frenchmen could only scratch their muddled heads and stare.

"*Diable!*" muttered Jules Gasconade, at length. "Vhat am de matter?"

"Nothing's the matter," returned Jack, ceasing his rat-a-tat. "I'm only waiting for you. March."

"Waiting for me?" echoed the corporal, in a mystified tone. "Vhat for you vait for me, eh?"

"Why, didn't you say——"

"Ah, yes, yes. *Vraiment!*—truly. I had forget. You shall come viz us to your mozer."

"No, thank you," said Jack, coolly.

"Vhat! not come?"

"No; you shall go with me instead."

"Go where?"

"To the English camp."

"*Le camp Anglais?*" echoed the Frenchmen, with one voice.

"Yes. As prisoners of war."

This idea quite tickled Jules and his comrade.

"Ha, ha! prisonairs of var," they grinned. "*Quel petit drôle!*—what a droll little fellow."

"Oh, I dare say you think it very funny," continued Jack; "but I'm in earnest."

Our hero spoke in such a decidedly stern tone for a youngster, that the Frenchmen looked at him in amazement, and, happening to glance aside, they caught sight of his comrades, Ned and Brian, who stood still as statues and upright as ramrods, musket in hand, waiting for the word of command.

The smile died out of the faces of the gallant adventurers, as they recognised their weapons in strange hands.

They realized, also, the fact that their legs were tethered together, that they were bound by a rope.

"*Sacré!*" burst out Jules, with a strong effort at bombast; "ve is sons of ze *grande nation*, and I demand my muskeet."

"Soldiers of France," joined in Pierre Pimpelot, "and I vant *mon fusil.*"

"Then you won't have it, either of you," returned Jack; "so get up and march."

"But, *diable!* how can ve get ope when some r—r—rascal villain have tie our two legs togezer?" growled Jules.

"I'll assist yez, mounseers," said Brian, as he gave the rope he held an encouraging jerk, and at the same time applied the point of the bayonet to the corporal's protuberant hindquarters.

He then performed a similar operation upon the spare anatomy of Pierre Pimpelot.

The effect was immediate.

"Oh, oh! *Je suis blessé à mort!*—I am mortally wounded," they each yelled out most piteously.

"Get up, then," grinned Brian.

Roaring like a couple of baited bulls, the "sons of the *grande nation*" scrambled to their feet.

"Now, then," cried our hero; "march."

The prisoners looked dolefully this way and that.

But there was no help for them.

Running away was impossible.

And so, with a rueful shrug of their shoulders, they resigned themselves to their fate.

With young Jack in front, rattling away on his drum, and followed by Brian O'Flinn and Ned Rattles, with pointed bayonets, the valiant Frenchmen shuffled along towards the English camp.

On their arrival there, it seemed as if fortune had especially intended to signalise our hero.

The first persons they met were Sergeant Crank, and the commander-in-chief and his staff.

The former chuckled to himself as he caught sight of the party, and heard the rattle of Jack's drum, and the earl exclaimed, in astonishment—

"Hallo! what have we here?"

"Prisoners of war, general," cried Jack, saluting respectfully.

"What! is it possible you have captured those men?"

"Yes, general," returned our hero, cheerfully; "we captured them between us."

"Where did you take them?" asked Marlborough.

"In the woods, general."

"And how did you manage it?"

"We took away their guns, tied their legs together, and led them along by a rope to the beat of the British drum, general," explained young Jack, naïvely.

"Bravo! excellent!" laughed the earl, heartily; then turning to his staff, he said to them—

"If that youngster lives, he'll make the foes of England remember one day that he is a Boy of England."

Jack Barrington heard this, and he placed it on the tablet of his memory, side by side with the other words the earl had spoken.

CHAPTER XVI.
CAPTAIN HECTOR TOMTONNERRE.

THE next day all was excitement in the English ranks.

Part of the French troops had advanced, and a body of the British had been ordered to attack them.

A sharp skirmish was the result.

Our hero, Ned Rattles, and Brian O'Flinn were present in the encounter.

The fight terminated in favour of the English, and the French were driven back into their entrenchments with considerable loss.

At the conclusion of the engagement, Jack and Ned Rattles were slowly returning across the field of battle, which was strewn with bodies, when suddenly they were arrested by a strange voice.

Gruff and harsh as its tones, and coming, they could not tell from whence.

"This is strange, isn't it?" said Ned Rattles.

"It is," said Jack.

Still the voice kept muttering in a low tone like muffled thunder.

"*Sacré!*" they heard it exclaim, in a deep, growling tone, "if ze cursed Engleesh had not run avay, I should have *écrasé*—crushed zem all. I should."

"Wherever does the voice come from?" said Jack.

"Hang me if I can tell."

They cast their eyes scrutinizingly about them.

On the ground at some little distance lay a large cannon that had fallen from its carriage, and been left upon the field.

This object attracted them.

As they stood looking at it, something rough and of a reddish hue was cautiously protruded, and almost immediately drawn in again.

"What was that?" exclaimed Jack.

"Looked something like a mop," Ned replied.

"Mops ain't red, though," remarked our hero.

"Not usually."

"Heads are, though, sometimes."

"Heads?"

"Yes. Heads of hair," said Jack, significantly.

".Ah! then where there's hair there's generally a head, isn't there?"

"Yes; and where there's a head there's usually a body as well."

"You think there's a body, then, in that cannon, eh?"

"I feel pretty sure there is."

"You mean to say there's a Frenchman there?"

Just at this moment they saw the bugler coming towards them.

"Here's Brian; hurrah," cried our hero; "we'll ask him what he thinks."

"There ye are, thin, me darlin's, all safe and sound," cried the Irish lad, joyfully.

Instead of answering his greeting, Jack put his fingers on his lips to enjoin silence.

"What's up, eh?" he asked.

Ned Rattles pointed to the cannon.

"There's a mystery in there," he said, with a subdued laugh.

"Oh, bedad, is there?"

"Yes. It's either a mop or a man, and we're not quite sure which," said Jack.

"We'll soon find out," grinned Brian; "let's come a little nearer."

They approached cautiously, and listened a moment.

The voice spoke again.

"Blood and blistairs, swords and pistoles! I shall kill zem all. Ah! *les maudits Anglais.* I shall annihilate zem, grind zeir bones."

These exclamations were uttered in a tone the most ferocious and bloodthirsty possible to conceive.

"What do you think of that?" asked Jack.

"Bedad, I think there must be an ogre inside there at the very least," replied Brian, with a comical assumption of dismay in his face.

"Don't he roll his r's?" remarked Ned Rattles.

"There's no doubt of that; he puts me in mind of Jack's dhrum."

"I think the best thing we can do is to get him out," Jack remarked.

"Right you are, me boy," said the bugler.

"Another prisoner," exclaimed our hero, exultingly.

"We'll soon see what he's made of," said Brian.

The above conversation had been carried on in a whisper.

And the Irishman, now, with a knowing wink at his companions, said aloud—

"I tell you it's loaded."

"I don't think so," returned Ned.

"You're wrong thin; didn't I see the gunner put in half a barrel ov gunpowther, and afore he could discharge it, didn't a ten-pound ball come and knock the poor divil's head clane off his shoulders?"

"Oh, if you saw him load the cannon, and then have his head blown off before he could fire it off, of course it's loaded," said Jack.

"Ov coorse, and I'll prove it to yer by firin' it off. Give me a light and bang'll go off the cannon."

At this the object inside the gun became decidedly uneasy.

"M—m—m—orbleu!" the voice was heard to mutter, "ze gun loaded! I shall be blowed into fragments; ugh, zese villains *Anglais!*"

The speaker's tone was very shaky.

"Hand me over the powder-flask," said Brian O'Flinn, after a moment.

A groan of mortal terror issued from the cannon.

"Here's the light," cried Jack, in a lively tone.

"Now, then, stand clear all of yez and put your fingers in your ears whilst I put the light to the touch-hole," bawled Brian.

These imaginary preparations were so appalling to the individual within that he uttered a doleful yell—

"Don't—don't—don't light ze powdare," he shouted; "zere ees somevon inside that vonts to get out."

"Someone inside!" echoed everybody, pretending to be very much astonished; "who is it?"

"It ees me, and I lob you all," wailed the voice.

"Who's me?" demanded Jack.

"Hector Gobelin Tomtonnerre, de noble soldier of France," was the answer.

"Well, then, Misther Goblin, p'r'aps you'll have the kindness to show us your physog," said Brian.

There was a slight pause, and then slowly a shaggy head of deep red hair protruded itself.

The head was raised and the features became visible, grimed and black with the gunpowder they had accumulated inside the gun, ornamented by a tremendous pair of moustaches and a long tuft on the chin, of the same Rufus-like hue.

"Behold me," exclaimed the smudged figure, in a deep, hoarse tone, and with a hideous grin on his face, intended doubtless to inspire the lookers-on with a proper dread of him, but it did not in the least produce this effect.

On the contrary, all present burst into a roar of laughter.

"*Sacr—r—r—é !*" growled the Frenchman; "vhat for you laugh, eh ?"

"Because we can't help it," replied our hero.

"Guns an' pistoles, I vill not be laughed at," exclaimed the red-haired man, fiercely. "I am a grand hero—a hero of France. Who dare to laugh at me shall die."

And the Frenchman pretended to draw his sword.

"Ha, ha ! hark at him," cried Brian. "Oh, sure the big boy will kill us. Ha, ha !"

And then, taking the hero of France by his nose, which was long enough to afford a good hold, he said—

"Now, then, mounseer, out wid yez."

"*Morbleu !* let go my *nez*—my nose."

"I'll be afther pullin' it off if you don't come out," returned Brian.

With much growling and spluttering the doughty Frenchman gradually poked himself out of the narrow quarters in which he had wedged himself, receiving much assistance during this operation from Brian's finger and thumb, which still kept a tight grip on the hero's proboscis.

"Phew !" he gasped, as he came to the ground on all fours, and, rolling himself into a sitting posture, extended his arms in the air with a great many wry faces, "my muscles is all cr—r—r—r—amps."

"Never mind your muscles," said Brian, "but tell us what you are."

"*Je suis soldat*—I am a soldier of ze *grande armée*—a hero of F—r—rance."

"A hero, ha ! Shure, are there many more of ye ?" grinned Brian and the rest.

"Can you play the drum ?" joined in Jack.

"Ze drom !" echoed the hero contemptuously. "Bah ! do I look like a drummer ?"

"Not much," Jack laughed. "Just now you're a great deal more like a sweep."

This created a general roar.

"*Sacré mille tonnerres !*" exclaimed the Frenchman, in a fury. "I do understand a little of de English, and you say a sveep !—me, Hector Tomtonnerre, captain of cuirassiers, a sveep ! Shade of Achilles ! I shall sveep him to destruction !"

This indignant burst caused a second explosion of laughter heartier than the first.

The speaker, with his ill-fitting jacket of tarnished yellow lace, and his baggy trousers thrust into a pair of boots like candle-cases, did not look at all like a captain.

But the laughter of the lookers-on increased his wrath.

He felt each of his sides and behind his back for his sword.

Not being able to find it anywhere, he shook both his fists and ground his teeth furiously at our hero.

"There, that'll do, mounseer," said Brian. "You'd better shut up, and come along wid us as our prisoner quiet and paceable."

"Come wiz you as your prisoner ?" yelled the cuirassier, puffing out his cheeks and grinning ferociously. "Nevair, nevair, nevair, nevair !"

Brian O'Flinn and his comrades quietly drew their short swords, and went up to him.

"You won't come, won't you ?" repeated the Irishman.

"Nevair !"

Brian gave him a slight dig with the sharp point of his sword.

Ned Rattles gave him another dig with his.

Jack Barrington followed with a little one in from his.

"Oh ! ugh ! oh !" howled the Frenchman; "it do hurt me all behind," as he danced about, rubbing the lower regions of his back with both his hands.

"Are you ready ?"

"Oh, yos, yos ; I am ready," groaned the captain of cuirassiers, "oh, oh !"

"Stop a minnit," said the bugler.

He took a piece of cord from his pocket and pinioned his arms.

"Now then, off we go ; march !"

Once more Jack's drum sounded, and the English party walked on, with their prisoner groaning and execrating by turns, in their midst.

The capture of Captain Hector Tomtonnerre being reported at headquarters, he was placed in confinement with the other prisoners.

CHAPTER XVII.
THE GAMBLERS.

IT was on the following day that the Frenchmen were seated in the open air, smoking their pipes.

The English did not, as a rule, shut up their prisoners of war in close, poisonous dungeons.

Consequently, Jules and his comrade Pierre and the redoubtable Hector Gobelin Tomtonnerre, although kept under vigilant watch, were allowed the free use of their limbs.

The mounseers did not like the idea of being in the power of the English.

The most discontented amongst them was the red-haired captain of cuirassiers.

The oaths he swore and the wrathful manner in which he twirled his moustaches and rolled his r's was something almost terrible to witness.

"Zose r-r-rascal *Anglais !*" he growled, "to dare to make me a prisoner ! me—Hector Gobelin Tomtonner-r-r-e. Guns and pistols ! if I had a weapon in my hands, I should do somesing terrible ; ha, ha ! I should kill von hundred of ze miserable English before my breakfast."

Jules and Pierre had very good opinions of themselves.

But they were nowhere by the side of their fierce countryman.

He could swear ten times louder and drink ten times deeper than they could.

They looked upon him, consequently, as a very terrible being indeed—a regular fire-eater.

"Do not excite yourself, *mon ami ;* vhat is ze good ?" said Jules.

The cuirassier captain turned upon him with a ferocious scowl.

"*Va t'en, misérable !*"

Which, in plain English means—

"Get out, you miserable wretch !"

Jules felt himself crushed.

Pierre came to his assistance.

"Calm yourself, *mon brave !*" he said; "here are the cards; let us play."

The vindictive Hector was about to consign the spectral-like guard to instant perdition, but catching sight of the cards, his mind altered suddenly.

"Ah, yes !" he exclaimed, reflectively, winding one of his long, wiry red moustaches round his finger like a corkscrew, "play; it ees a great *honneur* I do to play viz sosh as you; *mais n'importe*—no matter, I will condescend."

The bombastic captain did not join his *confrères* at once.

He took a few more turns up and down, but a close observer might have quietly noticed that he quickly thrust some cards up his sleeve.

This done, he stalked to the table, and seated himself with a terrific "Ahem !"

He then drew from his breast pocket a handsome morocco leather pocket-book, and slapped it down with a bang, that sent the hearts of his companions into their mouths.

It was just at this crisis Brian O'Flinn and Ned drew near.

They had been watching the manœuvres of Monsieur Hector for some little time.

"Two to one on the winner," said Brian.

The cuirassier uttered a savage grunt, and said—

"Let us put down ze stakes."

"How mosh ?" asked Jules.

"Five francs apiece," was the answer.

"I shall shuffle," the captain said.

Leaving the Frenchmen to continue their pastime, let us go to the quarters of Sergeant Crank.

Jack Barrington was with him when a note was brought him.

It was addressed to—

"General the Earl of Marlborough."

The sergeant took it, and, wishing to bring our hero as much as possible before the notice of the commander-in-chief, he said to him—

"Now, my boy, you see this despatch ?"

"Yes," said Jack.

"Well, go at once to the tent of the earl, and deliver it to him. Wait to know if there is any answer."

Away went Jack.

In a few moments he reached the general's tent.

"Your business ?" demanded the sentinel on duty before it.

"A despatch for the general," replied Jack.

"Enter."

The earl, who was writing when he entered, looked up.

"Ha, my young hero," he said, with a smile, "what brings you here ?"

"This, general," replied Jack, saluting respectfully, and holding forth the note.

The earl took it, examined the address attentively, and then opened it.

"Ha !" he exclaimed, in some surprise; "'tis from the French general, Marshal Boufflers; what can it be about ?"

Without further remark, he read the letter, to himself, but aloud.

"GENERAL,—You will probably be surprised at receiving a written communication from one who, by the rules of war, is your foe; but, although this is the case, the chivalry of nations still exists, and the name of Marlborough being a guarantee for all that is generous and honourable in man—all that is brave and skilful as a soldier—I do not hesitate to appeal to you.

"The cause of my addressing you is, that I have been robbed of five thousand francs by a scoundrel whom I had employed for a short time as my valet. It is supposed that he deserted after the engagement of yesterday, and that he has joined the English ranks. His name is André Fouet, and I shall esteem it a favour if you will cause inquiries to be made, and that, if found, he may be conveyed to the French lines, in order that he may be dealt with as he deserves. On my part, I promise a reward of two thousand francs to anyone who shall arrest the fellow. He is above the middle height, strongly built, wears neither beard nor moustaches, his hair a light flaxen.

"I have the honour to be,
"Yours,
"With much respect and admiration,
"BOUFFLERS.
"To the Earl of Marlborough,
"Commander-in-Chief of the English Army."

The earl, having finished the letter, said to our hero—

"Send Sergeant Crank to me."

In a few moments the latter obeyed the summons.

The general explained what had taken place, and ordered that strict inquiries should be made in the ranks after the culprit.

This was at once done; but no one answering to the description could be found.

When Sergeant Crank publicly announced that a reward of a thousand francs would be paid to anyone who should discover the thief, André Fouet, the French captain was simply furious.

"*Trente mille diables !*—thirty thousand devils !" he burst out fiercely; "do you dare to suppose zat any of us is tieves, eh, *coquin ?*"

"I don't think it at all unlikely," replied the sergeant, coolly.

"*Sacrebleu !*" yelled the captain; "he call me tief ! Oh, if I vas not a prisonaire, I should grind him to powdare."

"Oh, don't let that make any difference," said Benjamin Crank, coolly; "grind away if you think you can."

"Bravo, sergeant," cried Brian O'Flinn. "I say, captain, set to work."

"No, no," muttered the captain; "I shall spare him zis time; he is not vors my angaire. Go avay, go avay !" he cried, waving his arm grandly, "and leave us to fineesh our game."

The sergeant smiled with contempt, and snapped his fingers in his face, much too near his nose to be respectful.

"Ugh ! *maudit chien*—cursed dog," muttered the fire-eater, as he pocketed the affront and turned once more to his countrymen.

"Let us go on," he said.

"I have lost all my monee," exclaimed Jules Gasconade.

"And me too," added Pierre, with a very long face as he glanced wistfully at the heap of silver.

"Vhat! you mean to say you are broke clean out?" growled the captain.

"Zat is a fact," replied his companions, showing their empty purses.

"Nevair did I know soch bad luck," continued Jules.

"Bah! you are bad players and deserve to lose."

And the captain swept his winnings into his pocket-book.

It was of crimson morocco leather, massive and handsome, with a coat of arms emblazoned on it in gold letters, and underneath some initials also in gold.

Jack Barrington, who had accompanied Sergeant Crank to the spot, was struck with the imposing appearance of the pocket-book.

He had tried hard to discern the initial letters, but the captain had been too quick for him.

CHAPTER XVIII

A TRIPLE DUEL.

It seemed very hard to Jules and his friend not only to lose their money, but to be called bad players into the bargain.

Brian O'Flinn, from the discontent expressed in their features, foresaw that it would not be difficult to get up an "iligant little row between the mounseers," and nudging Ned Rattles to assist him, he whispered to Jules—

"Did you hear what that bounceable son of a gun (meaning the captain) called you?"

"Parbleu, yes; he call me a bad player," said Jules.

"The fact is you've been cheated," said Brian.

"Swindled right and left," said Ned.

"Diable!"

The two Frenchmen at this started up full of fury.

"Ha, coquin, voleur!—r-r-rascal, robbair."

"Miserable poltron—coward!" they cried, fiercely, shaking their fists at the winner.

"You have cheat us out of our monnaie!" they yelled together.

"Vhat!" shouted Hector Gobelin Tomtonnerre; "I sheat you?"

"Ah, oui—yes," they replied; "you got cards up you sleeve."

The captain sprang to his feet.

"Swords and pistoles!" he cried, "if I had but a veapon, I should cut you into mince-meat, you two lying cochons—pigs."

"And if ve had veapons, ve should ron you through ze heart, you pig rascal."

"Une épée—a sword, a sword!" cried Jules, extending his arms in a kind of frenzy. "Who vill lend me a sword?"

"Who vill lend me von?" joined in his equally excited companion, Pierre, as he waved his hands in the air.

The cuirassier captain shook his head and his clenched fists, and grinned at the excited pair like a ferocious tiger.

Brian, finding they were wound up to the proper pitch, stepped forward with his companions.

"I tell ye what it is, mounseers," he said; "there's only one way of settling this business comfortably; you must fight."

"Ah, yes, morbleu! ve shall fight," cried the Frenchmen, with one voice.

"The only difficulty," Ned remarked, "is that you have nothing to fight with but your fists, and you gentlemen are not very good at sparring."

"Non, non; no 'spar'—guns, pistoles, cannons," they shouted.

Young Jack now came in with a mild suggestion.

"Perhaps we could lend the gentlemen a cannon," he said, "and then they could fire at one another in turns."

"Ve moss have trois canons—three cannons —von apiece," they screamed.

"Well, me darlin's," said Brian, soothingly, "ye see it wouldn't be quite convanient to dhrag three big guns here; but I'll tell ye what—I'll purvide ache of ye wid an iligant pistol and as much powder and shot as ye like. Will that do for yez?"

But they did not seem quite as grateful as they might have been for this generous offer.

"You'll find pistols much more handy," said Ned Rattles to them, encouragingly.

"And you can pop away at one another till you're all three full of bullet holes," said Jack.

The countenances of the heroes became suffused with a slightly yellowish tint.

But Brian, without any delay, hurried off, and presently returned with three large horse pistols, a powder flask, and a bag of bullets.

"Now, then, me honies," said Brian, in the most cheerful tone, "I'll load the poppers, and while I'm doing that, you can make your wills, if ye've got anything to lave."

The loading went on briskly.

"How many bullets will you have in ache pistol?" asked Brian of the duellists, after a moment.

"You can have half a dozen if you like," suggested Ned.

The combatants seemed perplexed as to the number.

Jules murmured something to the effect that he thought "one" might be sufficient.

"It's as well to make shure," grinned Brian, "so I'll put in two; then, if one misses, there will be a chance for yez wid the other, don't ye see, darlings?"

The heroes did see, and shuddered inwardly at the prospect before them.

"There they are," said the bugler, as he finished priming the weapons, "loaded all right and tight——"

"Bang up to the muzzle," added Ned Rattles, as he cocked his eye down the barrels.

"Diable!" muttered the fire-eating Hector, who had become strangely moody during the preparations; "up to ze muzzel! Zey vill burst."

"Divil a bit, honey," cried Brian; "they'll blow you into smithereens sooner."

Everything being ready, all that had to be done was to place the combatants in their proper positions.

There was some little difficulty about this; but the fertile brain of the Irishman soon arranged it.

"Now, then, Misther Cuirassier, you'll stand here—you, Misther Jules, there—and you, Misther Pierre, there !"

As he said this, he marched each one to his proper position.

The figure they formed was that of a triangle, which the following slight diagram will fully explain.

HECTOR

JULES ◁◁◁◁◁ PIERRE

"Now, thin," continued Brian, as he placed the pistols in the hands of the duellists, "you'll have the goodness to take all signals from me."

The sons of France looked particularly nervous, Hector Gobelin especially.

Though the cheeks of all were pale, and their hands trembled, the teeth fairly chattered in the head of the fire-eating captain, and his knees knocked together.

"Stand at ease !" cried Brian, laughing.

The heroes looked towards him.

"Make ready."

They cocked their weapons.

"Raise your——"

"*Attendez !* — stay !" gasped the captain, whose complexion was of a light green.

"What's the matther ?" demanded the Irishman.

"I—I do not a—a—understand how ve is to to—f—f—fire," he stammered.

"Why, pull your thrigger ov course."

"Bote I have got two to shoot, and I have only got von pistole," remarked Hector Gobelin.

"But haven't you got two bullets, you unrasonable crathur ?" said the young bugler. "Hould your tongue and get ready to fire away at each other. Now then, attention !"

"Bote stop, stop ! I cannot kill both zose *cochons*—pigs, with von fire," cried Hector, glaring at his two opponents, who seemed almost paralysed with fear.

"Of course not," Brian replied; "you mustn't be in too much of a hurry. Listen to me, and I'll tell you what you're to do. Misther Hector'll fire at Mr. Jules—Misther Jules'll fire at Misther Pierre—and Misther Pierre'll fire at Misther Hector. D'ye understand now ?"

"But I do not vant to fire at my *cher ami* Pierre," cried Jules.

"Och, sure, but you must fire at him, honey, d'ye see ?" explained Brian.

"*Non*—no ; I do not see not at all."

"Well, niver mind," grinned the Irishman; "maybe you'll feel prisintly."

Jules groaned.

"Oh ! but I do not vant to shoot my friend Pierre."

"Well, it's ten to one you miss him," said Brian.

"And then, after the first round, you'll change places," said Ned; "that is, if you don't all kill one another at the first go off—and then your friend Pierre will have the chance of shooting you."

"Attention !" exclaimed Brian. "Have you cocked your poppers ?"

"Ah ! *oui*—yes," was the murmured reply.

"Then fire away."

The heroes shut their eyes, and finally pulled their triggers.

The pistols went off with a bang.

The English spectators gave a ringing cheer, and as the smoke cleared away, two of the heroes were discovered stretched full length on the ground.

The third, the redoubtable Hector Tomtonnerre, was curled up, nose and knees together, like a periwinkle.

"Well done !" cried Brian, as he sprang forward; "all dead at the first fire."

"And without bullets, too," grinned our hero.

They all gathered round the prostrate Frenchmen, and presently Jules Gasconade, opening his eyes, gasped—

"Ugh, *ma foi !* I do not sink I am dead quite ; please stick von pin in me, all behind me to see."

"Here's one not dead," exclaimed Brian.

"Nor me neizer," murmured Pierre.

"And here's another," called out Ned Rattles.

"*Morbleu !* give me a drink of *cognac*," whined the captain.

"And here's a third," cried Jack. "The hero of France is alive too."

"All alive oh ! by the powers," shouted Brian O'Flinn ; "up wid yez, while I load the poppers again."

The Frenchmen were hauled up on to their feet, and the brandy bottle passed round, during which Brian reloaded the weapons.

"We'll have betther luck this time, plase the pigs," he said, as he came forward with the pistols in his hand ; "there's three bullets in every mother's son of them."

The combatants now changed places, and each having received his weapon, Brian again gave the signal.

The pistols were again discharged.

But this time Jules and Pierre had drunk in a little more courage with their draught of brandy, and instead of firing according to the rules of the triangle, they fired at their mutual foe, Hector Tomtonnerre.

The wadding of their pistols caught him on each check.

"Oh, *diable*, I am shot !" he yelled, as he fell to the ground, and kicked his legs in the air ; "oh, moordare ! I am kill."

"Now's your time," whispered Brian to the Frenchman, "to get back your winnings."

"Ah, yos, yos, yos !" they cried ; "*voleur* —thief, r-r-rascal !"

With these words they threw themselves heavily upon the successful gambler, and endeavoured to tear open his jacket and secure the pocket-book.

This attempt at once brought the mortally-wounded cuirassier to his senses,

"Ah, *cochons*—pigs, *misérables poltrons !*" he raved, as he grasped them by the hair of their heads.

"'I AM AN ENGLISHMAN!' EXCLAIMED OUR HERO, PROUDLY.'"

The two *cochons* roared lustily, and they all rolled over.

"Give me my *monnaie*, let go my hairs!" shouted Jules Gasconade.

"Let go my hairs, give me my *monnaie!*" shrieked Pierre Pimpelot.

"Nevair," raved Hector.

The English party, roaring with laughter, cheered on the combatants.

"Go it, fatty," cried Brian, encouragingly.

"Stick to him, long 'un!" joined in Ned.

"Eat 'em both, Puffy!" called out our hero, to the red-haired cuirassier.

But while the struggle was going on, he kept very close to the latter.

The next moment with a desperate tug Jules ripped open the captain's jacket.

Out flew the morocco pocket-book.

It was this Jack had been eagerly expecting, and he pounced upon it like a hungry hawk.

Picking it up, he glanced hastily at the coat of arms and the initial letter B.

"Boufflers!" he cried to himself, exultingly. "Hurrah! I have found the thief!"

Just at this moment Sergeant Crank, aroused by the shouts and the report of fire-arms, was seen rapidly approaching with a dozen grenadiers.

"Hollo!" he cried; "what does all this mean?"

"It means, sergeant," returned Jack, confidently, "that I've found the thief."

"What! the man who robbed Marshal Boufflers?" inquired Benjamin Crank.

"Yes; the valet André Fouet. Get up," cried Jack, as he approached the robber; "you're wanted; rise, André Fouet, *alias* Captain Hector Gobelin Tomtonnerre. Ha, ha! you're caught nicely."

The gambler glared at his youthful accuser for a moment, and then springing to his feet with an oath, made a rush for escape.

But a couple of grenadiers quickly formed a barrier with their crossed muskets and naked bayonets.

"I am not André Fouet!" he growled, as he was brought to bay.

"He doesn't seem to answer the description," remarked Sergeant Crank.

"Well, no, this blackguard's head thatch is as red as a carrot," joined in Brian; "but," he added, lowering his voice, and winking knowingly, "there's ways and manes by which thaving varmints disguise themselves."

And without another word Brian approached the prisoner.

"Now, my noble hero," he said, with a grin, "I'm going to shave yez."

A very rapid and energetic motion of the Irishman's hands followed, and a loud yell from the party operated on.

The next minute Brian O'Flinn held up a red wig, and a pair of tremendous moustaches, together with a chin tuft, long enough for a billygoat.

The culprit, shorn of his disguise, stood revealed without a hair on his face.

The fire-eater was done completely.

His jaw fell.

"Away with him!" cried Sergeant Crank.

And amid the derisive cheers of the lookers-on, André Fouet was marched off.

"You've done a good thing for yourself, my dear boy," said Crank to him, warmly, as they went along; "there's a reward of two thousand francs for you."

"Not all for me," replied our hero, generously; "there are two others to share it."

"Two others?"

"Yes; Brian O'Flinn and Ned Rattles. We'll divide it between us."

Benjamin Crank was more delighted at this display of unselfishness on Jack's part.

"Share and share alike amongst comrades was always my motto, and I'm glad to see it is yours, my dear boy," he replied. "You'll never lose anything by it, depend on it, never!"

CHAPTER XIX.

BOUND FOR THE FRENCH CAMP.

STRAIGHT to the tent of the Earl of Marlborough went Sergeant Crank, taking young Jack with him.

The earl at once admitted his humble friend.

"Well, sergeant."

"The thief's found, general," returned Benjamin Crank, "and this pocket-book was found upon the thief."

"Indeed!" exclaimed the earl; "where was he discovered?"

"In the camp, general."

"Amongst the prisoners?"

"Yes, your grace. But he was disguised, and I think he would have escaped detection, had it not been for one pair of quick eyes."

"Ha! and pray whose quick eyes were it that found him out?"

As the commander-in-chief put this question, his eyes instinctively turned towards our hero, who stood there modestly enough.

"I think I can guess," resumed the earl, after a moment, with a smile; "it must be my young namesake, here. Am I right?"

"You're always right, general, always," burst out Benjamin; "it was Jack Barrington as discovered this thieving valet."

"And you say he was disguised?"

"Yes, general; his own mother, if he's got one, wouldn't have known the rascal."

The earl smiled at this, and turning again to Jack, said to him—

"I shall be glad to hear your account of this."

Our hero, in a very simple but graphic manner, explained to his illustrious inquirer all the incidents of the detection and capture of André Fouet.

Incidents which, being already familiar to the reader, need not be repeated here.

The earl listened with much interest.

"But how was it you came to be acquainted with the facts that first excited your suspicions—this pocket-book, for instance?"

"I heard you read the letter from Marshal Boufflers," replied our hero.

"Ha!"

"You read it aloud, so that I couldn't help hearing it," Jack added.

"True, true; but the letter was written in French."

"I understand French as well as English," answered Jack quickly.

"Oh, indeed," said the earl. "But the pocket-book was never mentioned in the letter."

"No, general. But I happened to catch a glimpse of it as the man was putting it into his pocket, and I fancied the letter on the cover looked like a B."

"And B you thought meant Boufflers, eh?"

"Yes, general."

The earl opened the pocket-book, and after hastily examining its contents, he said, with a smile of admiration—

"Your thoughts do great credit to your sagacity, my boy."

"Does the pocket-book really belong to Marshal Boufflers?" Jack ventured to ask.

"I think there's no doubt of it," the earl replied; "and I cannot suggest anything better than that you should yourself conduct the prisoner to the French camp."

"Oh, your grace," exclaimed our hero, "I'm afraid I'm not quite strong enough for that yet. He'd run away before I got him along twenty yards."

The earl burst into a hearty laugh, in which Sergeant Crank felt himself privileged to join.

And after a moment the earl said—

"It is not my intention to burden you with the responsibility of taking charge of this ruffian alone. You shall have a dozen grenadiers, with your friend Sergeant Crank at their head, to escort Monsieur André back to his old quarters."

Jack revived at once at this assurance.

"Oh, then I shall like to go very much."

But he stopped suddenly, and said—

"I forgot to say that I don't deserve all the credit of discovering this man."

"What, then," ejaculated the earl, "had you some assistant detectives?"

"Oh, yes, general; Brian and Ned helped me."

"Brian and Ned! Who are they?"

"O'Flinn and Rattles, bugler and drummer of the 47th, your grace," Sergeant Crank explained.

"Ah! I see; and they assisted you, did they?"

"Yes, general; it was Brian O'Flinn that pulled off André Fouet's red wig and whiskers."

"Ha, ha!" laughed the earl.

And then he added—

"I think all the more highly of you for not seeking to monopolise all the honour of this affair to yourself."

Sergeant Crank stepped forward, and spoke a few words in a low tone to the general, who then said to our hero, very good-naturedly—

"Well, then Brian O'Flinn and Ned Rattles shall accompany you to Marshal Boufflers. I think that will be fair for all parties."

Jack once more expressed his gratitude.

"Away with you," cried the earl, "and don't forget you will have to receive a reward of two thousand francs."

Jack Barrington hurried off full of joy, and hastened to his comrades.

"Och filliloo," cried Brian O'Flinn; "we'll have a roarin' time ov it amongst the mounseers."

Away he went or his bugle.

His aunt Biddy gave him a drop of whisky in a flask, and a bit of tobacco to smoke on the journey.

CHAPTER XX.

DESERTED.

LET us now go back to the time when Caleb Corder and Timothy Tootles were put to sudden flight by the sound of a drum, just at the moment when they had a good dinner in prospect.

After running some distance, their speed gradually slackened.

"I am tired of this game," muttered Caleb in a surly tone, as he came to a stand.

"So am I," returned his comrade.

"After all, if they are English soldiers we heard, we can manage to keep out of their sight behind the trees," continued the drummer; "suppose we go back?"

"I'm quite agreeable," assented Timothy.

Very cautiously they retraced their steps, and were not a little dismayed at the picture that presented itself to their view when they once more drew near the spot.

This picture being Brian O'Flinn, Ned Rattles, and Jack Barrington seated comfortably on the grass polishing off the remains of pies, tarts, and fruit, with wonderful energy, whilst the two Frenchmen lay stretched on the ground.

Caleb Corder swore and gnashed his teeth bitterly.

Timothy Tootles groaned inwardly, and rubbed his croaking stomach.

This was all they could do, so they remained with their mouths watering hopelessly behind the trees, watching the good things as they disappeared in rapid succession.

They had the full benefit, however, of observing all that passed, of hearing all that was spoken, and when at length the party moved off, both drummer and fifer understood perfectly that their comrades had taken the Frenchmen prisoners, instead of their taking them.

The thought was dreadfully galling.

"Now, vhy couldn't ve ha' gorn an' done that?" whimpered Timothy Tootles.

"Why, because they've got muskets and we haven't," growled Caleb, savagely.

"Well, never mind, it can't be 'elped," remarked the fifer; "p'r'aps they've left some of the grub be'ind 'em."

They advanced and examined the dishes eagerly.

Not a crumb was left, and the bottles were quite empty.

"Guzzling humbugs!" grated the disappointed drummer, between his teeth.

"Greedy pigs!" wailed the fifer; "wot's to be done?"

"I've made up my mind what I'm going to do," returned Caleb.

"Wot?"

"Desert."

"Desert?" echoed Timothy. "What, leave the English harmy and go over to the mounseers?"

"Yes; what's the good of going back? What chance is there for me?"

"Well, but if you goes, wot's to become of me?" asked Timothy, with a very piteous expression on his peppered face.

"You'd better come too."

"I'm 'alf afraid."

"Oh, well then, stop where you are," snarled Caleb; "I can go alone."

"Well, but 'ow d'yer know 'ow the mounseers will treat us?" argued Timothy; "p'r'aps they'll lock us up in a dungeon ever so fur hunderground."

"Bah! you're a coward; you've blown all your pluck away through the holes of your fife."

"No, I ain't," replied the spare youth, indignantly; "but I should like to see——"

"What?" demanded Caleb, irritably.

"Well, I only wanted to know wot sort of a story yer was goin' to pitch to the furreners," Timothy answered.

"I've made up my mind what to say, so you needn't trouble yourself about that," was Caleb's gruff rejoinder; "all you have to do is to bear me out in everything."

"Wot a orful lot of crammers I shall 'ave to tell," murmured Timothy, "and my poor mother's last adwice to me wos—'Tim, my boy, if yer wishes to prosper and become a gin'ral, allus tell the truth.'"

This was too much for his comrade, and he burst into a hoarse laugh.

"You become a general! Ha, ha! a poor, half-starved shadow like you!" he cried, contemptuously; "but there, do you mean to come or don't you?—because I'm off."

"I'll come, of course I will," returned the weak-minded Timothy; "'opes we shan't be caught by any of our own party. If we is——"

"Why, we shall be shot, and a good job too. It wouldn't trouble me much," growled the reckless Caleb, as he strode forward.

"Oh, Lor'!" murmured Timothy Tootles, shuddering all over from head to foot as he followed, "I shouldn't like to be shot."

The two deserters pressed forward.

It was sunset as they approached the boundaries of the French camp.

They were made aware of this fact in a somewhat startling manner.

A fierce-looking grenadier, with a thick, wiry moustache that gave him the look of a tiger, darted up, apparently out of the ground.

"*Qui va là?*—who goes there?" he shouted.

"Pretty vell, thank'ee," replied Timothy Tootles, who didn't understand French, and fancied the grenadier was inquiring after his health; "'ow are you?"

The soldier frowned and raised his musket.

The fifer was so appalled at this act that he hopped very nimbly behind his comrade.

"*Bung sore!*" cried Caleb Corder, putting on a bold face, and wishing the sentinel good evening in lamentably bad French.

But it seemed to have a good effect; for the guard, lowering his musket, inquired in broken English—

"Who are you?—what do you want?"

"We're deserters from the English lines,

and want to join you brave French heroes," said Caleb, going in hit or miss.

"Ye—es," stammered Timothy Tootles; "ve're brave English-French 'eroes."

"Ha! is it so?" exclaimed the sentinel.

"That's the exact fact," returned Caleb; "Monseer Somebody, who is a friend of ours, told us to mention his name to the captain of your regiment."

"Aha! *c'est bon!*—it is good," replied the grenadier.

He then signalled to a comrade who approached.

And handing over the English applicants to his care, they walked forward to the captain's quarters.

Having arrived there, the captain was speedily apprised of their arrival.

"Two deserters from the English army!" he exclaimed. "Bring them in."

The next moment the fugitives were escorted into his presence.

Captain Gravellotte—or Gasper Grimsby, for it was he—looked at them intently.

"Strangers," he muttered, inwardly. Then he said to them—"So you've deserted?"

"Yes, monseer," replied Caleb, astonished at hearing a Frenchman speak such excellent English.

"Why?"

"They didn't treat us well, monseer."

"No, monseer; quite t'other," joined in Timothy Tootles, who received a dig in the ribs for speaking.

"Umph! you don't look as if you had been particularly well treated," replied the captain, with a somewhat sarcastic smile; "didn't feed you sufficiently, eh?"

This was to Timothy.

"The grub wasn't so bad, but they was allus a-blowin' of us up, monseer."

This was an unlucky speech, and called attention to the physiognomies of both.

"Your appearance is that of persons who have been blown up," the captain replied; "who blew you?"

"Sergeant Crank."

"Sergeant Crank!" echoed the captain, thoughtfully; "and what reason had he to be always 'blowing you up,' eh?"

"Well, monseer, it was all on account of a young sneak."

"Oh; and pray what was this 'young sneak's' name?"

"Jack Barrington," said Caleb.

Captain Gravellotte started.

"He is an English boy, is he not?"

"He seems so; but he can speak French."

"Dark eyes and hair; rather sharp?"

"Sharp as a needle," replied Caleb, his eyes flashing; "you seem to know him?"

The captain did not make any reply to this, but continued—

"Then he is with the English army?"

"Yes, he's there safe enough," answered Caleb, bitterly.

Captain Gravellotte felt satisfied that the speaker was no friend to Jack Barrington.

He said no more on that subject, but asked Caleb and his comrade if they wished to join the French army.

"Yes, monseer," replied both the deserters.

"We belong to the band," Caleb explained.

Captain Gravellotte touched a bell.

An orderly entered.

"Send Jaques to me," he said.

In a few moments the dragoon entered.

His hand was still in a sling, and he looked like "the savage" he was called.

Glaring upon the deserters with his ogre-like eyes, he advanced.

His superior gave him some directions in a low tone, after which, Jaques beckoned to Caleb and Timothy to follow him.

The dragoon led them to a canteen.

Fixing his ferocious eyes upon the new-comers whilst he lit his cigar, he said abruptly, after a moment—

"You know zis Zhack Barringtone, you two; eh?"

"Yes, we know him," was the reply.

"You loave him ver mosh; eh?"

"No; I hate him!" growled Caleb Corder, his eyes glaring as fiercely as those of the man he addressed.

"Aha!" grinned Jaques; "I thought so. Vell, I hate him too; it was through him I got my wound in my hand—*sacré!* it vos all through him; and for sosh zere is only von sing to be done, to hang or shoot zem."

"I should be glad to see Jack Barrington hung or shot," exclaimed Caleb.

"Ver good zen; you do vot I tell you, and moss like you shall have zat *plaisir*, and somezing besides."

"What am I to do?" asked the drummer.

"Firs, you moss go back to ze Engleesh camp."

Caleb's countenance fell at once.

"I don't know whether I can."

"You don't know," exclaimed Jaques, sharply, opening his eyes as wide as saucers; "but I do. You must go back; *comprenez-vous?*—do you understand?—you moss."

"Well."

"You moss make friends wiz Mastair Zhack Barrytones; get him to come along viz you, do you see?"

"That won't be very easy, because he happens to know I hate him," Caleb explained.

"You moss change his mind; make him sink you loave him," replied Jaques, with a cunning grin.

"How can I?"

"Oh, give him brandee, cigar."

"He neither drinks nor smokes."

"Give him monnaie zen."

"It wouldn't do," said Caleb, despondingly; "and besides, he's too well watched. There's always a lot round him."

"Vell, he moss be got here by some means," said Jaques Sanglier, in a very positive tone; "if you promise zat, you shall be vell paid for your trobel, if nort—*diable!* you shall be shot, ze pair of you."

This rather excited Timothy Tootles, and he said, with his hair almost standing on end—

"Yer don't s'pose ve should be sich donkeys as to come back 'ere to be shot, does yer?"

The Savage gripped him sharply by the shoulder till the bones cracked again, and bending down with one of his awful chuckles, hissed out—

"Ha, ha! *mon cher*, I shall not vait for you to come back. In ordare to make sure of you, you vill be shot before you go."

These ominous words impressed the two deserters with the idea that they were not quite so safe as they had supposed, and that it might be as well to promise everything, even though they performed nothing, and Caleb said with a forced laugh—

"There'll be no need to shoot us. We'll do all we can. And I dare say we can manage to get hold of Jack Barrington, either by fair means or foul."

"Aha! zat vill do ver vell," cried Jaques, approvingly. "Only get him, and your fortune vill be made."

At this juncture, the fragrant odour of soup reached the spot, and travelled up the noses of the famished pair.

Timothy Tootles' mouth watered profusely, and he said to his comrade—

"Oh! vot a lovely smell of gravy, ain't there?"

"Yes; and I mean to have some, too," replied Caleb, who at once applied to Jaques. "We haven't had anything to eat or drink all day," he said, in a very decided tone.

"Zen come viz me," Jaques answered. "I shall take you vhere you can eat and drink."

"That's the ticket," cried Timothy Tootles. "I'll eat enough to last me a veek."

The eating and drinking were so good, that both the drummer and the fifer got extremely jovial over it.

Early the next morning, with aching heads and parched throats, they were routed out, and ordered to start.

The travellers did not hurry themselves, for they were rather undecided about the course they should pursue as regarded young Jack.

If they could contrive to inveigle him away from his friends and convey him over to the French lines, they believed they would be well rewarded.

But then in order to accomplish this, they must return to the English camp, where it was pretty certain they would be at once arrested for having been absent without leave.

"Phew!" exclaimed Caleb at length, in a grumbling tone, "my head's as heavy as lead."

"So's mine," assented Timothy, who looked particularly qualmish. "But have yer made up yer mind whether we're to go back to the camp or not?"

"Well, all things considered, I don't think I shall."

Caleb Corder was silent a moment, and then continued—

"Our only chance is to make our way across to the coast, and try to get aboard some vessel bound for England."

"That'd soot me uncommon vell," said Timothy, "and I knows mother 'ud be glad to see me."

"There's only one thing against us," continued Caleb. "Our uniforms; they might betray us."

"What?"

"Ah, yes. I'll tell yer vot ve must do; svop 'em wi' some peasant for 'is togs."

"Ah! yes," ejaculated the drummer; "that isn't a bad idea. We'd better make a start.

It's very like as Jack'll get a bullet in his nob afore long."

Caleb rose, and Timothy followed his example, but before they could take a single step in their new route, a voice cried impatiently—
"Stop !"

A French grenadier, musket in hand, stood close behind them, whilst at a short distance stood half a dozen of his comrades, all armed in the same manner.

The Frenchman Jaques, not feeling quite sure of the trustworthiness of his agents, had ordered this small escort to follow them.

"Oh, Lor' ! Oh, Lor' !" Timothy Tootles groaned to himself, "I shall never see mother ag'in ; ve shall be shot to a dead certainty."

"*Ecoutez, camarades !*—listen, comrades."

Those addressed by the French soldier, listened, of course, with great attention.

"Zat is your vay," continued the grenadier, significantly, as he extended his arm in a direct line with the English camp.

"Yes," muttered Caleb, rather doggedly.

"Don't forget zen. If you do, ve shall remind you, *mes braves garçons*, wiz a dozen bullets. *Avancez*—go on."

"Ve're in for it, anyhow," murmured Timothy to his comrade.

"Hark," cried Caleb, "to those sounds."

The sound of drums and a bugle at a distance was heard.

He stopped instantly, and looked behind him.

The soldiers were nowhere to be seen.

They, too, had heard the martial notes, and had at once concealed themselves behind the trees.

Caleb then looked anxiously ahead.

"I wonder who it is coming ?" he muttered to himself.

"They're Henglish, I'm sartin," said Timothy Tootles. "I could almost take my oath that was Brian O'Flinn's bugle."

"It sounds like it, the Irish beggar," growled Caleb, savagely. "Let's come on carefully. Mind how you walk, and keep behind the trees."

In a short time three figures in uniform appeared.

There was no mistaking who these three figures were, and Caleb uttered an exclamation of fierce exultation as he recognised them.

"The whole lot, by gosh !" he cried.

"So it is," said Timothy, with a nervous chuckle ; "but don't do anythink rash, or p'r'aps yer'll frighten 'em away."

Caleb Corder threw a sneering glance at his timid companion, and then said—

"I've settled what to do. Let us come back."

"To the mounseers ?"

"Yes."

They were not long retracing their steps, and soon came upon the escort quietly posted behind the thick trunks.

"The boy we want is coming," said Caleb, hastily, to the sergeant of the troop, whose name was Blaize Garnier.

"There are more zan von, are zere not ?" asked the soldier.

"Yes, three, but they are only armed with swords."

"*Bon !*" exclaimed the sergeant ; "zay will give us no trouble zen."

The sergeant then gave a few directions to his men.

The next moment not a soul was visible ; all had retired behind the trees.

Whilst every moment, coming nearer and nearer, were heard the sounds of Ned and Jack's drums and Brian O'Flinn's bugle.

Jack Barrington and his comrades marched forward, for, with the Earl of Marlborough's letter, and the pocket-book of Marshal Bouffiers in their possession, they had not the smallest apprehension of danger.

"Bedad, this is beautiful, isn't it ?" exclaimed Brian, as he withdrew his bugle from his mouth ; "won't the marshal be glad when he sees us ?"

As the sound of the bugle died away, a voice shouted loudly—

"*Halte !*—stop !"

The party instantly obeyed.

And looking before them they beheld with some surprise a French soldier, armed with a musket, standing right in their path.

The French sergeant held his musket with the bayonet pointed at them, and Brian bawled—

"What's the matther, ould feller ?"

"*Où allez-vous ?*" demanded the sergeant.

"What does the bla'guard say ?" whispered the Irishman.

"He asks where we are going," returned Jack, who acted as interpreter.

"Shure, me darling, we're blackberry hunting," said Brian.

The grenadier shook his head, and called again—

"*Eh bien !* you are my prisonairs, and moos come viz me ; *comprenez-vous ?*"

"I don't wish to hurt yer feelings, me honey, but we don't feel inclined to come," Brian responded, coolly.

The grenadier, who didn't understand what was said to him, looked very angry.

"*Diable !* if you do not obey, I shall fire," he exclaimed.

Brian and his companions disappeared in one bound behind the trees.

"Fire away now as fast as you like, me darling," returned the Irishman, jocosely.

Bang ! went the grenadier's musket.

And at the same moment Caleb Corder, followed by Timothy Tootles, emerged from behind an adjacent trunk.

"Don't let 'em escape ; they're spies," cried Caleb.

"Yes, they're sp-p-ies," stammered the lank fifer, in a very shaky tone of voice.

Brian peeped out at the speakers.

"Oh, it's you, you murdtherous pair o' spalpeens, is it ?" he said. "So ye're turnin' informers agin your own countrymen, are ye ? Bedad, I'd like to horsewhip the pair of yez."

Caleb Corder answered contemptuously—

"You may spare your tongue, Mr. Paddywhack, and if you'll take my advice, you'll all come along quietly."

"And where would you advise us to come to, Misther Knuckle-smasher ?" asked Brian.

"To the French camp, to receive the reward of your merits," returned Caleb.

"And, pray, what may that be?"

"The punishment of spies is a rope or a bullet, I don't know which," was the reply, accompanied by an ugly grin.

"They shoots 'em," replied his comrade, "like dawgs."

This was more than Brian O'Flinn could stand.

With two energetic springs he dashed forward, and before either the drummer or fifer was aware of his intentions, he was upon them, and had gripped them by the scruff of their necks.

"I know what the punishment of a pair of cowardly, black-hearted assassinatin' varmints ought to be," he cried, "and I'll give yer a specimen."

And with that he banged their heads together soundly.

Timothy Tootles yelled—"Murder!"

Caleb Corder shouted to the grenadier to fire.

But the soldier hesitated, fearing to shoot the wrong one.

But the moment the Irishman released his victims, the Frenchman, who had reloaded his musket, pointed it at Brian, and pulled the trigger.

Again the report echoed through the wood.

But Jack Barrington had darted forward, and given the arm of the French soldier a sharp jerk upwards.

The bullet had whizzed through the branches of the tree, instead of piercing the Irishman's body.

Brian was unhurt, whilst Ned Rattles, who was quite on the alert to assist his comrade, cleverly tripped up the heels of the grenadier, and laid him on his back.

In his fall his musket dropped from his hands.

Ned at once picked it up, and presented the point of the bayonet at the breast of the prostrate soldier.

"Surrender!" he cried.

The Frenchman, instead of admitting his defeat and yielding himself a prisoner, shouted loudly—

"*Au secours!*—help!"

In response to this some of his comrades sprang forth from behind the trees, and our English heroes, to their surprise and chagrin, found a dozen muskets directed against them.

"Och, murdher! we're settled now intirely," muttered Brian.

The overthrown grenadier sprang to his feet.

"*Avancez!*—advance!" he cried.

In an instant our heroes were surrounded and made prisoners.

It was just then that Jack Barrington whispered to Brian—

"Are they going to shoot us?"

"Shoot us, honey! I'd like to catch 'em at it," returned the Irishman, indignantly.

"They shot my father," was our hero's somewhat mournful reply.

"Ah! but that was a bit ov private grudge, I'm thinking."

"True, it was."

"I don't think they mean shooting us," remarked Ned Rattles; "but it's pretty certain we're prisoners."

"That's little odds," laughed Brian, "seeing as they'll only take us to the very place we were going."

"Don't say a word about the earl's letter," said Jack.

"Not a syllable, me darling."

"*Venez!*—come," said the grenadier, whose name was Blaize Garnier.

"All right, me boy," replied the Irishman, slapping the sergeant jovially on the back, "although we've had a bit ov a scrimmage, we'll be none the worse friends on that account. Will you take a small taste ov the crathur?"

As he spoke, he offered his flask to Blaize Garnier.

The grenadier, impressed by the genial tone and looks of the speaker, smiled, and accepted the offer.

After which they formed into rank, and the word of command being given, marched forward.

CHAPTER XXI.

MARSHAL BOUFFLERS.

DURING the journey Caleb Corder lost no opportunity of insulting his comrades.

Even Timothy Tootles, encouraged by his example, began to wax bolder, and hinted at sundry "rods in pickle" which were waiting for them when they reached the French camp.

The prisoners took little heed of these malicious remarks.

They were all in excellent spirits.

As they neared the French lines, curiosity was evidently excited.

"*Voilà des prisonniers Anglais!*—these are English prisoners," flew from mouth to mouth.

The escort moved on till it reached the quarters of Captain Gravellotte.

After a brief delay Caleb Corder and his comrade were summoned to attend Jaques Sauvage.

"So you have catch zis boy—zis Jack Barrytone?" he exclaimed, eagerly, as they made their appearance before him.

"Yes, we've got him, safe enough," chuckled Caleb, "and two other fellows with him—regular Tartars they are too—and they all hate the French."

"That they does, like p'ison," joined in Timothy.

"Ha, ha! do zey?" grinned the dragoon, with a kind of ferocious exultation; "zey shall have somesing to hate us for, now ve have got hold of zem."

He then inquired into the particulars of the method by which they had laid hands on the prisoners.

Caleb gave his own version of this feat, and drew a vivid picture of the desperate struggle he and his comrade had had before they could secure them.

The account seemed to interest the Savage immensely, and he smiled and showed his large teeth, and rolled his fierce eyes about in sheer delight.

"And now conduct me to zese *Anglais*."

They found Jack Barrington and his comrades standing chatting very cheerfully together.

"'OH! OH!' HOWLED THE FRENCHMAN, 'IT DO HURT ME.'"

Jaques Sauvage, thrusting his hands in his pockets, regarded them in silence for a second or two from under his knitted brows.

The prisoners looked at him in return.

"Oh, bedad!" muttered Brian O'Flinn to his companions; "he looks for all the world like Ould Nick's first cousin, don't he?"

The likeness of the dragoon to this dark personage was at once admitted by the rest, and when his hoarse voice addressed them, the idea was by no means dispelled.

"*Regardez-moi, coquins!*—look at me, rascals," he cried.

"We are looking as hard as we can at a rascal," replied young Jack, indignantly, in French.

Jaques made no reply to this.

He had no time to make any, for young Jack, with a sudden impulse, sprang forward, and gripping him by his belt, exclaimed excitedly—

"What have you done with my mother and my little sister?"

"*Morbleu!* vhat do I know about your mozer?" hissed the dragoon, between his teeth.

"You do know. You helped to carry them away," continued our hero, firmly, "and you must tell me—you shall."

Jaques Sauvage uttered a terrible imprecation, and, clenching his fist, he was about to bring it down with all his force upon Jack's head,

But this was frustrated by Brian O'Flinn, who strode forward and caught him by the wrist.

"Bad luck to yez, you half-bred spalpeen, would yer be afther hitting a boy like that?" he cried, indignantly.

And the brave Brian gave the Frenchman's arm a twist that made him nearly howl with pain.

"*Chien! Je suis soldat Français!*—dog, I am a French soldier," shouted the infuriated dragoon, as he snatched away his hand, and aimed a terrific blow at Brian's forehead.

The Irishman stopped it on the most approved scientific principles, and dropped the Savage one in return full on his nose, which sent him rolling over on to the ground.

"Ah! *sacré tonnerre!*" he yelled, as he lay on his back. "*Aidez-moi!*—help!"

Caleb Corder and Timothy Tootles, who felt themselves compelled to keep up their character for pluck, advanced to the rescue.

Sad to relate, in two seconds they were laid sprawling on the top of the dragoon.

"Long live the queen and Marlborough!" shouted Brian, as he danced a jig round the prostrate trio.

"Hurrah!" echoed Jack and Ned.

The shouts drew attention to the proceedings, and a number of French soldiers came hurrying up.

Jaques Sauvage was hoisted on to his feet, swearing fearfully.

The dragoon's nose was bleeding, and he glared at Brian O'Flinn with terrible vindictiveness, as he cried hoarsely—

"Avay wiz zem all to prison!"

Several soldiers advanced, when Jack Barrington said to them in French—

"*Ecoutez-moi, messieurs*—listen to me, sirs!"

This appeal in their own language caused the men to pause.

"You must not take us to prison," continued our hero.

"I say yes, zey are spies," shouted Jaques, who looked, with his face smeared with blood, hideous.

"I say no," shouted our hero; "take us to Marshal Boufflers."

A bitter ironical laugh burst from the lips of Sauvage the dragoon, as he yelled—

"You shall not see the marshal; off viz you."

"I tell you we must see him," cried Jack.

"Take them away," shouted the dragoon.

They were quickly seized, and with bayonets flashing around them on all sides, they were hauled along.

Their situation had now become extremely critical.

Even Brian O'Flinn, who was of a sanguine temperament, and had a happy knack of hoping for the best, whispered to his comrades—

"I'm afraid we're settled entirely this time, me darlin's."

It was just as he uttered this that a voice cried—

"*Attendez!*—stay!"

Everyone knew that voice, and the soldiers looked towards the speaker with profound reverence and submission.

Even Jaques Sauvage smoothed his ferocious countenance in the presence of the commander-in-chief, for it was he who had spoken.

Marshal Boufflers, mounted on his charger, was before them.

The very man, beyond all others, Gallant Jack wished to see.

CHAPTER XXII.

TWO WITNESSES.

THE marshal was a man past middle age, of soldier-like aspect and imposing presence.

For a moment he glanced in silence at the group.

Then he said—

"Who are these?"

"English spies, general," answered Jaques.

"No, general, we are not," cried Jack Barrington, at the top of his voice.

"Divil a spy is there amongst the lot ov us, yer honour," joined in Brian O'Flinn.

"It is true, general, zey are spies," repeated the dragoon; "zey have tried to tamper wiz our men."

"If ye plase, gin'ral, it's a big lie that ugly bla'guard's telling," shouted the Irishman, determined to be heard.

"Yes, it's a lie," echoed Jack.

The general, who understood English, knitted his brows for a moment, and then said to Jaques in a sharp, quick tone—

"Bring them to my tent. I will examine them myself."

With these words he rode on briskly.

Jaques dared not disobey the orders he had received.

Brian was beside himself with joy.

"Hurroo! Ould Ireland for iver!" he shouted. "Three cheers for Marshal Bufflers!"

His comrades joined in with all their hearts as they marched towards the tent.

Jaques Sauvage beckoned to Caleb Corder and Timothy to join him, and they walked along behind the rest.

The countenance of the dragoon exhibited much perplexity.

"*C'est malheureux!*—it is unfortunate, zis meeting viz ze marshal," he said to them.

"Ve shall have to tell some lies. I suppose you do not mind zat."

"Not I; I'll tell as many as you like," said Caleb, readily.

"So'll I," added Timothy.

"It is necessary; if you don't, ze whole affair will be discovair, an' you vill bote be shot."

This pleasing intelligence quite determined the drummer and fifer to swear to anything, even that black was white, if necessary.

*   *   *   *   *

Marshal Boufflers had a few letters to write; and having dispatched these, he ordered the prisoners to be brought before him.

Although Sergeant Crank had not yet arrived with the absconding valet, they felt themselves now to be on safe ground; and, in order to see what their adversaries would say and do to support the charge against them, Brian suggested that they should not produce the earl's letter, or the marshal's pocket-book, until the close of the inquiry.

"It'll be a glorious thrate to hear what the bla'guards have got to say agin us," he said.

"Especially as we can bowl 'em out so nicely at last," said Ned Rattles.

With this determination, Jack and his comrades entered the tent of the commander-in-chief.

Jaques Sauvage accompanied them, the guard remaining without.

The marshal fixed his keen eyes scrutinisingly on the English lads for a moment, and then at once commenced his inquiries.

"*Ces jeunes hommes sont espions, vous dites?* —these young men are spies, you say?" he said to the dragoon, in a sharp, magisterial manner.

"Yes, general."

"They have been tampering with our men?"

"They have, general."

"That is serious, very serious," remarked the marshal, smoothing his grey moustaches with his hand.

Turning to the prisoners, the marshal asked them—

"What have you to say to this charge?"

"It is false, general," they answered.

"You mean you are not spies?"

"No, general."

"You have not been tampering with our men?"

"Not in the least."

"Oh, *miséricorde!*" groaned the accuser, with well-assumed horror. "Vot lies!"

The marshal turned towards him and said—

"Where are the men who have been tampered with?"

"I can fetch zem eef you vish, general," was the reply.

"*Certainement*—certainly, I wish. I must hear both sides of the question. Bring them before me at once!"

Jaques Sauvage executed a deprecatory shrug of his shoulders and left the tent.

As soon as he was gone, the marshal pointed to an inner compartment of the tent, before which a curtain was suspended.

"Go behind there," he said to Jack and his comrades.

They at once obeyed.

And in less than no time they had made three small holes in the draped partition through which they could see all that was passing on the other side.

In a short time Jaques returned, ushering in two semblances of French soldiers.

"Och, filliloo!" whispered Brian O'Flinn in an ecstasy of glee, as he recognised the drummer and fifer, in spite of their foreign uniforms; "look at 'em; ain't they a pair of beauties?"

The commander ran his eye over them in silence for a moment.

"*Regardez-moi!*—look at me."

Caleb Corder obeyed at once.

Timothy Tootles rolled his eyes in a wandering and distracted manner round the tent, and at length contrived to bring them to bear upon Marshal Boufflers.

"I understand you have been tampered with by certain English soldiers," said the marshal to Caleb. "Is that the case?"

"D'ye hear that, boys?" grinned Brian from behind the curtain; "he's done now; divil a word of French does he know."

But Caleb was not done just yet, for he began to talk on his fingers with great rapidity.

"*Diable!*" growled the commander, "I don't understand that language. Use your tongue."

"He is dumb, poor boy," said Jaques.

The poor boy shook his head mournfully in attestation of this fact.

"Umph!" grunted the general.

Then looking towards Timothy Tootles, he said—

"Perhaps you can explain this tampering business?"

Timothy looked at him with a vacant stare and made no reply.

"*Parbleu!* is he dumb too?" demanded the marshal, somewhat irritably.

"No, general, *il est sourd*—he is deaf," once more explained Jaques.

"*Peste!*" cried the general, in a passion, "what is the use of witnesses who can neither speak nor hear?"

"I dare say I can get ze truth from zem," returned the dragoon.

With this he began what appeared to be an animated conversation on his fingers with the afflicted soldiers.

They answered in the same manner.

Caleb Corder and Timothy Tootles were standing with their backs to the curtain behind which their comrades had retired.

And just as they were congratulating themselves how capitally they were getting on, they felt some sharp instrument probing their legs.

This was not singular, considering that their comrades on the other side of the partition were probing them through the drapery with the points of their pocket knives.

Conscious that the eyes of Marshal Boufflers were fixed upon them, the two deserters strove hard to endure the torture unflinchingly, but it was too much for them.

Caleb, forgetting he was dumb, roared out fiercely—

"Be quiet."

"*Parbleu!* the dumb can speak," exclaimed the marshal.

"Yes, and so'd you, ole feller," almost shrieked Timothy, "if someone was behind you as was a-sticking spikes into you every minute."

"And, *ma foi!* the deaf can hear," cried the general.

"Yes," called out Jack, from behind the curtain; "they're a couple of humbugs."

"Aha! I thought as much," said Marshal Boufflers. "Come from behind the curtain, all of you."

The prisoners instantly obeyed.

The marshal looked at them an instant, and then said—

"Who was it that spoke in French?"

"I did, general," our hero replied.

"And you know these men?"

"Yes, general; they're no more deaf and dumb than I am."

"Oh, vot a vicked lie," shouted Timothy Tootles; "ve is."

"Silence!" remarked the marshal, rather sternly.

Then, turning to Jack, he said—

"Go on."

"They're not Frenchmen, either," Jack continued.

"It is evident that they have accomplices in our own ranks, went on the marshal, looking keenly at Jaques Sauvage. "Who supplied them with French uniforms?"

The marshal turned to Jaques.

"What explanation have you to give of this matter?" he asked him.

"*Parbleu!*" answered the latter, shrugging his shoulders, "I know nothing about it, marshal."

Caleb, finding matters going decidedly against him, determined to let his employer have his full share in the concern, and he said bluntly to him—

"How can you say you know nothing about it, when it was you gave us the uniforms yourself?"

"Yes, and told us to sham as we was deaf and dumb into the bargain," joined in Timothy Tootles.

The dragoon glared at the informants like an incarnate fiend, but made no reply.

"I must inquire into this," said the marshal, after a moment; "it is serious."

Then, addressing himself once more to our hero, he said—

"How is it you are here?"

"I and my comrades were sent to you with a message from the Earl of Marlborough," the latter replied.

"Ha! indeed."

"Yes, marshal. You remember writing to the earl, saying you had been robbed of five thousand francs?"

"*Certainement!* yes; by my valet, André Fouet."

"Well, monsieur, we are here to bring back your money, and to tell you we have caught the thief."

The marshal started up with surprise.

"Aha! *c'est bon*—it is good," he cried, eagerly.

"Here is the pocket-book," continued Jack, as he stepped forward and handed it to the general; "is it right?"

"Ah, yes, yes; it is mine; the one I lost," exclaimed the marshal, in a tone of much gratification; "how can I thank you?"

"Shure, thin, the pleasure we have in servin' yer honour'll be paymint sufficient," interjected Brian.

"It is very kind of you to say so," returned the commander, courteously; "and you shall not find me ungrateful; but did you not say you had caught the thief?"

"Yes, marshal."

"Where is he?"

"He did not accompany us. He is on his way from the English camp under guard of an escort."

At the precise moment these words were uttered, an orderly entered the tent, and spoke in a low tone to the marshal.

"Ha, just in time," cried Marshal Boufflers; "let them come in."

The next moment footsteps were heard, and a file of English soldiers entered headed by Sergeant Crank, with the redoubtable Hector Gobelin Tomtonnerre—*alias* André Fouet, in their midst.

All the bully had been taken out of the valet by this time, and he presented a very abject appearance.

It took but a very short time to adjust matters.

The culprit, who had nothing to say for himself, was ordered at once to prison.

Jaques Sauvage was placed under arrest, Caleb Corder and Timothy Tootles were handed over to Sergeant Crank as deserters, and our hero having been complimented highly for his courage and discernment, received the promised reward of two thousand francs, with the addition of a handsome ring, which Marshal Boufflers begged to present in memory of the event to the Earl of Marlborough.

Everything being settled, the English party took their departure.

CHAPTER XXIII.
TO BE SHOT AT SUNRISE.

THE British troops were now posted before the city of Liege.

Two days had elapsed.

Sergeant Crank received a summons to attend the general in his tent.

He at once obeyed.

"I have sent for you, sergeant," said his superior, "to tell you that to-morrow I recommence hostilities."

"Very good, general."

"But that is not the only thing I had to

say. I have been thinking a good deal about your clever *protégé*."

"Jack Barrington?"

"Yes; at the same time I am doubtful," the earl continued, "whether he is not almost too young yet to be exposed to the heat of action."

"He is young, your grace, certainly," admitted the sergeant; "but then he's wonderfully plucky; I never knew a boy to have so much pluck. I really don't think he'd be happy to be left out."

"Well, you will see how he regards the prospect of steel and lead that is before us to-morrow."

"I will, general."

Sergeant Crank saluted his commander, and was about to retire, but stopped suddenly.

"Oh, general," he said, "what is to be done with the two deserters—Corder and Tootles, the drummer and fifer?"

"They must be shot, as an example to the rest of the troops."

"Very good, your grace," replied Benjamin Crank; "when is the sentence to be carried out?"

"Early to-morrow morning; and as these fellows have shown such murderous intentions towards Jack Barrington, let him convey to them the intelligence of their fate."

The sergeant, having received these orders, left the tent, and hastened to his own quarters.

Jack was there with Brian O'Flinn and Ned Rattles.

Benjamin Crank was on very friendly terms with our hero's comrades, and encouraged them to keep together.

"I've got something to say to you, my boy," he said to Jack, as he entered.

"Then you'll be wantin' us out ov the way, won't yez?" remarked Brian, as he rose to depart.

"No, you needn't go; I can trust you," the sergeant replied, as he seated himself.

All being gathered round him, he went on—

"To-morrow we begin to fight again."

"Hurroo!" cried Brian.

"I shall be ready with my drum," joined in Jack, cheerfully.

"Just as I expected," said Benjamin Crank; "but the earl (God bless him!) thinks you're a trifle too young to stand the 'tug of war' just yet."

"Oh, no, I'm not too young!" cried our hero, eagerly; "I've been in one action, and I stood that well enough, and I can stand another."

Sergeant Crank smiled again at his *protégé*, as he remarked, admiringly—

"Well, my dear boy, if there isn't a great deal of you at present, dash me if you're not game to the backbone."

"If it's game not to be frightened then, I think I am game," laughed our hero, "for I don't mind the bullets a bit."

"There's no doubt you were born to be a soldier. So, then, you're determined to go in with the rest, are you?"

"Certainly," said Jack; "Ned will be with me."

"I'll stick to you too, like a leech, old fellow," protested Ned Rattles.

"And if I see a cannon ball coming widin half a mile of yez, me darling, I'll stop it wid my fist," cried Brian O'Flinn, in his merry style.

"Well, Jack, you shall go to battle to-morrow. And now," resumed the sergeant, "you're to go to the cell where Caleb Corder and Timothy Tootles are confined."

"And what am I to do there?" asked our hero.

"It's nothing to do, but something to say," Sergeant Crank informed him.

Jack turned quite pale at the terrible announcement.

"Don't kill them, sergeant, don't!" he entreated earnestly.

"Odds bobs," cried Benjamin, "it isn't me that's pronounced sentence; it's the Earl of Marlborough—Heaven bless him!—and how can I stop it?"

"And why should the sergeant stop it, honey?" exclaimed Brian O'Flinn, who was not quite so forgiving as his young companion. "Shure, the blackguards desarve what they're going to recave."

"That's just my opinion," said Ben Crank.

Jack's face exhibited more dismay than any present had ever before seen in it.

But he could not refuse to obey orders, and, accordingly, he accompanied Sergeant Crank to where the culprits were confined.

At a signal from the sergeant, the door was unlocked, and our hero stood in the presence of his comrades.

The moon's rays, falling through the grated window, revealed the prisoners.

"Who's there?" asked Caleb, aroused by the opening of the door.

"It is I," replied the visitor, speaking in as firm a tone as he could; "Jack Barrington."

"Well," grunted Caleb Corder, the prisoner, in his usual surly tone, "and what brings you here, Jack Barrington?"

"'Ave yer come to let us out of this 'ole?" whimpered Timothy Tootles, dolefully. "Do let us out, that's a good cove."

"I can't," replied Jack, mournfully. "I wish I could."

This was perfectly sincere on his part.

But his tone of sympathy took little effect on Caleb Corder.

"If you can't let us out, what do you want with us?" he growled.

"I am come to bring you a message from the Earl of Marlborough," replied our hero, in a choked voice.

"Um!"

"A dreadful message, too."

"Oh, Lor'!" shuddered Timothy, his teeth chattering together.

"Well, what is it?" asked Caleb, doggedly.

"That you're both to be shot to-morrow morning in presence of all the troops," answered Jack, his voice faltering, and the tears coming into his eyes.

Caleb Corder, even at this announcement, evinced no remorse.

He simply muttered—

"A good job too; there'll be an end to us, then."

Timothy Tootles now began to bellow, piteously—

"Oh, dear! oh, Lor'! I'm a-goin' to be shot. I shall never see poor old mother never no more. Oh, oh!"

Our hero pitied his condemned comrades sincerely.

But especially the weak-minded Timothy.

"I'm very sorry for you both," he said, earnestly. "I don't suppose you think so, but I am, indeed."

"I don't care a straw whether you're sorry or not," returned Caleb Corder, bitterly.

"Oh, don't say that," interposed Timothy, with the tears trickling down his face. "I thinks it's werry kind of Jack to be sorry for us, arter tryin' to blow 'im up in the hair, and get 'im taken prisoner arterwards."

Jack stepped forward, and took the luckless youth by his manacled hands.

"Keep up your spirits as well as you can," he said, soothingly, to him.

"I vill, Master Jack, so I vill; but it's 'ard for a cove to keep up 'is sperrits when 'e knows 'e's a-going to be shot afore breakfast to-morrer—oh, oh!"

Timothy continued his wailings, but suddenly he stopped, and said to our hero—

"I say, Muster Jack, couldn't yer put in a vord for us to the hearl? 'E'd be sure to listen to you, cos you're sech a pet of 'is."

"I'm afraid I couldn't do much for you," said Jack, after a moment.

"Vell, vill yer do vat yer can?"

"I will."

"You promise?"

"Yes."

"Ugh!" sneered Caleb Corder, "a fat lot he'll do; he'll be too glad to get rid of us."

Jack made no reply to this embittered speech, and having wished his comrades good-night, he tapped at the wicket to be let out.

The door opened, and the next moment our hero found himself once more in the open air.

"Well," said Sergeant Crank, as he joined him, "how did they receive the news?"

"They didn't like it at all."

They reached their quarters in silence, and after a short time, Jack, having a plan in his head, slipped away.

*   *   *   *   *

The attention of the sentinel who stood at the entrance of the Earl of Marlborough's tent was suddenly aroused by the approach of a slight figure.

"Who goes there?" he demanded.

"Jack Barrington."

The name was familiar to the guard, and he asked—

"What business?"

"I have something particular to say to the commander-in-chief," Jack answered.

Our hero being regarded as a privileged person, the message was at once transferred to the soldier within the tent.

The next moment the word was passed—

"Let him enter."

Our hero found himself once more in the earl's presence.

We need not linger to give the conversation that ensued in detail.

Enough that the earl's last words were—

"I cannot undertake to spare these two delinquents, although I think your intercession in their behalf is a noble proof of the generosity of your disposition. But one thing I promise, that they shall not be executed till after to-morrow's battle."

CHAPTER XXIV.
THE FIRST CANNON.

IT was about three in the morning when the English camp was broken up, and began to move forward towards the French entrenchments without the city of Liege.

A dense mist hung suspended in the air, so that the advancing force could approach without being seen. Soon the order came to halt.

The Earl of Marlborough then, having arranged his plan of attack, placed his troops in order.

The English formed the central body, supported on the right and left by the allies.

All was in readiness.

Profound silence prevailed amongst the ranks, during which, divine service was performed at the head of each regiment.

This being done, they waited until the morning light should enable them to commence the attack.

Slowly the dawn crept onwards from the east.

The gallant troops were eager for the contest to commence.

The earl mounted his horse, and with his telescope in his hand, waited patiently till the mist should clear off and permit him to reconnoitre the foe before him.

One person only was close to the commander.

This was Sergeant Crank.

"Our position is excellent," said Marlborough to him; "could not be better, but yet we may have a sharp struggle."

"Short and sweet, general," remarked Benjamin, with a grin.

The atmosphere was cleared, and the hostile force appeared fully revealed in the morning light.

The sight of the foe before them made the English soldiers long for the signal to advance.

This was on the eve of being given, when suddenly a white puff of smoke was belched forth from the French batteries, accompanied by a deep boom.

It was the first cannon fired by the enemy.

The distance had been well calculated, and the ball struck the ground almost close to the spot where the earl had taken up his position, causing his horse to rear, and enveloping him in a cloud of dust.

A cry of alarm burst from those around.

But the voice of the commander reassured them.

"I am unhurt," he cried, raising his hat from his head, and smiling at those around him.

A shout of exultation came from the soldiers.

"Our foes have set us an example," continued the earl, "and we must not be slow to follow it."

With these words, he gave orders to the artillery to open fire.

The thunder of the cannon rolled across the plain.

The blue sky above was obscured by dense clouds of smoke.

Once more the din and crash of war had commenced.

CHAPTER XXV.

THE BATTLE WITHOUT THE WALLS.

THEN came the word of command to the right and left wings—

"Advance!"

The order was obeyed with alacrity.

The Dutch and German cavalry rode forward.

The enemy were evidently prepared for their approach.

As they drew nearer, and the cry "Charge!" was given, they were met by the French and Bavarian troopers.

After a sharp but fierce encounter, the latter gave way.

Their place was immediately filled by the infantry, who were opposed by the soldiers of the English allies.

The Earl of Marlborough rode from post to post.

His voice was heard in every quarter, exhorting his men to use all their exertions to drive back their foes.

"I told you that we might expect a sharp struggle," he cried, as he galloped up to the spot where his English troops waited.

"Aye, aye, general," returned Sergeant Crank.

Up to the present time, the earl had confined his attacks to the right and left wings of the enemy, making use of his foreign allies only for that purpose.

But now the moment for the decisive blow had come, when the English, who formed the main body of the army, were to throw their weight into the scale of conflict.

Striking spurs into his horse's side, Marlborough shouted in ringing tones—

"Forward, my English lads."

With a ringing shout, the cavalry dashed forward, right into the very heart of the enemy's ranks.

They were supported by the English grenadiers.

The entire number of the vast host was now engaged.

Amidst the rattle of musketry the roar of cannon, the shouts of men, and the clash of steel, the terrible strife continued.

"Short and sweet, my boys," remarked Sergeant Crank to our hero and his comrade, as they rolled their drums in the thick of the fight.

The sergeant had been many times in action, and he knew from experience that the fiercer the battle waged, the nearer it was to its termination.

This was soon evident in the enemy's flanks.

They began to fall into disorder, and to lose ground.

Two regiments of British cavalry, dashing in upon them, completely put them to the rout.

At the same moment, a squadron of dragoons bore down upon the main body of the French army with the fury of an avalanche.

This blow was decisive.

Their ranks were broken up and thrown into utter confusion.

"*Sauve qui peut*—save himself whoever can," was the general cry, as they rushed in disordered masses towards the entrenchments.

"Hurrah, lads," shouted Sergeant Crank, cheerily, as covered with dust, he hurried along with his comrades. "The queen and the Earl of Marlborough. Hurrah!"

"The queen and the Earl of Marlborough!" echoed those who heard him.

The victory was virtually gained.

The French and their allies were pouring in at the city gates.

The English cavalry scoured the plain in pursuit of stragglers.

It was at this time that our hero and Ned Rattles, who had been separated in the *mêlée* of conflict, found themselves together again on the bloodstained field.

"Hallo! old chap," cried Ned, "it's been sharp work, hasn't it?"

"Rather."

"Well, and how are you by this time? All right."

"Quite right, thank you. And you?"

"Ditto!" Ned replied. "Can't say as much for my drum though."

"What's the matter with it?"

"Shot clean through the body in two places," laughed Ned; "mortally wounded."

"Well, better your drum than yourself."

"Decidedly; I can get a new drum easier than a new body."

"Yes. Have you seen Sergeant Crank lately?"

"Not for some time."

The two comrades glanced around them.

On all sides were stretched the wounded, the dead, and the dying.

"War's an awful thing after all, isn't it?" remarked Jack.

"Yes; you find it out when it's all over," Ned replied. "You've no time to think about anything while the hurry scurry's going on."

"That's true," admitted our hero, "but it seems awful to see so many poor fellows lying on the ground never to rise again."

"Well, suppose we get back to the camp," said Ned, after a moment.

"Come on, then."

They went on, but had hardly taken half a dozen steps, when they heard sounds of grief.

A few paces from them a pretty young French girl was seated on the ground, weeping bitterly.

She was dressed in the costume of a vivandière, and carried a keg at her side.

So absorbed was she by her grief, that she did not notice the approach of the lads.

"What's the matter with her?" said Ned. "Speak to her. Ask her what it is. She'll understand you."

They drew near, and our hero said to her, kindly, in the French language—

"What's the matter, mademoiselle?"

The young girl, hearing herself addressed in her own language, looked up, and seeing Jack

"THE FRENCH SOLDIER FROWNED, AND RAISED HIS MUSKET."

looking down upon her with much sympathy expressed in his face, replied with sobs—

"Alas! I am sick at heart."

"Won't you tell me why?"

"On account of my lover, *mon pauvre* Jeannot."

"Is he dead?"

"I know not."

"Then why do you sit here weeping?" asked Jack.

"Because I fear he may have been hurt in the battle, and I cannot find him."

The girl threw her eyes hurriedly over the field as she spoke.

"Is your lover a soldier?" said Jack.

"Oh, yes, a brave soldier," returned the girl, her eyes sparkling with sudden animation; "handsome, gallant."

"And you have not seen him since the fight began?" asked Ned Rattles, who knew just enough of the French tongue to understand this.

"Alas, no! I shall never see him again, *mon cher, mon brave* Jeannot," cried the vivandière, with a fresh burst of grief.

"Perhaps he has been taken prisoner by our troops," remarked Ned Rattles; "if so, he's sure to be well treated."

"Ah, yes, yes; the English always treat their prisoners well," returned the girl, consoling herself with the thought.

"Perhaps we may see something of him," Jack continued.

"Oh, if you do," exclaimed the vivandière, eagerly, "will you please give him this?"

As she spoke, she took from her bosom a scrap of paper, round which was tied a lock of dark hair, and placed it in our hero's hand.

"Give him this," she repeated; "his name is Jeannot Roussel."

"Jeannot Roussel. I won't forget to seek for him."

"Tell him Fanchette sent it with her love, will you?"

"I will, I promise."

"Heaven bless you!" exclaimed the young girl, fervently.

Then pressing our hero's hand to her lips with much emotion, she hurried away.

Jack Barrington and Ned Rattles stood looking after Fanchette as she went along, pausing only to glance at the bodies as she passed, until she was lost in the crowd of stragglers hurrying in the same direction.

"Poor girl," said Ned.

The words had hardly passed his lips when he heard a distant shout.

"Hallo! what's up now?" cried Ned.

Two figures were scudding across the field towards the town.

One short and fat.

The other tall and thin.

They had no weapons, and were in a state of *deshabille*, being without either coats or hats.

As they drew nearer, our hero recognised them.

"It's Jules Gasconade and his *cher ami* Pierre," he said.

"They're running away, I think," added Ned Rattles.

"There's not much doubt about that," laughed Jack. "See how the fat corporal puffs and blows."

"Shall we stop them?" said Ned.

"No; let them go," returned our hero; "we're not supposed to have seen them, and I don't think they can hurt the English much."

"Very well; we'll allow them to escape. But I should like to give them a parting——"

"Shot?"

"No—fright; it won't do them any harm."

"What shall we do?"

"Imitate me," said Ned, as he picked up a musket.

Jack did the same.

Messieurs Jules and Pierre were stepping along at much more than double-quick time, when suddenly two voices shouted—

"Halt, there!"

The Frenchmen paused, and Ned and Jack presented their unloaded muskets.

"You are escaping," they cried; "yield yourselves prisoners, or we fire."

The fugitives uttered a groan of disappointment and dismay, and fell on their knees.

"Oh, *diable!* Don't fire! don't! you might shoot us!" they yelled.

"Very likely," returned Ned Rattles; "it's quite right to shoot prisoners if they are caught attempting to escape."

"Oh, no, no! ve do not vish to escape. Ve vas take a leetle excursion, dat vas all," explained the civil guard, trying to laugh.

"Oh, well, you can go then," said Ned; "but you'll be sure to come back?"

"Oh, yes, yes! sure to come back," replied both the Frenchmen, eagerly, as they sprang to their feet.

"Off you go then," called Ned.

Away went the Frenchmen and were soon out of sight.

Our hero and his companion continued their course, until they reached a spot where the strife had been especially fierce.

Here the dead lay piled in heaps, and the ground was dark and crimson with blood.

So terrible and ghastly was the sight that the lads shuddered.

They were about to turn away when they caught sight of a wounded soldier, who was lying with his back propped up against the lifeless bodies of friends and foes.

He was young, and evidently a Frenchman from his uniform.

He turned his eyes imploringly upon them and murmured—

"Water, for the love of Heaven!"

They had none to give him; but fortunately just at that moment they descried Biddy O'Flinn.

The old Irishwoman, with her kegs of cordials slung at her side, was going her rounds to administer relief to the wounded.

At the sound of Jack's voice, she hastened forward.

A cup of water was speedily held to the parched lips of the young Frenchman.

This done Biddy, after exchanging a few words, continued her charitable labours.

Jack knelt down by the side of the wounded man.

"You are badly hurt, I fear."

"Yes," replied the soldier; "my leg was shattered by a cannon ball towards the close of the engagement. It is all over with me."

"Oh, no; you should hope for the best," said Ned Rattles, cheeringly.

The Frenchman shook his head.

"I shall die," he said, presently; "but it matters not. Why should I live since France is beaten, and Fanchette hates me?"

"Fanchette!" exclaimed Jack; "are you Jeannot Roussel?"

"I am," returned the soldier, surprised at the question.

"Then Fanchette doesn't hate you," cried Jack. "We met her not long ago, and she gave me a letter for you in case we came across you."

One glance at the dark tress was sufficient.

The pale face of the young Frenchman lighted up with hope.

"Ah, yes, yes; *c'est vrai!*—'tis true. Oh, Fanchette loves me," he cried, joyfully. "I wish to live now."

"Then here's a chance for you," said Ned; "see who comes."

It was the vivandière.

Her quick eyes had descried her lover, and in an instant she was at his side.

"Jeannot; *mon cher* Jeannot!" she exclaimed, as she threw her arms round him.

"*Ma chère* Fanchette," murmured the wounded soldier.

But the joy he felt was too much for him.

His head sank upon her breast, and he fainted.

The next moment he was lifted into the ambulance, which moved on to collect other victims.

But the lovers were together once more.

Again Jack and his comrade were moving on towards the English lines, when once more their progress was arrested by the report of a musket.

It came from the direction of the wood which lay on the right.

Looking towards it, they saw three figures engaged in what appeared to be a deadly encounter.

Suddenly our hero exclaimed—

"It's Sergeant Crank."

"Where?" cried Ned Rattles, eagerly.

"Yonder; fighting, I believe, with two others."

"Let's go and help him, then."

In an instant they had snatched up two guns with bayonets fixed, and were hurrying forward to the scene of conflict.

CHAPTER XXVI.
A SINGLE COMBAT.

TOWARDS the end of the battle, Sergeant Crank found himself separated from his comrades.

Suddenly he perceived a French officer galloping towards him.

The Frenchman dashed onward at a rapid pace.

But suddenly, as he passed, he raised his sword, and delivered a sweeping blow at the sergeant's head.

Fortunately for Benjamin Crank, a quick backward step forestalled the deadly intention.

All that the stroke accomplished was the cutting off of a portion of the sergeant's hat.

Almost at the same moment the officer's horse stumbled and fell, carrying his rider with him to the ground.

Instantly the sergeant was upon him, and ere he could rise, had dragged him from the saddle.

A desperate tussle took place upon the green sward.

Captain Gravellotte—for it was he—had lost his sword in the fall.

The sergeant had laid down his musket, in order that he might have his hands at liberty.

Both were wiry and strong-limbed.

Both were English, although one wore the French uniform.

The struggle was fierce and prolonged, being simply hand to hand, without any weapons but those which nature supplied.

At length the renegade captain began to show signs of exhaustion.

"Yield!" cried Sergeant Crank, "yield yourself prisoner."

"Enough; I yield," returned the other breathlessly.

He spoke such excellent English that his victor was astonished.

"You are no Frenchman," exclaimed Benjamin Crank.

"No matter what I am," returned Gasper Grimsby, sulkily. "The fortune of war has given you the victory. Be content, and ask no questions."

"Oh, I'm quite content, if you are," replied the sergeant, with a grim smile, "and so come along with me to the English camp."

These words were spoken as they lay on the ground.

But on the captain declaring himself beaten, Sergeant Crank relaxed his grip and allowed him to rise, still holding him by his belt.

But the officer was by no means satisfied with the result of the encounter.

Freedom was his object.

As soon as he regained his feet, he slipped the buckle of his belt, which he left in the sergeant's hand.

Having thus set himself at liberty, he darted upon his sword, which lay at a little distance from him.

Benjamin Crank at once snatched up his musket, with the formidable bayonet at the end.

Captain Gravellotte did not renew the contest, but set off at full speed towards the wood that lay before him.

The sergeant, chagrined at the manner in which his prisoner had slipped out of his clutches, after the trouble he had taken to secure him, shouted—

"Stop, or I fire."

A mocking laugh was the only answer he received.

Benjamin Crank, true to his word, raised his musket and fired after him.

But his long wrestle had made his aim unsteady, and he missed his mark.

This put him thoroughly on his mettle, and

vowing in his mind to recapture his prize, he gave chase.

He was an excellent runner, and rapidly gained ground, coming up with the fugitive almost on the borders of the wood.

Finding him close upon him, the latter stopped and turned.

The combat now recommenced with sword and bayonet.

Captain Gravellotte was active, and a skilful swordsman, but Sergeant Crank was equally efficient with his bayonet, and it was not long before he had given his opponent a thrust in the arm.

"I'll have you yet, my friend," he cried, "either dead or alive."

The officer ground his teeth with rage, and continued the contest with fierce intensity.

But it soon became evident that he was growing weaker, and Benjamin Crank felt certain that the victory would be his after all.

It was just as he was quietly exulting over this thought, that two Bavarian troopers emerged from the shadow of the wood.

"Au secours—help!" shouted Captain Gravellotte to them.

The troopers, who were armed with sabres, ran forward, and Sergeant Crank found himself very unexpectedly opposed to three men instead of one.

But he was a man of strong nerve and dauntless spirit, and far from being dismayed at the odds against him, he prepared himself—although it was somewhat a forlorn hope—to conquer or die.

He had reloaded his musket as he ran, and as the Bavarians advanced, he fired.

One fell dead.

The odds were now only two to one.

Planting his back against a tree, he, with his bayonet, successfully parried their attacks, until, at length, by a skilful thrust, he stretched the second trooper on the ground with his companion.

Captain Gravellotte had taken the opportunity to bind up his arm.

The slight rest had also, in some degree, revived his failing strength, but now, finding his colleagues slain, he, with a last effort, putting aside the bayonet, rushed in upon his antagonist, bringing his sword down upon his head.

The hat averted the full effects of the blow, but it was still sufficient to inflict a scalp wound, and the blood poured down the sergeant's face like rain.

At the same moment, and whilst a thousand lights were flashing in his eyes, Captain Gravellotte sprang upon him, fastening his nails in his throat with the desperate ferocity of a wolf.

Wearied with his protracted exertions, and weakened from loss of blood, Benjamin Crank was no longer able to cope with his adversary.

He began to reel and stagger like a drunken man.

He felt the breath being choked out of him under the violent pressure upon his windpipe.

It was at this critical moment, just when the brave sergeant had made up his mind for death, that a ringing shout was heard.

Captain Gravellotte thirsted for the destruction of the man he held in his power, but he loved his own life still better, and on hearing the shouts, he thought it time to provide for his safety by flight.

But his fingers still lingered on his victim's throat, as though loth to loose their grasp, when suddenly he received a tremendous thwack on his back, followed by another on his sconce, and a voice shouted—

"Hould, yer murdtherous bla'guard, is it sthranglin' the poor man you'd be afther?"

The captain, with haggard face and glaring eyes, turned and looked over his shoulder.

Biddy O'Flinn stood before him.

Biddy, red as a turkey cock, flourishing her shillelagh in the air.

"Bad luck to yez, you spalpeen," she continued, "lave go. Take that, ye divil."

Down came the "illigant twig" once more on the head of the renegade, whilst the shouts of those approaching rang also in his ears.

He waited no longer, but with a bitter execration of mingled rage and pain, he released his grasp, and suddenly darted off towards the wood.

In those dark shades he quickly disappeared.

One exclamation from a boy's voice, however, followed him as he ran.

"That's the man who killed my father!"

The next moment our hero and Ned Rattles came hurrying up, with a couple of formidable muskets on their shoulders, accompanied by Brian O'Flinn, who had met them by the way.

Sergeant Crank, by the time they reached the spot, was seated on the ground.

Biddy was supporting him with one arm, whilst with the other she held to his lips a flask.

"A taste ov the crathur, sergeant darlin'; it'll set you right if anything will," she said, assuringly.

Although a staunch teetotaller, Sergeant Crank at that moment felt vividly that he required something considerably stronger than tea to dispel the faintness that had seized upon him, and he took a good pull at the potheen.

Brian O'Flinn, who was much attached to the brave grenadier, dropped down by his side and wiped the blood from his face.

"Cheer up, sergeant darlin'," he said, soothingly; "only parsevere wid the whisky, and if that won't keep you up, nothing will."

Benjamin Crank had already felt the reviving effects of the stimulant, and fancying he had caught a glimpse of his protégé a moment before, he said—

"Didn't I see my boy Jack?"

"Oh, yes, he's here right enough," returned Brian.

"Where?" inquired the sergeant, as he glanced anxiously around.

The inquiry was repeated, but no answer came. Jack Barrington was no longer in sight.

He and his comrade Ned Rattles had disappeared.

The sight of the captain had recalled the dark and terrible tragedy of which he was the author.

Young as our hero was, it had stirred his soul to its very depths, and he had gone in pursuit of the man who had murdered the father he had loved.

CHAPTER XXVII.

CAUGHT AT LAST.

THE murderer not only heard the words of young Jack, but recognised the voice that uttered them, and it seemed to retard his footsteps by a kind of fascination.

Having gained the covert of the wood, in spite of the pain of his wound, he paused, and remained peering forth from between the trees.

He could see gallant young Jack.

"The whelp will follow me, I believe," he muttered to himself. "Let him; he may find it harder to return."

Hardly had he uttered these words when Jack and Ned plunged into the thicket.

Concealing himself behind one of the trunks, Captain Gravellotte allowed them to pass, and then followed cautiously in their wake.

For more than a mile the young soldiers pushed boldly on.

But without overtaking the object of their search.

"I'm afraid we've lost him," said Jack at length, as he came to a stop.

"Seems like it," replied his companion.

"I'm sorry for it," said our hero, "for he killed my father."

"I meant to have shot him if I could have caught him," continued Jack, after a pause; "but I'm afraid he has got away."

Jack had almost made up his mind to return, when he heard the sound of footsteps.

He looked round.

Between the trees he saw advancing a pale, ghastly-looking figure.

At first he did not remember him, but as he drew nearer, he recognised the well-known features of Caleb Corder.

He glared at them for a moment like some frightened animal, suddenly surprised by hunters.

"Well, I'm not shot after all," he said, at length, in a tone of bravado.

"So I see," answered Jack; "but how is it you're at liberty?"

"Took French leave of course. Cut and run," was the reply, accompanied by a grin.

"Do you mean to say you've escaped?" asked Ned Rattles.

"That's just it. I was tired of confinement; and while the English and French were pummelling one another, I slipped my chains and bolted."

As he spoke, he held up his wrists round which the handcuffs with the link broken still clung.

"And what are you going to do now?"

"I'm going over to the French lines," was the dogged answer.

"You'd better take care you're not caught before you get there," counselled Jack.

"Ugh! you'd like to see me dropped upon, wouldn't you?" exclaimed Caleb, bitterly.

"Not at all," replied our hero. "I'm very glad you've got away."

"Oh, yes, I dare say you are very glad."

"I am indeed. If I'd wished you to be shot, I shouldn't have asked the earl to let you off."

"Go on; tell that to the marines" cried the deserter, in a mocking, incredulous tone; "you know that you did all you could to get us executed."

Jack made no reply to this.

It was clear enough that his assurances of good feeling were entirely discredited.

"Good-bye, Caleb," he said; "I hope you'll get on better with the French than you have with the English."

"No fear. There are no sucking heroes there."

"Oh, come on; let's leave the sulky brute to himself," cried Ned Rattles, in disgust.

Nothing loth, Jack Barrington turned away with his comrade.

"They're a nice pair," said Caleb Corder to himself, as he stood looking after them; "but they stick together, anyhow."

He was about to move on, when suddenly a hand was placed upon his shoulder.

He turned and found himself face to face with Captain Gravellotte.

The face of the renegade was pale and besmeared with blood and dust.

So much so, that Caleb did not at first recognise him.

"We have met before," said the officer, as he looked at him earnestly.

"Yes, I—I think so," returned the deserter, puzzling his brains to know where.

"You were employed by Jaques Sauvage."

"Yes, to capture Jack Barrington, and I did capture him."

"True."

"But I was never paid for my services."

"Indeed!" exclaimed the officer, affecting surprise. "Well, never mind; you shall be remunerated handsomely; and if you wish to double the reward, you can do so."

"How?"

"You know who goes yonder?"

"Yes."

"Well, come with me, and help me to secure them. I should not need your assistance had I not received a severe hurt," and the captain held up his wounded hand.

"I'll come," said Caleb.

On they went together in pursuit.

*   *   *   *   *

Suddenly, as Jack Barrington and his comrade were quietly pursuing their way, they heard a hoarse shout.

The next moment they were surrounded by half a dozen French and Bavarian soldiers.

Before they had time to inquire what they wanted, Captain Gravellotte strode forward with Caleb Corder at his side.

"Arrest these fellows," cried the former, "and convey them at once to the common gaol."

Our hero turned his flashing eyes upon him.

"You've no right to stop us, and you'll repent it, you murderer, you!" he exclaimed.

Captain Gravellotte cast a sneering scowl at the young speaker, but made no reply.

"He, he!" grinned Caleb, "I hope you'll get on as well in the common gaol as you did out of it."

Jack turned from him with contempt.

The next moment, the soldiers hurried him and his companion along through the dense wood.

At length the town was reached, and they were marched through the gates.

On every side the greatest confusion prevailed.

Soldiers and citizens were mingled together. The wounded, dying, and dead lay in all directions.

The general topic of conversation was the defeat of that day, mingled with execrations against *les maudits Anglais*—the accursed English.

Many a scowl and bitter malediction was cast upon the young English soldiers as they walked on between their guards.

As they were going along, a young girl glanced at them from a window.

It was Fanchette.

Jack caught a glimpse of her and she of him.

"The preserver of my Jeannot a prisoner!" she cried, as she hastily disappeared.

But before she could reach the street, they were out of sight.

On they went, until at length they arrived at a dark stone building.

They were conducted beneath its gloomy portals.

When the sun went down, they saw his last rays glimmering through the bars of a French prison.

CHAPTER XXVIII.

IN PRISON.

SERGEANT CRANK experienced great anxiety when he learnt that his *protégé*, Gallant Jack, and Ned Rattles, were missing.

It seemed to trouble him far more than his wound.

"He must be found—Jack must be found!" he cried, fretfully.

"So he shall, sergeant darlin'," said Brian O'Flinn, assuringly. "No doubt he's only strayed away into the wood; I'll look afther him."

This promise comforted the sergeant, and instructed by him, Brian O'Flinn, armed with no other weapons but his sword and a flask of the crathur, plunged into the wood in search of our hero.

* * * * *

Jack Barrington and Ned Rattles were locked up in their gloomy cell.

The only light they had now that day had departed was the rays of a solitary oil lamp that hung suspended from the ceiling.

"How do you like being in prison?" said Ned Rattles, at length, ruefully.

"Not at all," Jack replied.

"That's just how I like it," said Ned. "It is a miserable hole."

"It isn't very pleasant, certainly; but there's one thing I like about it."

"What's that?"

"We're alone."

"Not quite," remarked Ned; "look yonder."

As he spoke he pointed to a hole in the corner.

A small animal with a long tail glided forth.

"It's a rat, isn't it?" said Jack.

. "Yes."

"Oh, never mind the rats. I'd rather have them than a lot of people."

"So would I," replied Ned, "although beggars. I've heard they eat prisoners sometimes."

"We must give them a share of our supper, then."

"If we get any."

"Ah, true. I begin to feel rather hungry."

"So do I," said Ned; "I could eat the head of my drum if I'd got it."

"I'll tell you what we must try to do," said Jack.

"What?"

"Escape."

"Escape!"

"Yes; prisoners do sometimes," said our hero. "Many a one has picked away the mortar from the wall with only a rusty nail, and got out that way."

"We haven't got even a rusty nail," said Ned.

"Perhaps we may find one somewhere when the daylight comes."

Just at this moment the key turned in the lock.

The door opened.

A little old man with grey hair, dressed in a coarse serge suit, and wearing a red woollen nightcap on his head, entered.

It was Ferron, the gaoler.

Altogether the appearance of the old man was not unpleasant.

He looked at them for a moment, and then said with a smile—

"Aha, there you are, my dears, safe enough."

"Yes, here we are," said Ned Rattles.

"Zat ees right; I like boys."

"English boys?" asked Jack.

"*Ma foi*, it is no mattair for zat. Engleesh or French, eet ees mosh ze same. You are good boys. I like good boys."

"You like tobacco, too, don't you?" asked Ned, as he noticed the pipe stuck in the band of the gaoler's red cap.

"Ah, *oui; je l'aime beaucoup*—I like it much."

"Here's some for you, then."

As Ned spoke, he took from his pocket a pouch and threw it towards him.

"That's Brian's pouch, isn't it?" whispered Jack.

"Yes."

Gregoire was delighted at the present, and commenced smoking at once.

"You are verree kind—verree. I shall not forget you," he said, his rubicund face glowing with satisfaction.

"I hope you won't forget to bring us some supper," said Jack.

"Vell; I shall see if I can get you a loaf presently, vhen all ees quiet."

"It seems pretty quiet now," remarked Ned.

"Ve moos vait a leetle. Zere may be some von come yet. Hush!"

At the same time the door opened, and a figure with a cigar in its mouth looked in.

It was Caleb Corder.

The gaoler stared at him in surprise.

"You needn't be astonished at me, mounseer," grinned the deserter. "I'm one of the *grande nation* now."

Gregoire shrugged his shoulders and puffed at his pipe.

Caleb advanced with his hands in his pockets.

He contemplated his comrades with insolent exultation.

"It's your turn, now," he said, at length, in jeering tones. "I hope you find it as pleasant as I did."

"When you were in prison, we did not come to mock you," said Jack.

"You didn't come and tell me I was to be shot, did you?" returned Caleb, spitefully.

"I was obliged to deliver the earl's message."

"I don't believe the earl sent any such message, at all."

"He did."

"The shooting didn't come off, anyhow, for here I am, alive and kicking," sneered Caleb.

"You may thank Jack for that," interposed Ned Rattles.

"Thank him—pooh!"

"'Pooh' as much as you like; but if he hadn't begged the earl to spare your life, you'd have been dead long ago."

"I'm not going to die just yet," exclaimed Caleb, boastfully. "I'm going to be a great man presently."

"Oh, indeed! Is that what you came to tell us?"

"No, it isn't. I came to tell Master John Barrington that he may expect a visitor presently."

"Whom?" Jack asked.

"You'll know when you see him," was the reply.

Our hero was not left long in doubt, for just then footsteps were heard in the passage, and the next moment Captain Gravellotte entered.

He glanced at Caleb and the gaoler, and said abruptly to them—

"You can go."

He then called to our hero—

"Come here."

Jack approached him.

For a moment the captain stood with his eyes fixed upon his young prisoner.

"You remember me?" asked the officer.

"Yes. I shall never forget you," answered Jack.

"Where is it you have seen me?"

"In the wood. You are the murderer; you killed my father," our hero replied, his lips quivering.

"I killed your father!" echoed Captain Gravellotte. "You are quite mistaken; I wished to save him."

"No, you didn't; for I heard you order the soldiers to fire," returned Jack, boldly.

"Nonsense, boy," exclaimed the other, with suppressed anger; "you are full of fancies."

"That isn't fancy; and I believe you know where my mother is, too," our hero continued.

"Supposing I do, you would like to see her again, perhaps?"

"I should very much, and sister Lyddy as well," replied Jack, eagerly. "May I?"

Without answering this question directly, the captain said—

"I suppose a clever boy like you can write?"

"Oh, yes."

"Very well, then, I'll supply you with pen and paper, and you'll write to your mother."

"Willingly."

"Listen. You will write and tell her how very kind I've been to you, and how very fond you are of me. Do you understand?"

"No, I don't," was Jack's answer.

"You will if you consider a moment."

"No, I shan't," continued our hero, shaking his head; "because you haven't been kind to me in the least, and I'm not at all fond of you. I loved my father, but not you."

The renegade captain smiled at this candid avowal, but it was an ugly, spiteful smile, and he replied—

"What you say is, I have no doubt, quite true, but, nevertheless, you must write as I tell you."

"I will not," said Jack, firmly. "If I write, I shall say you are the murderer of my poor father."

"You refuse, then?"

"Yes."

"Psha! the boy's a fool," growled the officer, between his teeth.

"No, I'm not," said Jack; "but I'll tell you what, if you'll let Ned and me out of prison, I'll write and tell mother what you've done for us."

"You'll write as I dictate."

"I won't write anything that's untrue," insisted our hero, firmly.

"Wonderful boy!" cried the captain, in a tone of mock admiration. "But suppose your life depended upon your writing this letter—what then?"

"Well, then I wouldn't write it."

"You mean that?"

"Yes, for I know you to be a villain."

Captain Gravelotte went to the door and tapped against it angrily.

The gaoler and Caleb Corder re-entered.

"Let these fellows have nothing but bread and water—do you hear?" he growled to the former, as he strode out.

"And not too much of that," added Caleb, with a malicious grin, as he followed his new master.

Ned Rattles, who had taken off one of his boots to be ready for any emergency, shied it at Caleb's head, but he was a little too late, and the boot only struck against the edge of the door.

"*Ma foi,*" exclaimed the gaoler, as he picked up the useful article and returned it to the thrower, "if you had hit him, you should have knock his head out of his brains."

"You mean his brains out of his head," said Jack, in French.

Gregoire Ferron was surprised to hear himself addressed by our hero in his own language.

"Poor boys," he murmured; "and only bread and vatair for zem, zat is hard."

"You were saying not long since that prisoners might have anything to eat if they paid for it," said Jack.

"Truly."

"JACK BARRINGTON GAVE THE SOLDIER'S ARM A JERK UPWARDS."

"Well, then, get us something nice for supper, will you?" said our hero, as he placed five francs in his hand.

"Five francs!" exclaimed Gregoire, in profound astonishment.

"You won't forget the grub, will you, old fellow?" asked Ned Rattles, earnestly. "I'm so precious peckish."

"Oh, no; I shall not forget. But I was joss thinking how I should get ze supper for you. I cannot leave ze prison myself."

"But can't you send someone?" inquired Jack.

"*Hélas!* I have no von to send, unless my daughter should come here to-night," replied the gaoler.

"Do you think it's likely she will come?" asked the hungry prisoners very eagerly.

"I hope so," replied the old man, "or I shall have no supper for myself; but——"

He broke off suddenly and listened.

"Ah; zere she is. I hear her step. Fanchette, Fanchette, *ma chérie*," he cried, as he hurried out, forgetting to shut the door in his excitement.

Not that it mattered much.

Jack and his comrade had been too much struck with the name they had just heard to think of taking advantage of the omission.

"Fanchette!" exclaimed Jack. "Did you hear?"

"Suppose it should be the same we spoke to after the battle?"

"Ah!"

"Wouldn't it be strange?"

The next moment the gaoler entered the prison, accompanied by his daughter.

"Zere are ze boys," he said to her.

There was a mutual exclamation of surprise and delight, as the parties recognised each other.

It was the veritable Fanchette of the battlefield.

CHAPTER XXIX.

A FRIEND IN NEED.

THE young vivandière flew towards them, and, throwing herself on her knees, embraced them as warmly as though they had been her own brothers.

"It is they, it is they," she cried, excitedly. "*Ces chers garçons*—these dear boys. It is to them I owe the life of my Jeannot."

The old gaoler looked on in extreme wonder.

But his daughter quickly put him in possession of the facts, and his gratitude to his captives increased a hundredfold.

Fanchette undertook to go to market, and quickly returned with some savoury pies, fruit, and coffee, and a bottle of wine.

No more visitors being expected, Gregoire relaxed the strictness of the prison rules.

"Now, my boys," he said, "if you vill promise not to try to run avay, you shall have suppare in my private room."

The boys promised readily.

It was not till after breakfast on the following morning they again found themselves in their old quarters.

"Well," said our hero to his comrade, "who'd have thought of our meeting Fanchette in this place?"

"It's a proof that a kind action brings its reward."

It was about noon when Gregoire Ferron entered the cell with a nice meal of soup, white bread, and fruit, and to have a pleasant chat with them.

His daughter was with him.

After a slight pause, Jack said to Fanchette—

"You would like to see us free again, wouldn't you?"

"Oh, yes. I should rejoice so much," answered Fanchette.

"Well, then, I think you might get us our liberty."

"How?"

"Do you know Marshal Boufflers?"

"Oh, yes. He is the commander-in-chief of the French army," said Fanchette.

But she sighed as she thought of the pitiable plight in which that army was just then.

"Well," continued Jack, "the marshal was very kind to us a few days ago because we did him a service."

"Indeed. You did him a service?"

"Yes, we discovered the thief who had robbed him of five thousand francs, and brought him back, and the money too."

"Ha! vas it you did zat?" asked Ferron, eagerly. "Aha! you bring back André Fouet! Zat vas good, ver' good," chuckled the old gaoler.

"Do you know André Fouet?" asked our hero.

"He is a rascal, coward!" cried Ferron, vehemently.

"The marshal gave us two thousand francs as a reward," said Ned.

"Yes. That's how it is we happen to be so rich," said Jack. "And he gave me this ring besides."

As he spoke, he took the ring from his pocket, and handed it to Fanchette.

She examined it with interest, and, at the same moment, a grinning face rose up slowly behind the grated window and peered through the bars.

It was the face of Caleb Corder.

And he, too, fixed his eyes greedily upon the golden hoop in Fanchette's hand.

"I've been thinking," continued our hero, "that if I could send that ring to the marshal and let him know we are locked up here, he would order us to be set free."

"Ah, yes. I am sure he would," cried the vivandière, eagerly, "and I will take it to him."

"*Vive le maréchal!*" cried Gregoire Ferron, waving his red cap with enthusiasm. "You shall be at libertee, my boys, in less than two hours, *mes braves garçons*."

Fanchette sprang to her feet, and, bidding her young friends to keep up their spirits, left the cell with her father.

The dark face disappeared from the grated window at the same time.

Fanchette hastened from the prison, holding the ring in her hand.

Her eyes sparkled with hope and animation as she hurried along on her errand of charity.

The streets were in dire confusion, presenting a painful realization of the horrors of war.

In order to avoid molestation, Fanchette avoided the more public thoroughfares, and made her way through the narrow bye ways that intersected the city, unconscious that a figure was dogging her steps, and only waiting for a favourable opportunity to rob her of her treasure.

This quickly came.

As she turned into a narrow alley, the figure sprang forward, and, throwing his arm round her neck so violently as almost to strangle her, snatched the ring from her hand and fled with the speed of a greyhound.

Fanchette was, for a moment, completely bewildered by the sudden attack, but she was a brave girl, and, quickly recovering her presence of mind, set off in pursuit of the thief, but he had got too good a start.

All pursuit was vain.

She sank down upon a door step and wept, but she did not weep long.

A sudden determination came across her.

She would not be daunted at the mischance that had befallen her, but seek the marshal at once and relate the entire affair, trusting to his penetration to see that she was speaking the truth.

With this intent she rose and hurried forward to the quarters of the commander-in-chief.

But, alas, on arriving there she was informed that he had left Liege, and that a stranger had taken his place.

It is scarcely necessary to state that it was Caleb Corder who had snatched the ring from the hands of Fanchette.

He was rapidly progressing from bad to worse.

When once evil passions are allowed to enter the soul, from that moment it becomes filled with the very spirit of evil.

So it was with Caleb Corder.

Envy, hatred, murder, and theft were now familiar objects—his bosom companions.

"Ha, ha!" he cried; "they thought this ring was going to get them out of prison, did they? No, no. Old Marshal—what's his name —Buffers shall never see it, and they shall starve and rot in gaol. The ring is mine; I shall sell it, and——"

His voice suddenly ceased as a pair of strong hands gripped him.

Turning his head, he found himself confronted by a pair of hideous countenances, more resembling wild beasts in their ferocity than human beings.

They addressed him in a hoarse *patois*.

Caleb did not understand their language.

But he perfectly comprehended from their looks and actions that they wanted the ring he held.

"I shan't give it up, you pair of ugly thieves," he shouted, as he struggled violently to get away.

Those addressed did not attempt to argue the point.

One of them raised his clenched fist, of the colour of mahogany, and brought it down like a sledge hammer on Caleb Corder's skull.

He remembered no more, but fell to the ground like a log.

When he came to his senses it was growing dark.

Dizzy, faint, and sick, he dragged himself to his feet.

The ring was gone. All he had gained from his base attempt was disappointment and a fearful headache that almost drove him mad.

CHAPTER XXX.

TO THE RESCUE.

It was with no little dismay that Jack and his comrades heard of the incident that had destroyed their hopes of deliverance from captivity.

But they did not blame the kind-hearted vivandière, seeing how heart-broken she was at her loss.

"If we could only let Sergeant Crank know where we are," said Jack, suddenly, to Ned Rattles.

"Vat ees zat ; who ees Serzheant Crank?" asked Gregoire, as he caught the sound of the name.

"He is a brave English soldier, and a very dear friend of ours," Jack informed him.

"And he does not know you are here, eh?"

"No ; we left him badly wounded. He may be dead," said our hero, sorrowfully.

"I don't believe he's dead," said Ned Rattles. "He's precious tough, is Sergeant Crank."

"He is with the Engleesh armee, I suppose?" said Gregoire.

"Yes. I wish we could find someone to send," exclaimed our hero.

Fanchette had been sitting listening.

Now she looked towards Jack, and said—

"Could I go?"

"I daresay you could, if you would," was Jack's answer.

"But, *ma chérie*," interposed the gaoler, anxiously, "they will not let women out of the gates whilst the enemy is in sight."

This was a blow at once to all their hopes.

"Don't despair," said Fanchette. "I've thought of a plan."

"What is it?"

"Suppose I were to disguise myself as a man?"

"You?"

"Yes, I. As a soldier."

"I should think you would make a capital soldier," said Jack, flatteringly. "Then, are you willing to go?"

"Quite. And I promise to be more successful this time than I was with the ring."

"I shall have to write a letter for you to take with you."

Gregoire Ferron, having supplied paper, pen, and ink, the despatch was soon indited.

"I have addressed it to Sergeant Crank, Biddy O'Flinn, and Brian O'Flinn," said our hero.

"I can give it, then, to either ?"

"Yes."

Fanchette having received the letter, gave her young friends a kiss, and departed.

* * * * *

Brian O'Flinn wandered in the wood till he was tired, and very narrowly escaped being made prisoner himself by a party of the enemy.

When, at length, he regained the English camp, it was with the disheartening intelligence that he had seen nothing either of Jack Barrington or his companion.

The effect of this news upon Sergeant Crank was serious.

What with that and his wound he became delirious, and raved wildly about his "dear boy," as he called his *protégé*.

"Shure," said Brian O'Flinn, "it's the mounseers have got hould on 'em."

It was the evening of the second day after their disappearance.

Brian was sitting thoughtfully at the door of his aunt's canteen.

His pipe was in his mouth, but he was so absorbed in his reflections that it had gone out.

Whilst so engaged, a couple of grenadiers approached, conducting between them a very young-looking, handsome French soldier.

Having reached the canteen, the men, pointing to Brian, said—

"There's the man you want."

As soon as the guides had retired, the young Frenchman approached the bugler.

"Are you Monsieur Brian O'Flinn ?"

"Brian O'Flinn widout the mounseer, if you plase, honey," was the Irishman's reply.

"Then this is for you."

The speaker at the same moment handed him the letter.

Brian glanced at it for a moment, and then sprang up with a cry of delight.

"It's Jack's handwritin'," he shouted.

Without further delay, Brian opened the letter and read it.

"Och, murther !" he muttered to himself, as he came to the end, "Jack is in prison, an' that thafe of the world, Caleb Corder, hangin' about, too. That's the divil an' all."

He looked up suddenly at the presumed soldier, and inquired—

"Have you seen the darlin' boys, mounseer ?"

"Oh, yes," Fanchette replied, blushing as she spoke.

"Well, Jack writes that he's been kindly treated, and so I s'pose we must thank you for that same, but come along to the sergeant ?"

It revived the wounded Sergeant Crank wonderfully to hear that Jack was alive.

"Something must be done for the dear boy."

"Something shall be done," cried Brian O'Flinn ; "and at once."

"What do you propose ?" asked Crank.

"Why, I mane to be off at once, an' if I don't get our comrades out by hook or by crook, I'll forfeit my right to be called a son of Ould Ireland."

"Heaven bless your efforts," murmured the sergeant, earnestly ; "I am yet too weak to help you, and the earl is now far away. Give my love to Jack."

"Shure, I will," said Brian ; "an' I'll state publicly, that if any harm happens to the lads, we'll blow the town to smithereens."

It took the bugler but a few moments to make his preparations, and in the darkness he started off with his companion.

"What's your name, honey ?" he asked, as they went along.

"Jeannot," returned the supposed Frenchman, adopting the name of her sweetheart.

They went on for some time in silence, and then Brian, who was thinking of the work he had to accomplish, burst out suddenly—

"I say, me darlin', I've been wondtherin' how I'm to get into the town."

"Through the gates, I suppose," laughed Fanchette.

"That won't be so aisy, I'm thinkin'. There's a guard there."

"Yes."

"They'll niver mistake me for a Frenchman, because in the first place I can't speak a word of French, an' next I wear an' English uniform."

"I've been thinking of that myself ; but I think I can manage it very well if you leave it to me."

They continued their course, not in a straight line, but making a considerable circuit, until at length they stopped at a small cottage, that stood in a very retired spot.

"We must call here," said Fanchette, as she knocked at the door.

The inmate of the cottage had long since retired to rest ; but after some little delay footsteps were heard within, and a voice inquired—

"Who's there ?"

"It is I, Dame Margot," Fanchette replied.

The tones of the speaker were sufficient, and the door was opened at once.

An old woman appeared.

She evinced great surprise at the appearance of two soldiers, but Fanchette stepped forward quickly and whispered a few words in her ear.

The old woman seemed satisfied, and asked them to enter.

A few moments elapsed, and Fanchette brought a bundle of clothes, and placed them before Brian O'Flinn.

"Put on these," she said.

The Irishman turned them over, and found they consisted of articles of female attire.

"Oh, bedad, is it goin' to turn me into a woman you are?" he asked, with a grin.

"It is the safest disguise you can wear," Fanchette replied.

"All right, honey; if I can only get Jack Barrington out of prison, I'm parfictly willin' to be transmogrified into one ov the fair sex."

"So you ought to be," returned Fanchette, "since in order to accomplish that, I have transformed myself into a man."

Having thus explained herself, and before Brian could recover from his surprise, she went out of the room.

The bugler quickly invested himself in the garments.

Last of all he put on the cotton night-cap, and a large cloak with a hood.

"Aha!" laughed Fanchette when she returned; "it is capital. No one would ever suspect you were anything but what you seem to be."

"Oh, no, shure," grinned Brian, "it's your granny I am, darlin', for the prisint; but what am I to call yez?"

"Call me Jeannot, although my name is Fanchette."

*   *   *   *   *

Very early in the morning the pedestrians approached the city gates.

The guard challenged them as they arrived.

"Who are you?" he demanded.

"Jeannot Roussel, private of dragoons," answered Fanchette, speaking in a gruff voice and twirling her false moustaches.

"And who is that with you?"

"My *grand'mère*."

"You can enter," said the guard.

The next moment they had passed through the gates.

———

CHAPTER XXXI.

CLOUDED PROSPECTS.

THE next morning, when Jack's gaoler made his appearance, his countenance beamed with satisfaction.

"All is well," he exclaimed, as he entered.

"Has Fanchette come back?" asked the prisoners, eagerly.

"Ah, *oui, oui!* and she have bring somevon viz her."

"Who—Sergeant Crank?"

"No," said Fanchette, appearing at the door, and placing her finger on her lips to imply caution; "your comrade, Brian O'Flinn, disguised as my granny."

Great was the joy of the captives at this welcome intelligence.

A grand consultation was held as to the best course to be pursued.

"I vish I could let you go!" said the old gaoler, earnestly, "but I dare not. I should be shot eef I let you escape."

At this moment the cautious creak of a footstep caused Jack to start.

The outer door grated on its hinges, and closed with a slight snap.

The gaoler looked round.

"Could somevon have been listening?" murmured he, half to himself.

"Oh, no, *mon père*," replied his daughter, assuringly; "who could have listened? There is no one here but ourselves."

This served to restore confidence.

But it was misplaced.

For a figure in a blouse had been posted in the passage for some time, and was now skulking away with the information he had gathered, to impart it to his superior.

*   *   *   *   *

Barely an hour had elapsed, when the prison gate swung open on its hinges, admitting Captain Gravellotte and Caleb Corder. The latter entered the cell where our hero and his comrade were confined.

He looked awfully ghastly, his head was swollen, and he had a very ugly contusion on his forehead.

But in spite of this his vindictive spirit was as lively as ever.

He stood rubbing his hands together, looking at his old comrades with a smile of a particularly fiendish character on his face.

"Ha ha!" he laughed at length, "you're precious clever, you two, ain't you?"

There was no reply to this.

"You're in very snug quarters here, eh?"

No answer.

"Gaoler a kind old buffer, gets you nice grub—something better than bread and water, don't he?"

Still silence.

"Pretty daughter Fanchette to pet you too?—he, he!"

The prisoners began to feel rather uncomfortable at these remarks, but they had not heard the worst.

For the malicious speaker continued—

"I fancied I saw Brian O'Flinn lurking about. What does he want, eh?"

"I don't know what you mean," exclaimed Jack at length, irritated at the sneering mockery of the tormentor.

"Oh, yes, you do. You know well enough. You think he's going to make it all right with old red nob, and get you out of prison, don't you? But here you are, and here you'll stop, till——"

"We go," interrupted Jack passionately.

"No, a little longer than that. You'll stop till——"

"Well, how long?"

"Till the rats gnaw the flesh from your bones," hissed the speaker.

Before our hero had time to reply, Captain Gravellotte and the gaoler entered the cell.

The countenance of the old man expressed intense anxiety, but he endeavoured to control it as much as possible.

The captain threw a keen suspicious glance around. First at the stone walls, and next at the prisoners.

Then turning to Gregoire, he said to him sternly—

"Circumstances have come to my knowledge, which prove you to have been unfaithful to the trust reposed in you."

"*Moi, monsieur!* I unfaithful!" asked the old man aghast.

"Yes, you. You have been feeding these culprits with dainties, instead of bread and water, as I ordered."

"*Diable!* how did he know that?" muttered Gregoire.

"You have lodged them in your own room instead of this cell."

The gaoler groaned inwardly.

"And finally, you have transmitted a letter from them to the English lines; in consequence of which, one of their comrades is in the town disguised. Do you dare to deny this?"

The unfortunate old man was completely staggered, and remained silent.

"For what you have done, you are dismissed from your post," continued Captain Gravellotte; "therefore, be gone at once, and thank your stars you have no severer punishment."

Gregoire threw a pitying glance at the boys he had befriended, and with quivering lips, and aching heart, went out to prepare for his departure.

As soon as he was gone, the captain fixed his malignant gaze upon the prisoners, and said—

"You'll find the new gaoler I am going to appoint a stricter disciplinarian than the old one."

"Here he is." shouted Caleb Corder.

The next moment heavy footsteps came clattering along the passage, and Jaques Sauvage strode into the cell.

"I give these fellows into your care," said Captain Gravellotte.

Jaques nodded.

"Hitherto they have been enjoying themselves, and feeding upon luxuries, but now I wish them to know what prison fare really is."

"*Begar!* they shall, *mon capitaine!*" returned the dragoon with a hideous grin.

The captain spoke a few words apart to the new gaoler.

After which, they left the cell together.

Caleb Corder followed last of all.

"It will be all over with you two soon," he hissed at them over his shoulder. "Starvation—rats! ugh!"

Then the door slammed to.

The key was turned and the prisoners were alone once more.

Jack and Ned Rattles looked earnestly at each other for a moment, as if to see what each thought.

"We're done for now, I'm afraid," said Ned, ruefully.

"I'm afraid so, too," admitted Jack, in a low tone. "I can't help thinking that they mean to kill us."

The day passed.

They began to feel terribly hungry.

The weather was hot, and they were parched with thirst.

In vain they implored for a cup of water.

A mocking laugh was their only answer.

In vain they knocked at the door of their cell.

CHAPTER XXXII.
UNDER FALSE COLOURS.

IT was with great concern that Brian O'Flinn heard from Fanchette the sudden unfortunate turn which circumstances had taken.

Jaques Sauvage, who was not at all sorry to be released from more active duty, took it easy in his new employment.

What was it to him that the boys lacked food and water whilst he had plenty of brandy to drink and cigars to smoke?

It was growing dusk when a loud shout reached his ears.

His brains were by this time tolerably muddled with drink.

"*Sacré!*" he growled, "what a row they make yonder! Is the town on fire?"

He had hardly uttered this supposition when the shout was renewed.

A girl came suddenly hurrying round the corner as if pursued.

For an instant she paused in uncertainty.

Then fixing her eyes upon Jaques, who was winking at her in return, she rushed towards him.

"Och, thin, good misther officer, will you take compassion on a poor young woman?" she cried excitedly, as she threw herself at his feet.

Jaques Sauvage, brute as he was, had a certain amount of the natural gallantry of his nation.

And besides, he was half drunk, and that gave an impetus to his feelings.

"Vot is ze mattair, *ma belle?*" he asked.

"Och, shure, it's a lot of sogers was running afther me to give me a kiss," replied the young woman, "and I didn't want to be kissed."

"*Certainement non!* you shall not be kissed by anyone but myself," exclaimed Jaques, in a tone of inebriate assurance.

But the damsel did not seem at all annoyed.

On the contrary.

She smiled and affected to blush, as she replied, archly—

"Arrah! now get along wid your blarney."

To the unsteady eyes of the dragoon, the young Irish girl appeared a perfect beauty.

"*Parbleu, mademoiselle,*" he said, "you shall have suppare viz me. Vill you honour me viz your company?"

"Oh, yes, wid pleasure, if you won't think me intruding," returned the fair one, modestly.

"Oh, no, no, *mon bel ange*—my fair angel," remarked the enraptured Jaques. "I love you."

"Oh, Misther Officer, you don't mane it?"

"*Sur mon honneur*—on my honour I do. Vot is your name?"

"Kathleen, if you please, mounseer."

"Cat-lean ! ver goot. Zen coam in, Cat-lean, and let me drink your hels in a glass of Cognac."

The dragoon led the way with a somewhat unsteady step, and the Irish girl followed, with most bewitching confidence.

So delighted was Jaques that he could not refrain from chucking her slightly under the chin, which favour she returned with a playful dig in the ribs with her forefinger.

"Oh, *diable !*" grinned her admirer, "vot a playful leetle cat you are."

The door being closed, the dragoon resigned himself entirely to the fascinations of his fair companion.

What with his brandy and the society of Kathleen, he grew quite amiable.

The evening wore on, when suddenly a knocking was heard at one of the doors in the building.

"Hallo, Misther Officer, what's that ?"

The knocking was continued, and a voice was heard to cry, imploringly—

"Water, water !"

"Bedad ! somebody wants wather, I'm thinking," said Kathleen.

"It is onlee some of ze prisonairs," returned Jaques, rather indifferently ; "nevair mind zem."

He rose as he spoke, and, going to the door, shouted—

"Be quiet, you two boys, or I shall coam and cut you in pieces viz ze cudgel."

His fair companion was highly indignant at this.

"Bad luck to yez, you unfeeling, ugly bla'guard," she cried, as she seized him by the back of his collar ; "give the poor fellows some wather. If you don't, I'll spifflicate yez."

Fortunately, Jaques Sauvage had drunk so much brandy that his senses were quite in a fog.

"Nevair mind zose boys, zey are Engleesh. *Sacré !* I hate ze Engleesh ; zey are our enemies."

"Hould your row, you drunken baste," cried the Irish girl, "and show me the way to the pump."

"*Morbleu, ma chère ;* ze pomp ees yonder, in ze yard."

He pointed lazily as he spoke, but made no attempt to move.

"Hurroo !" chuckled Brian (for of course Kathleen was no other than himself in disguise) ; "it's all going on beautiful ; in less than half an hour I'll have the dear boys out of this infernal hole."

It took the Irishman a few moments to find his way to the courtyard at the back of the prison.

But having accomplished this, he quickly filled the can and returned to the room.

Jaques Sauvage had fallen asleep, and was snoring loudly.

The keys dangled at his waist.

Brian, without losing an instant, detached

them, and as he did so, he again heard the voice crying—

"Water, water."

"I'm comin', me darlin's," as he hastened out can in hand.

Guided by the sound, he soon reached the cell in which the prisoners were confined.

"Are ye there, honeys ?" he sang out.

"Yes, yes !" was the eager answer.

"I'll be wid yez in two twos."

There was a slight delay whilst Brian selected the key, and then the door opened and he sprang inside.

"Ould Ireland and the Queen for iver !" he shouted, with enthusiasm.

"And the noble Marlborough !" joined in his comrades, but more faintly.

"And now, afore ye talk, dhrink," said Brian, as he held forth the can.

Parched, and sick with thirst, Jack and Ned Rattles quickly emptied the vessel of its contents.

"How did you get in ?" asked the lads, in a breath.

"Ha, ha !" laughed the Irishman ; "it was these illegant petticoats got me here. Mr. Whiskers has fallen in love wid me."

"Ho, ho, that's capital !"

"Can't we get out ?" asked Jack.

"Ov course ye can. Come on."

They all three turned towards the door, when a savage yell greeted them, and Jaques Sauvage staggered in, his features inflamed with intemperance, and a heavy dragoon sabre in his hand.

He closed the door by reeling against it, and stood flourishing his weapon, and glaring like a fiend upon those before him.

"*Sacré !*" he shouted, "vot you do here, Ma'amselle Cat-lean ?"

"Make room for us, you black-muzzled varmint," cried Brian.

A yell, deeper and more ferocious than the first, answered this, and, with a savage imprecation, the drunken ruffian prepared to slay Brian and the boys.

CHAPTER XXXIII.

THE CITY TAKEN.

BRIAN in a moment threw off his cap and head-dress, and stripping off his bodice, tucked up his shirt sleeves, displaying a pair of brawny, muscular arms.

"Now I'm ready for yez," he cried.

"*Mille tonnerres !*" growled Jaques, savagely ; "you are no *demoiselle*—you are a man, after all."

"Right you are, black muzzle," Brian replied, "and, plase the pigs, I'll let you know it."

"I shall chop you into mincemeat," shouted the dragoon.

As he spoke, he staggered forward. Raising his formidable sword in the air, he made a tremendous slash at Brian ; but his aim was anything but steady.

"'IT WILL BE ALL OVER WITH YOU TWO SOON,' SAID CALEB."

The Irishman easily avoided the stroke by stepping aside.

The sword descended, and striking the stone floor, snapped in half.

At the same moment Ned Rattles gave The Savage a sharp kick, and knocked his legs from under him.

Down he went with a crash, the back of his head coming first in contact with the ground, on which he lay stretched, stunned and motionless.

"Hurrah!" cried Brian. "Now, then, me boys, let's put the bla'guard where he can't do any harm to anybody."

With this they dragged the prostrate dragoon to the wall, where a chain hung fastened by a strong staple.

With this they encircled his body, and made it secure.

"Now, me boys," cried Brian, "come on; the sooner we're out of this dirthy hole the better."

The last word had hardly left his lips, when the outer door of the prison opened with a sharp, jarring clang, and a strange sound, like the murmur of voices, mingled with the clatter of arms, burst upon their ears.

"Hollo, what's up?" exclaimed the Irishman, as he and his comrades hastened to the door of the cell.

The grey of early morning was just stealing upon the darkness of night, and in its light they could see, as they looked down the passage, the street without thronged with soldiers.

"What the divil does it mane?" muttered Brian to himself, in a perplexed tone.

The explanation came at once in the person of Captain Gravellotte, who entered hastily, followed by Caleb Corder, the latter attired in a French uniform.

The captain dashed open the door of the gaoler's private room as he passed, and looked in.

Not finding him there, he withdrew his head.

His eyes glanced to the end of the corridor, and saw the door open and Brian O'Flinn in his petticoats with the two prisoners at his side.

An oath burst from his lips as he rushed forward.

"What, in the devil's name, is the meaning of this?" he demanded, as he entered the cell.

"It means that that fellow in the woman's togs belongs to the English army," shouted Caleb Corder, who followed.

"What are you doing here, sirrah?" continued the captain, to Brian.

"I might ax you what you're doin' wid the French uniform on your back, fightin' agin your own countrymen, Misther Gasper Grimsby?" returned Brian.

The blood flushed into the renegade's face, but he replied contemptuously—

"Answer my question, fellow. Why are you here?"

"I'm here to pretect the boy whose father you murdthered in cowld blood, you treache-

rous, cowardly miscreant," was the bold reply.

The guilty man turned ghastly pale, as he said—

"Leave the prison, fool."

"I will wid all the pleasure in life," returned Brian, "but I'll take my comrades wid me."

"They are my prisoners. I will detain them."

"Marshal Boufflers would set them at liberty if he was here."

"Marshal Boufflers is not here."

"Thin, by the powers, I'll wait till he comes."

Captain Gravellotte ground his teeth with rage.

"Harkye," he said; "do you intend to leave the prison?"

"Yes, but not to leave the boys behind."

Just at that moment Jaques Sauvage's voice was heard.

He had come to his senses, and, growling with rage and pain, was striving to get loose.

His superior officer perceived him for the first time.

"Who placed you there?" he demanded.

"I did," replied Brian, boldly, "an' if you don't give us free passage, it's more than likely you'll find yourself on the top of him in about half a second."

This was too much for Captain Gravellotte.

With a yell of rage he dashed out of the cell and rushed towards the door, hastily followed by Caleb Corder.

"A musket," he shouted, as soon as he reached the portal.

One was instantly handed to him.

He raised it, and taking deliberate aim at Brian O'Flinn, pulled the trigger.

The report reverberated through the silent passages.

There was a cry and the sound of a body falling.

At the same moment from without came another sound, far more terrible and significant.

It was the thunder of English cannon.

The bombardment of the town had commenced, and the crash of bursting shells was already heard in the streets.

Captain Gravellotte stood listening like one who had received a sudden shock.

Whilst he did so, a dragoon came up.

"You are waited for at the general's quarters, captain," he cried, hastily. "Quick, you must come with me."

Gasper, unwilling to lose sight of his prisoners, still lingered.

Again the roaring of the artillery rolled across the heavens.

Not daring to remain longer, he beckoned to Caleb, and, shutting to the door, locked it.

"You must keep watch here," he said to him, "and rather than let this Jack Barrington escape, shoot him."

He placed a pistol—which he took from one of the troopers—in his hand, as he spoke.

"I will, captain," grinned Caleb; "trust me."

"You will have no difficulty, since that Irish ruffian is put out of the way."

"Oh, no, not the least; I'll manage it now O'Flinn's dead."

With the cannons thundering, and in the midst of masses of sulphureous smoke, Gasper Grimsby sprang on to his horse, and rode off, followed by his troop.

Caleb, exulting in the commission he had received, took up his post at an angle of the prison, from which point he could see the front door and also the barred window of the cell in which the prisoners were.

Could he have looked inside at this moment, he would have been much surprised.

He would have found Brian O'Flinn as much alive as ever he was, whilst Jaques Sauvage was as dead as he could possibly be.

How this came about was that The Savage, by a desperate effort, had loosened his chain, and sprang towards Brian, as Captain Gravellotte pulled the trigger of the musket.

He was just in time to receive the bullet in his heart, instead of the victim for whom it was intended, and now lay stark dead on the dungeon floor.

* 　 * 　 * 　 * 　 *

Boom! Boom!

Crash! Crash! followed in rapid succession, whilst the shouts and cries of the inhabitants were borne upon the air to the lonely prison.

It began to grow terribly exciting.

And Brian said at length—

"Bedad, I'd like to see what's goin' on, anyhow."

With this, he sprang from the ground, and catching the iron bars of the window, dragged himself up, till he could look out from the grating.

The only living object that met his gaze was Caleb Corder, posted at the corner, with his eyes fixed upon the window as eagerly as a hungry cat watches a mouse-trap.

"Ugh! you sneakin' varmint!" muttered Brian, "I'd like to——"

He suddenly broke off.

Bang! went a pistol.

Down dropped Brian.

"Are you hurt?" cried his companions, eagerly.

"Divil a bit," returned the Irishman, cheerfully.

"Was it Caleb fired at you?" inquired Jack.

"Shure it was, the bla'guard! I didn't see what he'd got in his hand, or I'd have been more careful."

Some time had elapsed, when the occupants of the cell heard footsteps and the murmuring of voices without.

The door was not opened.

Some operation seemed to be going on outside the prison.

"What's up now, I wondher?" said Brian to himself, thoughtfully.

"It's the English soldiers, perhaps," Jack suggested.

"No, honey, it isn't the English," replied the bugler, after listening; "it's only the jabberin' of the mounseers I hear."

"What are they doing?"

"That's more than I can tell."

The voices ceased.

The footsteps died away.

Nothing was heard but the roar of cannon as before.

Suddenly, however, a crackling noise was heard.

Caleb's exulting laugh reached them.

"Whin the divil laughs, it's sartin there's mischief afoot," remarked Brian.

The mysterious crackling continued.

Presently Ned Rattles said—

"Don't you smell something burnin'?"

"By the powers, so I do!" said Brian.

"And see, see!" cried our hero, "there's smoke coming in at the window."

"And under the door, too."

Brian O'Flinn knitted his brows and remained for an instant silent.

The terrible thought of the truth flashed across him.

"Bedad! they're either goin' to roast us alive, or else smoke us to death in this stone cage," he said, at length.

He was perfectly correct in his supposition.

Rather than that his prisoners should escape, the atrocious captain had doomed them to this merciless fate.

This appalling prospect struck them all with dismay.

Well it might.

They were powerless to resist the progress of the suffocating vapour.

They had no weapons with which to break down the stone walls.

There seemed no resource but to perish miserably.

Each moment the heat grew more intense, the smoke more thick and stifling, blinding their eyes, and penetrating to their lungs at every breath they took.

Their position now began to be most agonizing.

"Oh, I'm stifling!" gasped Jack, as he staggered against the wall.

"Lie down, me boys," said Brian, who could scarcely speak himself; "keep your faces close to the ground."

They did so, and for a moment experienced some relief.

But only for a moment.

A deadly faintness seized upon each one of them.

The place appeared to reel round and round.

Through all this torment they could hear Caleb Corder's fiendish laughter.

Suddenly a great shock, a crash, and a ringing shout.

They remembered no more.

When Jack and Brian recovered their consciousness, they were surrounded by English soldiers.

The first countenance they recognised was the anxious face of Sergeant Crank.

"You're safe, my dear boy," he said, affectionately, to our hero.

"Have the English taken the city?" asked Jack, faintly.

"Yes," returned the sergeant; "Liege is ours."

"Hur-roo! Ould Ireland for iver!" cried Brian O'Flinn, with an effort.

"Long live the queen and the Duke of Marlborough!" joined in Jack and Ned Rattles.

A hearty English cheer echoed them.

"Long live the queen and the Duke of Marlborough!"

For the news had just reached the camp that the earl had been made a duke.

CHAPTER XXXIV.

YOUNG SWEETHEARTS—ENGLAND.

It was a lovely night in August.

The spacious rooms of Marlborough House were in a blaze of light.

The duke had returned triumphant from his long campaign, in honour of which a grand *soirée* was being held at his princely mansion.

The exploits of the renowned John Churchill were on everyone's tongue.

And not his exploits alone.

There was another who, though much humbler in station, came in for his full share of the general interest.

This one was no other than young Jack Barrington.

Everywhere the great earl had spoken of the orphan boy in the highest terms, predicting for him a future of honour and renown.

That the Duke of Marlborough had fully determined to honour our hero may be gathered from the following conversation.

It was in one of the smaller rooms of the mansion four persons were assembled.

The four were Sergeant Crank and his *protégé*, with Brian O'Flinn and Ned Rattles.

On the table at which they sat was spread a costly dessert, consisting of all the luxuries of the season, and glittering cut-glass decanters full of the richest wines.

"Your fortune's made, my dear boy," said Sergeant Crank to our hero. "The honour his noble grace—God bless him—is going to do you will be your stepping-stone to fame and glory."

"Am I really to go into the room where the guests are?" inquired Jack.

"Aye, that you are," returned Benjamin Crank; "and more, his grace will introduce you to them publicly."

Jack's cheeks glowed again with pleasure.

Some time passed, during which the sweet strains of music floated to their ears.

At length, a footman, in a gorgeous livery, entered, and, having spoken a few words to Sergeant Crank, retired again.

"Get ready, all," said the sergeant; "her grace will be here shortly."

"Do you mean the Duchess of Marlborough?" Jack asked.

"I do, indeed," returned Benjamin. "There's an honour for you."

"I saw her once," said Brian O'Flinn, admiringly. "By the powers, it's a rale beauty she is, and no mistake."

"Hush!" exclaimed the sergeant, in a hasty whisper. "I think I hear her step."

He was right.

The next moment the door opened, and there entered Sarah, Duchess of Marlborough, a queenly, beautiful woman, arrayed in a gorgeous robe of blue velvet, and resplendent with costly diamonds.

Her dark, lustrous eyes smiled a general welcome upon the party at the table, whilst she honoured Jack with a more marked regard and a sweeter smile, as she said to him—

"Come, young hero, you are waited for."

Jack rose at once, his cheek flushed with expectation, and his heart throbbing more rapidly than it had ever done on the battlefield.

The duchess observed his excitement, and perfectly comprehended the cause.

"How handsome he looks," she murmured to herself; "as handsome as he is brave."

With this, she took him cordially by the hand, and led him away.

She did not, however, conduct him at once to the grand saloon, but to her own private boudoir.

Here she seated herself for a moment, bidding Jack seat himself beside her.

"You are not afraid of company, my dear, are you?"

"No, your grace," returned Jack, with a little hesitation, "I am not afraid."

"That's right; heroes never are," was the assuring answer.

"But I think I should feel a little shy if you were not with me, madam," continued our hero.

The duchess evidently felt flattered at the boy's confidence in herself, and she smiled as she said—

"You need not feel shy. You will meet none but friends, who think very highly of you."

This was very assuring, and Jack smiled in return, as he said—

"I won't be shy, then."

The duchess then called—

"Flora!"

A girl about the same age as our hero, with long golden curls, came tripping forth from the adjoining ante-room.

"Come here, love," she said, "I wish to introduce you to one of the heroes of the day."

The little maiden advanced with mingled curiosity and timidity at the sight of the handsome lad in his uniform.

"There he is, Flo; what think you of him?"

Flo smiled and blushed, as she said candidly—

"I think he's a great deal prettier than the heroes in the picture gallery. I don't like them at all."

"Then I suppose you do like this one?" laughed the duchess.

"Oh, yes; I think he's the prettiest soldier boy I ever saw."

This was extremely flattering, and as Jack looked upon the speaker as the loveliest little girl he had ever seen, it was no wonder that he blushed at the compliment up to the very roots of his hair.

"Ah!" said the duchess, good-naturedly, "I can see you were intended for each other."

And with this remark she left the room, taking our hero with her.

"Good-bye, soldier boy," called Flora, after him.

Jack looked over his shoulder at her and smiled his farewell, and all the way he went along he was thinking what a beautiful little blue-eyed fairy she was.

His meditations were suddenly interrupted by the opening of a door.

A burst of music rang in his ears.

A blaze of light flashed in his eyes, and he found himself in the grand saloon, surrounded by a crowd of magnificently-dressed guests.

The sight of the duchess leading her young *protégé* by the hand excited general attention.

The queenly Sarah conducted her charge through the suite of rooms till she reached the spot where her noble husband awaited her.

The Duke of Marlborough rose as the young drummer boy approached, and taking him by the hand, exclaimed—

"Allow me, my friends, to introduce to you the bravest lad I know at the present time— Jack Barrington. Young as he is, he has already been present at two engagements and one siege, and in each and all he has conducted himself as one who, if he lives, bids fair, not only to make the name of soldier honourable, but to render signal service to his native country."

At the end of this flattering address some of the highest and noblest in the land pressed forward to shake our hero by the hand.

Some of the fairest dames and maidens of the English aristocracy patted him on the head and wished him go on boldly in the course he had commenced.

Jack's head was in a whirl.

He had never been so praised in his life.

With his heart thrilling within him, and the blush of youthful modesty kindling his cheek and lighting up his dark eyes like diamonds, he stood listening to the oft-repeated congratulations of the multitude.

More than one high-born beauty whispered, as she gazed upon him—

"Brave as handsome, handsome as brave."

But there was more than this to come.

It was when the excitement was beginning to subside that a handsomely-dressed man approached Jack, and looked at him earnestly.

At length he said to him—

"Do you remember me?"

Our hero fixed his eyes upon the speaker intently.

He fancied he recognised the foreign accent and the features of the stranger, but could not for a moment recall where he had met him.

"I think I have seen you before," he said, at length, thoughtfully.

"Do you not remember the grenadier at Nimeguen?" said the gentleman, presently.

"Ah, yes," exclaimed Jack, quickly; "you saved my mother from that peasant fellow."

"And you repaid the debt afterwards by saving my life when I was wounded; you recollect?"

"Oh, yes, yes; you came to the cottage where we had taken shelter."

"I did, and you let me in."

"You gave me this," said our hero, as he produced the ring from his finger; "and your name is Victor Montsorel."

The gentleman smiled, and clasped Jack's hand warmly.

"You are right; it is," he said.

Then turning to those around him, he continued—

"Yes, my lords and ladies, I owe it to this brave boy that I am here at this moment."

"Indeed!" they exclaimed.

"'Tis true. Being in disgrace at court, owing to some political offence, I had joined the army as a common soldier. I was wounded, and must have died upon the field had not my young friend bound up my leg and procured me the assistance of the English doctors. I owe my life to him. The brave boy, also, at the risk of his own life, took in his hands and threw from the window a shell that exploded the next moment."

This declaration on the part of the Count Victor De Montsorel brought down a fresh volley of congratulations on our hero's head, which lasted until the Duchess of Marlborough, thinking so much praise might be wearisome, if not injurious, led him from the saloon.

"There, my dear boy," she said to him, kindly, as she bade him good night, "you see what your friends think of you; all you have to do is not to disappoint their expectations."

"I never will, your grace; never," replied Jack, warmly.

"I believe you, young hero," was the duchess's reply.

There was only one more incident to happen.

But it was not the least important in Jack's estimation.

As he was passing the boudoir of the duchess, a head was protruded, and a fair face smiled at him through a cloud of golden hair.

It was Flora.

"There you are again," she said, with evident pleasure in her tone; "I'm so glad to see you once more."

"Not more glad, I think, than I am to see you," Jack ventured gallantly to reply.

"Well, we're both glad, then, to see each other, ain't we?"

"Yes."

"I've been waiting ever so long to wish you good night."

"Have you? How kind."

"What a time you've been gone."

"It didn't seem very long to me," said Jack; "but I had to shake hands with a great many, and I suppose it did take up some time."

"More than an hour; but I was determined not to go to bed till I'd seen you again. Good night."

The little beauty held out her white hand to Jack as she spoke.

Jack took it quite reverentially, and not knowing what better thing to do with it, pressed it gently to his lips.

"Good night," he replied.

But Flora had not quite done with him yet.

Holding him by his coat, she shook her bright curls from off her face, and looking up at him with an extraordinary amount of earnestness in her speaking blue eyes, she said seriously to him—

"You're going to battle again some day, aren't you?"

"Oh, yes," returned Jack, with conscious pride; "I'm going to try to be a captain."

"That's right. Be very brave, and then you're sure to be one. The duchess says so."

"Does she, really?"

"Yes. She's my godmamma, and you know the duke is her husband, and he can make as many captains as he likes," said Flora, significantly.

Jack smiled as he remarked—

"I hope he'll make me one some day."

"He will, you may depend on it; be very brave; mind and don't get killed, and then when you're old enough, and I'm old enough——"

"Yes," said Jack; "what then?"

"You shall be my husband, and I'll be your wife. Would you like that?"

"Shouldn't I!" exclaimed our hero, fervently.

Flora hesitated an instant.

Then she said a little timidly—

"I've got a present for you, if you will accept it."

Jack looked his thanks from his eyes.

"Here it is; a piece of my hair. I cut it off on purpose."

As she spoke, she gave him a golden lock, tied with a piece of azure blue silk.

"Oh, thank you, thank you!" cried our hero; "I'll never part with this as long as I live."

"Won't you give me a lock of yours?"

"You may have it all if you like," returned Jack, magnanimously.

"One curl will do. Wait a minute."

Flora slipped in at the door, and almost instantly returned with a pair of scissors.

The curl was quickly cut off.

"Good night," said Jack, regretfully.

"Good night."

The next moment Flora had darted into the boudoir, and the door was closed.

The young sweethearts had separated.

Not to meet again for years.

CHAPTER XXXV.
AFTER MANY YEARS.

OUR hero fully realized all the expectations his patron, the Duke of Marlborough, had formed of him.

He accompanied the commander-in-chief in all his campaigns.

His courage, activity, and amiable, honourable temper made him invaluable to the earl.

If any service of especial importance or especial danger was to be performed, our hero was sure to be entrusted with it; and he never failed.

Nor was he alone.

His old comrades, Ned Rattles and Brian O'Flinn, were remembered by him.

The three staunch companions clung together through thick and thin.

Sergeant Crank had impressed upon them that comrades were like a bundle of faggots—unconquerable whilst they remained united, and only to be overcome when they separated from each other.

Consequently they never did separate.

In many a hard battle the three "invincibles," as they were called, fought side by side.

The drums and the bugle had been long since laid aside, and our heroes had been made cornets in a cavalry regiment, that being the capacity in which their energies could be most effectively employed.

* * * * *

Years had passed.

The battle of Malplaquet was not long over.

The army had again returned to England.

The city of London was full of rejoicing, and the shouts of the loyal citizens followed the great Marlborough wherever he went.

* * * * *

In one of the turnings leading out of the Haymarket was a coffee-house familiarly termed "The Road to Ruin."

The house itself was of very bad repute, being the resort of the most noted card-sharpers, gamblers, and duellists of the day.

At one of the tables in the public room sat two persons, who carried in their dress and appearance the aspect of those who were fighting a hard battle with fortune.

One of these was in the prime of life, the other many years younger, but both looked years older than they were.

Both were attired in something like the fashion of the period, but the shabbiness of their garments was perceptible.

No one who had not been well acquainted with them would have recognised Gasper Grimsby and Caleb Corder, after the lapse of years, yet there they were, floating along down the stream of time, companions in fortune and in crime.

As they sat sipping their coffee, Caleb said, at length, fretfully—

"I say, captain."

"Well."

"You've told me a good many times our luck was going to turn."

"I'll tell you so once more if you like," rejoined his companion, with a laugh.

"You needn't do that; but I should like to know when the turning point's going to be arrived at."

The captain's only reply to this was an impatient grunt, whilst he continued to look down the newspaper he was perusing.

Suddenly he uttered an exclamation.

"By Jove! here's a chance at last," he cried.

"What is it?" asked the other, eagerly.

"Listen."

Lowering his voice almost to a whisper, he read the following advertisement—

"Should this meet the eye of Ruth Stanmore, she is requested to communicate at once with her father at Camden House, Islington."

"What's that to do with you?" remarked Caleb; "you're not Ruth Stanmore."

"I'm quite aware of that, but I intend Ruth Stanmore to be mine, and then I shall have an interest in her."

Caleb looked mystified.

"I don't know anything about Ruth Stanmore," he said, at length, sulkily.

"There is in reality no such person," Gasper replied.

Caleb looked more mystified.

"No such person?" he echoed.

"No. There was, but she changed her name."

"Oh!"

"You remember that clever youth, Jack Barrington?"

"Oh, yes, I remember him. I hope he's dead."

"Well, then; his mother's name was Ruth Stanmore before she married his father."

"I see," said Caleb; "then it's Jack Barrington's grandfather who put that advertisement in the paper?"

"Yes; and as he's my uncle, I'm going to try and make money out of him," said Gasper.

Hardly had he said the words when a handsome young man pushed open the door with a bang, and entered the coffee-room.

It was the Marquis De Hauteville, a French refugee, rich, and one of the most reckless and dissipated noblemen in the metropolis.

"Well, captain," he said, familiarly, "I've a job for you—that is, I think so, if you are ready to undertake it."

"I'm ready for anything," replied Gasper; "what is it?"

The marquis seated himself and spoke for some time in a low tone.

"Are you willing to undertake this little commission?" he asked, when he had finished.

"Yes," answered Gasper; "but as it is one that requires tact and determination, I must be well paid."

"What's your price?"

"Two hundred guineas. One hundred down, and the other when the job is done."

Without the least hesitation the nobleman took from his pocket-book notes to the amount, and thrust them into his agent's hand.

Gasper put them into his pocket with eyes gleaming with satisfaction.

"I shall expect you to be ready at any moment I may require you," said the marquis.

"You may depend on me."

The nobleman walked away.

"The turning point in our fortune has arrived," cried Gasper, starting up exultingly; "come and let us recruit our damaged wardrobes, and then for Islington."

* * * * *

The Marquis De Hauteville, on leaving the coffee-house, called a chair, and having been conveyed to the ferry at Lambeth, crossed the river, hired a vehicle, and proceeded at once into the country.

Bidding the driver wait, he left the carriage, and passing through the gates of a park, walked towards the house.

There were two fair girls in the grounds.

One of these was the Lady Flora Greville—that same Flora who, ten years, before had given one of her golden tresses to Jack Barrington, and had cut off one of his dark locks in exchange.

She had now grown into a beautiful maiden.

But as she saw the marquis swaggering along the path, her fair brow clouded, and she exclaimed—

"Oh, see, Jenny, that tiresome marquis."

Jenny Heathcote was the orphan daughter of a colonel, and Flora's companion.

"What brings him here again?" she said. "He was here yesterday."

"He comes to make love to me," returned Flora, pettishly.

"I shan't be long, Jenny dear," she said to her companion as she left her. "I'll send this marquis away for good this time."

The next moment she was in his presence.

With all the effusion of French gallantry the marquis approached her, and taking her hand in his, raised it to his lips.

"You see, beautiful Flora, I cannot keep away from you," he said.

"So it seems, marquis," she replied, coldly, "but I fear you are giving yourself a great deal of useless trouble on my account."

"Nay, it is no trouble, it is the greatest pleasure in the world to me," the marquis assured her.

From the expression of Flora's countenance, she did not at all reciprocate this pleasure.

"Allow me to offer you my arm, *carissima*," said the gallant, as they stepped from the large window on to the terrace.

"You are very kind, marquis, but I can walk alone," was the chilling reply he received.

He bowed courteously, but bit his lip, nevertheless, at the same time.

"Mademoiselle," he said, "you know I love you."

"You are very kind."

"Deeply, devotedly."

"Oh, marquis, you flatter me too much."

"No. I don't flatter you," returned the other. "I am in earnest; why are you not the same?"

"For a very good reason; I don't love you."

"Not love me?" exclaimed the marquis; "is it possible—is it possible?"

"Quite possible. It's a positive truth."

The countenance of the foreigner, which had been a moment before wreathed in smiles, darkened.

"Why do you not love me?" he asked.

"I am not obliged to explain why," returned the young beauty, with cold hauteur. "It is enough to tell you I do not and cannot."

"But you must tell me why, mademoiselle," cried the marquis, passionately.

"Your character is against you. I cannot love you."

The marquis turned livid with rage.

"Well, at least, I love you. And you must love me."

"Must?"

"You must—shall!" cried the ruthless mar-

GALLANT JACK WRESTED THE WEAPON FROM HIS GRASP."

quis, as he clasped her in his arms. "And you shall ask my pardon, too, for this insult."

"Never ! It is you who should ask my pardon," returned the young girl, tremulously, as she caught sight of the glittering eyes of her captor.

"Ha, ha ! you shall give me a kiss into the bargain."

"Desist, villain," cried Flora, indignantly.

"Not till I have my kiss !" almost yelled the marquis, as he sought to press his lips to hers.

But he was foiled.

For suddenly releasing her arms, Flora gave her assailant a stinging box on his ear with her fair hand.

"*Sacré !* you shall pay for this," raved the baffled nobleman.

As he spoke, he sprang forward to seize his prey, when suddenly he was gripped by a strong hand from behind, and, by a vigorous jerk, laid sprawling on his back on the grass.

CHAPTER XXXVI.
SWORD-PLAY AND LOVE-MAKING.

IN a furious rage he sprang to his feet, burning to resent the supposed indignity to which he had been subjected.

He found himself confronted by two handsome young men, who wore the uniforms of English cavalry officers.

These were Jack Barrington—now a captain in the dragoon guards—and his comrade Ned Rattles, a lieutenant in the same regiment.

After glaring at them fiercely for a moment, the marquis said, in a voice hoarse with passion—

"Which of you was it dared to offer me this insult ?"

"I did," returned Jack, coolly, but with suppressed indignation in his eyes.

"*Sacré !*" swore the Frenchman, "do you know who I am ?"

"I neither know nor care," replied our hero, contemptuously. "I found you insulting this young lady, and I treated you as I should any other ruffian under similar circumstances."

"You are a scoundrel !" foamed the nobleman.

"You are a coward and a scoundrel !" retorted Jack.

This was too much for the marquis.

Livid with rage, he drew his sword, and made a desperate lunge at the speaker.

Flora uttered a scream of terror.

But there was little cause for alarm.

Our hero adroitly parried the thrust with his arm.

Closing with his assailant, Gallant Jack wrested the weapon from his grasp.

Then snapping the blade in halves against his knee, he threw the two pieces at the assailant's feet.

The marquis picked them up.

Every feature in his face was quivering with rage.

Looking towards our hero with a malignant scowl, he hissed between his clenched teeth—

"We shall meet again, when you shall have cause to remember this day."

"I am here now, coward," cried Jack; "try your strength against mine if you like, and I will place you again on your back in the dirt."

"I will have revenge," shouted the Frenchman.

With these words, he walked hastily away towards the gate.

Jack did not condescend any further reply.

Probably he did not hear the threat.

He had approached Flora, and was endeavouring to reassure her after her alarm.

"I am not generally a coward," she said ; "but that dreadful Frenchman was so violent, and when he drew his sword, I was so alarmed on—on your account that I—I——"

The fair speaker faltered and blushed as she saw the dark admiring eyes of her handsome young protector fixed on hers.

Jack relieved her by saying—

"All danger is over now, Lady Flora, and as for that marquis, he is not even worth a thought."

"Oh, but he is vindictive, I am sure. The look he cast upon you before he went away was terrible," said Flora, earnestly.

"I've no fear of him," laughed Jack, lightly. "I have observed that men who insult women are invariably braggarts and cowards. Think no more of him."

At this juncture, Jenny Heathcote, who had heard angry voices, came to the spot.

"But I am forgetting my mission," said Jack, presently.

With these words, he presented a note to Lady Flora.

"From my godmamma," she said.

Hastily tearing it open, she ran her eyes over its contents.

"An invitation for both of us to Marlborough House !" exclaimed the young girl, her fair face beaming with pleasure.

"Oh, how glad I am !" joined in her companion Jenny.

"The duchess gave us permission to escort you, Lady Flora, if you are disposed to ride on horseback to town," said Jack.

"Oh, I should like to ride extremely."

"Jenny, *ma chère*," said Flora, "lead the way to the house, and we'll follow you. The gallant soldier at your side—I regret I don't know his name——"

"I'm sure I beg your pardon," interposed Jack ; "this is Lieutenant Rattles of the Dragoon Guards."

"Thank you. I'm sure Lieutenant Rattles will honour Miss Heathcote with his arm."

Ned at once availed himself of the privilege.

"I have been wondering how it is you seem to know me so well," Flora said, glancing up at Jack archly.

"Your name was on the note," replied Jack, somewhat evasively.

"Ah, yes ; so it was. But you seemed to meet me more like an old friend than a stranger. Can you explain that ?"

A smile glimmered in our hero's eyes as he answered—

"I think I can."

"Oh, pray do, then."

"I must trouble you to go back a long time."

"How long ?"

"Quite twelve years."

"Oh, dear, that is a long time!" exclaimed Flora, in a serio-comic tone. "Makes one feel quite old, I declare."

"Well, then, can you recall one night when there was a grand assembly at Marlborough House?"

"There have been so many such grand assemblies there," said Flora.

"Ah, yes; but there were some particular incidents that mark the night I speak of."

"What were they?"

"A drummer boy was introduced to the company."

"Oh, yes, yes; I remember that perfectly," exclaimed Flora, with animation. "His name was Jack Barrington, and a very pretty boy he was too."

"Do you remember also a very pretty girl with beautiful long golden hair?"

"Ye-es, I think I do," returned Flora, demurely.

"Do you remember her giving this drummer boy a lock of her beautiful golden hair?" Jack continued.

"I do, and I remember, too. that she cut off one of the pretty drummer boy's beautiful dark locks in exchange."

"Quite true; she did. And now, sweet Lady Flora, deign to look at me, after twelve long years have rolled away. I am Jack Barrington."

The young girl turned her lovely blue eyes tenderly upon him as she replied—

"And I am Flora."

There was a slight pause as they stood gazing thus at each other.

Then Jack said to Flora—

"And do you still think as kindly now of the 'soldier boy' as you did twelve years since?"

"First tell me, do you still think as kindly of the golden-haired little girl?" she replied.

Jack thrust his hand into his breast pocket, and brought forth the tress of hair she had given him.

"This is my answer," he said, as he held it towards Flora. "I have worn this next my heart ever since, for your sake."

Flora drew from her bosom the dark lock she had severed.

"And I have worn this next my heart ever since, in memory of you," she replied.

There needed no more explanations.

The next moment the young lovers were clasped to each other's hearts.

CHAPTER XXXVII.
DEAD.

In the high road, now known as the Essex Road, Islington, there stood, in former times, a substantial brick building, known as Camden House, the residence of John Stanmore, a retired merchant.

At that period the locality was entirely rural, the house being surrounded by fields and orchards and an atmosphere filled with the fragrance and freshness of the country.

In a room at the back of the mansion that looked out upon a spacious garden, sat the proprietor, an old man more than sixty years of age.

"Twenty-one years," he soliloquized, "since, by too much harshness, I drove my poor Ruth from her home. Twenty-one years! What can have become of her during all that time?"

He sighed, and having shifted his position, continued—

"Is she still alive?—and if so, will she see the advertisement I have put in the papers? Pray Heaven she may! for I am growing old, and would fain see my child once more before I die."

He paused and ran his eye over a parchment document before him.

"Ha, ha!" he laughed bitterly to himself, as he read—"'Last will and testament of John Stanmore.' And this is what I've toiled for; to amass wealth I cannot enjoy, to leave to one who may not be alive to inherit it. Oh, pray Heaven my dear girl may be restored to me."

As he said this, there was a ring at the gate bell.

Coming as it did so immediately upon the words he had just uttered, it struck him as remarkable.

"Can this be she?" he murmured, anxiously.

The door opened, and his housekeeper—an elderly lady of his own age—entered.

"Well, Mrs. Marchmont, do you bring me good news?" he asked. "Is it—is it Ruth?"

"No, sir."

The old man's countenance drooped, and he sighed wearily.

"It is a young gentleman," said Mrs. Marchmont, "who wishes to see you on important business in connection with the advertisement."

"What is his name?" inquired John Stanmore, eagerly.

"Captain Barrington, sir."

The face of the old man underwent an instantaneous change.

"Show him in—show him in at once," he cried, excitedly.

Mrs. Marchmont retired, and presently returned, bringing with her the stranger.

The door closed upon him, and he and the merchant stood gazing at each other long and earnestly.

There were evidently some tender feelings working in the old man's heart, as he looked at our hero.

At length he said, in a tone husky and faltering from emotion—

"Your name is Barrington?"

"Yes, sir."

"Are you the son of Edward Barrington?"

"I am, sir."

"I need not ask who was your mother, for in your features my dear girl lives again."

"My mother's maiden name was Stanmore," said our hero.

"I know, I know! She was my own daughter," cried the old man, with a burst of remorse. "You are my own flesh and blood. Come near me, my dear boy."

Jack approached and knelt reverently before his grandfather.

The old man embraced him with intense emotion.

"What is your Christian name?" he asked after a few moments.

"John. I was christened after you, sir, my mother has often told me."

"Ah! poor, dear girl. I was harsh to her; steeled my heart against her, and all because she loved your father."

"What was my father's fault, sir?"

"He had no fault. He was a worthy, honourable man; but he was not rich. On that account, I forbade your mother to marry him. She disobeyed me, and I drove her from me with a curse."

"Is it possible—your own child?"

"Alas, yes," went on his grandfather, tearfully. "But all that is past; I am a changed man now. Heaven has softened my stony heart, and I wish to make atonement."

"I fear it is too late," said Jack, in a mournful tone.

"Too late!" echoed John Stanmore, gazing at him, in a kind of horror. "Is—is your mother dead?"

"She may be still alive; but I am not certain," returned Jack, sadly.

"How is that?"

"She was carried off more than twelve years ago, and I have never seen her since."

"Carried off!" gasped John Stanmore. "By whom?"

"By the man who murdered my father," Jack replied.

The merchant fell back in his seat, as if the terrible intelligence he was listening to paralyzed him.

"What is the murderer's name?" he asked, at length.

"He usually calls himself Captain Gravellotte."

"Is he a Frenchman?"

"I think not. The name is only an *alias*, and not his own. I believe him to be an Englishman and a relative, for I remember hearing my father call him cousin."

"Then you are not acquainted with his real name?"

"No."

"But you know him by sight?"

"Perfectly well," said Jack; "we usually remember our foes; and this man has been a deadly one to me. He would have destroyed me as well as my father if he could have done so."

"The wretch!" exclaimed John Stanmore, who, now thoroughly roused to indignation, begged his grandson to relate to him minutely all that had happened in the past.

Jack did so, omitting nothing concerning either his parents or himself.

The old man listened with trembling earnestness.

"And where do you believe your mother to be now if she is alive?"

"The last I heard of her was at Liege in the Netherlands. But though I searched and made every inquiry, I could not discover her, and that is twelve years ago," said our hero, with a mournful sigh.

"It is a long time, indeed," said his grandfather. "But let us not despair. Can you get leave of absence from your regiment?"

"I have no doubt I can, for a time."

"Then we will go together in search of your dear mother. Money is no object to me, and if she be alive, though it cost me half my fortune, I will find her."

Having said this, he pointed to the parchment before him.

"This is my will," he continued, "in which I leave all I possess to my daughter. But I shall add a codicil, bequeathing it in the event of her death to yourself."

Our hero thanked him and prepared to take leave.

"When shall you be ready to start?" asked the old man.

"In a few days."

"The sooner the better. We may have far to go, and life, even at the longest, is but short."

"I will be here in three days from this time," Jack promised.

This satisfied John Stanmore, and our hero, receiving from his newly-found relative a cordial adieu, took his departure.

* * * * *

The third day had arrived, and again the gate bell of Camden House rang.

This time, a dark-complexioned man of middle age stood there.

He was dressed soberly but well.

He, like our hero, had come on important business, respecting the advertisement.

He was accordingly shown into the library, where John Stanmore sat amongst his deeds and documents.

The stranger having been asked to a seat, lost no time in coming to the point.

"I am here on behalf of my wife, sir," he said.

At the same time his eyes wandered to the table, and fastened, instinctively it seemed, upon the will that lay there.

"Have I the pleasure of knowing the lady?" asked John Stanmore.

"I should think so," returned the other, with a bland smile, "considering she happens to be your daughter."

The old man uttered a sudden cry, that almost startled his visitor, as he sprang up from his seat.

"Do you mean my daughter—my daughter Ruth?" he demanded excitedly.

"Yes, my dear sir, your daughter Ruth," was the calm reply.

The placidity of the speaker had effect upon the listener, and controlling his emotion by a strong effort, he said—

"May I ask your name, sir?"

"Certainly; I was about to tell you. It is Gasper Grimsby."

"Gasper Grimsby!" echoed John Stanmore, sharply. "That is not the name of my Ruth's husband. She married Edward Barrington."

"Quite true, sir, she did," admitted the other, with perfect composure; "but he, poor fellow, was shot by a Frenchman more than twelve years ago. I am your daughter's second husband."

This seemed possible to the merchant, and he asked—

"Where did you meet my—my Ruth?"

"In the Netherlands. It was my good fortune to rescue her from the brutality of a French officer there."

" The name of that officer ?" demanded John Stanmore, eagerly.

" Captain Gravellotte."

This seemed to tally so exactly with the account John Stanmore had received from Gallant Jack that he could but believe the speaker was uttering the truth.

" And so you are my child's husband ?" he said, after a moment.

" Yes, sir, I have that honour, and a loving, amiable wife she is," replied Gasper, with well-assumed warmth.

" And where is she now ?" inquired the old man.

" In Paris."

" Why did she not accompany you ?"

" Alas ! her state of health will not permit her to travel."

" She saw my advertisement then ?"

" Yes, in the London papers. And begged me to come at once to England, to let you know she was alive, and to assure you of her love and duty to you, sir."

" Did she send no particular message—no letter ?"

" She was too weak to write at the time I left her, sir," said Gasper, shaking his head mournfully, " but I may tell you, that owing to the wars between England and France, my fortune has become greatly impaired, and she bade me say that she rested upon your fatherly kindness and generosity, to assist us in our need."

" Poor girl, poor girl," murmured the repentant parent ; " she may do that."

He paused a moment, and then said—

" I was on the point of starting in search of my dear child, but since you are here, sooner than the friend I was going with, I will accompany you to Paris."

A shadow of disappointment flashed across the features of Gasper Grimsby at this announcement, but he controlled it and said—

" The state of affairs abroad is very unsettled, sir, and at your time of life——"

" No matter," interrupted John Stanmore quickly. " Let us start at once."

" That is impossible, sir," returned Gasper ; " business matters will detain me several days."

" Business ! and your wife ill," exclaimed John in surprise.

" It is business on her account," returned the other soothingly ; " but I have a friend who starts for Paris to-day, by whom I can forward anything your bounty pleases to send her."

" There will be no need, as I shall start myself," said the old merchant, sharply. " I long to clasp my dear child once more to my heart."

A close observer might have seen Gasper Grimsby was bitterly chagrined at this determination, and rising, he approached the table at which John Stanmore was seated.

" Husband and wife are one flesh, sir," he said, with a smile ; " may I request you, for your child's sake, to advance me a hundred pounds for present expenses ?"

The old man looked up at the speaker, whose eyes were riveted eagerly upon the will.

There was an expression of such intense greed in them, that John Stanmore paused before he replied.

Then he said deliberately—

" I should of course, be happy to assist my daughter's husband in any way I could."

" A hundred pounds is not a large sum," interposed the other.

" It is not the amount," returned John ; " it would matter little to me if it were a thousand."

The eyes that looked down into his flashed eagerly.

" You can make it a thousand, if you like, sir," he said ; " when I have recovered my losses, I will repay you without fail."

This was an imprudent speech.

He who made it did not know what a shrewd, keen man of business he was speaking to, or he would never have spoken so.

For it excited in the mind of John Stanmore a sudden and strange suspicion, and he replied, in his former clear, deliberate tone—

" I am perfectly willing to lend you the sum or any further sums you may require——"

" Oh, my dear sir ; you are too kind !"

" Stop, I haven't done yet. I was going to say, I decline advancing a single farthing, until I am fully assured you are my daughter's husband."

" Can you doubt me ?" cried Gasper Grimsby, losing his self-control, and glaring fiercely at the merchant.

" I doubt everything, until I have sufficient proof," returned Stanmore coolly ; " all I want is proof."

" I have no immediate proof," said Gasper Grimsby, sullenly, " beyond my bare word ; that must be enough."

" That is insufficient," answered John Stanmore, " since you are an entire stranger to me, and since—not wishing to offend you—there are so many impostors in the world."

At this home thrust, Gasper compressed his lips in evident rage.

" Am I then to understand that you refuse me any pecuniary advance ?" he asked after a moment.

" Yes !"

The sallow countenance of Gasper darkened, and his brows became knitted into a stern frown, and just at that moment the gate bell rang loudly again.

Mrs. Marchmont entered, and approaching close to her master, whispered something to him.

Gasper Grimsby started as his listening ear caught one name—" John Barrington," and an expression like that of a fiend came over his face.

The merchant seemed delighted, and said to the housekeeper eagerly—

" Let him come in."

As soon as she had departed, and ere a word could be uttered, Gasper sprang forward.

With a hasty sweep of his arm, he snatched up a heavy stick that was close to the old man's chair.

Whirling it through the air, he brought it down twice with terrific force upon the head of the old merchant.

A faint groan was all that was heard, followed by a rustling of paper and the rattle of gold, and then the sound of a window opening, and all was silent.

*   *   *   *

Our hero entered hastily, looking as if he fully expected to meet someone.

But no third person met his sight.

"Strange," he said to himself; "the housekeeper told me there was a stranger here."

He turned to the armchair.

A cry of horror burst from his lips.

His grandfather lay there lifeless.

His skull fractured and his brains scattered upon the chair back.

"Merciful Heaven!" exclaimed Jack, aghast, "it must have been that murderous wretch who passed me. He has been here, and this is his atrocious deed."

He looked on the table.

The will was gone.

He glanced towards the window.

It was open.

The murderer had escaped. Nor could any trace of him be found.

CHAPTER XXXVIII.

FOREBODINGS OF DANGER.

It was a lovely August night.

The gardens at Ranelagh were filled with a splendid company.

Dukes, lords and marquises were there.

Officers in the army with their rich uniforms, and beautiful women, glittering with costly gems, strolled along the illuminated paths, whilst the strains of sweet music added to the enchantment of the scene.

In a somewhat retired spot sat our hero and Lady Flora Greville.

The Duchess of Marlborough fully sanctioned their mutual attachment, and they were now affianced lovers.

Not far from them were Ned Rattles and Miss Jenny Heathcote, who seemed fully to appreciate the attention paid to her by the young lieutenant.

Whilst a little further off still, Ensign Brian O'Flinn lounged luxuriously on a garden seat; having no fair attraction to occupy his thoughts at present, he was placidly enjoying a cigar.

All were in excellent spirits, but one.

This one was Jack Barrington.

Although seated by the side of the girl he loved, he looked pale and abstracted.

Although some weeks had passed, he had not yet recovered the shock of his grandfather's death.

That death, so strangely, terribly mysterious.

He had no doubt in his own mind as to the murderer.

But the absence of any clue to his discovery, and of any positive proof of his guilt even if discovered, rendered the prospect of bringing him to justice hopeless.

Flora noticed his abstraction, and she said at length—

"How pale and depressed you are to-night, Jack dear."

"I am, I confess," he replied. "Pray pardon me, but I cannot throw off the gloom that oppresses me."

"I can quite understand. You are thinking of the terrible tragedy of Camden House."

"Yes, love. But that is not all that weighs upon my spirits."

"What else?" asked Flora, anxiously.

"I can hardly define what it is," returned Jack; "but I have a presentiment of impending danger."

"Oh, you are low-spirited, dear," said Flora, soothingly. "What danger could possibly threaten you?"

Our hero made no reply, and at that moment Brian O'Flinn came up to him.

"I say, Jack, honey," he said.

"What is it?"

"Do you know that extensive person yondther, in the gould-laced coat and the flowing wig?"

As he spoke, he pointed to a spot at some little distance that was partly in the shadow.

There stood a gentleman of distinguished appearance, who was evidently closely watching him.

"Do you know him?"

Jack looked earnestly at him for a moment and then replied in an undertone—

"Yes. It is the Marquis De Hauteville, I believe, whose sword I had the pleasure of snapping in half a few weeks since."

"Oh, bedad!" laughed O'Brian; "that accounts for the interest he takes in you."

Flora's quick ear caught the words, and looking round, she too caught sight of the marquis.

"That man here," she exclaimed, as she clung closer to her lover. "What does he want?"

"Nay, that's more than I can tell," Jack replied, with a forced laugh.

"I fancy I can see the scowl upon his face at this distance," murmured Flora, in an anxious tone; "I feel half afraid of him, for I am sure he is revengeful."

"A fig for his revenge," replied our hero. "I'm not afraid of him."

"He's seen as much as he cares to see," said Brian O'Flinn, "and has walked off."

The evening wore on.

Ned Rattles and Brian O'Flinn had strolled into the saloon.

Our hero, his betrothed and Jenny Heathcote were left together.

A servant in livery approached with a note, which he handed to Lady Flora, and instantly retired.

"What can this mean?" she said, as she recognised the hand of the Duchess of Marlborough.

Having opened and read the note, she cried—

"Our relative, Lady Ormond, has been seized with a sudden and dangerous illness."

"Dear, dear! how sorry I am to hear that," exclaimed Jenny.

"She is at Herne Hill, is she not?" asked Jack.

"Yes; and as it is feared she is dying, the duchess wishes us to return thither at once, instead of returning to Marlborough House."

"I and my comrades will escort you," our hero replied.

Flora pressed his hand gratefully.

"And perhaps, dear, you will see if our carriage is near," she said.

"I will, most certainly," was Jack's reply, "if you will wait here."

The young ladies promised, and he hurried away.

* * * * *

As Ned Rattles and Brian O'Flinn were strolling leisurely along, two persons passed them.

They were well-dressed and wore high-heeled shoes, elaborate cravats and ruffles, and full flowing wigs.

The young officers, struck by the fixedness of their gaze, looked at them earnestly in return.

"Did you see that pair of big wigs?" asked Brian of his comrade, after they had passed.

"Yes. How they stared at us."

"Yes, bedad! they screwed their eyes into us like gimlets. Where the devil have I seen their physogs? By the powers, I've got it now! I know who they are!" he exclaimed, suddenly.

"Who?"

"Guess."

"I can't recall them," said Ned.

"Have you forgotten that illegant specimen of a turncoat, Captain Gravellotte?" asked Brian.

"What! was it he?"

"Shure as fate, he was one of them, and the other was that thafe of the world, Caleb Corder."

"I think you're right, old fellow. I believe it was them."

"I feel shure it was."

"What do you suppose they want here?" Ned Rattles asked.

"That's more than I can tell; but unless they've altered greatly for the betther, it's no good they're afther, you may be shure."

"I wonder how Jack will take it, when he hears these fellows are here?"

"I don't suppose he'll throuble himself much about 'em."

In a few moments they had reached the spot where they had left Jack.

He was no longer there. The young ladies were alone.

Ned and Brian were soon informed of the calamity that had befallen Lady Ormond, and having exchanged a few words with their fair companions, they departed, expecting to find Jack Barrington at the gates.

They were not disappointed.

As they approached, he came hastily towards them, holding an open letter in his hand.

"I'm glad you're here; you're the very two I was wishing to see," he said.

"Anything particular happened?" asked Ned Rattles.

"Oh, no, but here is a summons from the Duke of Marlborough."

"The duke!" echoed his comrades, simultaneously.

"Yes, he writes to say we are to attend him directly at the War Office."

"Phew!" whistled Brian, "is there goin' to be another fight wid the mounseers?"

"I don't know, I'm sure," exclaimed Jack,

"but we'll go back to the ladies and tell them why we cannot accompany them."

Flora was greatly chagrined at the intelligence.

"I am very much disappointed myself, love," returned Jack, "but you know we must obey orders."

"Oh, yes, I know that," replied Flora, her fair face full of regret.

She bent down to her betrothed and whispered earnestly—

"I do hope after we're married, you'll leave the army. I shall want my husband all to myself."

Jack smiled as he pressed her hand in his.

"A soldier is the property of his country, darling," he replied, with a chivalrous smile; "even our noble commander-in-chief has to leave his wife when duty calls him."

"Ah, yes, so he does," sighed Flora; "well, then, if we must go alone, we must. But we shall see you at the park to-morrow?"

"If I can possibly get away, you may depend upon me."

And with an affectionate good night the lovers separated.

* * * * *

"Hollo, captain!"

"Hollo, sergeant!"

This was in reply to the hail given by Sergeant Crank to our heroes, as they were riding sharply along towards the War Office.

They pulled up their horses at once.

"Whither bound, captain?" inquired the sergeant, who, as an old comrade, was rather familiar in his speech.

"To the War Office."

"The War Office?"

"Yes. We have been summoned to meet the duke there."

The sergeant's face exhibited profound surprise, as he exclaimed—

"Impossible! The duke started for Scotland this evening, and will not return for a week."

"But here is his letter," said Jack, as he took it from his pocket.

"May I look at it, captain?" asked Benjamin Crank.

"Certainly," Jack replied, as he handed it to him.

The sergeant looked at it earnestly by the light of a carriage lamp.

"This is not the duke's handwriting," he exclaimed after a moment.

"Not!" echoed his hearers.

"No, it's a wonderful good imitation; but still it's not the duke's, I'll swear."

Brian O'Flinn whistled apprehensively to himself at this.

"Whose can it be then?" said Jack.

"It must be a hoax," returned Benjamin.

"If so, then perhaps the other letter was a hoax also."

"What other?"

"Why, the note sent by the duchess to Lady Flora Greville this evening."

"A note. What was it about?"

Jack informed him.

"Oh, hang it all," burst out Sergeant Crank, "this is too bad. It's a confounded lie."

"What, then, isn't Lady Ormond dangerously ill?"

"HE BROUGHT THE STICK DOWN WITH TERRIFIC FORCE ON THE OLD MERCHANT'S HEAD."

" Not a bit of it. She arrived at Marlborough House, not two hours ago."

There was a pause of silence after this.

Suddenly the Marquis De Hauteville recurred to our hero, and he exclaimed in a troubled tone—

" I'm afraid there's some villany afoot."

" Bedad !" ejaculated Brian O'Flinn, " I shouldn't be surprised if there was, considtherin' who was in the gardens to-night."

" You mean the French marquis ?"

" An' two others besides him."

" Who ?"

" Captain Gravellotte and Caleb Corder."

" Were they there ?" cried Jack Barrington excitedly.

" Yes ! by the powers, Ned an' myself saw the pair ov them."

A thousand bewildering thoughts and suspicions rushed in a torrent through our hero's mind.

" I told Flora that I had a foreboding of evil, and it seems I was right," he murmured.

Then turning suddenly, he shouted—

" Comrades, let us return to the gardens at once ; we may yet be in time to save the ladies."

" Hurrah ! On we go, then," cried Brian.

Away they went, and paused not till the gates were in sight.

Here, from the crowd of carriages, they were compelled to stop.

Dismounting from their horses, they made their way into the gardens, and directed their course to the spot which they had occupied during the evening.

It was entirely deserted.

Hastily they hurried through the various walks.

They looked in at the saloon.

It was empty.

The company were taking their departure.

" We are too late," said our hero at length.

" Whose carriage do you want, sir ?" asked one of the gate-keepers.

" Lady Flora Greville's," answered Jack eagerly.

" Gone long ago, sir," said the man.

" Then we must follow," cried Jack excitedly. " To horse ! to horse ! lads, for I'll not rest till I have Lady Flora safe by my side."

" Hurroo !" joined in Brian O'Flinn ; " to horse !"

The next minute they were in their saddles, dashing along the road in the clear moonlight, as though they were leading a charge.

CHAPTER XXXIX.

CARRIED OFF.

IT was with mingled feelings of disappointment and depression that Flora Greville and Jenny Heathcote got into their carriage. Both were grieved at the dangerous condition of their kind guardian, Lady Ormond, and disappointed at the enforced absence of their brave protectors.

" Well, we must make the best of it," said Flora, as she nestled herself into a corner of the carriage.

" Oh, yes," replied Jenny ; " there's nothing like philosophy in these cases."

" And we shall see our heroes to-morrow," said Flora.

The carriage rumbled away.

At that period, there were comparatively few houses on the outskirts of the town, and they were soon in the country.

It was a lovely night, and the bright moonlight, the cool fresh air, and the sweet perfume of the hay, made the journey at least very enjoyable.

The road towards Herne Hill was solitary enough.

Not a single person, not a vehicle did they pass.

It was when they were within two miles of Herne Hill they heard the sound of horses' hoofs behind them.

Was it their admirers coming after them, or some midnight desperadoes following on their track to rob them ?

Nearer and nearer came the hurried footsteps.

Presently several mounted men dashed past the carriage, and wheeling suddenly round, shouted to the coachman to stop.

At the same time, in order to ensure obedience to this injunction, two of the party seized the horses' heads, whilst a third dragged the coachman from his box, and bound and gagged him.

The next moment two figures looked in at the carriage windows.

These were Gasper Grimsby and Caleb Corder. Both were masked.

The fair occupants of the vehicle were no cowards, and therefore did not faint or scream.

" Lady Flora Greville ?" said Gasper, at length, inquiringly.

" I am Lady Flora Greville," returned the young beauty, with dignified hauteur ; " what is your business with me ?"

" My business was to stop your ladyships," answered Gasper, coolly ; " and having done that, I await further orders."

" You are acting for another, then ?" said Flora, with wonderful presence of mind.

" You've just hit it, mademoiselle," laughed Caleb Corder ; " and we're waiting till the other comes."

" By whose orders do you stop us on our journey ?" continued the young girl.

" Ah ! Now you want to know a trifle too much, my beauty," grinned Caleb.

" Ask no questions and you'll learn all in good time," remarked Gasper, coolly.

The familiar tone in which she was addressed annoyed Flora, who was of high spirit.

She compressed her lips and remained silent.

A few moments had elapsed, when the rattle of wheels was heard, and a close travelling carriage came up and stopped by the side of the other.

The door opened, and a gentleman descended.

It was the Marquis De Hauteville.

He approached the vehicle in which the ladies were seated.

" Open the door," he said to Caleb Corder.

The door was opened, and he looked in upon the fair inmates.

" Well, sweet Flora," he said, complacently, " all is fair, you know, in love and war."

The young girl turned her head scornfully away, without condescending any reply.

"You scorned my love, if you remember," continued the marquis, "and have driven me to this."

"Wretch !" murmured the maiden, "you will answer for this outrage to Captain Barrington."

"We need not waste time," the Frenchman went on ; " I do not wish to detain Miss Heathcote ; she can proceed. but you, beautiful Flora, must accompany me."

"Never, villain," she cried, her blue eyes flashing with mingled scorn and terror.

"You shall not take her, you vile man !" exclaimed Jenny Heathcote. "Help ! help !"

"You may spare your outcries," said the marquis, "there are none to listen to you."

"It's not the least use your screeching," joined in Caleb, officiously ; "it won't do any——"

He was suddenly stopped, and knocked on one side by a sharp blow on the ear, administered by Gasper Grimsby.

"You are here to obey orders, not to dictate," said the latter.

Caleb growled, and swore he wouldn't be knocked about for anybody.

The marquis then, looking towards his agents, said in an undertone—

"Now, then, you can get her into my carriage without loss of time."

Caleb Corder, at a sign from his companion, left off rubbing his ear, and sprang into the carriage.

"Now, then, out we come," he said to Flora.

As he spoke, he sought to grasp her by her wrists, but all he caught was a second box on his ear from the white hand of the indignant beauty, whilst Jenny Heathcote, clenching her small fists desperately, punched him with all her might ; but resistance was impossible for long, and in a moment or two, Flora was dragged out.

Gasper Grimsby secured her, and with the air ringing with her cries, he bore her to the other carriage, where the Marquis De Hauteville waited.

Terror and exhaustion had its effect, and she fainted in the Frenchman's arms, but ere he had time to deposit his prize on the luxurious cushions prepared for her, the sound of horses' hoofs became audible in the distance.

"There is someone approaching," said Gasper Grimsby, hastily.

"*Diable !*" muttered the marquis, after listening an instant, "so there is."

Then thrusting his head from the window, he shouted to the postillions—

"Drive on as hard as you can ; fifty guineas extra if you reach your journey's end in safety !"

With this prospect, the men cracked their whips, and dug their spurs furiously into the horses' flanks.

The vehicle rolled away at a rapid pace, and was soon out of sight.

The sound of the hoofs was drawing nearer, and Gasper Grimsby said to his companions—

"Having performed the work I undertook, I have nothing more to do, and intend to decamp."

"So do I," said Caleb Corder.

The next moment, they had sprung over the hedge, and become invisible amidst the trees that skirted the road.

The two men who had held the horses' heads also decamped.

By. the time our hero and his comrades came up to the spot, not one was to be seen.

Lady Flora's carriage, with its doors open, stood on one side of the road.

The coachman, with his wig off, his arms pinioned, and his mouth propped wide open by the gag, was seated ruefully on the path.

Jack Barrington rushed at once to the carriage, and looked in.

He saw Jenny Heathcote reclining languidly in one corner, just recovered from a swoon, and as yet scarcely conscious, but his betrothed he found not.

"Where is Flora ?" he cried, in an agony of apprehension.

"Carried off," replied Jenny, in a tone scarcely audible.

"By whom—whither ?" were our hero's distracted questions.

"The Marquis De Hauteville," gasped the young lady, as she burst into tears, but in what direction, she knew not.

But Jack had heard enough, and he cried fiercely—

"The cowardly villain ! he shall pay for this outrage with his life."

Turning from the carriage, he said to his comrades—

"I am off in pursuit of this libertine Frenchman. It will be with us a case of life and death."

Hardly had he uttered the last word when the report of a pistol rang through the trees.

Brian O'Flinn uttered a sharp cry.

"It's death for me, me boys, I'm thinkin'," he murmured, faintly, as he fell forward on his horse's neck.

His comrades, dismounting, lowered him to the ground.

"You will look to him," said Jack, in a somewhat bewildered tone to Ned Rattles.

Then bending down to his wounded friend, he said to him—

"God bless you, old fellow ; I'm sorry to leave you, but I must go. Flora is carried off, and every moment's of consequence."

"Aye, shure ; don't mind me, me boy, I'll do well enough," said Brian, as he took the hand extended to him. " If this is to be a settler for me, an' we niver meet ag'in alive, good-bye an' God bless yez, an' the dear young lady too."

Jack looked down sadly at his old friend's pale face, and the next moment was in his saddle again. Bang !

A second shot, with murderous intent, was fired at him, but the ball whizzed past without effect, and without even heeding his peril, he dashed forward in pursuit of his beloved.

CHAPTER XL.

A HARD RESCUE.

SHOUTING the name of Flora, he rode on at a reckless pace, but saw no signs of the carriage.

Perplexed, bewildered, desperately anxious, he stopped at length.

"I must have overtaken it if that rascally marquis had kept to the road," he muttered, fretfully, to himself.

He listened intently.

There was not the slightest sound of whip or wheel, nor the faintest echo of the cry of the postillions urging on their horses reached him.

"Gracious Heaven!" he exclaimed, "is my darling to be torn from me in this atrocious manner? Oh, guide me, guide me to her, that this dire peril may be averted."

As if in answer to this petition, a cry came wailing to his ear from the distance.

He started and looked round.

The cry was not before, but behind him, but it gave him new hope.

"'Tis Flora's voice," he exclaimed, breathlessly.

Then, wheeling his horse round, he retraced his steps with all his former speed.

But the cry had ceased, and he still saw no thing.

Again despair was beginning to fasten upon him, when suddenly from across the fields he heard once more the signal of distress—

"Help, help!"

"With my life," was his reply, as he dashed forward, seeking for some opening in the thick plantation that bordered the road through which he might pass.

*　　*　　*　　*　　*

The Marquis De Hauteville was glad when his fair captive fainted.

It stopped her cries, and so spared him the trouble of soothing or threatening her.

As the carriage rumbled on at the quickest speed possible, he examined the flints of a pair of pistols, and having re-primed them, placed them in one of the carriage pockets.

It was just as he had done this, he heard shouts behind him in the distance.

"Sacré!" he muttered to himself, "are they pursuing? If so, mounted on horseback as they are, I cannot fail to be overtaken."

He looked out anxiously from the window as he spoke.

The carriage was just opposite a gloomy-looking lane, branching off from the main road, whose dark-embowered recesses seemed to promise concealment at least.

This at once suggested to the marquis what to do, and he shouted to the postillions—

"A la gauche, coquins! à la gauche!—to the left, rascals, to the left!"

They pulled up, and one replied—

"There is no thoroughfare that way, milord."

"Peste! so much the better," cried the Frenchman. "Proceed."

The men shrugged their shoulders as they obeyed the order, and the carriage went lumbering up the dark lane.

It led into a field of standing corn.

It was at this juncture that Flora opened her eyes.

"Where am I?" she murmured, faintly.

"Quite safe, ma belle, with him who adores you," was the reply she received.

The tones of the speaker's voice recalled the peril she was in.

"Help, help!" she shrieked, wildly.

It was this shriek that had reached the ear of her lover.

Again came the cry, and up the lane Jack rode, a straggling branch sweeping his hat from his head at the first step.

He did not pause to pick it up—it was fortunate he did not, as it afterwards proved —but pressed forward, intent on rescuing his betrothed.

As soon as he reached the end of the lane, he espied the carriage in the open field before him.

It had got into a deep, entrenched furrow, which the corn concealed, and had fallen over almost on to its side, where it remained motionless like a water-logged barge.

Certain now that he should soon be at the side of her he loved, he shouted—

"Flora, love, I am here to save you."

And then he dashed on.

The young girl heard his voice, and looked forth from the window.

The marquis instantly dragged her back.

But Jack was now almost close upon the vehicle, when suddenly his horse plunged violently into a furrow like that which had overturned the carriage, and fell, sending its rider flying over its head.

The thick corn broke the force of the fall, and Jack was unhurt.

At the same moment the marquis discharged one of the pistols at him.

The Frenchman's aim, owing to his excitement, was unsteady, and he missed his mark.

The marquis, with an oath, was about to try his other pistol, but was anticipated by Flora, who had taken it whilst his back was turned, and he now found the muzzle pointed at his breast.

"Coward, let me get out," cried the young girl, "or I fire!"

With a scornful laugh, the nobleman seized Flora's delicate wrist, and turned the weapon upwards away from himself.

There was a sharp bang, and the ball lodged in the roof of the carriage.

Flora uttered a cry.

Jack Barrington, having regained his feet, sprang forward.

"Scoundrel!" he shouted, to the marquis; "if you dare to injure her, your life shall answer it."

"Seize that fellow," cried De Hauteville, contemptuously, to the postillions, from the window; "bind and gag him."

The men darted upon Jack.

But our hero, who in his desperation, seemed to have the strength of a giant, seized them instead with a grip of iron, and after knocking their heads together till they rattled like a couple of empty cocoanuts, he flung them from him.

By the time he had done this, he found himself confronted by the marquis, sword in hand. His own sword quickly flashed from its scabbard.

"Misérable!" hissed De Hauteville, from between his teeth; "your time has come."

"Braggart, coward!" shouted Jack, furiously ; "look to yourself; Gallant Jack fears not twenty Frenchmen."

The attack commenced.

Flora, hearing the clash of steel, looked from the window.

"Oh, pray—pray, Jack, do not fight on my account !" she cried, imploringly.

"Don't fear for me, my love," returned Jack, as he looked towards her.

The marquis took advantage of his momentary abstraction.

By a sharp lunge he wounded him in the arm.

"I shall leave you as full of holes as a cullender," said De Hauteville, with a bitter, sarcastic laugh.

The wound was not serious.

But it increased our hero's irritation, it warned him that he must be cautious.

The marquis was a perfect master of his weapon, and fought with his French rapier.

His lunges were decided, and quick as lightning.

Again he drew blood from his opponent.

Flora could endure her suspense no longer, but sprang from the carriage and advanced towards the scene of strife.

The sight of her inspired our hero.

Whirling his sabre in the air, he brought it down with resistless force on the head of the marquis.

The Frenchman was utterly powerless to guard the blow.

Cutting clean through the hat he wore, it cleft him to the skull.

Drenched in blood, the libertine fell backwards.

Dead !

The corn, closing over him, shut out from sight the ghastly object.

Pale and breathless with his exertions, Jack Barrington clasped Flora to his heart.

Supposing the immediate danger to be over, he rejoiced in her safety.

Not suspecting any fresh attack, he made no further effort to protect himself.

He did not perceive a rustling in the corn, under cover of which two forms had been gradually approaching.

The report of a pistol, and a bullet whizzing close by his head, aroused him to a sense of danger.

But he could see no one.

"Return to the carriage, dearest," he said to Flora, after a moment, "you will be safer there than here ; fear not for me."

With these words, he led her to the vehicle and placed her inside.

He had hardly accomplished this, when a hoarse laugh that sounded familiar to his ear caused him to look round.

Two men—apparently strangers—confronted him.

Each was armed with a horse pistol, and looked bitterly malignant.

After a moment's earnest scrutiny Jack recognised them.

Gasper Grimsby and Caleb Corder.

"Ha, ha, brave captain ! we have you at last, in spite of your cleverness," cried the former.

"Yes, and we'll pay off old scores, too,"

joined in Caleb, malignantly, "and the noble marquis shall have the dainty Flora, in spite of you."

Our hero was beginning to feel much exhausted from loss of blood.

But the sight of these men gave him a momentary energy.

He cried fiercely—

"You pair of cowardly, contemptible murderers, you lie ! The scoundrel who employed you has met with his deserts. Beware, lest you receive the same death."

With this, he was about to spring forward, sword in hand, when he was suddenly seized by the postillions, who had crept round by the carriage.

For a moment he struggled to get free, but the exertion was too much for him.

His wounds burst forth afresh.

A deadly faintness seized him.

He sank down insensible.

Flora, seeing her lover lying prostrate on the ground, sprang from the carriage.

"Wretches, you have killed him !" she exclaimed, as she rushed forward and interposed herself between him and his foes.

"Your ladyship is mistaken," replied Gasper Grimsby, with mock politeness ; "we haven't killed him yet, but we shall."

"Oh, yes , we're going to, before we've done with him," added Caleb, brutally.

Flora uttered a cry of horror.

But at a signal from Gasper the postillions dragged her back.

He then approached our hero's unconscious form.

Having cocked his pistol, he turned to the horror-stricken girl, and said to her in a jeering tone—

"Has your ladyship any message to the other world ?"

Flora strove to reply.

But the words seemed to freeze upon her lips.

She was silent.

Gasper deliberately raised the weapon.

Having pointed it at Jack's breast, he pulled the trigger.

The hammer fell.

A piercing shriek of anguish burst from Flora's lips as she covered her eyes with her hands.

But there was no report.

"Sacré !" muttered Gasper, "the priming has fallen out."

"It won't take a second to re-prime," grinned Caleb. "Here's the powder-flask, captain."

He handed it to his companion as he spoke.

But ere it could be used, the rattle of arms and the trampling of horses were heard, and the voices of Sergeant Crank and Ned Rattles.

Gasper Grimsby dropped the flask with an oath.

"Quick, away !" he cried, as he plunged into the corn and hurried off with desperate haste.

The rest followed his example.

By the time the sergeant and his comrades reached the spot, there was no one to be seen but our hero lying upon the ground, and Lady

Flora Greville supporting his head in her arms. This sight stopped all further pursuit.

Benjamin Crank dropped from his horse and knelt by the side of the young soldier.

"How is it with you, captain?" he asked, anxiously.

"Oh, he is wounded—dead!" wailed Flora, in piteous accents.

"Not so bad as that, your ladyship, I trust," said the sergeant; "let us see."

The military coat, soaked with gore, was quickly taken off, and the crimson shirt-sleeve tucked up.

Two small but deep rapier thrusts in the arm became at once visible, from which the blood oozed in thick clots.

Benjamin Crank placed his hand upon our hero's heart.

"Thank Heaven! there's plenty of life in him yet," he said, after a moment. "He's only faint from losing somewhat too much of the vital fluid."

With this remark he proceeded at once to bind up our hero's wounds.

He then compelled Jack to drink a little brandy from a flask he carried.

In a short time, our hero revived and opened his eyes.

"You here, sergeant?" he said, in some surprise, as he recognised his friend.

"Yes, captain, here I am. Not before I'm wanted, it seems."

"How did you find me?" asked Jack.

"You were kind enough to drop your hat at the entrance of the lane, captain, and that served as a clue," answered Ben, with a smile.

"Ah, true; so I did."

Flora Greville now spoke.

"Will he live?" she asked, anxiously.

"Live, your ladyship, of course he will," returned Sergeant Crank, heartily; "he's not one of the dying sort."

This cheered Flora, and her lover completed her happiness by taking her hand and pressing it to his lips.

"You are safe, my beloved," he murmured. "So I shall live for you."

"And now where's the enemy?" asked Benjamin, looking round.

"You'll find the leader not far off," answered Jack, as he pointed amongst the corn.

The sergeant went to the spot and looked down.

"Ah, yes, I see," he said, after a moment; "he won't lead anyone into trouble any more. And the rest?"

"Fled when they heard your voices," replied Flora.

"Ah, well," muttered Benjamin; "let 'em go. They'll have run the full length of their tether before long."

With some trouble the carriage was got out of the rut into which it had fallen, and our hero, Lady Flora, and Ned Rattles, proceeded in it to Beechwood Hall, whither Jenny Heathcote and Brian O'Flinn had already gone.

The wound of the latter, though very serious, was not mortal, as it had at first appeared.

Both the invalids gave promise of a speedy recovery.

CHAPTER XLI.

THE DUTCH SKIPPER'S MISSION.

GASPER GRIMSBY and his myrmidon, Caleb Corder, got safely off.

But the narrow escape they had had took but little effect upon them.

As for the former, he had by no means given up his designs against our hero.

Having registered a vow to destroy him, he thirsted for his death like a ravenous wolf, whom nothing but blood could appease.

* * * * *

Some weeks had passed.

The Dutch sloop, "Vrow Griet," from Amsterdam, lay moored in the Thames.

The skipper, Hans Oudenwold, whilst his cargo was being unloaded, remained on board, sipping his schnapps, and smoking his pipe with much complacency.

This being done, he prepared to execute some other commissions with which he had been entrusted.

Opening a strong iron box, which was a fixture in his cabin, he took from it a letter.

This letter was addressed in a very beautiful female hand.

The address was—"To John Barrington, soldier."

Hans Oudenwold looked at it for some time thoughtfully.

"*Teufels!*" he exclaimed, "how shall I find dis Zhon Barringtone vid a direction like dis here?"

He took several puffs at his pipe, and a good pull at the schiedam bottle at his side.

Between the two, he became a little more hopeful.

Having made up his mind, he went to the door, and struck a bell.

The summons was answered by a most peculiar-looking individual.

He was something like the mathematical definition of a straight line—length without breadth.

He wore the Dutch nautical costume.

But his face had not altered in the least during the last twelve years, and anyone who had known him at that period, would have recognised him at once as Timothy Tootles, the once military fifer.

Time had passed lightly over his head.

Perhaps, from his extraordinary spareness, the old gentleman with the scythe had failed to notice him.

He did not look an hour older.

His hair still hung long and lank on each side of his lantern jaws, and his eyes still rolled in all directions when he was addressed.

Perhaps from the constant motion of the vessel they had acquired a knack of rolling more than ever.

He entered the cabin, and stood before the skipper.

"Tim," said Hans, in a solemn and impressive tone, "I am going to leave der vessel. I may be avay for a day or two."

"Oh!" said Timothy.

"You know I have mosh confidence in you, Tim."

Tim rolled his eyes twice round in his head, and finally fixed them on the scheidam bottle.

"Mosh confidence—take a leetle drop of schnapps ?"

Tim at once availed himself of the offer.

"Now, Tim," went on the skipper, "I want you to keep a sharp look-out in the ship vhile I am avay, you onderstand ?"

"Oh, yes ; I know how to look six ways at once."

"Ha, ha !" laughed Hans, "you are a goot fellow, a very goot fellow, onlee you von't get fat. Vhy don't you get fat like me ?"

"I s'pose it ain't my natur," answered Timothy Tootles, with a grin.

"Vell, den, now I am off," said the skipper ; "I shall leave you some schnapps and tobacco, and you can smoke and drink as mosh as you like, only mind you don't get dronk."

Tim rolled his eyes round thrice, and vowed he wouldn't.

His master went on shore, and at once set about accomplishing his mission.

Anyone observing the Dutchman's round, barrel-like form as he made his way along the streets, would have set him down as a man of an easy-going, contented turn of mind.

Anyone happening to come suddenly *vis-à-vis* to him turning round a corner, would have seen in his round, smooth, unctuous face nothing but charity and benevolence.

He could be good, bad, or indifferent, just as it suited him, and according to the profit he was to get.

With his natural shrewdness, he went to the nearest barracks, and inquired there after "Zhon Barringtone."

At length he encountered a soldier, and from him he learnt that there was a Captain Barrington in the 5th Dragoon Guards.

"Ha, ha ! dat is someting," he said to himself.

And away he went to the place where that regiment was quartered.

In answer to his application, he was told that there was such a person as Captain John Barrington, but that he was out of town invalided.

"Ha, ha ! dat is someting more," thought Hans.

And then he asked in what part of the country he was staying.

"Beechwood Park, Herne Hill," was the answer he received.

"Ha, ha ! dat is bettair still," he chuckled.

As he was approaching the park, he encountered a man who looked like a tramp.

"I say, mein friend," he called to him, "am I near Beechvood Park ?"

"It is about half a mile along the road," returned the man, coming to a stop.

"Tank you."

"Have you business there ?" asked the tramp.

"Yah, of course, I have, or vort shoult I vornt dere ?"

"I suppose you want to see someone up there, eh ?" continued the man.

The round, dark eyes of Hans Oudenwold peered at his questioner for an instant, then he said, with a bland smile—

"Excuse me, mein friend, I nevair tell mein pusiness to nobody."

And the cunning Dutchman rolled on his way.

The tramp, or rather Gasper Grimsby, for it was he, looked after him.

"Business at Beechwood Hall," he muttered to himself ; "a Dutchman too. What business can it be ?"

He went on a little further and whistled.

Another tramp (Caleb Corder) sprang out of the hedge.

"You see that Dutch barrel ?" he said to his co-mate, as he pointed to the receding figure of the rotund skipper.

"Yes ; I see him."

"He is going to the Hall."

"I know he is ; I heard him say so."

"Well, follow him, and at any risk, short of actual discovery, find out what he wants there. Are you armed ?"

"All right ; I have something here that will not miss fire," returned Caleb, with a nod, and scrambling up the bank, he plunged through the hedge and disappeared, intending to make a short cut to the park.

Jack Barrington was lying dreamily on the grass, thinking of the stirring incidents of his past life, when a footman brought him word that a person wished to see him.

"Who is it ?" he asked.

"A stranger, sir, a foreigner."

"A Frenchman ?"

"No, sir, a Dutchman ; a sailor by his dress."

"You can bring him here," said our hero.

The domestic departed, and presently returned, conducting Hans Oudenwold.

"You wished to see me ?" said Jack.

"Yah, meinheer," replied the latter.

"What is your business ?"

"Vell, meinheer, I come from Amsterdam, and a ladee dere vish me to find out Zohn Barringtone."

The colour flushed into the pale face of our hero at these words.

"My name is John Barrington."

"You are a soldier too."

"Yes, a captain of dragoons."

"I tink den it moss be you ; eef so, I have a lettair for you."

"A letter ?" exclaimed Jack.

"Yah."

Jack glanced at the strange address—

"To John Barrington, soldier."

"It is from my mother, I feel sure it is ; and, dear soul, she had no other clue but this by which to find me," said Jack.

With trembling hands he opened the letter, and read as follows—

"Amsterdam, Brack's Hotel,
"Oude Doelen.

"MY DEAREST BOY,—With many earnest prayers, yet scarcely daring to hope that this will reach you after so many years, I write. I had long mourned you as dead. It was only during the last month I heard a young girl I met accidentally in Paris speak of one whom, from her description, and from the name, I felt must be my lost son. That you were a soldier I had no doubt, and I therefore address this letter vaguely, as you see, with the earnest hope that God, in his good providence, will guide it to you. Should this be permitted, you will know that your poor mother, after

"AT THAT MOMENT THE MARQUIS DISCHARGED ONE OF HIS PISTOLS AT JACK."

being much persecuted by that monster in human shape, Gasper Grimsby, your father's murderer, has escaped his clutches, and is still alive and in tolerable health, and longs to clasp once more to her widowed and solitary heart the son of her love. Should this reach you, you will, I know, write at once, or what would be better still, come over to Amsterdam, where you will find me at the above address.

"Your loving mother,

"RUTH BARRINGTON."

"P.S.—I grieve to tell you that your sister Lydia, driven to desperation by the cruel insults of Gasper Grimsby, disappeared some years ago. I have never seen or heard of her since, but I hope we may all be spared to meet yet."

It was with feelings of intense emotion our hero perused this letter.

Forgetting that he was not alone, he read it aloud.

Consequently Hans Oudenwold heard every word of it with much interest, and so also did another listener, who was concealed in the shrubbery close by.

As soon as Jack could command his voice sufficiently to speak, he said to the skipper—

"When shall you be returning to Amsterdam?"

"In von veek from dis time."

"You could receive a passenger on board, I suppose?"

"Yah, meinheer."

"Very well, then, I will sail with you."

"Ver goot, meinheer. You shall be ver comfortable on board mein vessel."

"Where is she lying, and what is her name?" asked Jack.

"She lies at der London Bridge wharf, and her name is der 'Vrow Griet.'"

Our hero made a note in his pocket-book of these particulars.

"Then you may depend on my accompanying you," he said.

The arrangement seemed to be completed, but the skipper, instead of taking leave, lingered and scratched his head.

"Pardon me, meinheer," he said, after a moment, "it vill be necessary to pay something down, in order to ensure your berth."

"Ah, true! I quite forgot!" exclaimed our hero; "here are five guineas. Will that be sufficient?"

"Qvite, meinheer," returned Hans, his round face beaming with smiles. "I vish you a ver goot day."

And with a profoundly respectful salutation, the skipper steered once more for the park gates, and the concealed listener followed him.

CHAPTER XLII.

ON BOARD THE "VROW GRIET."

IT was a misty evening, early in September, when Jack Barrington went on board the Dutch sloop.

Having been up very late on the previous night at the Duke of Marlborough's, he sought his cabin at once, intending to refresh himself with an hour or two's sleep.

Consequently, he knew nothing of the perils that surrounded the "Vrow Griet" as she strove to make her way out of the nest of vessels that hemmed her in on all sides.

Hans Oudenwold was on deck, encouraging his vessel with his voice, as though she had been a living thing capable of understanding.

"Steady! steady, mein beautiful maid!" he cried; "now den, pop your pretty head in dere, dat's goot; now den, shake your sides a leetel. Ha, ha! dat's petter, now you get through; did I not tell you so?"

In this way, slowly but surely, the skipper got his pet, at length, into tolerably clear water.

Deptford and Greenwich were passed.

At Woolwich, two other passengers came on board, loosely wrapped in cloaks, to keep out the evening mist.

They brought with them a large sea chest, and had altogether a mysterious appearance.

It was evident Hans Oudenwold expected them, and he received them, as they came up the ship's side, with a "Good evening, meinheerren," and winked to them to go below into his own cabin.

But there was one whose attention the newcomers especially excited.

This was Timothy Tootles.

In spite of the gloomy night, and the manner in which they were muffled up, there was something about them that set his weak mind thinking.

"Seems to me as if I'd met them two afore, some'eres," he thought to himself, as he crept close behind them.

This opinion was confirmed when he heard one say to the other in a low tone, as they descended the cabin steps—

"All right thus far."

To which the other replied—

"All right, captain!"

Timothy recognized the voice of the last speaker, and he muttered in a tone of profound surprise—

"Caleb Corder, as sure as my name's Tim!"

The sloop was soon under way again.

The wind had freshened; the atmosphere had grown clearer, and she now went on steady enough.

Finding himself now in smooth water, the skipper, after giving a few directions to the man at the helm, went below.

Timothy Tootles remained on deck in a brown study.

"Wotever can Caleb Corder want aboard this 'ere wessel?" he asked himself repeatedly; "and 'oo's that other cove vith 'im?"

His meditations were interrupted by the sound of the skipper's bell.

"I'm vanted," he exclaimed; "I vonder vhether they'll remember me?"

In a very doubtful state of mind, he descended to the cabin.

On entering, he saw several flasks and bottles on the table with tobacco and cigars.

Preparations seemed to be on foot for making a night of it.

The two passengers had removed their cloaks, and were now seen to be dressed in pea-jackets of a coarse frieze, and thick sea boots, and disguised by large beards.

Timothy Tootles had only to roll his eyes once round in his head, to take in all these particulars, and to be quite certain, that one was his old comrade, Caleb Corder, and the other, a certain Captain Gravellotte, whom he had met once or twice a long time ago.

"Clean glasses," cried the skipper.

Tim disappeared, and presently returned, bringing the glasses with him.

"Now den," said Hans to him, impressively, "you can go on deck, and stop dere ; I don't vant to be interrupted."

The two strangers were lighting their cigars, and had not noticed the spare youth, much to his satisfaction, and he quickly removed himself up above. But Tim's mind was busy, as he stood looking out upon the dark sea, and listening to the monotonous plash of the waves.

He could not get the disguised men out of his head, and he found himself murmuring over and over again—

"Vot do they vant 'ere ?"

The waves seemed to be answering in a subdued whisper—

"Listen and hear—listen and hear !"

"Blest if I don't too," said Tim.

Having made up his mind to this, he crept down the hatchway, and cautiously approached the cabin door.

The door was thick.

So also were the cabin walls.

But there was a slight crevice, to which he applied his ear.

At first, owing to the creaking of the timbers, the sough of the sea, and the flapping of the sails, he could hear nothing.

But gradually by intense effort, he could catch a word or two.

Little as it was, it made him very uncomfortable.

Someone it seemed (no name being mentioned) was to be put out of the way.

He caught the words—

"Years ago—sneaking hound—put out of the way—drug wine—chest—overboard—safe —fifty pounds," uttered at different times.

He then heard the skipper, in his full, round tones say—

"Monee foorst, meinheer, monee down."

Then there was a rattle of gold, followed by a long silence.

Timothy began asking himself all sorts of terrible questions.

"Who was meant ?—who was the sneaking hound that was to be put out of the way ?"

The words " years ago " seemed to give him a clue.

A dreadful clue it was too.

It must be himself the conversation pointed at.

His comrades had found him out and determined to get rid of him.

He was to be drugged with wine.

Locked up in the chest whilst unconscious, and thrown overboard to the fishes, and his master, the skipper, whom he had always thought so full of the milk of human kindness, was to have fifty pounds for conniving at the atrocious act.

No wonder the lank hair of the spare youth began to bristle on his head.

Yet it seemed strange to him that Caleb Corder should desire his death .

They had always been friendly.

Timothy grew quite bewildered and perplexed.

"I'll die precious hard, any'ow," he said to himself, with determination.   "They ain't a-goin' to get me into that there chest without a kick for it, I knows ; and as for vine, I won't taste a drop nor sperrits neither."

Just as he said this, he heard footsteps approaching.

He had only time to draw back and spring up the cabin steps, when the door opened and he heard the skipper say—

"I will show you to your berth meinself, meinheer."

"You're very kind," replied Gasper Grimsby, in a thick tone, as if he had been drinking. "Then we'll leave you to manage the rest."

"Yes, we'll leave you to—hic—pack the chest," joined in Caleb, with a drunken grin.

"Yah, yah ! I shall see to dat," returned the skipper.   "Don't talk so loud, and come on."

They disappeared, leaving Timothy Tootles in an intense state of mental agitation.

"Vot a cold-blooded lot they is," he muttered.   "Vot am I to do ?"

He was interrupted by the voice of Hans Oudenwold calling him.

"I von't go.   I'd rather die fust."

As he said this, he walked towards the ship's side with a half-formed intention of throwing himself overboard.

Again he heard his master's deep tones.

"Tim, Tim ! why der teufels don't you come when I call ?"

Tim hesitated, and finally descended to the cabin.

"Donder unt blitzen, vort a time you have peen," grunted Hans.

"I didn't hear you, captain," said Timothy, looking very white and scared.

"Vot's der matter vid you ?" asked the skipper.

"N—n—nothing pertickler," stammered Tim ; " it's only a touch of the mullygrubs vot's got 'old of me."

"Here den, take a drop of schnapps ; dat vill send dem flyin' into der Red Sea."

As Hans spoke, he handed Timothy the scheidam flask.

"N—n—n—no, th—th—th—ank'ee," gasped the spare youth.   " I don't vont no schnapps ; it allays makes me wus."

As he spoke, he extended his arms to keep the deceitful spirit as far from him as possible.

"Oh, vell, if you von't drink den," cried Hans, " I vant you to go to der cabin of der young shentelmansh dat come on poard early dis evening."

Timothy knew nothing whatever of our hero's arrival, and he asked innocently enough—

"Vot young gen'lman do you mean ?"

"I mean der von vot occupies der first cabin.   Go to him vid my complement an' say I shall pe happy to see him in my cabin."

Tim, whose ideas, on hearing of the young gentleman, had taken a fresh turn, went as he was ordered.

As he was going, he encountered several of the crew, who glared at him in the dim light suspiciously; but they were new hands, who had just joined the ship, and being strange to them, he did not speak, but went on till he came to the door, at which he tapped.

"Come in!" cried a voice.

Timothy at once obeyed.

A handsome young man in a military undress uniform, stood before him.

"What cheer, mate?" asked the latter, smilingly.

"Please, mynheer, the captain sends his compliments, and vill you—vill you—vill——"

The speaker's voice died gradually away.

His mouth opened, and he stood gazing idiotically upon the occupant of the cabin.

At length, he burst out—

"If it ain't his blessed self, I vish I may be turned into a Dutchman."

"You know me?"

"Yes; and you knows me, too."

"I fancied I did. It's Timothy Tootles, isn't it?"

"As much as is left of him. And you're Jack Barrington, ain't you?"

"I am."

To our hero's astonishment, Timothy fell on his knees at his feet, and burst into tears.

"Oh, Mister Jack, old comrade, forgive me for trying to blow you up, pray do," he sobbed, as he clasped his hands imploringly.

"I forgive you, my boy," Jack replied, touched at his evident remorse.

"Thankee, Mister Jack, for forgiving me; I should never have thought of such a piece of villany if it hadn't have been for Caleb Corder."

"I believe you," returned our hero; "and as twelve years have elapsed, forget it as I have done."

"Shake 'ands with us, please, Mister Jack," pleaded Timothy, humbly.

Jack took his long bony fingers, and pressed them cordially.

The warm, friendly grip seemed to put new life into the weak-minded youth, and to unlock all his faculties in a miraculous manner.

Jack's presence on board, coupled with that of the disguised men, seemed to explain the mysterious words he had heard.

It was our hero who was to be put out of the way, not Timothy.

Observing his agitation and confusion, Jack, in order to recall his faculties, said to him—

"You have a message to me from the captain, haven't you?"

"Yes, yes! I 'as, I 'as!" replied Tim, excitedly; "'e wants to see yer in the cabin. But don't go; pray don't."

"Why not?"

"Cos if yer does, yer'll be drugged, and put in a chest and shied overboard to the fishes, as sure as my name's Tim."

"The deuce I shall," laughed our hero; "that would be serious indeed."

"Offul, I thinks," shuddered Tim.

"And how did you learn that this fate was in store for me?" asked Jack.

"By listenin' at the cabin door, and 'earin' 'em talk about it."

"Hearing 'them,' you say?"

"Yes."

"Who do you mean by 'them'?"

"Capting Grawelpop—"

"Gravellotte," corrected Jack.

"Ah, yes; Gravellotte, and Caleb Corder."

"Are they on board, then?" asked our hero, without evincing any surprise.

"Yes. And they've give my master, the skipper, fifty pounds to make you drunk with drugged wine."

"And I suppose it is for the purpose of performing that interesting operation he wants me now?"

"Yes; that it is. But don't go."

"Oh, yes, I shall," said Jack, positively. "I suppose I may depend upon you?"

"That yer may to the backbone," protested Timothy Tootles, eagerly; "I'll die for yer, if yer vants me, Mister Jack."

"I wish no one to die for me, nor do I wish to die myself," replied our hero, as he approached the door, and threw it open.

Then, turning to his former comrade, he said—

"Go to the skipper, and tell him I'm not in my cabin, but on deck."

And with these words he went out and ascended the companion ladder.

"'Ow cool 'e takes it," thought Timothy; "vot a lot of pluck 'e's got."

CHAPTER XLIII.

PLOT AND COUNTERPLOT.

TIMOTHY TOOTLES, on returning to the skipper's cabin, found him quite prepared to receive his visitor.

He had removed the empty bottles, and placed fresh ones on the table.

"Vell," he said, as soon as he caught sight of his servant, "is der young shentlemans coming?"

"He isn't in his cabin, meinheer," replied Tim.

"Where is he den?"

"On deck, meinheer, I thinks."

"Vell, go and him find den," said Hans, in a growling tone.

Timothy disappeared quickly up the hatchway steps.

When he reached the deck, the wind was blowing freshly; he could just see the tall, shapely figure of Jack Barrington as he stood, talking to several sailors.

When Timothy approached, they left him.

"The skipper's wery anxious to see yer, Mister Jack," he said wistfully, "but——"

Our hero checked him as he said—

"I don't believe in 'buts' or 'ifs.' Listen to me."

Timothy Tootles listened with all his ears, whilst Jack spoke a few hasty words.

"All right," replied Tim at length.

"You understand?"

"Puffec'ly."

Jack Barrington then went below once more.

"Ah, mein tear young friend," exclaimed

Hans cordially, as he entered; "I am ver' glad to see you. Pray sit down."

Jack went straight to his seat, whilst the skipper quickly bolted the door and followed.

Our hero noted this act, and he said with a smile—

"I see you like to make all sure

"Eh? Ah! yos, yos," returned the Dutchman, in some little confusion at finding his guest had observed him; "besides, de vind blow der door open sometimes, you see."

Hans filled his pipe.

"You smoke, meinheer?" he asked.

"A cigar, thank you."

Lights being applied, and the clouds beginning to float upwards, the skipper passed one of the bottles to his visitor.

"Dis ees splendid sherry," he said.

"It looks capital," replied Jack.

"Eet ees capital; try eet."

Jack poured out a glass.

"Shall I fill for you?" he asked.

"Vell, no, tank you."

"Don't you drink then?"

"Not vine; it do not agree vid me. I shall drink schnapps."

He gave proof of this by pouring out a bumper of the fiery spirit.

"Goot hels, meinheer," he said, as he took a tremendous gulp.

Some time passed, during which the skipper and his guest chatted and smoked and drank.

The sherry in the decanter grew less and less, and still the young "shentlemans" was as lively as at first.

Hans was puzzled.

"He moss have got iron in his head instead of brains, to stand dat," he thought.

But the fact was, Jack had not swallowed a drop, having emptied the contents of his glass from time to time, when Hans was not looking, into the spittoon, instead of down his throat.

Still he seemed to drink, and at length the bottle was empty.

"*Teufels!*" growled Hans to himself, "he have swallow every drop, and it take no effect, not at all."

It was just as he was pondering upon this extraordinary circumstance he happened to look towards his guest.

His guest had his eyes fixed intently upon him.

So earnest was the gaze that the suspicion, if not the conscience, of the skipper was aroused.

"You look at me very earnestly, meinheer," he said, at length.

"Yes," returned Jack, without removing his glance, "I am wondering."

"Ah, inteed; vot about?"

"Whether you are an honest man, or a rogue."

"*Donder unt blitzen!*"

"Whether I can trust you."

"Ha, ha! what a droll idea!" laughed the Dutchman, who was beginning to feel particularly uncomfortable; "veder you can trust me, eh?"

"Yes."

"Vhy?"

"I'll tell you," said our hero, impressively.

He leant forward across the table, and in a voice of increased earnestness, continued—

"You have at this moment, on board your vessel, two cowardly and atrocious murderers."

"Mein Gott!" exclaimed the skipper, his eyes beginning to roll in his head, "you don't say so?"

"It's a fact; and I intend to capture them."

"You do?" gasped Hans.

"Yes."

"*Teufels!*" muttered the skipper.

"There is no better field, you know, for taking a pair of scoundrels prisoners than aboard ship, meinheer; they can't run away," said Jack, with a smile.

"Ha, ha! no; dat is true," returned Hans, with a ghastly grin; "dey can't run far."

"Therefore, you see, we are sure of our prey."

"We are sure," said the skipper. "Dey are your prey, not mine."

"You are the captain of this vessel, are you not?" asked Jack.

"Certainlee I am."

"And you are an honest man?"

"Vell, yos—of coorse."

"Very well, then, I expect your assistance."

"But——"

"Nay, more, I demand it!"

Before Hans Oudenwold had time to offer any objection, he found the muzzle of a pistol pointed at his head.

His jaw dropped hopelessly, as he sat gazing at it.

"Now then," said Jack coolly, "unless you wish me to seize you also, as an accomplice of the murderers, you will prepare to act as I direct."

The Dutchman groaned, and looked very much inclined to fall off his seat with perturbation.

"Vot do you vont me to do?" he gasped at length.

"Precisely as I tell you," Jack answered, "in which case you will keep your character as an honest man, and earn a hundred pounds."

These last two words produced an immediate revolution in the mind of the skipper.

"Von hondred pounds!" he exclaimed, all his embarrassment vanishing at once, and his eyes twinkling greedily.

"Yes! I promise you if these two scoundrels are handed over to justice, through your means, you shall have that sum."

"You vill give me your note of hand for dat?"

"This moment, if you can supply me with pen and ink."

"It is here," said the skipper, eagerly.

Jack at once wrote him a promissory note, payable at sight.

This quite satisfied Hans Oudenwold.

And he was now virtuously as indignant against the two murderers as he had a short time before been ready to assist them.

As for the fifty pounds he had received from them, he had forgotten all about it.

Hans entered into the plan of our hero with great alacrity.

*   *   *   *   *

A short time had elapsed, when a tap was

heard at the cabin occupied by Gasper Grimsby and his confederate.

"Who's there?" asked the drowsy voice of the latter.

"It ees me," answered the skipper; "are you avake?"

"Yes."

"Open der door, den."

The door was opened, and Hans went in.

The two occupants were terribly drowsy from the effects of the wine they had drunk, and looked as stupid as a pair of owls in the sunshine.

"All's ready," said the skipper.

"Is he fast off?" asked Gasper.

"Fast as a church, meinheer," answered Hans, chuckling; "I left him snoring like von peeg."

This intelligence roused up the muddled pair.

On entering the cabin, they found Jack Barrington stretched on the ground breathing heavily.

With malicious exultation, Gasper Grimsby and Caleb Corder stood looking down upon him.

"He'll do," remarked the latter, at length, with a chuckle, "and the sooner he's in the chest the better."

This receptacle stood in the corner of the skipper's cabin.

Gasper Grimsby taking a key from his pocket, unlocked it.

It had in it some straw and a quantity of old iron and lead, to ensure its sinking.

"Now then, in with him," said Gasper, impatiently; "lend a hand."

Raising the body between them, they placed it in the chest.

"A very nice snug box to travel in," grinned Caleb, without the least remorse, as he shut down the lid.

"Hist!" exclaimed Hans, in a sudden and somewhat startled tone; "hark!"

"What is it?" inquired Gasper.

"I fancy I hear voices on deck," replied the skipper. "You go an' see if der coast ees clear; ve don't vant any ozer eyes bote our own about."

"Certainly not," Gasper answered.

He and his companion hastily left the cabin, and were gone several minutes on their errand.

At length they returned.

"Is all quiet?" asked Hans.

"Quite. The men have gone below, and the night's as cloudy as if it had been made expressly for us."

"Dat's right," returned the skipper, as he locked the chest. "Goot-bye, mein tear young friend," he said, and going to the cabin window, he opened it, and threw the key into the waves.

"He find dat useful p'r'aps, if he vont to let himself out vhen he get to der bottom of der sea," he grinned.

At this excellent joke the two miscreants laughed aloud.

"And now for the launch," said Gasper, after he had finished his burst of fiendish merriment.

"Can we get it up the steps?" said Caleb Corder, looking at it ruefully. "It'll be precious heavy."

"Teufels! Yes. Ve shal. have to put our shouldare to der vheel to lift him."

"Come on," said Gasper; "all together with a will."

Opening the door, they dragged the chest out, and raising it by their united strength, succeeded at length in getting it to the top of the stairs.

Panting with their unwonted exertion, here they paused to rest awhile.

"Phew!" gasped Caleb; "it tries your muscles, doesn't it?"

"Never mind your muscles, when the fishes are waiting for their suppers," growled Gasper, grimly; "let's get it over."

By a second effort they dragged the ponderous chest to the side, and hoisted it on to the ship's side.

Here they supported it poised for an instant, and Gasper Grimsby exclaimed, derisively—

"Good bye, Gallant Jack, pride of the British Army, and a pleasant voyage to the bottom of the sea."

With these words, they tilted the chest over the side, and it fell with a heavy plunge into the dark waters.

The ominous sound had hardly passed away, the would-be murderers were still looking over the ship's bulwarks, when a bright light beamed around them, and a hand was laid upon each of their shoulders.

They turned quickly with a sudden terrified start.

A wild yell of horror and surprise burst from their throats.

There before them stood the man they thought in the depths of the ocean, Jack Barrington.

Around him were a body of sailors with lanterns.

On one side stood Hans Oudenwold, with a smile of virtuous complacency on his round, fat face.

For an instant there was a dead silence, during which the guilty men stood with distended eyes, and quivering lips, gazing awe-stricken at our hero, in doubt whether he was living or dead.

But his voice soon revealed the truth to them.

"Seize those murderers!" he cried.

Instantly two of the sailors sprang forward, and gripped them by the collars.

In spite of the nautical dress they wore, the culprits had no difficulty in recognizing in the disguised sailors the well-known features of Brian O'Flinn and Ned Rattles.

"It's run to earth ye are this time, you pair of venomous snakes," said Brian O'Flinn, with intense indignation.

But Gasper Grimsby, having recovered from the first shock of the surprise he had received, replied, in a tone of bravado—

"This is a very pretty piece of pantomime. But by what right do you pretend to arrest us? Have you turned warrant officers?"

"Oh, no," Brian answered; "but in order to make sure of yez this time, we've taken care to have the law on our side."

As he spoke, he looked over his shoulder and called—

"Step forward, gentlemen."

Two special constables advanced, with their staves in their hands.

And one, who held in his hand an official document, said—

"We arrest you, Gasper Grimsby, and you, Caleb Corder, in the name of the queen, on the several charges of murder and conspiracy. You are both our prisoners."

The accused ran their eyes moodily over the forms of the agents of the law.

They saw now there was no hope for them, and maintained a moody silence.

They were handcuffed, and without offering any resistance, conveyed below, and consigned to the darkness of the hold, till the vessel should reach port.

Their desperate plot against the life of our hero had been foiled, and his counterplot had afforded a convincing proof of their guilt, and nothing remained now but for the law to take its course.

The "Vrow Griet" reached the port of Amsterdam safely.

Our hero at once dispatched a note to the hotel, informing his mother of his arrival, and shortly after he bent his steps towards the Oude Doelen.

It was with a strange feeling of eagerness and anxiety he entered the hotel.

He was shown into a private room.

Whilst he waited there, who could attempt to describe his sensations, or the thousand conflicting thoughts that thronged into his breast?

After twelve years' separation, he was about to meet the mother he loved once more.

The delay until she came, although only a few moments, seemed an age.

At length he heard hurried footsteps without.

With throbbing heart, and every nerve in his body trembling with emotion, he beheld the door open.

The rustling of a silk dress was heard, and a handsome woman, of some thirty-five years of age, entered.

She was attired in black.

For a moment she stood silently gazing upon the manly, handsome young man before her.

He, as though unable or unwilling to break the stillness, remained gazing upon her.

At length the tears welled up into the eyes of both.

The lady's lips quivered, and in a faltering tone she murmured two words, two only—

"My son !"

But their magic was enough to break the spell.

"Mother !" burst forth from Jack's lips, as he sprang forward, and clasped his beloved parent to his heart.

There needed no further proof as to identity; the likeness between mother and son was sufficient, whilst the responsive voice of nature in their hearts bore witness to the ties that bound them together.

For a long time they could only sit gazing at each other, through tears of grateful joy.

And when at length they grew more com-

posed, how many questions were there to be asked and answered !

But as these would have little interest for the reader, let us leave the long-sundered relatives to themselves, whilst we return on board the " Vrow Griet."

*   *   *   *   *

It took several days to unload the sloop. It being determined to keep the prisoners on board, rather than transfer them to a gaol on land, they were removed to a cabin, in which they were strongly locked and barred, and guarded night and day by one of the constables, who was stationed at the door.

In one circumstance, Gasper Grimsby still triumphed.

The will of John Stanmore was missing.

It was not in Gasper's possession, but he knew where it could be found.

But on this point he was obstinately silent.

Neither threats nor entreaties could induce him to disclose where he had concealed it.

With mocking defiance, he taunted our hero with the assurance that not a farthing of the splendid legacy should ever come into the hands of his mother or himself.

The secret, he vowed, should die with him.

The thought was maddening, but there was no resource, and the operation of reloading being completed, Jack Barrington brought his mother on board the sloop, intending to take her back with him to England, Brian O'Flinn and Ned Rattles going with them.

The morning for sailing had arrived, when the constables suggested that the prisoners should be once more transferred to the hold of the vessel, that being the most secure place of confinement for criminals as desperate as they were.

This being determined on, the door of the cabin was unlocked.

The constables looked in, but fell back, utterly aghast.

The handcuffs lay on the floor.

But those who had worn them were no longer there.

A plank in the partition wall of the adjoining cabin had been removed during the night, and it was evident enough that through the aperture the culprits had effected their escape.

After all the trouble they had caused, they were still at large, still at liberty to devise schemes of evil.

The constables were full of chagrin.

Nor were our hero and his comrades less dismayed.

Brian O'Flinn was the first to recover himself.

" Don't fret about it, honey," he said to Jack ; " the divil gives his slaves a long chain sometimes, but he's shure to pull 'em up with a short turn at last."

Our hero could but smile wistfully and shake his head.

And Mrs. Barrington remarked—

" I have noticed that when events fall out in an unusually strange and unexpected manner there is always some sufficient reason for it."

" You think then, mother," said Jack, " that

"THE DUTCHMAN GROANED, AND LOOKED INCLINED TO FALL OFF HIS SEAT."

the escape of these scoundrels is permitted for some ultimate good?"

"I do, my dear boy," she replied. "I believe that in allowing these men to gain their liberty Providence may be carrying out some wise design which this event alone could accomplish."

Jack bowed his head in submissive deference to his parent's opinion, although in the heat of his disappointment he did not fully share her confidence in the certainty of retribution overtaking the villains.

But, afterwards, he had good reason to own that he was wrong, and that his mother was right.

CHAPTER XLIV.
A NIGHT ADVENTURE.

JACK BARRINGTON, on reaching England, was proud to introduce his mother to his noble patrons.

The Duke and Duchess of Marlborough received her with open arms, and showered every possible kindness and courtesy upon her.

Jack's beautiful betrothed fell in love with her the moment she saw her; and, having no mother of her own, adopted her instinctively from that time. There was another also who beheld Mrs. Barrington with strong admiration; this one being the Count Victor De Montsorel, who was a refugee in England. He well remembered the care he had experienced at her hands when he was helpless and wounded; and he sought now to return it by the most grateful friendship.

It was at this time that the torch of war between England and France was again to be lighted.

The first intelligence of this was brought to our hero by Sergeant Crank.

"The mounseers are going to give us a little more work, captain," he said to him one day.

"Is war declared, then?" Jack asked eagerly.

"It is; as sure as this boot's a boot," answered Benjamin, lifting up his foot.

His listener's countenance did not light up with its usual enthusiasm, and he replied in a coldly-resigned tone—

"I am ready, if it must be. I must postpone my marriage until after the battle—that is, if I live to be married at all."

"Live to be married! Of course you will, my dear boy, and so shall I to dance at your wedding!" exclaimed Benjamin, hilariously; "and I tell you what, your fair bride-elect will profit by the delay."

"How so?" Jack asked.

"Why, she'll marry a colonel instead of a captain, that's all."

The idea of promotion pleased our hero, and he smiled.

And now the news spread widely; north, south, east, and west—nothing was talked of but the forthcoming war.

Then came those frequently recurring episodes in a soldier's life. The sad partings—the bitter tears—the fervent prayers that the loved ones about to risk their lives in the service of their queen and country might be spared to return in safety and honour.

This last painful ordeal over, amidst the rolling of drums and the clang of trumpets, the British troops marched away to meet their foe.

* * * * *

The English army, with their German and Dutch allies, was commanded by Prince Eugene and the Duke of Marlborough.

It numbered about fifty-two thousand men, and was composed of troops who had long been familiar with victory; and who had seen the French, the Turks, and the Russians fly before them.

The French, with their Bavarian allies, amounted to sixty thousand, the majority of whom were veterans who had shared in the conquests of their *grand monarque* Louis XIV., and who were now commanded by the two most distinguished generals of the time, Marshal Tallard and the Duke of Bavaria.

Both armies, after many marchings and counter-marchings, approached each other.

The French were posted on a hill near the town of Hochstet.

Their right covered by the Danube and the village of Blenheim.

Their left by the village of Lutzengen, and their front by a rivulet, the banks of which were steep and the bottom marshy.

The right wing of the French was commanded by Marshal Tallard.

Their left by the Duke of Bavaria.

Their position being advantageous, they were willing to await the enemy, rather than offer battle.

Such were the relative positions of the forces as the sun went down upon the British lines.

Night shrouded the camp in darkness.

Our hero and his comrades were seated in one of the tents.

Amongst them a young German officer, Ernest Von Steinberg.

A capital fellow was he, who had made himself a general favourite by his genial temper and amiable manners.

But on this night it was observed that he was particularly silent.

He smoked his cigar without joining in the general conversation, whilst an expression of profound melancholy rested on his usually animated features.

"You seem out of spirits this evening, mein-herr," said Jack Barrington to him.

"Yes, I confess I am," he replied.

"May I ask the cause?"

"Oh, he's thinking of the darlin' fraulein he's left behind him," said Brian O'Flinn; "am I not right, honey?"

"Yes," returned Ernest, with a sad smile; "but that is not all."

"If it isn't a secret, would you object to tell us what is on your mind?" asked Ned Rattles.

The young German hesitated a moment, and then said—

"Well, then, I will."

He looked round at his companions as he asked—

"Have any of you ever had a warning?"

"A warning?" they echoed.

"Yes, I mean of some impending calamity."

"No," they replied.

"I have," said Ernest.

"What was it like ?" asked Brian.

Ernest continued—

"I was standing on the plain, watching the sunset this evening. Gradually it grew less and less distinct, till it faded away into the bosom of the ocean."

"Yes ?"

"I still lingered in the grey twilight thinking of my Adelaide, and wondering whether I should ever see her again."

"Very natural, too, under the circumstances," remarked the Irishman ; "but pray go on."

"It had grown almost dark, when suddenly I heard a deep sigh."

"The wind, perhaps," said Ned Rattles.

"No. I turned at the sound, and perceived at a short distance from me a figure, the exact counterpart of myself."

"That was strange," remarked our hero, much interested.

"I thought so, especially as it had a shadowy, unsubstantial appearance, like that of a spirit."

"Bedad, it's the first time I iver heard of one's seeing his own ghost," laughed Brian.

"Are you sure it wasn't fancy ?" inquired Jack Barrington.

"Quite sure ; and the moment after it was joined by another form."

"Who was that ?"

"Adelaide Von Sheben, my betrothed."

"Is it possible ?"

"The two shadowy forms stood speaking together. Suddenly I heard a report as of a cannon ; one fell to the ground with a cry of pain."

"Which one ?" asked everybody eagerly.

"That which resembled myself, and the form of Adelaide knelt down, and clasped it in her arms."

"Yes."

"After a few moments, I heard a clock strike three, when they both faded away."

"And you saw them no more ?"

"No."

"And what do you infer from this ?" asked Jack.

"That my death is determined, and the hour," said Ernest. "I believe that at three o'clock to-morrow, I shall be no longer in this world," was the solemn response.

There was so much deep seriousness in the tone and look of the speaker, that all present were greatly impressed.

Just at that moment Sergeant Crank entered the tent.

Having saluted, he said—

"Captain Barrington and Lieutenant Rattles, the duke desires to see you."

The young soldiers rose at once and left the tent.

"Well, my dear boys," said the commander-in-chief, as they appeared before him. "I know you are always pleased to be entrusted with commissions of importance."

Jack and his comrade bowed at this compliment.

"What can we do now, general ?" they asked, eagerly.

"I wish to gain some intelligence of the enemy's plans. And I must depend upon you to procure it."

"Your grace shall not be disappointed," said Jack. "Before midnight you shall know all that can be known."

"Go then and prosper," said the duke, encouragingly, "and remember, after this battle is over, there is promotion for those who distinguish themselves."

And with a kind smile he dismissed them.

"Sergeant Crank was right," laughed Ned Rattles. "You'll be a colonel before you're a husband."

In a few moments they were in their saddles, and making their way as rapidly as possible, consistent with caution, towards the village of Lutzengen, which flanked the enemy's left wing.

The night was misty, and they had to listen from time to time in order that they might not come unprepared upon a body of French scouts.

They had been on the road for a couple of hours without encountering any adventure.

"I'm afraid we're not destined to pick up any important intelligence whatever," said our hero, at length, to his comrade.

"So it seems," replied Ned Rattles.

"I should be sorry to return without some information ; we should lose our characters for vigilance."

"That would never do. But how is the information to be arrived at ?" Ned asked.

"We must get as near as possible to the enemy's outposts."

"All right, there's plenty of fog to screen us."

"And if we're challenged by a sentinel, we can both of us mumble a few words of German."

"Yah, meinherr !" laughed Ned.

Hardly had he said this, when he received a check from his comrade.

"Hush ! don't you see a light glimmering yonder ?"

"Where ?"

"Right ahead."

"Yes," answered Ned, "I think I do."

"I'm sure I do," said Jack, eagerly. "Let's push on, but be cautious."

Walking their steeds, they rode forward.

They found as they drew nearer, that the light they had seen came from a fire that had been kindled at the entrance of a wood.

Round the fire were seated several French dragoons, their horses being tethered to the branches near them.

Very cautiously keeping behind the trunks, our adventurers approached sufficiently close to see and hear all that was going on.

The men were smoking their pipes and solacing themselves with cheap brandy which they drank from a flask.

"When are we going to begin fighting ?" asked one.

"Parbleu ! we are not going to begin at all, I think," replied another.

"How is that ?"

"Why, old Tallard knows when he has a good position. And it's my opinion he'll stay where he is and let our foes open the ball."

"It all depends on the answer he receives from General Villeroy."

"Our captain has gone for it, has he not?"

"Yes; and he ought to have returned ere this."

"If he hasn't fallen into the hands of the *maudits Anglais*."

"The marshal must be anxious to receive this answer, I should think."

"You are right. If it be favourable, he won't forget to reward the messenger, depend on it."

As these words were spoken, one of the dragoons, who had been lolling in the background listening attentively, rose, and creeping to his horse, mounted it and rode quietly off.

But quickly as he had done this, our hero had time to recognise him, and he exclaimed, excitedly, in an undertone—

"Caleb Corder, as I live."

"Are you sure?" said Ned Rattles.

"Yes, I'll swear to him."

"If we could take him prisoner, that would be something, wouldn't it?"

"I don't think he's worth the trouble," Jack replied; "but it strikes me, from the sneaking manner in which he left his companions, that he meditates some manœuvre."

"Shall we follow and see?"

"Yes, this way."

They walked their horses on in the direction Caleb had taken.

"I tell you what I mean to do if I can," said Jack, presently.

"What?"

"Get hold of the letter from General Villeroy. You may depend that would be of importance to the Duke of Marlborough."

"No doubt. Well, all that will have to be done, will be to intercept the French captain, and make him disgorge his prize."

"Which I most decidedly will if I can manage to come across him."

They kept on, guided by the sound of the hoofs of the horse ridden by Caleb Corder.

Suddenly the latter stopped, and reining in his steed beneath a tree, awaited there.

This compelled those who followed him to stop too.

"What the deuce is he up to?" asked Ned Rattles.

"Some rascally trick, no doubt," answered Jack.

"Suppose we get a little nearer; I'm curious to know. Gently!"

Proceeding very cautiously, they got within twenty yards of the crafty Caleb.

He kept on his saddle, little dreaming who was so near him.

They had not waited long, when the sound of another horse's hoofs became audible.

At the sound Caleb Corder became on the alert immediately, and he snatched a pistol from one of the holsters.

The steps of the approaching steed became now more distinct, and presently the moon shining out through the darkness, revealed the face and form of Captain Gravellotte.

This unexpected meeting of these two scoundrels at such a time, and under such circumstances, was so strange and unexpected that Jack Barrington could only sit and gaze in silence.

On rode the captain at full speed, till he passed the tree where his quondam comrade waited for him.

Then suddenly the latter raised his pistol and fired.

The horse reared up with a snort of agony, and fell prostrate to the ground, dragging his rider with him.

In an instant Caleb Corder had leaped from his saddle, and sprung like a panther upon the bewildered half-stunned captain.

In an instant he had cut the strap of the leather letter bag he carried across his chest; and snatched from it the letter it contained.

"Hurrah!" he muttered, exultingly; "all's fair in love and war—my fortune's made!"

But he was premature in his self-congratulation.

For as he sprang to his feet the letter was suddenly snatched from his grasp, and he received a straightforward blow between the eyes from Jack Barrington's fist that floored him like a dead log.

"The scoundrel is silenced for a time," cried our hero, looking at Caleb.

"Could we manage to take them with us?" asked Ned eagerly.

"We'll try, anyhow," returned Jack.

But just at that moment, the sound of voices in the distance caught their ears, and they had barely time to get under some of the trees, when the dragoons came galloping up to the spot.

Without waiting to see what followed, our adventurers hurried away as quickly as possible.

"Our journey hasn't been fruitless after all," cried Jack; "we've got the letter."

"We have!" echoed Ned Rattles; "hurrah"

And spurring their steeds, they dashed ⟨ wards.

CHAPTER XLV.
CAPTURED.

ON reaching the English lines, our hero and his comrade hastened at once to the tent of the Duke of Marlborough.

The eyes of the general sparkled with satisfaction as he perused the intercepted letter.

"You have done excellently, my young friends," he exclaimed, warmly.

He held forth the paper as he continued—

"From this dispatch, I understand that Marshal Villeroy is preparing to cut off all communication between our forces and the Rhine."

He paused in silence for a moment, and then, looking towards our hero, said to him—

"I must dispatch you on another enterprise."

"I shall be willing and proud to undertake it, your grace," answered Jack, eagerly.

"I am quite sure of that," returned the general, flatteringly; "and have, moreover, every confidence in your tact and courage to carry it out successfully."

Jack bowed low at the compliment, and asked—

"When are we to start?"

"If you are not too fatigued, the sooner the better."

"I am not fatigued in the least," said our hero.

"Nor I," joined in Ned Rattles.

"Very good; then my wish is that you should start at once."

"What are our instructions?" Jack inquired.

"You will make your way to the Rhine; approach as near as possible—without risk of discovery—to the banks, and bring me word what preparations are on foot to hem us in. Haste! for every moment is of consequence."

"We will be in the saddle in less than half an hour, general," Jack assured the duke.

It took our heroes but a short time to swallow their supper, and having provided themselves with what they deemed necessary for their enterprise, they procured fresh horses and started once more.

*   *   *   *   *

The principal incident related in the former chapter will afford one among the many proofs that thoroughly bad men cannot be true even to each other.

Caleb Corder and Gasper Grimsby had become partners in crime.

At first they stood in the relation of master and servant to each other; but as time went on the difference of position was dropped, and they came to regard one another as equals.

Having escaped from the cabin of the Dutch sloop, they had made their way back to France, and war having broken out again, they found plenty of employment.

Caleb began to be seized with an ambition to rise in the world.

He had no scruples as to how he should accomplish this.

Whether by sacrificing his colleague or any-one else.

It was then the opportunity arrived by which Caleb fancied he would be able to bring himself into notice.

By striking down his comrade on the road and robbing him of his dispatch, he felt he should gain his end.

As it happened, however, all he got for his pains was to be knocked down himself and to lose the prize he coveted.

So suddenly had the blow been struck that Caleb could hardly distinguish the form of the striker, but he fancied he recognized Jack Barrington; and whether his suspicions were true or not, he hated him more vindictively than ever, and the bitter thought of his heart was—

"Oh, that I might find him where I might get a fair blow at him, a blow that would send him out of the world at once and for ever."

As for Gasper Grimsby, shaken as he was by his fall and bewildered by the suddenness of the attack, he could not positively swear to the identity of his assailant.

Yet still he had a kind of glimmering perception that it was Caleb Corder who had caused his failure.

But when the dragoons arrived, and he rose to his feet and found Caleb stretched half stunned upon the ground, he hardly knew what to think.

Caleb was quite ready with his account.

He had—so he declared to him—witnessed the attack made by a party of English troopers, headed, as he believed, by Jack Barrington.

That, having shot down his horse, the leader had wrested the despatch from his pouch.

In endeavouring to prevent this act of spoliation, he—Caleb—had himself received the blow which had laid him senseless.

With this explanation, whether it satisfied him or not, Gasper Grimsby was compelled to be content.

And then came the question—how was the disaster to be remedied?

"There's only one way," said Caleb, when he came thoroughly to the use of his faculties.

"What is that?" asked Gasper; "to pursue the robbers?"

"No; to return by the way you came."

"To the Rhine?"

"Yes."

"Umph! to say I've been plundered of the despatch, and that it has fallen into the hands of the English? A pretty account to give to Marshal Villeroy," growled Gasper, gloomily.

"You wouldn't be quite such a fool as to tell him that, I should think," said Caleb.

"How can I account, then, for its loss?"

"You can say the strap of your knapsack gave way, and that you left it behind in the forest."

"Ah, true; I might say that," replied Gasper.

"Of course you might; who could dispute it?" rejoined Caleb. "If you take my advice, you'll start at once. I'll accompany you, if you like."

Gasper made no objection, and being supplied with a fresh horse in the place of his own wounded steed, he and his treacherous comrade started for the Rhine, the object being to obtain a fresh despatch from Marshal Villeroy.

On they went through the darkness.

*   *   *   *   *

The grey dawn was breaking, when from out a wood near the Rhine there emerged two young men, evidently, from their dress, French peasants.

None would have suspected they were not what they appeared, had not one of them drawn a telescope from beneath his blouse, and commenced reconnoitring the river's banks, which already appeared alive with troops.

"They evidently mean stopping the English here," remarked one, after a moment.

"If they can," added the other.

"I tell you what I've a mind to do."

"What?"

"Our horses are safe in the wood."

"Quite."

"And our disguises perfect."

"Yes."

"Well, then, I think we may safely venture a little nearer, and try and pick up a little decided information."

"I think so, too. We can't fail, especially as you speak French like a native."

"Come on, then."

And with these words, Jack Barrington and Ned Rattles—for it was they—walked forward towards the river.

It was evident, as they approached, that determined preparations were on foot to block up all communication or supplies from reaching the English by the way of the Rhine ; and observing a group of French grenadiers standing together, our heroes sauntered up to them, throwing an expression of innocent curiosity into their faces.

"*Ma foi, messieurs!*" exclaimed Jack, in a well-assumed *patois;* "are you going to empty the river?"

"No, my boy," returned one of the grenadiers ; "we are rather going to fill it."

"Fill it?" was the wondering reply ; "what with—stones?"

"No, no ; with impediments."

"Impediments ; we don't understand."

"Do you understand this?" asked one of the grenadiers, as he advanced his musket with its bayonet fixed at the end of the muzzle.

"Ah, yes ; we understand that."

"And so will the English," returned the soldier, "when they find the Rhine banks bristling with French bayonets."

"Backed by arguments such as those," interjected one of the soldier's comrades, pointing to a number of pieces of ordnance that were being placed at intervals in front of the river ; "our foes will know they are not to pass. Do you see now?"

"Oh, yes, we see now," said the fictitious peasants, affecting to be very much enlightened ; "the *grande armée* will gain the victory, eh?"

"*Sans doute — sans doute,*" returned the grenadier, confidently, smoothing his moustache ; "our troops have got a fine position, they are masters of the situation. *Comprenez-vous?*—do you understand?"

"Not quite," said Jack, shaking his head.

"Ah, *imbécile,*" cried his instructor, indignantly ; "what fools you peasants are."

Our heroes, admitting the fact, humbly asked—

"Where is the *grande armée* posted?"

"On the hill of Hochstet," explained the soldier, exultingly ; "*une position magnifique,* guarded on all sides."

"Ha, ha! yes ; old Tallard knows what he is about," joined in the rest with equal enthusiasm.

"Then I suppose, having this magnificent position, the marshal will not make the attack?" said Jack, inquiringly.

"*Certainement non;* he will remain on the height and wait for the foe to attack him."

"Suppose they won't attack?"

"Well, then he will wait, tire them out, starve them ; you see, that is why he is going to block up the passage across the river ; our enemies will not be able to procure supplies ; ha, ha! *c'est une grande idée, n'est-ce pas?* ha, ha, ha!"

"Ha, ha, ha! capital!" joined in the peasants, apparently quite delighted at what they heard.

"*Vive le* Maréchal Tallard!" cried the Frenchmen unanimously ; "no one can equal him."

"They say there is one on the English side who is far superior," Jack remarked, quietly.

"Who is that?"

"The Duke of Marlborough."

"*Parbleu,* no! You will see he will eat up this Engleesh duke and his followers, as a crane would swallow a lot of frogs."

The peasants laughed at the idea, being pretty confident, in their own minds, who the frogs were that were to be so unceremoniously doomed.

Just at this moment the sound of horses' hoofs was heard, and a captain of dragoons, accompanied by another, galloped up and sprang from their saddles.

These were the renegade Captain Gasper Grimsby and his colleague Caleb Corder ; our heroes recognised them at once.

"Phew!" murmured Jack ; "who'd have thought of seeing them here?"

"What's to be done?" whispered Ned Rattles.

"Nothing, keep still ; evince no concern ; ten to one they won't notice us."

This seemed very probable, as both the new comers appeared to be occupied with their own matters.

"Where is Marshal Villeroy?" asked Gasper of the soldiers.

"In his tent, *capitaine,*" answered one of the grenadiers ; "he is giving audience to a visitor, who only arrived from Paris this morning."

"Do you know who the visitor is?" Gasper inquired.

"Monsieur le Comte Victor Montsorel," returned the soldier.

"How strange!" whispered Jack Barrington, pressing his comrade's arm as he caught the name.

"I have particular and important business with the marshal, and must see him at once," said Gasper.

Then turning towards Caleb Corder, he said—

"Come!"

But the latter took no notice of the injunction.

His attention was absorbed in the two peasants, on whom his eyes were riveted.

"What are you staring at?" asked Gasper, as he plucked him by the sleeve.

"Hush!" he exclaimed in a sharp whisper ; "there's something to make you stare!"

"Where?"

"Yonder!"

Gasper looked in the direction towards which his comrade nodded.

He started violently, and a vivid flush rushed into his sallow face, as he answered—

"Jack Barrington ; and disguised too!"

"Yes!" almost hissed Caleb in his ear ; "the same that shot your horse, and robbed you of the dispatch."

"His course is run then," returned Gasper. "He shall find that in coming here he has run into the lion's den."

Then, suddenly pointing to our heroes who, conscious of their critical position, stood with averted faces talking together a short distance off, he shouted loudly—

"Arrest those fellows ; they are English spies!"

With an indignant yell the grenadiers rushed upon them.

It was too late to retreat ; resistance against

such overpowering numbers would have been worse than useless.

The next moment Jack and his comrade found themselves in the grasp of their enemies.

They uttered not a word in self-defence. Neither did Gasper Grimsby make any accusation against them at the time.

All he said to those who held them was—

"Bring them after me to the marshal's tent."

He then walked on himself, whilst the prisoners followed in the midst of their custodians.

"This looks ominous, I'm afraid," said Jack to his comrade, as they walked along.

"I am afraid so too," Ned replied.

"Well, it can't be helped. It's only one of the freaks of *la fortune de la guerre.*"

"We mustn't look for much favour here."

"I don't expect any, and am prepared for the worst."

"So am I."

"Remember one thing; when we are questioned, as we certainly shall be, keep a silent tongue."

"I will; depend upon it."

"Explain nothing; confess nothing that may give our foes any advantage."

"Not a word."

"Then if we are shot, we shall at least die knowing that we have done our duty."

"Hurrah! Long live the queen!" cried Lieutenant Rattles, loyally.

"And the Duke of Marlborough!" joined in Captain Barrington.

CHAPTER XLVI.
THE PLACE OF EXECUTION.

La fortune de la guerre, or the fortune of war, has many vicissitudes.

Our heroes had already experienced some of these, and they were now called upon to endure another more perilous, perhaps, than any that had preceded it. Surrounded by enemies who were embittered by continual defeats, they had everything to fear and little to hope; but the young soldiers evinced no shadow of trepidation, and as they stood waiting outside the tent till they should be summoned to the presence of the commander-in-chief, the grenadiers who guarded them could not help admiring the cool *nonchalance* they exhibited.

At length the order was brought that the prisoners should be admitted.

The next moment they stood in the presence of Marshal Villeroy.

The marshal peered sternly at them through his half-closed eyes, as though he would have probed their very thoughts if he could.

Had he possessed this power he would not have been greatly flattered at the disclosure he would have arrived at, for both Jack and Ned were thinking at that moment how like an old baboon in regimentals the marshal looked.

After scanning them in silence for some time, the marshal exclaimed suddenly—

"So you are English, you two?"

"We are, monsieur," was the reply.

"Officers, I am informed?"

"Yes."

"Your being found in the French camp dis-

guised, is sufficient proof as to your motive in venturing there; you are spies?"

No answer.

"You have been dispatched to watch our proceedings?"

No answer.

"Which you are commissioned to take back to the Duke of Marlborough. Is it not so?"

No answer.

"You are, of course, aware of the punishment due to those who come prying amongst us with sinister motives?"

Still no answer.

"I will tell you this, since you are so doggedly silent; the penalty is—death!"

This elicited a reply from our hero.

"You must first prove us to be spies," he said.

"We have proof sufficient," responded the marshal. "Did you not rob this gentleman of an important despatch?"

As he spoke he indicated Gasper Grimsby, who stood by, by a motion of his head.

"I see no gentleman," returned Jack.

"*Parbleu!* You must be very short-sighted then," exclaimed the marshal; "why, you are looking at him now."

"I am looking at a scoundrel," replied our hero, his eyes flashing with the fiercest indignation.

"What say you?" cried Marshal Villeroy, starting from his seat. "Do you dare call an officer in the French army a scoundrel?"

"I dare to call anyone a scoundrel who deserves the title," returned Jack boldly, "and I denounce that man not only as a scoundrel, but as a robber and a murderer!"

As he uttered these words, he fixed his eyes full of withering scorn upon the renegade captain.

Gasper Grimsby turned livid with rage.

"The fellow lies!" he gasped in a scarcely audible tone.

"*Assurément!*" cried the marshal, crimson with rage; "but we will soon set this matter right. These men are spies and shall be shot without delay. Order a dozen men to be in readiness for their execution, which I leave to you to see carried out."

With an evil gleam of exultation in his face that made him look perfectly demoniac, Gasper Grimsby left the tent.

He had scarcely departed when a soldier entered with a message to the marshal, who replied—

"Tell the comte I will attend him instantly."

He then turned to the sergeant of the grenadiers, and having commanded him to look well to the prisoners, he went out.

The period intervening between the sentence of death and its fulfilment is to most an awful pause, and it was not different in the case of our heroes.

But the doom they were to meet was no more than they expected, and so they offered a silent prayer to Heaven to prepare them for the momentous change, and calmly awaited the time of execution.

"I should like to have been able to send a farewell message to my comrades," said Jack, after a time, "and," he added, his lips quivering slightly, "to dear Flora."

"And I, too," said Ned Rattles, "but that seems impossible."

"Nothing's impossible," returned our hero, suddenly recovering his self-possession.

Taking his companion by the hand, he continued—

"Remember we are accused by a man whose character is odious in the sight of God and man."

"Bu that does not make our condition any the more favourable," remarked Ned.

"I think it does," Jack replied; "and desperate as our case seems at this moment, I do not despair."

"Have you any reason to hope?" asked his comrade.

"Yes."

"On what grounds?"

"Heaven's justice! I believe God will not permit us who are simply performing our duty, to fall a victim to the vindictive malice of Gasper Grimsby."

"He was permitted to kill your father," said Ned Rattles, seriously.

"True, he was. But that is no reason he should be allowed to destroy his son."

"You expect that some miracle will be vouchsafed then in our behalf, do you?" asked Ned, with a faint smile of incredulity.

"Oh, no," returned Jack; "if Heaven wills that we are to be saved, it will be brought about by natural, not miraculous means."

His comrade was less hopeful, and only shook his head; and at the same time the rolling of the drums was heard without.

"You know what those sounds mean?" said Ned. "Are they not ominous?"

"Not to my mind. I don't consider myself any nearer my end, because I hear them," replied Jack, calmly; "I have often listened to them on the battle field, and still lived."

"Well, we shall see," said Ned, who marvelled at his friend's confidence.

"Yes, old fellow, we shall, and pretty quickly now, for I hear the tramp of the guard outside."

Hardly had our hero spoken these words when Gasper Grimsby stalked into the tent.

The same evil, bitter smile was on his face as he cried—

"Conduct the spies to execution!"

At once the soldiers who had been left to guard the condemned formed into order, and the prisoners being pinioned, were placed between the ranks and marched out.

On emerging into the open air it was much lighter.

At no great distance, the young Englishmen could see a compact body of grenadiers leaning on their muskets, and they knew full well they were to be their doomsmen.

The drums still continued to beat as they marched slowly forward.

On their way they passed another group, this being the Marshal Villeroy and his visitor, surrounded by a staff of officers, who watched the condemned men as they wended their way to the place of execution.

They came to a stop here for a moment, and the drums ceased whilst the commander-in-chief gave a few directions to Gasper Grimsby.

During this brief interval Jack Barrington looked with calm steadiness at the faces of this assembly.

Suddenly he started as he recognised amongst them one he knew well.

It was the visitor of the marshal who had thus attracted him, and who proved to be the Count Victor De Montsorel.

The friend of our hero and his mother.

How the count should have come there, or what brought him to that spot at that moment, we need not pause to inquire.

There he was, his handsome features contracted into an expression of regret at the thought of what was about to take place.

It was quite evident he did not recognise Jack Barrington in his peasant's costume, and after glancing a moment at the mournful *cortége*, he turned his head away as though the sight was displeasing to him.

In vain Jack looked earnestly towards the spot where he stood.

He did not look round again, and the rattle of the drums being resumed, rendered any attempt on Jack's part to call him by name hopeless.

But suddenly our hero bethought him of the ring which the Count Victor had presented to him years before, in the poor cottage at Nimeguen, and which he had never parted with.

Quickly he thrust his hand into the inner pocket of his vest, and drew forth the ring.

Just as he was doing this, the order was heard—

"Forward!"

In something like desperation, Jack sought to leave the ranks.

But his malignant foe, who never removed his eyes from him, prevented him with his drawn sword.

"Coward, villain!" murmured Jack bitterly; "your day of retribution will be a bitter one for this."

Gasper answered him only with a mocking smile, and bade him roughly—

"March on."

"Would I could convey this ring to the count," thought our hero, as he slowly moved forward; "it would save our lives."

Just at that moment they passed a group of French dragoons.

Jack observed that one of them looked earnestly at them, with an expression of deepest sympathy in his face, as though he knew him.

After an instant's reflection he remembered his features.

It was Jeannot Roussel—Fanchette's Jeannot.

Suddenly an idea flashed across his brain, and he held out the ring as well as he could towards him.

Jeannot seemed to comprehend, and took it at once, inquiring—

"For whom?"

"The Comte Victor Montsorel," Jack answered, joyfully. "Haste; life or death hangs upon it."

All this passed so rapidly as to effectually frustrate any attempt to stop it.

Jeannot had disappeared with the ring.

Whilst amidst the rattle of drums, the procession with monotonous regularity of tread moved onwards.

* * * * *

The Comte De Montsorel was standing thoughtfully a little aloof from the rest of the party, when Jeannot came hurrying up to him and placed the ring in his hand.

The nobleman glanced at it, and his features in an instant lighted up with intense eagerness.

"Who gave you this?" he asked, quickly.

"Jack Barrington," was the eager answer.

"Where is he?"

"Yonder, on his way to death!"

A cry of horror burst from the count's lips.

"Merciful Heaven!" he exclaimed, "this must not be."

At once he rushed through the throng to Marshal Villeroy.

"My dear friend!" he cried, excitedly; "I entreat you to stop, or, at least, suspend this execution."

"*Mais pourquoi, mon cher comte?*—why, my dear comte?" asked the commander, shrugging his shoulders.

"Because this young Englishman, whom you would send to an untimely grave, is an honour to his country and humanity," the count replied.

And then, briefly, but vividly, he narrated the incident of his preservation.

"You must save him for my sake, marshal," he cried as he concluded, in a tone of strong entreaty.

"*Morbleu!* if it is as you say, the young man certainly deserves a better fate than shooting," the marshal replied. "Let us go forward."

* * * * *

The cortége had reached the scene of execution.

The party who were to fire stood with their muskets in their hands.

The prisoners were conducted to the fatal spot, and ordered to kneel.

"All's over," murmured Jack, with a sigh; "the ring must have miscarried."

"Make ready!" shouted the eager voice of Gasper Grimsby.

The rattle of the muskets sounded ominously in the ears of the victims.

"Present!" cried the vindictive captain.

The crisis of doom seemed to have arrived, but ere the last fatal order could be given to "fire," a loud shout was heard.

"*Arrêtez!*—stop the execution!"

It was the marshal's voice, and at the sound the grenadiers lowered their muskets.

The prisoners sprang to their feet.

Gasper Grimsby, pale and baffled, and chafing like a bloodhound who has been suddenly held back when he has scented blood, muttered a fierce oath, whilst Marshal Villeroy and Victor De Montsorel, accompanied by the staff, galloped up to the spot.

At once the count dropped from his saddle, and rushing towards our hero, clasped him to his heart with all the warmth of paternal affection.

A moment after Jack and his comrade were unbound, and Marshal Villeroy said to them—

"Messieurs, you are free; thanks to the in-

tercession of the Comte De Montsorel. Take my advice, mount your horses, and begone at once, while you are safe."

Having thanked the commander for his clemency, and spoken a few words to his kind friend, Jack left the spot, accompanied by his comrade.

With hasty steps they plunged into the wood, and mounting their steeds, paused not till they had left the Rhine banks far behind them.

Their enterprise, though it had so nearly proved fatal to themselves, had been the means of securing valuable information.

So much so, that the Duke of Marlborough, after listening to it, said briefly—

"Very good, indeed; we commence the attack to-morrow."

CHAPTER XLVII.

A NIGHT'S ADVENTURE.

THE night closed in misty and chill, when a young girl, with faltering, weary step, might have been seen making her way along the road leading towards the village of Blenheim.

At length, having reached a spot where the routes ceased, she paused, as though uncertain which way to proceed.

"Oh, would, would I could reach the English camp!" she exclaimed aloud, in earnest accents; "Heaven guide me!"

She had hardly said the words when the sound of horses' hoofs and the rattle of military accoutrements were heard.

These sounds became rapidly more and more distinct.

It was evident the steeds were approaching. But the gloom of night was such as to prevent the fair pedestrian from discerning the forms of the riders, or from being able to ascertain from their uniforms under which flag they served.

The young girl, from her accent when she uttered her brief soliloquy, was unmistakably English. But alone in that solitary spot she hesitated to apply for guidance, fearing to encounter some rude, licentious trooper, whose companionship might be far more perilous than the darkness and the silence of the dreary road; accordingly, as the horsemen drew near, she remained crouching behind a tree, with her ears listening intently to catch, if possible, the sound of their voices.

If she could discover that they were her own countrymen, she would not then hesitate to trust herself to their honour and humanity.

This was soon made palpable, for they were talking rather loudly as they passed.

What they said she did not particularly notice; it was sufficient for her that they spoke the English language, and advancing from her place of concealment, she called to arrest their attention—

"Gentlemen!"

The horsemen checked their steeds at this appeal, and one of them called in reply—

"Who speaks?"

"Someone who doesn't know us evidently," chuckled his comrade, facetiously.

"It should be a woman by the voice," remarked the first inquirer.

And then he cried again—

"Who is it?"

"An English girl and a stranger," was the reply, uttered in a timid, but singularly sweet tone.

"Where are you?"

"Here, at the side of the road."

The next moment a lantern flashed its rays through the darkness, revealing the well-known forms of Gasper Grimsby and Caleb Corder.

Presently the light which was in the hand of the former fell upon a girlish figure, enveloped in a cloak, the hood of which was drawn over her head.

In spite of this not particularly becoming attire it was easy to see that she whom it covered had the manner and bearing of a lady, and that she was also beautiful. The sombre colour of the garment she wore brought out in more distinct contrast the clear paleness of her complexion, whilst her dark eyes, with their wistful, anxious, upturned glances, had in them a wondrous power of fascination.

Gasper Grimsby gazed at her in a kind of reflecting, dreamy manner, like one in a trance. Those dark, expressive orbs had set him thinking; they reminded him of another face he knew. At length, coming out of his reverie, he said to the young lady—

"May I ask if you have travelled far?"

"Yes; from Paris."

"Paris!" echoed Gasper, in much surprise; "you must have some strong motive for coming such a distance alone and unprotected."

"That is just it; I have a strong—a very strong motive."

"May I inquire what it may be?"

"I am seeking a mother and a brother, from whom I have been severed for years."

"And know you where to find them?"

"Alas, no! but I think if I could once reach the English camp, I might, perhaps, be able to get some information there of those I love."

"I am an Englishman, and if you will condescend to tell me your name, perhaps I may be able to direct you in your search."

"Oh, thank you, most generous soldier!" exclaimed the young girl with grateful earnestness; "my name is Barrington—Lydia Barrington."

Gasper Grimsby's heart began to throb violently at these words in spite of himself. No wonder her face was familiar to him; but subduing his excitement, by a strong effort he replied—

"I know your brother well; and if you will place yourself under my protection, I will conduct you to the camp myself."

"I shall be most happy to do so," said Lydia, with entire confidence; "and I thank Heaven that permitted me to meet you as I was beginning to lose my way."

"You must be fatigued," remarked Gasper; "let me lift you up into my saddle; it will give you a rest."

Without the least hesitation the young girl consented, and Gasper, bending down, placed his arm round her waist, and raising her up, placed her before him on his saddle.

But had Lydia Barrington known the man who thus supported her, she would have shrunk from him as from the clutch of a fiend.

It was evident that Gasper intended to take the fair wanderer to the French camp, where he would detain her under plausible pretences until the battle was over.

It was necessary for his plans that he should discover the retreat of Ruth Barrington, and he felt that whilst he held possession of her daughter, he had in his hand a powerful instrument for that end.

One thing he was fully resolved upon, and that was to make Ruth his wife by fair means or foul, since it was only in this way he could lay hands upon the property.

That property left her by that dead parent, whose last will and testament Gasper had safely in his hands.

It was with a certain kind of desperate satisfaction he guided his steed along the gloomy road, with his confiding charge before him.

Her head almost resting upon the breast beneath which throbbed the heart that was all the time full of evil designs against herself and those she loved.

Caleb Corder followed with a peculiarly sinister smile upon his features.

He had acted as jackal to the lion long enough, he thought, and had now resolved to secure some pickings for himself.

He had already made one determined attempt in this direction, and though it had failed, he was not by any means disheartened, but vowed inwardly to try again at the first opportunity.

The two confederates in crime went along in the gloom, each planning in his short-sighted folly the game he was to play, ignorant that fate was quietly directing their course towards the dark abyss, over which in stern characters was written the end.

* * * *

They had proceeded some distance, when the voice of one of the sentinels on the outposts challenged them.

"*Qui va là?*—who goes there?" he asked.

"*Soldats Français!*—French soldiers."

"*Le passe parole?*—the password?"

"Tallard and Eugene!" answerd Gasper.

"*C'est bon!* it s good!" was the reply, and they passed on.

It struck Lydia, who understood French perfectly, as strange that English soldiers should give their signals in the language of their foes, and she asked why her conductor had done so.

The question seemed somewhat embarrassing to him, for he did not at once reply.

But Caleb Corder, who heard her words, answered for him—

"We give and take the signals in French, miss, in order to blind our enemies if they should come upon us in the dark."

"Yes, that is the reason," joined in Gasper, glad to be able to creep out of the difficulty.

"The man who just now spoke to you was a Frenchman, evidently," remarked Lydia thoughtfully.

"Yes, and if I had not replied as I did, he would have given the alarm, and we should in a few seconds have been surrounded, and perhaps shot."

At this the young girl shuddered slightly.

But she was well educated, and not entirely

ignorant of military customs, and she remarked after a moment—

"It seems to argue much carelessness in discipline, does it not, that the French should allow the English to become acquainted with their watchword?"

This was another rather pointed question.

So much so that it made Caleb Corder relax from his moody frown and grin considerably, as he muttered to himself—

"These Barringtons are a deuced sharp family."

All that Gasper Grimsby replied to Lydia's inquiry was the cool remark—

"The French soldiers are proverbially careless."

The young girl said no more.

But presently they encountered on the road a body of French cavalry.

In an instant the lanterns of the troop were turned upon them.

"Ah, Captain Gravelotte, it is you, then?" said the leader to Gasper, as he recognised him.

Captain Gravelotte frowned, and muttered something under his teeth, and was moving on, when the other caught sight of the cloaked figure, from beneath the hood of which the fair face and dark eyes of Lydia Barrington peered anxiously forth, and he exclaimed—

"*Parbleu!*—what angel is that?"

"She is a young lady," almost growled Gasper, "whom I am taking to the camp."

"*Ma foi*, she is lovely. Whose friend is she —the marshal's, or Prince Eugene's?"

"She is mine," snarled Gasper, fiercely, as he spurred his steed forward.

But the suspicions of Lydia Barrington had been aroused by what she had just heard.

She was no longer passive as she had been before, and she said hastily—

"Where are you taking me?"

"To the camp," answered Gasper, his voice husky with the irritation he felt.

"But is it to the English camp?"

There was no answer, save a dig of the rider's spur into the flank of his horse.

"You are not taking me to the English camp," cried Lydia, now fairly alarmed, as the steed, under the influence of the goad, plunged forward.

"Why, where should I be taking you?" growled Gasper.

"There is no Marshal Tallard—no Prince Eugene amongst the English," Lydia continued; "you are deceiving me, and are carrying me to the French lines."

"I am conducting you where you will be safe, foolish girl," exclaimed Gasper. "What have you to fear?"

"Your name is Captain Gravelotte, is it not?" asked Lydia, suddenly.

"It is. Does my name offend you?"

"Yes. So much that I request you to release me at once."

Gasper uttered a sharp angry laugh, and still kept on.

"Set me down!" cried Lydia. "I would rather find my way alone than trust any longer to your guidance. Do you hear me?"

"Oh, yes, I hear; but I do not intend to obey," was the mocking rejoinder.

"I will not go with you; you have no right to take advantage of your strength to compel me."

"I detain you for your own good. How could you choose your path by yourself? Content yourself, and you will be perfectly safe."

But Lydia would not listen to these arguments.

"If you do not set me down at once," she exclaimed, desperately, "I will spring from the saddle."

"And be dashed to pieces for your pains."

"Better that than to be where I am."

And as she spoke, with a sudden and unexpected effort, she pushed aside the arm that encircled her, and sprang, or rather threw herself from the back of the steed.

Gasper Grimsby, in spite of his irritation, uttered a cry of alarm as he checked his steed.

"Fool!" he muttered; "she must be dashed to death."

With these words he descended from his saddle, and, lantern in hand, proceeded to search for his prey, fully expecting to find her lying in the dark road senseless and bleeding, if not dead.

But to his surprise and chagrin, he found no traces of her whatever.

In a sharp, angry tone, he shouted to his companion—

"Come out of your saddle, will you, and help me search for this vixen."

Caleb, with a malicious smile on his face, lowered himself lazily to the ground, and came forward.

"I tell you what, captain," he said; "it strikes me these Barringtons are more plague than profit."

"Curse them!" growled Gasper, as he threw the rays of light around.

"It seems to me they've as many lives as a cat," Caleb continued, facetiously.

"Where can she have crept to?" muttered his superior, as he walked forward along the road.

The rugged pathway was lined with trees.

Suddenly, as he flashed his lantern hither and thither, he caught sight of the cloaked figure, just as she was about to seek the shelter of the covert.

With an exclamation of triumph, he sprang forward.

"Not so," he cried, as he stretched forth his hand to grasp her.

To his great dismay she thrust it aside, and dashed the lantern to the ground.

It fell with a clatter, and became at once extinct.

With a shrill cry of united excitement and terror, Lydia Barrington plunged into the wood.

Her would-be captor was left standing in the road, shrouded in total darkness.

CHAPTER XLVIII.
BRIAN O'FLINN'S LUCK.

ON this particular night Brian O'Flinn had wandered from camp.

He was—wonderful to state—in a thoughtful mood; and he had ridden forth in the gloomy mist, in order to indulge in his reflections undisturbed.

The young Irishman was not as a rule given to meditative fits; but he had been turning over matters in his mind, and felt somewhat perplexed in consequence.

He saw his comrades, Jack Barrington and Ned Rattles, the heroes of several daring adventures and hairbreadth escapes, which had raised them in the estimation of the whole army.

Whilst he alone had done nothing.

Brian was not envious or jealous of his brother officers, but he felt that their exploits were a reproach to himself.

"Bedad!" he muttered to himself, "it's only an idle, skulking rapparee I am, widout a morsel of energy in me. It must be so; for whilst Jack and Ned have been riskin' their lives for the general good, I haven't got a single heroic act tacked to me name."

Shaking his head dolefully, he rode on.

Presently he continued—

"Jack and Ned have got swatehearts, too; two charmin' young crathurs, each one of whom's worth her weight in gould. I haven't. No bright eyes to smile on me. No gentle, tender heart looks for me. An' how should it, seein I've done nothing to deserve it? Luck's against me, that's what it is; but I must make an effort, that I must. Oh, that it would plase the powers to send me some adventure; something that would render me worthy of——"

He stopped his soliloquy suddenly, as a shrill cry was borne to him from the distance.

"Something at last!" he cried, joyfully; "that was a woman's shriek, if iver I heard one."

He urged his horse on at a swift pace, listening intently as he rode.

Presently, he heard hoarse voices shouting, and the female tones were again audible.

"Where the divil are they?" he murmured to himself fretfully. "I'm just as badly off as iver, in the dark."

Hardly had he uttered these words when the sound of light footsteps hurrying towards him caught his ear.

*   *   *   *   *

Gasper Grimsby did not remain long pondering upon his loss.

Finding his prey had slipped through his fingers, he as quickly as possible relit his lantern.

Then, remounting his steed, and ordering his companion to follow him, he turned into the wood, and started in pursuit.

As fate decreed it, he happened to hit upon the right path, and it was not long before a faint rustling amongst the leaves on the ground informed him that he was not far from the fair fugitive.

"There she is," cried Caleb, as he pointed out the fragile figure, hurrying at the top of her speed, not far from them.

"Forward!" shouted Gasper, eagerly.

She heard the voice, and, with a wild cry of despair, darted onwards like a startled hare, her pursuers on her track.

Fortunately for her the thick growth of the trees impeded the progress of the horsemen, so that she was enabled to keep well ahead of them.

It was only a strip of wood into which Lydia had plunged, and she had not run far when she found herself once more in the open road.

For an instant she paused, looking this way and that, uncertain which way to go.

It was just then she heard the sound of hoofs that seemed to be coming towards her, and, determined to risk any peril rather than fall again into the hands of Captain Gravelotte, she uttered another cry for help, and once more resumed her flight, going in the direction of the advancing horseman, this horseman being Brian O'Flinn, who, fortunately for her, was hurrying anxiously to meet her, but little dreaming who it was that needed succour.

*   *   *   *   *

Brian, as the footsteps drew near, checked his steed, fearing lest, in the darkness, he might run over her he wished to help.

He had not long to wait.

Hardly had he stopped when Lydia, panting for breath, came staggering up.

"Whoever you are, protect me, I entreat you," she gasped.

"Shure, and I will, me darlin', as long as I've got a breath in me body," cried Brian, chivalrously.

And, with this, he glided from his saddle, just in time to catch the fair suppliant, who sank exhausted and fainting in his arms.

"Bad luck to the bla'guards who could injure a helpless girl," muttered the young Irishman, indignantly, under his breath.

He looked down at her anxiously.

But nothing but darkness met his sight.

"Seeing's impossible," he continued; "but I feel shure she's a beauty from the sweet tones of her voice."

Once more he bent over her, and murmured a few soothing words in her ear.

But she heard him not.

"She's gone off into a dead faint, poor dear," he said, with much sympathy.

It was the first time in his life that he had ever found himself supporting a fainting young lady in his arms, and it somewhat perplexed him what to do with her.

This question became more imperative, as he heard the voices of the pursuers in the distance.

"I'll put the darlin' gently down on the bank at the roadside," he mused, "and then I'll have my hands at liberty to defend her from the rapparees, if they come."

He accordingly carried his unconscious burden to the spot he had mentioned, and found to his great satisfaction that there was a quantity of dry grass heaped up there.

Whether it had been collected for fodder for the horses he knew not.

But it afforded an excellent bed for the fainting girl.

Having placed her on it as tenderly as if she had been an infant, he listened.

The voices had ceased.

Not a sound was heard but the faint murmur of the night wind as it passed by.

"The bla'guards are off the scent," thought

Brian, " but, by the powers, I'd have liked to have had a cut at them."

In order to be quite ready for any emergency, he took his pistols from the holsters and re-primed them, and having replaced them, he led his horse to the side of the road, and then bent down once more over the young girl.

A sigh announced that she was coming to herself again.

Brian took from his pocket a small flask, and removing the cork, he said to her persuasively—

"Will you allow me, miss, to offer you a small sip of this? It's only whisky, but you'll find a taste ov it'll do you a power ov good. Dhrink, me darlin', if you plase."

As he spoke he raised her head, and placed the flask to her lips.

Faint and trembling, Lydia did not refuse the draught so kindly offered.

She drank a little, and its effects were soon perceptible.

In a few moments she was able to sit up.

"You are betther now, miss?" said Brian to her.

"Oh, much! I am almost myself again, sir, thanks to your kindness," she replied.

"Oh, pray don't thank me," entreated the Irishman, "you wouldn't if you knew how obliged I am to you."

"For fainting as I did?" asked Lydia, smiling in the dark as she spoke.

"Yes, shure, an' for givin' me the opportunity of bein' of service to yez."

"And my pursuers?" asked the young girl, listening anxiously; "where are they?"

"That's more than I'm able to tell you, miss," Brian answered. "I've seen nothing of them."

"All the better," returned Lydia, in a tone of relief; "though in this darkness it is impossible to distinguish friends or foes."

"That's thrue, miss. I haven't even had the pleasure of seein' your sweet face, though it's certain I am it's a pretthy one, from the tone of your voice."

"As certain as I am that you're a brave and honourable man, from the sound of yours," said Lydia, flatteringly.

Brian O'Flinn was delighted, and after a moment he said—

"An' pray, in what direction might you be thravellin', miss?"

"I wish to find my way to the English camp," she replied.

"The English camp!" echoed Brian; "then shure it's meself can take you, for I'm going there."

"Oh, how glad I am!" exclaimed Lydia, "how very glad."

"You wish to see someone there?"

"Yes."

She paused a moment, and then asked—

"Is there an officer there named Barrington?"

"Is it Jack you mane, miss?"

"His name is Jack Barrington."

"Oh, yes, he's there safe enough."

"You know him, then?"

"Know him!" exclaimed Brian, in a paroxysm of delight. "Is there anyone that doesn't know Captain Jack?"

"He's a captain, then, is he?" continued Lydia, with evident gratification in her tone.

"That he is, an' the dearest friend I've got in the world."

Lydia did not reveal her name to her protector, nor did she disclose the relationship that existed between herself and Jack Barrington, and Brian O'Flinn was too much taken up with the agreeable adventure that had befallen him, to think of asking any questions.

"Oh, how thankful I am that I met you," exclaimed the young girl after a moment, warmly; "you will take me to him, won't you?"

"Aye, shure, that I will, me darling," replied Brian; "an' I think the sooner we start, the better."

"I am quite ready," said Lydia, "but I wish it wasn't quite so dark."

"It will be lighter before long," returned Brian.

The young Irishman had never made a truer assertion than this in his life.

Hardly had he spoken the words when his horse gave a hasty spring back, as if something had startled it.

"Steady, boy! steady," cried Brian. "What's the matter wid yez?"

His question was answered by a sudden flash, like the explosion of gunpowder, and at the same moment, the heap of dry material on which Lydia had been lying a few moments before, burst into a blaze, revealing two men in French uniforms.

These were Gasper Grimsby and his comrade.

They had heard the sound of voices, and dismounting, had quietly advanced on foot, leaving their steeds behind at a short distance.

Lydia uttered an exclamation of dismay at the sight of them.

Brian O'Flinn, throwing his arm round her delicate form, gazed sternly at the two intruders from under his knitted brows.

"What do you want?" he asked after a slight pause.

"I want that lady," returned Gasper gruffly.

"Do yez? Well, then, all I have to say is, I wish you may get her—that is, unless she desires to accompany you."

"Oh, no, no; I do not! Heaven forbid!" exclaimed Lydia, in a tone of horror, as she clung to the lieutenant.

"Don't be afraid, me darlin'," whispered the latter, soothingly to her.

Then addressing himself to the soldiers, he continued—

"You hear what the young lady says; she doesn't wish to have anything to do wid yez."

"She belongs to me, nevertheless," growled Gasper.

"Of course she does." joined in Caleb Corder; "she's his niece."

"No, no; I am not indeed! Don't believe him; he is not speaking the truth," cried Lydia, indignantly.

"I don't belave anyone but you, me jewel," returned Brian.

"Whether you believe or not, matters nothing to me," said Gasper, contemptuously. "I intend to have the girl, so just withdraw your arm from her and give her up; do you hear?"

"I'll see you at Jericho first, and then I won't," cried Brian.

"Then we must compel you."

"Ha, ha! don't be too shure of that. It's an Irishman you've got to deal wid, and before I'll allow a pair of lying, blustering spalpeens like yourselves to lay a finger on this pretty crathur here, I'll shed iv'ry dhrop of blood in me body."

Gasper muttered to his comrade in a hasty undertone—

"Look you to the girl, whilst I give this chivalrous champion his quietus."

Brian heard this, and, hastily drawing Lydia with him towards his steed that stood quietly by, he snatched a pistol from the nearest holster, and cocked it.

"Now, then, you cowardly rapparees," he cried, "if you advance a single step, I'll let a little of the night mist into your bodies."

As he spoke, he raised the weapon.

"Upon him!" shouted Gasper.

He sprang forward as he spoke.

Brian pulled the trigger.

But no report followed.

"Ha, ha!" laughed Caleb, mockingly, "you don't suppose we were so green as to leave you any priming, do you, Misther Brian O'Flinn?"

The tone of the speaker's voice threw a new and sudden light into the mind of him who listened to it.

At first he had not recognised his assailants.

He did now perfectly.

"So it's you, is it," he cried, "Captain Turncoat, and Caleb Corder?"

"Yes, it is; what do you think of us?" chuckled the latter, jeeringly.

"I think you're a pair of the biggest scoundrels unhung," returned Brian, emphatically.

And as he spoke, he hurled the pistol full in the face of Gasper.

It missed him, and, passing over his shoulder, took effect on his colleague's frontispiece.

With a howl of pain, the latter rolled over on to the ground.

"Don't lie yelling there," shouted Gasper, furiously.

Then, drawing his sabre, he, with a desperate bound, sprang forward.

Brian had had time to place the girl he championed behind him, and, sword in hand, waited the attack.

Fiercely the weapons clashed.

Both were good swordsmen, and the contest commenced with intense energy.

Striking sparks from their well-tempered blades, that glittered in the light of the blazing fire, they wheeled round and round in the dusty road.

Pale, and with her lips quivering with the terrible excitement she endured, Lydia Barrington withdrew to a short distance, and stood with her hands clasped nervously together, watching the encounter she could not prevent, and in which she was powerless to assist, save for her prayers, which she offered fervently for her brave protector.

But when she caught sight of Caleb Corder, who was working his way round to attack Brian from behind, all the spirit that was in her burst into a flame of indignation.

With her dark eyes flashing fire, she watched the skulking traitor as he crept forward, and just as he had raised his sword to inflict a deadly thrust, the brave girl frustrated the cowardly attempt.

Hastily darting forward, she threw her cloak over his head and shoulders, and dragged him backwards, sprawling once more to the ground.

Caleb's sword fell from his hand, and when at length he disentangled himself sufficiently to look up, he found Lydia standing over him, with the point of the weapon directed against his throat.

"Remain where you are, coward," she cried, imperatively, "or I will strike."

Caleb pushed aside the blade with his hand, and sprang to his feet with a savage oath.

"Give me that sword!" he yelled.

The yell subsided quickly into a gurgling cry, as the strong arm of Brian O'Flinn encircled his throttle, and bore him, almost strangled, to earth again.

The lieutenant had just disarmed Gravelotte in time to accomplish this feat.

But in the meantime, Gasper recovered his weapon, and rushed forward with renewed energy to the attack.

Brian was quite ready for him, and again the contest raged, during which Lydia kept Caleb Corder crouching on the ground, by means of the sword she held.

Suddenly a sharp, ringing snap was heard.

Brian O'Flinn's weapon had snapped short off at the hilt.

With an exultant shout, his adversary whirled his sabre in the air.

Brian's head was the mark he aimed a blow at.

But Lydia sprang to his side, and placed Caleb Corder's sword in his hand, in time for him to guard the deadly blow.

"Blessings on yez for that," he murmured, fervently.

And then resumed the conflict.

But Caleb, being no longer kept in check by the steel point, edged himself gradually along on the ground towards them.

Lydia, absorbed in the fierce struggle, did not observe his approach.

Suddenly he sprang up, and, throwing his arms round Brian, pinioned him.

The Irishman, finding himself gripped, by a rapid movement, swung round, and the clever Caleb, who was holding on to him, went round also.

Swish! went Gasper Grimsby's sabre.

Fortunately for Caleb, it fell short.

But the sharp point swept across his back, cutting through the cloth of his regimental coat as keenly as a razor would have done, but inflicting nothing more than a handsome scratch on the flesh beneath.

Nevertheless, it was the narrowest escape Caleb had ever experienced in his eventful life.

And feeling the smart, and being under the impression that he was cut in half, he cried out dolefully.

But he had little time for lamentations, for Brian, with a sudden jerk, sent him flying over his head.

At that moment, the stirring blast of a

trumpet was heard, followed by the trampling of horses' hoofs.

The fire suddenly became extinct, and they were once more shrouded in darkness, whilst the hearty English "Hurrah!" came echoing cheeringly along the road.

"It's our comrades coming, darlin'," whispered Brian to Lydia, as he draw her a little distance to the side of the road, and stood with his outstretched sabre to be ready for any renewal of hostilities.

But none came, and in a few moments lights were seen approaching, and a body of English cavalry, with Ned Rattles at their head, dashed up to the spot.

"Bravo!" cried Ned, as he caught sight of his friend, "I thought we should find you at last."

"Bedad! you've come at a most convanient time, me boy," returned Brian, breathlessly.

"Anything the matter, old fellow?" asked Ned, observing that his comrade looked rather flurried.

"Well, yes," replied the latter. "But before you ask any questions, help me to lay hould of these cowardly varmints yonther."

"Where?" inquired Ned, as he looked in the direction of Brian's outstretched finger; "I see no one."

Gasper Grimsby and Caleb Corder were no longer visible, having wisely mounted their horses, and beat a hasty retreat.

"You've had a bit of a scrimmage on the road, haven't you?" asked Ned.

"Something like it," was Brian's indifferent response.

At this instant, Lydia Barrington stepped forward to surprise them all.

Ned Rattles caught sight of the lady, and, having raised his cap politely, he said in an undertone to Brian—

"Who is that pretty girl?"

"She's my property," returned the young Irishman, in an exultant whisper. "Hould your whist," he added; "the darlin's Mrs. Captain O'Flinn that is to be."

A few words passed, and then, Lydia being lifted into Brian's saddle, the escort turned once more towards the British lines.

*   *   *   *   *

When Jack Barrington and Ned Rattles rode to the camp, they proceeded at once to the tent of the Duke of Marlborough.

The general had been waiting for them with much anxiety.

But he did not evince any of this in the presence of the staff officers that surrounded him.

It was only when alone with his humble, faithful follower, Sergeant Crank, that he had given expression to his thoughts.

He knew that the young soldiers were on an expedition of danger.

He knew, also, the affection the warm-hearted sergeant bore to them, but especially to Jack, and he felt sure Sergeant Crank would enter into his feelings as regarded their safety.

It was with great satisfaction that he received the announcement of their return.

They were at once admitted, and the general listened with intense interest to the information they had gained and the peril they had undergone.

"You have had a narrow escape indeed," exclaimed the duke, as our hero concluded his account; "but I will take care that you are recompensed for your services."

Then, as they had had a long and fatiguing journey, he kindly bade them seek repose, that they might be ready for the struggle of the coming morrow.

Not sorry for the opportunity of rest, they retired, and were soon buried in profound repose.

*   *   *   *   *

The hours rolled on.

Night had come, and still the wearied young men slept on.

But the excitement of the scenes in which they had been engaged, still clung to them even after sleep had rendered them unconscious, and their dreams were of the wildest and most extravagant description.

As for our hero, there seemed no end to the extraordinary adventures in which he was engaged.

At one moment he was on a vast plain surrounded by the enemy, fighting desperately against them single-handed.

Suddenly they vanished, and he found himself in a dense forest, hemmed in by a number of roaring lions.

He rushed in upon them with his sword, and the lions disappeared, leaving him face to face with a huge two-headed giant.

The peculiarity of this monster was that one of his heads resembled that of Gasper Grimsby, the other that of Caleb Corder.

It would be a good thing, he thought in his dream, to rid the world of two such pests, and with a wonderful leap, he sprang up in the air, and with a sweeping blow of his sword, cut off the two heads.

They rolled along on the ground, spouting forth jets of blood.

But now came a new marvel; wherever the blood dropped, there started up a wolf.

Grey, gaunt and fierce; but each one having in its face the human expression of one of the rolling heads.

With terrible glaring eyes they gathered round him, gnashing their teeth and opening their formidable jaws, that dripped with gore; but ere he could attack them, he heard the baying of dogs, and the next moment three noble hounds came dashing up to the spot, scattering the wolves helter-skelter, and then coming to him and fawning upon him.

On looking at them he perceived, to his astonishment, that their faces bore a strong human likeness to his best friends, Sergeant Crank, Ned Rattles and Brian O'Flinn, but before he could ask them any questions, they had vanished, and the scene had changed again.

He was now in a dark road, bound fast to a bare and withered trunk, whose ghostly branches waved and creaked in the wind, over his head.

Suddenly a cry reached his ears.

It was the cry of a woman in distress—but he could not stir.

"HE RECEIVED A BLOW BETWEEN THE EYES FROM GALLANT JACK'S FIST."

Presently, two soldiers appeared, struggling with a delicate female form, whom they were dragging along.

A pale, unearthly light seemed to encircle them, and he could see them distinctly.

It was Gasper Grimsby and Caleb Corder, again.

With a desperate effort (people are wonderfully strong in their dreams), he burst the thongs that held him, and was about to spring forward to the rescue, when suddenly the straggling branches bent down to the earth, all around him.

Small twigs entwined themselves between the larger stems, and he found himself in a cage, from which there was no escape.

In the midst of his despair, the young girl uttered a piercing shriek.

It was answered by a shout he knew well, and the next moment a fourth figure came up, wearing the form of Brian O'Flinn.

In a moment his sword flew from its scabbard, and he attacked the other phantoms, fiercely.

At the first blow, they vanished, and he heard a voice calling him.

It was his mother's voice.

He was once more free, standing in what seemed to be a tent.

Before him stood his parent, holding by her hand the young girl he had so lately seen.

Gradually the former seemed to fade away, and be replaced by his comrade, Brian, who took her place.

He was just marvelling to himself what this all meant, when he felt himself shaken rather violently, and a voice cried—

"Jack! Jack, me darlin'! wake up, will yez?"

The phantoms vanished, and he sprang up in his bed, to find himself face to face with Brian O'Flinn, who, lantern in hand, stood by the side of his pallet.

"I thought you was niver goin' to wake any more, honey," said the Irishman.

"I'm awake," said Jack, drowsily; "you and the sergeant sent those wolves flying capitally."

"Sent the wolves flyin'?" echoed Brian, with a grin.

"Yes; in the forest, you know. And—and how did you get on with the others?" inquired Jack.

"Who do you mane?" asked Brian, much surprised.

"Why, I mean the human wolves; those scoundrels, Gasper Grimsby and Caleb Corder."

Brian opened his eyes and his mouth, too, in wonder.

"You astonish me, intirely," he exclaimed, after a moment.

"Why, you attacked them, didn't you?" continued Jack, "and rescued the young lady?"

"How the divil did you know that?" asked Brian.

"Why, didn't I see you just now fighting with them in the road?"

"Oh, murther!" almost gasped Brian, his hair almost standing on end at the words he heard; "what's come to him?"

"He's been in bed for the last five hours, I can take my oath," said Ned Rattles, who had woke and was sitting up.

"Oh, shure it's dhramin' he's been," exclaimed the Irishman.

"I really think I must have been," returned Jack, rubbing his eyes, and blinking at the light of the lantern.

Then, bursting into a laugh, he added—

"Yes, yes, it's a dream after all. What a donkey I am."

Brian O'Flinn looked at his friend with peculiar earnestness.

"I tell you what it is, me boy," he said, seriously; "it sthrikes me you're possessed of the faculty of second sight."

"I was not aware I was the owner of any such gift," said our hero.

"Dhrames, you know, are sometimes sent as warnin's."

"Do you regard mine in that light?"

"Well, I don't know what to say about the wolves," Brian replied; "but as far as the fight in the road, it's intirely thrue."

"Indeed!" exclaimed Jack; "have you really been fighting?"

"Look here. *Ecce signum*, as they say in the classics."

As he spoke, he pointed to his arm, that was bound round with a handkerchief stained with blood.

"You have been fighting, then?"

"Hard, me boy, an' wid those two identical bla'guards you mintioned."

"What, Gasper Grimsby and Caleb Corder?" asked Jack, breathlessly.

"Yes; an' in defence of a young lady, too," was Brian's emphatic answer.

It was now our hero's turn to be impressed, and he exclaimed in a tone of wonder—

"Is it possible?"

"It's not only possible, honey, but it's a fact. An' what do you think besides?"

"What?"

"Why, I've brought the young lady wid me here to the camp."

"Indeed!"

"Yes; she wished to come here to find a certain person she wanted."

"And who is that?"

"Guess."

Brian's eyes twinkled so mischievously that Jack almost caught the clue from him.

"Not me, surely," he said.

"Yes, you; your own blessed self, me honey. The young lady wanted to find a soldier of the name of Barrington, an' so I brought her; an' here she is, an' waitin' to see yez."

"It's Fanchette," exclaimed Jack, with a sudden thought, as he sprang from his couch eagerly.

"No, it isn't," replied Brian, quickly. "Fanchette was a very nice girl, but this young lady takes the shine out of her all to nothing."

"Who can she be? What can she want?" soliloquized Jack, as he hastily put on his undress uniform.

"I can't gratify you on these points," returned Brian. "All I know is, she's the sweetest darlin' I ever clapped eyes on."

Jack Barrington laughed, in spite of the

strange curiosity he felt about this mysterious beauty, and he said—

"Didn't this young lady reveal her name?"

"Divil a bit," returned Brian. "An' upon me honour, I niver thought to ask her."

"Decidedly oblivious," said Ned Rattles.

"Ah, well, it doesn't matter," remarked our hero. "I suppose we shall know all about her in a few moments. Where is she?"

"In Sergeant Crank's tent."

"Very good," said Jack, as he gave a finishing touch to his hair. "Then I suppose I'd better go there at once."

"I'll run on ahead an' prepare her," exclaimed Brian, eagerly, as he bolted out of the tent.

Jack followed more leisurely, racking his brains all the way about the visitor, wondering who it could be that at such a time had travelled a dark and dangerous route to the camp to see him, but never once dreaming of the truth.

Never.

CHAPTER XLIX.

BROTHER AND SISTER.

ON reaching the tent, Brian O'Flinn found Sergeant Crank and the young lady.

The sergeant, not having retired to rest at the time of her arrival, had politely resigned his quarters to the fair traveller, and was now performing the duties of hospitality assiduously, waiting upon her, and expatiating at the same time upon the virtues of his *protégé* Jack, mingled with congratulations on her own escape from the hazards to which she had been exposed.

Lydia listened to the worthy grenadier politely—as a lady would—whilst she partook of the refreshment before her.

But when Brian entered, there was a sudden and marked change in her looks and manner.

Her eyes brightened with pleasure, her features lost their wearied look, and became full of life and animation at the sight of her protector, whilst last, but not least in Brian's estimation, the smile and blush with which she greeted him sent his heart beating at double quick time.

But he had no opportunity of whispering any little sweet word in her ear, owing to the sergeant's presence.

Brian announced officially—

"Captain Barrington is at hand."

In a few moments footsteps were heard, and our hero made his appearance.

He had determined in his own mind to be perfectly calm and composed, and he entered without haste, or betraying any anxiety, although his heart beat strangely, in spite of himself.

The young lady rose as he came in, and inclined her head in answer to the courteous bow Jack made her, and remained with her face inclined downwards—perhaps to hide the emotion she felt.

Sergeant Crank not wishing to appear intrusive, took the arrival of our hero as his cue to depart.

Brian O'Flinn, with a farewell glance towards the fair girl who had so impressed him—but which she did not see—went out too.

Jack Barrington and the lady were the only occupants of the tent.

There was a slight pause of silence, and then the former opened the conversation by saying—

"I was informed you wished to see me, miss."

"Yes," replied the young lady, and her voice as she spoke was faltering, and the tone husky, as if she was struggling with some deep feeling.

"May I ask what business you have with me?" Jack continued with much courtesy.

Without answering, the girl raised her head, and looked long and earnestly at him.

Jack looked at her, and as he did so, he could see the tears gathering in the dark eyes, and he felt a strange inclination—without quite knowing why—to shed tears himself.

At length the young lady said—

"You will pardon the question, but have you a father living?"

"No," returned Jack in a voice by no means steady; "he died many years ago."

"And—and your mother; is she dead too?"

"No, she is alive."

"Alive!" exclaimed Lydia, with a sudden burst of joy and surprise; "are you sure?"

"Yes; but it is only very lately I discovered her. I had been separated from her for twelve years, and never expected to see her again."

"Then you have found her at last?"

"At last, yes."

"Oh, thank Heaven for that! and where is she now—not here?"

"No; she is in London."

"And is she well?"

"Quite well."

The young lady clasped her hands gratefully, and her lips moved as if in silent prayer.

Presently she continued, and her voice was now more faltering than before—

"And you—you had a sister once—a little sister——"

"Ah, yes!" exclaimed Jack, the past seeming to roll back in an instant, and bring the childish form once more to his side; "my dear little sister, Lyddy."

"And where is she?"

Jack sighed, and the tears trickled down his cheeks as he murmured—

"Alas! I know not; I have never seen her since we were children."

The young lady stifled a sob as she asked—

"Have you any recollection of her?"

"My only remembrance is of a pretty little prattling thing with bright eyes and light brown curling hair. Ah! poor little Lyddy, she must have died long ago."

"No, no; she is not dead. She lives, she lives!"

"Lives?" echoed Jack, gazing at the excited girl, eagerly.

"Yes; I am she. I am your sister," cried Lydia, with a burst of emotion. "Jack, my dear brother. Come, come to me."

And with eager steps she rushed towards him, and throwing her arms round his neck, sobbed upon his bosom.

A muffled "Hurroo!" from without the tent recorded the fact that Brian O'Flinn sympathized warmly in this happy reunion, and after a time, when the emotion of the restored relatives had somewhat subsided, his voice was heard at the entrance of the tent.

"May I come in?" he asked, modestly.

Jack responded by going at once, and hauling him forward by the arm.

Lydia at once began to narrate the brave manner in which he had protected her from her assailants.

"But for this gallant soldier," she said, with grateful warmth, "I do not believe you would ever have seen me again."

"God bless you, old fellow!" exclaimed our hero, fervently, as he grasped his comrade's hand; "I shall never be able to repay you for this."

"I'm sure I never shall," protested Lydia.

But the brave Irishman, his honest face radiant with joy, declared that he was already more than repaid.

And he whispered some little secret into Lydia's ear which made her blush deeply, but she looked very happy notwithstanding.

Sergeant Crank and Ned Rattles now made their appearance, and having offered their congratulations, the former said—

"As to-morrow will be a busy day for all of us, I propose that everyone retires to rest. You know the old adage—

"'Early to bed and early to rise,
Makes a man healthy——'"

"An' ate lots ov pies," laughed Brian.

Everyone joined in the laugh, and Lydia, being much fatigued, was left to repose.

CHAPTER L.
GOOD-BYE, SWEETHEART.

THE next morning dawned chill and hazy.

A dense mist being in the atmosphere, nothing could be seen of the surrounding objects.

And as Brian O'Flinn stepped forth from his tent, he remarked, facetiously—

"Bedad, we'll have to put on our spectacles to fight to-day."

The Duke of Marlborough, after the intelligence he had received from Jack Barrington, had resolved not to delay the attack.

It was still early when Jack Barrington repaired to the tent where his sister was located.

The rolling of the drums and the tramp of many feet had aroused her, and she was up and dressed.

When he applied for admission, she came at once and let him in.

Jack was in full uniform, and in excellent spirits.

After welcoming him with a loving kiss, Lydia remained for a moment, contemplating him admiringly.

"I don't wish to flatter you," she said, at length; "but I must say I think I ought to be proud of my handsome brother."

Jack smiled, as he replied gallantly—

"I think that brother may well return the compliment by being equally proud of his beautiful sister."

These little affectionate flatteries being over, Jack said to Lydia—

"You have come at an eventful crisis."

"How so?" she asked.

"To-day we strike the decisive blow at the enemy."

"Do you mean that there is to be a battle?"

"Yes. And if I am not mistaken, a hard one."

The colour fled from Lydia's cheeks at this announcement, and her lips quivered as she said—

"You will take part in it?"

"Most certainly," replied Jack proudly.

"And—and the brave fellow who risked his life for me last night?"

"Brian O'Flinn?"

"Ah, yes."

"Oh, he'll be in it, and Ned Rattles also. Depend upon it, we shall all have our work to do."

"Heaven preserve you, my dearest brother," exclaimed Lydia fervently, "and your gallant comrades too."

"We have been signally favoured hitherto," said Jack cheerfully.

"You have not been wounded then?"

"Never, beyond a scratch or two not worth mentioning."

"It seems miraculous how you could have escaped."

"It does; but we have, nevertheless. In the thickest of the fray, when our comrades have been mowed down on every side of us, we have remained unscathed. On that account we have been christened the 'invulnerables.'"

"Oh that you may come safely out of this day's strife," exclaimed Lydia fervently, as she embraced her beloved brother fondly.

"I have no fear, dear," he replied; "but if it should be Heaven's will that a bullet or a sabre thrust should lay me low, I should wish to speak with you a little about the future."

The tears were trickling down Lydia's cheeks at this sad prospect.

But Jack at once sought to check them.

"Come, come, sister, don't weep before there is any occasion," he said, cheerfully; "a soldier is not a whit nearer his end for speaking of it than another person may be to death because he makes his will."

And then he spoke to her of much that had happened in the past.

Especially the determined and desperate attempts against his life by the recreant Gasper Grimsby and his accomplice Caleb Corder.

He also told her the fact that the former had been the murderer of John Stanmore.

"I could almost fancy," Jack continued, "that this miscreant was under the protection of some invisible fiend, so constantly has he eluded the hands of justice."

"He cannot be far off now," remarked Lydia, with a shudder.

"No; he is a renegade, fighting on the French side against his country."

"You may meet him in the strife," said Lydia, apprehensively.

"Heaven grant I may!" exclaimed Jack, his cheek flushing, and his eyes brightening with indignation; "I should wish nothing better than to meet him and his cowardly companion on the battlefield."

"Two of them? Heaven forbid!"

"Oh, I should know how to deal with them in open fight," returned our hero; "it is only in their treachery they are dangerous, like snakes in the grass."

At this moment a soldier, hastily passing, rustled the canvas of the tent, causing the drapery at the entrance to wave aside.

Our hero started and drew his sword, as if half expecting to see the form of his serpent-like foe.

But no one appeared, and resheathing his weapon, he went on—

"I am most anxious about our grandfather's will."

"Did you not say it was in the possession of this Gasper Grimsby?"

"Yes, though where he has concealed it, no one knows but himself. It is of vital importance that we should recover that, or every farthing of the splendid fortune it bequeaths us will be lost."

Jack had no time to say more, for the drums began to roll, and Sergeant Crank entered the tent.

"Good morning, my dear young friends," he said, cheerfully.

The blast of a bugle rang out at that moment.

"Ah! there's the signal to march," cried Jack. "Good-bye, Lyddy darling, and God bless you."

"I won't say good-bye, Jack," returned his sister, as she embraced him; "but I will pray God to bless and preserve you."

Jack hurried away, and the next moment Brian O'Flinn appeared.

"I've come to take lave of you, miss," he said, with considerable emotion in his tone. "I feel I'll fight betther afther shakin' hands wid you."

Lydia held out her white hand at once to the brave lieutenant.

Eagerly he took it in his own, and raised it tenderly to his lips, and continued—

"You'll pardon my boldness, won't you, miss? But p'r'aps this is the last time I may iver have the happiness of lookin' upon those bright eyes——"

"Oh, I trust we shall often meet again," said Lydia, earnestly, but blushing at the same time.

"You'll think of me, then, during this day's fight?"

"Could I forget him who risked his life for me? Oh, no, I am not so ungrateful," Lydia assured him.

"Bless you, Miss Lydia, for those words," murmured Brian, once more pressing the hand he held reverently to his lips. "Would I could take this wid me."

Lydia smiled as she answered—

"I cannot very well dissever my hand, but perhaps this will serve as a substitute."

And as she spoke, she drew a small pair of scissors from a case that hung at her girdle, and, cutting off a lock of her rich, dark hair, presented it to her honest admirer.

Brian's good-looking face glowed with delight as he received it.

"Dear angel," he exclaimed, fervently, "I'll wear this precious gift on my heart to-day. It will make me fight like a lion."

"Mind you bring it back, and yourself too, in safety," said Lydia, with a sweet smile.

Again the bugle sounded, and with one last murmured "Good-bye, darlin'," the young Irishman hurried away.

All was ready without, and our heroes had just time to mount, when the word "Advance!" was given, and the living mass moved on, like an army of shadows, in the dense grey mist.

CHAPTER LI.

THE CANNONADE.

WITH steady, regular motion the allied forces continued to progress, till they reached the plain at the foot of the hill of Hochstet.

Here they halted.

The hill itself was, owing to the haziness of the atmosphere, totally invisible to those beneath, whilst the presence of the English army was, from the same cause, entirely unsuspected by their foes on the heights above.

In solemn silence the troops were ranged in order of battle, the men cheerful and confident, and only desiring that the mist should clear off, that they might commence their work.

Gradually, as the sun rose, this was accomplished.

As the luminary mounted into the heavens, the vapour, heated by his rays, floated upwards into space, revealing to the astonished eyes of the French sentinels the British squadrons outstretched in glittering masses upon the plain.

In no little dismay, the tidings were quickly conveyed to Marshal Tallard, the commander-in-chief.

"*Diable!*" they exclaimed at the intelligence, "who would have expected they were so near us?"

In a very short time, the French camp was in a state of wild excitement.

Not expecting so sudden and close an approach of their foes, they were not properly prepared for such a conflict as they knew must take place.

But though the French were thus almost caught sleeping, they soon made preparations for a desperate resistance.

Amidst the rolling of drums, the blast of bugles, and the shouts of officers, the French legions were hastily marshalled into order.

But the sudden surprise had not been without its evil effects; and though the first excitement had passed off, the entire body had received, as it were, a kind of shock, and their spirits had scarcely recovered from it.

The word of command being given, the cannonading began on the English side.

The mouths of the English artillery belched forth fire and destruction unremittingly for more than three hours.

Where the mist had been, the white smoke from the guns rolled over the plain, and up the sides of the hill.

The Duke of Marlborough, mounted on his charger, stood calmly biding his time until the decisive moment for the attack should arrive.

At his side were three dragoon officers, on whom he chiefly depended for the success of that day.

These three were Jack Barrington, Ned Rattles and Brian O'Flinn.

Sitting erect in their saddles, calm but confident, they remained with their drawn swords in their hands, waiting the word that should send them to win a soldier's glory or a soldier's grave.

It was just at that time that the young officer, Ernest Steinberg, galloped up to them.

"Well met, comrades," he exclaimed, as he saluted them; "I rejoice to see you."

"The pleasure is mutual," replied those he addressed.

"And how is it with you, mein herr?" asked Jack, cheerfully.

"Well, quite well, my friend," said Ernest.

But though he said this, there was something in the pale hue of his features, and the deep melancholy of his eyes, that told of some inward foreboding, and Brian O'Flinn, in order to divert his attention, said he, as pointed to the ascent before them—

"We'll be havin' some uphill work presently, honey, I take it."

"Yes," was the gloomy reply; "many will go up there, but all will not come down again."

"Well, I tell you what, my boy," said Ned Rattles, "we've made up our minds to go up and come down too."

"Of course we have!" cried Brian, with enthusiasm, as he thrust his hand into his pocket, and pressed the lock of hair that rested next his heart.

"You may," returned Ernest, in the same mournful tone; "but I shall not."

"Oh, nonsense; I don't believe it," said Jack Barrington, anxious to rouse him out of his despondency.

The young German only shook his head.

"You will see I am right," he said; "that is why I was so glad to meet you before the struggle begins, and I now wish you farewell."

Having thus spoken, he shook hands with his comrades all round.

But Jack still maintained his opinion that they would meet again.

"Whether we do or not," said Ernest, solemnly, "I feel I am doomed. You remember the time?"

"Four o'clock," returned Ned Rattles.

"Yes; at four o'clock I shall be no more. If you see me, it will be only my lifeless clay that you will gaze upon."

And with a deep sigh, Ernest Steinberg wheeled his horse round and galloped away to join his regiment.

His singularly morbid state of mind had had a somewhat depressing effect upon those who listened to his words, till Brian O'Flinn burst out—

"Oh, bedad! it'll niver do to go into action in the dumps like this. Cheer up, me boys, and we'll give the mounseers and their allies up there such a run down hill prisintly as they'll remimber for the rest of their nat'ral lives."

Again a tremendous volley of ordnance was discharged, making the solid ground tremble beneath them.

* * * * *

In one of the French tents might have been seen an officer in full uniform.

It was Gasper Grimsby.

He was just about to go forth to place himself at the head of his troop.

But he had one thing to do first, and it was this.

He dug up from the ground beneath his tent a small tin box.

Having opened this box, he took from it a parchment deed.

It was John Stanmore's will.

"This is valuable. Where I go this goes," he said to himself with a cunning smile.

With these words he placed the parchment inside the lining of his regimental coat, and having spread it carefully and smoothly over his chest, he buttoned the coat and hurried out.

But he was not aware that there was one who had been watching him all the time from a rent in the canvas.

That one was Caleb Corder, who had seen what he did, and heard what he said.

"So, so!" he chuckled, as his superior disappeared; "it's valuable, is it? Look out for yourself then, Captain Gravellotte; I'm fond of valuables."

And with an ugly grin on his pale face, and amidst a fresh peal of thunder from the English guns, the traitor went to his place in the ranks.

CHAPTER LII.
THE BATTLE.

AND now the grim dogs of war, having for a long time listened to the fierce music of the cannon, and inhaled the sulphurous vapours which they vomited forth, became madly impatient, chafing like hounds in the leash to be started forth.

The Duke of Marlborough could see this, and the crisis having arrived, he called Jack Barrington to him, and gave him hastily a few directions.

Then galloping to the left wing, he cried—

"Charge!"

With a ringing, enthusiastic cheer the cavalry bounded forward with their noble commander at their head.

Splash! into the stream they go.

The opposite bank is quickly gained, and dashing boldly up the ascent, they attack the cavalry of Tallard with dauntless bravery.

The marshal was away at this critical moment, reviewing the disposition of his troops higher up the hill.

But his cavalry, having sustained the first onset of the English, fought on determinedly in the absence of their general.

The latter, hearing that they had engaged, flew to put himself at their head.

The encounter continued with increased fury and desperation.

The Duke of Marlborough's steed was shot under him, and fell, bearing its rider with it to the ground.

"A horse ! another horse !" cried the duke, as he rose to his feet.

In an instant a horse was brought him by his aide-de-camp, Captain Rodwell, whilst Colonel Billington, his equerry, held the stirrup.

The duke sprang to the saddle, but uttered a wild cry of horror as he did so.

The colonel still stood erect grasping the stirrup, but he was headless.

A cannon ball had decapitated him, and the next moment his lifeless trunk fell heavily to the ground.

The duke was bespattered with the blood of the unfortunate soldier.

But there was no time then for regrets, and, spurring on his steed, he rode at once to his troop.

Twice were the French cavalry driven back.

But they rallied again, and still held their ground, though evidently weakened.

Then were heard the shouts of the German troopers, as they galloped forward to charge the cavalry of the Elector of Bavaria on the left.

The assault was deadly and terrible, and well sustained on both sides.

It was at this moment that Marshal Tallard, finding his position growing imminent, despatched orders to a large body of reserve troops in the village of Blenheim to hasten to his relief at once.

The Duke of Marlborough heard the order, and counteracted it by an instant message to Jack Barrington and his comrades.

It was this—

"Intercept the reserve body on the right; let them not advance."

"Something to do at last," cried our hero, joyfully.

"Hurroo !" shouted Brian O'Flinn.

And having given the signal to advance, they galloped forward at the head of their troops.

The reserve corps was already winding round the brow of the hill, when the English squadrons came down upon them.

Their further progress was checked at once, and instead of joining the main body as expected, they had much difficulty in holding their ground against the determined onslaught of their assailants.

It was now, when the affray was at its height, that an ensign, carrying the French colours, appeared, urging on the men, and waving the banner in the air.

It struck our hero that he would, if possible, capture this trophy.

"I must have that flag," he cried to Brian.

"Fire away, me boy, an' good luck to yez," shouted the latter, in return.

The next moment, Jack was riding at full speed towards the banner bearer.

The latter saw him coming, and, guessing his purpose, was prepared to meet him.

"Yield your colours," cried our hero, as he dashed up to him.

The ensign smiled scornfully, and made a fierce cut at Jack with his sabre.

Jack guarded the blow, and returned it.

The fight was sharp and desperate.

But at length our hero, locking his hilt in that of his adversary, hurled his weapon from his grasp.

Sheathing his own sword, he then rode in upon him, and, seizing the flagstaff, a desperate hand-to-hand struggle took place for the coveted prize.

Both were young men in the prime of life, both strong-limbed and active.

But Jack's determination was the most intense, and at last, by a sudden and rapid shifting of his hands, he whirled the staff round, and wrenched it from his opponent's grip, whilst, by a vigorous blow of his fist, he sent him flying out of his saddle.

With a shout of triumph, he was about to rejoin his men, bearing aloft the trophy he had won, when he found himself confronted by two dragoons, the identical two men he had wished to meet, Gasper Grimsby and Caleb Corder.

The expression of their faces was full of hate, and the former cried to him jeeringly—

"You think you're going to carry that away with you, don't you ?"

"One thing I know," returned Jack, his eyes blazing with indignation, "it will take more than a couple of cowardly cut-throats like you to stop me."

"We'll see," said Gasper, as he drew one of his pistols from his holster, and fired it full in our hero's face.

A rapid side movement on the part of the latter saved him from the deadly bullet.

Instead of entering his brain, it only grazed the edge of his cap ; but it redoubled his fury, and without pausing to reflect, he lowered the flagstaff, which terminated in a sharp spear-like point, and couching it as a lance, he gave his steed the spur.

The animal bounded forward, and like a knight of old at a tournament, he dashed at his antagonist, and with a well-delivered thrust, drove the steel through his opponent's stock, the point protruding at the back of the neck.

The shock was so violent that it completely hoisted his enemy out of his seat, and he fell with a heavy thud to the ground, the staff breaking short off with his weight as he descended, and leaving the end imbedded in the wound.

The flag still remained in our hero's grasp, whilst he who had disputed his right to retain it, lay stretched upon the earth, motionless, and to all appearance dead.

"You have your deserts at last, you despicable wretch," cried our hero.

And then he looked round for Caleb Corder, but the jackal was not to be seen.

The fate of his superior had taken such an effect on his nerves, that he had thought it prudent to remove himself.

Just at that moment a ringing "Hurrah !" from the English caused Jack to look round.

The reserve body had given ground at length, and were in full retreat towards the open country at the rear of the hill.

Without pausing another instant to look after an enemy he so thoroughly despised, he urged on his steed, and quickly joined his comrades.

He was scarcely out of sight, when Caleb came once more up to the spot.

Pale and eager, as though he had something very important to perform.

This was nothing less than to rifle the dead body of his colleague of the valuable document he carried in his breast.

Pulling up his steed sharply, he dropped from the saddle, and approaching the prostrate body, bent down to drag open the military coat.

His hand was on the first button, when to his intense astonishment he received a tremendous blow on the nose from the clenched fist of the dead man.

Hundreds of coloured lights danced in his eyes, and he fell on his back with a yell.

"Take that, you infernal thief!" growled Gasper, as he sat up.

The spear point on the colour staff had only pierced the collar of his coat, and grazed his neck; and apart from being somewhat shaken, he was as much alive as ever.

"I—I really thought you were killed," whispered Caleb, apologetically.

"You should have been quite sure I was before you attempted to help yourself to any property of mine," returned his master, sternly.

"I will next time," Caleb muttered to himself.

It was not a time or place to indulge in recriminations, and Gasper, rising from the ground, and bidding his treacherous colleague follow him, mounted his horse and rode off.

*   *   *   *   *

Hardly had the French reserve corps been put to flight, when the English bugle sounded the recall.

Pursuit was at once checked, and Jack Barrington, Brian, and Ned Rattles galloped back with their men to their former station.

They arrived just in time to receive fresh orders from the duke.

These orders were that they were to advance between the engaging wings, and attack the French troops posted at the summit of the hill.

With joy they prepared to obey, and the next moment were mounting the ascent at the head of their gallant dragoons.

They could see that this was a most important commission.

If they could throw into confusion the body against which their attack was to be directed, if they could dislodge them from their position, the battle would be won.

With resolute hearts, and determination flashing in their eyes, our heroes pressed onward.

On either side of them was the din and conflict, the smoke and carnage of battle.

As they were proceeding, Ernest Steinberg appeared, riding across from the right.

He was carrying a dispatch from Prince Eugene to the Duke of Marlborough, on the left, and passed in front of the advancing columns led by Jack Barrington.

They saw each other and raised a mutual cheer.

The young German's face was calm and resolved.

But there was the same foreboding expression in his eyes, as he waved his hand to his English comrades.

Brian, to inspire him, cried out—

"Not dead yet!"

"It is not yet four o'clock!" was the significant reply of Ernest Steinberg, as he galloped onwards, and was lost in the smoke.

Our heroes continued steadily to advance until they came in sight of their foes.

It was evident from the manner in which the latter were placed that they were prepared for the attack, and a deadly volley of musketry saluted the British cavalry.

For an instant it threw the ranks into some confusion.

Many a brave fellow dropped lifeless under that terrible discharge.

But the gaps which death had caused were quickly filled up, and Jack Barrington cried—

"Charge!"

On dashed the dragoons with a ringing "Hurrah!"

They were met by the French troopers, who rode down upon them with all the advantage of the descent to increase the fierceness and impetuosity of their attack.

But the English withstood it with the firmness of rock.

And then commenced the furious onslaught—the deadly hand-to-hand struggle, which so particularly distinguished this memorable battle.

Each side knew well that on the issue of that struggle the success or loss of the day depended, and they fought with the desperation of men who had determined to die where they stood rather than retreat.

Jack and his comrades fought like lions.

Wherever the contest raged the fiercest, there were they, cheering, rallying, and encouraging their men.

"The Queen and Marlborough!" cried our hero, as his blood-stained sword flashed in the air.

"England and victory!" joined in Ned Rattles.

"For the honour of Ould Ireland, me bhoys," shouted Brian, who was like a jungle tiger in his excitement.

It was just at this moment a French officer pushed through the *mêlée* towards Jack Barrington, and drawing his pistol, fired at him.

The ball whizzed over our hero's shoulder and entered the breast of the man behind him.

Jack uttered an exclamation of surprise as he beheld his adversary.

It was Gasper Grimsby who had discharged the pistol, the man whom he had left—as he thought—lying lifeless on the plain.

Our hero knew not the cause of his preservation, and the seeming miracle of a dead man fighting amongst the living, for a moment unnerved him.

"Some supernatural power protects him," was his thought.

But in an instant it passed off, and rallying his senses, he urged his steed forward to reach his antagonist; but he was no longer to be seen, and the stirring incidents by which Jack was surrounded, quickly banished him from his memory.

The deadly strife continued with unabated fury.

The air rang with the shouts of the combatants, and the fierce sharp clash of steel.

Twice were the English beaten back.

Twice did they rally and force their foes to retreat.

Time was going on.

The engagement had lasted almost seven hours.

It was approaching four in the afternoon.

It then struck our hero that some skilful *ruse de guerre* must be employed to turn the tide of battle.

Quickly he communicated with his comrades, who, begrimed with dust and smoke, but still untouched, were scarcely distinguishable.

Suddenly, in the midst of the strife, the English troops gave way in the centre.

Like a torrent let loose, the French cavalry poured in at the breach, and rushed down the hill.

The *ruse* had succeeded, and the English wheeling round right and left, dashed up the ascent and took their places.

The relative positions of the conflicting bodies were now reversed, the British were above, the French beneath.

Jack Barrington and his comrades uttered a shout of triumph.

They knew now that the advantage was on their side.

That virtually the struggle was over, that victory was in their hands.

The French quickly saw the error they had committed.

But it was too late to retrieve it.

They made a desperate effort to recover their lost ground.

But in vain.

Exhausted with their prolonged exertions and depressed by the loss of their position, they were gradually forced back.

Again the cry of the English captains rang on their ears—

"Charge!"

And as the British cavalry came thundering down upon them, they gave way utterly, and turning, fled in wild confusion.

The panic of the defeat now spread simultaneously to the right and left wings.

The rout became general, and the flight precipitate.

The consternation of the French soldiers was such that they threw themselves into the Danube, without heeding whither they fled.

The victory was complete.

The Battle of Blenheim was one of the most splendid triumphs ever recorded in the annals of warfare.

It was in the midst of the confusion of flight, that once more Ernest Steinberg and our heroes crossed each other.

Jack Barrington congratulated him warmly.

"You see your fears were groundless, my dear meinherr," he said, in a cheerful tone.

The other only shook his head, and returned the old reply—

"It is not yet four o'clock."

Barely had he said the words, when a stray bullet struck him in the breast.

He fell from his horse with a cry.

In an instant, Jack and his friends dismounted and raised him.

He was deadly pale, and the blood poured in torrents from his wound.

It was evident it was mortal.

"You see my dream did not deceive me," he gasped. "Poor Adelaide, we shall never meet again."

With tears in their eyes, our heroes surrounded the dying soldier, on whose brow the shades of death were fast gathering.

After a pause, he asked faintly—

"What is the time?"

Jack Barrington having looked at his watch, told him—

"Three minutes to four."

A ghastly smile flitted over the white lips of the young German as he murmured—

"In two minutes I shall be no more."

Our hero, his timepiece in his hand, sadly counted the seconds.

At the precise time prophesied, the dying eyes became upturned.

A vacant, glazed look passed into them, and all was over.

Ernest Steinberg was dead.

When four o'clock came, his soul had passed away, and as he had predicted, his comrades looked only on his lifeless clay.

CHAPTER LIII.

WHEREIN CALEB CORDER POSSESSES HIMSELF OF THE WILL. ENGLAND ONCE MORE.

CALEB CORDER had determined in his own mind to possess himself of the document he had seen his master thrust into his vest, and he never lost sight of this intent.

During the strife he hovered about him like a vulture over his prey.

At length, at a time when the captain's attention was occupied, he crept behind him and dealt him a tremendous blow on the head with the butt-end of a pistol.

Down with a crash fell Gasper, totally unconscious.

Caleb was about to leap from his horse and possess himself of the document, when he saw a number of mounted men riding towards him.

It was more than probable that they were English, and, consequently, it would be dangerous to stop where he was.

So he determined to ride off and return when a better opportunity presented itself.

But, so that in the event of Gasper recovering ere he could return, he could not ride away, Caleb deliberately shot his horse dead.

Then, taking particular notice of the spot where Gasper lay, he rode away like the wind.

In less than a quarter of an hour, when he saw that the coast was clear, he returned.

Gasper was, to all appearances, dead.

Very closely did Caleb examine him.

"Yes," he muttered, "he's dead enough. Good! The will is mine."

Thereupon he tore open Gasper's coat and seized the document.

But Gasper was by no means dead.

No, he had recovered consciousness, and was just about to attempt to rise, when he saw Caleb cautiously riding towards him.

At once he knew it was he who had dealt the blow from behind.

As he was unarmed, he concluded that it would be better to sham death and allow Caleb to possess himself of the will.

And as we have seen, so well did he sham death, that Caleb was entirely deceived.

Securing the document about his person, Caleb rode away.

Then Gasper, with much difficulty, got upon his feet.

He looked wildly around him.

The battle was still in progress, but the combatants were getting further and further away.

"But for a drop of water!" he murmured —"the wretch—or brandy—anything! The hound—the brutal blackguard! But let him wait," he whined, as he gnashed his teeth. "I will be even with him. I shall not die. No— no. I will *not* die! Ah, who comes this way?"

It was an English soldier.

Wounded, and seriously, there was no doubt.

As he came closer Gasper saw that he had lost his left arm, while the greater part of his clothing was torn to ribbons.

Gasper called to him:

"What ho, friend?" he cried; "a drop of water for the love of God!"

The wounded man tottered towards him.

"French?" he murmured.

"Yes—yes," said Gasper, I am a Frenchman, it is true; but I have been for many years in your country. I am badly wounded. Have you a drink?"

The soldier detached his flask, and handed it to Gasper, who seized upon it, and at once placed it to his lips.

It contained brandy and water, and the spirit revived him to no small extent.

The unfortunate soldier sank down at Gasper's side.

"I am done for," he said—"bleeding to death. You could not bandage my arm?"

"I am unable to move," replied Gasper.

This was a lie.

He could have moved now had he chosen.

But, though the young soldier had given him what he wanted himself, he would not do anything for him.

"How are you wounded?" he asked Gasper.

"Broken leg." Another falsehood.

"Ah, that is but little. By and bye a doctor will set your leg, and you will be able to be removed. Listen, you said you had been many years in England?"

"Ay, in London. That was where I learned the language."

"Are you poor?"

"Very—very poor."

The young soldier took from his breast a pocket-book, and handed it to Gasper, who eagerly opened it.

Imagine his joy when he found that it contained a number of bank notes.

"It is of no use to me," said the soldier, with a deep sigh. "They are yours if you will make me a solemn promise."

"Speak."

"You will swear in Heaven's name that you will take the letters you will find in that pocket-book to the persons to whom they are directed."

"I swear."

"It is enough. I believe you."

Gasper, in defiance of the fact that his wound on the head nearly drove him mad, endeavoured to ascertain the soldier's history.

He felt certain that, although in the garb of a private, he was a person of superior position.

But he failed.

Gradually consciousness left the young fellow, and when the shades of evening began to draw over the terrible field of battle, he breathed his last.

Gasper at once searched him.

But all he found was a locket—a small gold one, attached to which was a tiny chain.

This he pocketed.

Hour after hour went by, the sound of fire-arms became less and less distinct, and, finally, a dead silence ensued.

"No one is about," murmured Gasper. "Now is my time. By Heaven, I seem to be going round and round. If I could but reach yonder wood I shall be safe. It is more than likely that I shall find some one willing to assist me. Ha! What is this I see? Some one advances."

Yes. Lights were advancing in the distance.

Gasper thought it must be the despoilers of the dead, who usually made their appearance in the silence of the night.

But he did not wait to see.

With all speed he searched for firearms, and,

having found them, made all haste towards the wood.

Had he waited he would have seen that the persons with the lights were Jack Barrington and his friends.

Our hero was, of course, anxious to possess himself of the will, and, thinking that he would find Gasper among the dead, he made this search.

Of course it was fruitless.

"The wretch has that important document," muttered Gasper, as he dragged himself through the dark wood, "and will, of course, use it to his own advantage. It would be of no use searching for him in France. Nay, he will proceed to England with all speed; but I will not be far behind him, curse him! But I must be careful, or he will get to know I am on his track, and give me the slip."

He struck a light and examined the notes in the pocket-book.

A grim smile of intense satisfaction rested upon his features as he saw there were two fifties and six fives.

"One hundred and thirty pounds!" he chuckled. "Here, indeed, is a splendid start for me!"

He did not take the trouble to look at the letters, nor the few other papers the pocket-book contained.

Replacing it, he again went on, and after another hour's weary trudge, he reached a small hut.

It belonged to a charcoal-burner. On account of the battle which for so many hours had been raging close by, he considered it likely that he should find the hut deserted, but no; when he knocked, the door, to his great joy, was at once opened, and an old man appeared.

He looked somewhat alarmed, but when he recognised the French uniform, fear fled.

"I have been wounded, my friend," said Gasper, "and would purchase a little spirits of you if you chance to have such a thing."

"Yes," was the reply; "enter, captain, and I will get you some Cognac."

Gasper was quickly seated in the comfortless hut.

The charcoal burner seemed as poor as a church mouse, but, nevertheless, the Cognac he produced was of first-class quality.

Gasper had some loose money, and he paid him well for it.

While he drank the liquor with much relish, he closely scrutinised the man before him.

Presently he said:

"I dare say you may think I make a strange offer, but I would pay you well for the clothes you wear. You are about my height."

The man certainly *did* look very much astonished.

"The fact is," continued Gasper, "my friends, who ought to have stuck to me, deserted me as soon as I was wounded. No doubt they think I am dead, and so I want to surprise them. Do you understand me?"

"*Oui*—yes captain."

"Do you agree?"

"I have another lot of clothes just like this, and you can have them for twenty francs."

"Good—bring them here."

The charcoal-burner opened a box, took out a lot of clothes, and handed them to Gasper, who examined them and said they would do well.

He paid the money, and requested the man to assist him in taking off his uniform.

The change was soon effected, and the charcoal-burner suggested that, in order to make the disguise perfect, Gasper should blacken his face. This he did, with charcoal, and the result was that he was completely altered.

The charcoal-burner thought it likely that the "gallant" captain would leave his uniform behind.

He was mistaken.

Gasper requested the loan of a knife, and he deliberately cut the uniform in pieces, and threw them upon the fire.

"*Ma foi!*" thought the charcoal-burner, as he attentively watched him, "I quite understand *now*. He would desert. *Peste*, he is a coward! No matter; I have profited by it."

Thanking the man, and bidding him adieu, Gasper departed and continued his way through the lonely wood.

"In some snug little spot I will rest until morning," he muttered, "and then I will push on. By easy stages I will go on until Paris is reached. Once there I am safe from all, and I shall have every opportunity to perfect whatever plans I may form."

*   *   *   *   *

The following day the Duke of Marlborough sent for our hero and his friends.

After warmly extolling their gallant conduct and the valuable services they had rendered to their Queen and country he promoted them.

Jack, who was already a captain, he presented with a colonelcy.

His comrades, Brian and Ned, he made captains.

Six days after this our hero, Brian, Ned, and Lydia were once again on the road to England.

CHAPTER LIV.

HOW GASPER POSSESSED HIMSELF OF A PILE OF MONEY, AND HOW IT FELL INTO THE HANDS OF CALEB CORDER.

ONE evening, a month after the incidents related in the last chapter, a person who had the appearance of a gentleman, was seated in a small room of the Royal Hotel, Piccadilly. He had been there three or four days, and, much to the astonishment of the servants, had never once gone out.

His name, as he had entered it in the visitor's book, was Robert Verrell.

It is probable that he would have remained in Paris for many months had it not been for the fact that his companions were arrested.

As soon as he found this out he disguised himself as a sailor, and thus made his way to England.

On a little table stood a bottle of wine, pens, ink, and paper, and the pocket-book handed to him upon the battle-field by the dying soldier.

For the hundredth time Gasper was examining the contents of the latter.

The most important, as it seemed to him,

DUNN FELL, PIERCED TO THE HEART.

But the reader will not be at all astonished to know that this person was none other than Gasper Grimsby.

He was in every respect much altered.

His hair was very fashionably dressed, his face clean shaven, and his clothes of the best make.

Nor was this all.

Gasper could now sign a cheque for a couple of thousand pounds.

In Paris he had associated himself with a number of blacklegs, and assisted them in their swindles.

The result was that he made a large amount of money.

document the book contained was as follows :—

"We are just about to fight what is supposed to be a decisive battle; and as, like many another, I may live but a few more hours, I take this opportunity of writing a letter of explanation, trusting that it may find its way into the hands of those for whom it is intended.

"I am known in the 40th Regiment as Private John Ward, but my real name is Frederick West.

"For many years I resided at Thames Ditton. It was there that my father died, and I inherited his wealth, which was considerable.

"Unfortunately I had formed the acquaint-ance of a number of men whom, too late, I found were the scum of society.

"Blindly acting on their advice, I soon ran through my fortune, and was compelled to sell even the residence.

"But this was not all.

"I had formed the acquaintance of Miss Nellie Farmer, the daughter of one of the wealthiest landowners in Kent, and I was under the impression that my attentions were by no means displeasing to her.

"But I discovered that a young fellow of the name of Stephen Dunn was paying his addresses to her, and, after several letters, I met him.

"A terrible quarrel ensued. I grossly insulted him, and he challenged me.

"On the following day we fought a duel beside the marshes, and Dunn fell, pierced to the heart.

"My friend had assisted me to place my coat on when there was a sudden rustling, and the next instant, to my intense astonishment, who should stand before me but Miss Farmer.

"How she had obtained the information which enabled her to be present I never learned.

"But as she wore a riding habit I thought it possible that she had been riding in the neigh-bourhood.

"I was just about to rush towards her when she waived me off, and in tones which I shall never forget—so full were they of scorn and loathing—she advised me to leave the country.

"She informed me—while my friends and the friends of Dunn listened—that she had long ago ceased to think of me, because she did not think me an honourable man.

"She mentioned the names of several of my companions, and asked me if I had ever dared to mention her name to them.

"'Go, Frederick West!' were her last words; 'and wherever you are do not forget that Nellie Farmer hates you with all her soul, for you have murdered one of the finest men who ever walked God's earth.'

"I said nothing. I was too crushed. She departed, after seeing Dunn taken away, and I have never seen her since. But I know that she still lives at her father's at Thames Ditton.

"I entreat of the one into whose hands this may fall to go to Miss Farmer and say how deeply I regret the past, and ask her to pray for me. Tell her that, gambler though I was, and the associate of blacklegs, I died a true soldier.

"Then take this letter to Mr. Marshall, whose address will be found on one of the letters herein.

"The money in this book is payment for what I ask.

"FREDERICK WEST."

"Hem!" muttered Gasper, as he carefully folded the letter and replaced it in the pocket-book. "And this portrait is, of course, of Nellie Farmer."

He opened the locket he had taken from the dead soldier, and gazed upon the portrait of a young girl.

"Decidedly handsome," he muttered; "but I suppose it would be no use trying my luck in that direction.

"No; no use at all. I am afraid I have not yet acquired the art of love-making.

"Now that I am a swell of the first rank—I don't think *that* can be questioned, since I *look* it—I must study the matter.

"But the most interesting part of this letter - at least to *me*—is where it says that Mr. Farmer is a very wealthy man. No time must be lost. If I am careful I may be a few hundred pounds richer in a day or so."

He rang the bell and directed the servant to inform the manager that it was his inten-tion to at once depart.

The manager quickly appeared with his bill, which Gasper paid.

"Chair, sir?" asked the polite manager.

"No; I am not going far—only to a friend's, and therefore I will leave my portmanteau with you."

The manager bowed.

"We will take every care of it, sir," he said.

Gasper buckled on his sword, saw to the priming of his pistols, and went at once to an innkeeper close by.

From him he hired a powerful horse, and having inquired the quickest way, rode off to Thames Ditton.

* * * * *

Yes, there was no doubt about Mr. Farmer being a wealthy man.

Besides being a large landowner in Kent, he had a large share in a well-known London banking business. He was a man of about sixty, and though he suffered severely from gout at times, he was as active in his business as he was when quite a young man.

A great deal of this business he transacted at his house at Thames Ditton—"Ditton Lodge," and he received very great assistance from his only child—his beautiful daughter Nellie.

Who did not know her as the rich heiress?

How many gentlemen occupying good positions had sought her hand and been refused?

They were all told the same thing.

It was to the effect that her love was buried with Stephen Dunn, and that she had no intention of marrying.

Her father was wise enough not to urge her one way or the other.

He let her please herself; though, to be sure, he secretly cherished the hope that one day she would marry.

It was about nine o'clock, and Mr. Farmer and his daughter were engaged in conversation concerning some business matter, when the servant informed them that a gentleman, who gave his name as James Lestall, and who had come straight from London, desired to speak with them.

"Lestall?" said Mr. Farmer. "I know of no such person."

To the servant:

"What is he like?"

"He is a handsome, well-dressed gentleman, sir," replied the servant.

Handsome! The servant was "wool gathering."

"Well, show him in. You will stay with me, Nelly."

Another moment and Gasper was ushered into the room.

"Looks a person of some position," thought Mr. Farmer; "but rather foppish."

"You are from London, sir?" asked Mr. Farmer.

"Yes, sir; from London direct."

"Will you please state your business?"

"My business, sir, concerns one Frederick West."

Nelly started up, her face turning deathly pale.

Mr. Farmer frowned.

"Frederick West?" he said, sternly. "We know no such person."

"Excuse me, you *did* know him."

"My daughter was acquainted with him. I am glad to say that I knew but little of the man. He proved himself a villain, sir."

"So he admits."

"He admits?"

"He does. He——"

"Where is the man now?"

"Where many a thousand Englishmen are, sir. Beneath French soil."

Mr. Farmer, in great agitation, stood up.

As for Nelly, she had fallen into a chair, and buried her face in her hands.

"Explain," said Mr. Farmer, in low and tremulous tones.

"He enlisted as a private soldier, was in several engagements, and, finally, at the great battle of Blenheim, where he was killed. Just before he died he placed this pocket-book in my hand.

"Here, sir, is a long letter in which he refers to your daughter."

"May I read it?"

"Certainly!"

Mr. Farmer, with many pauses and comments, read the letter.

Then, with a deep sigh, he returned it.

"Certainly," he said, "he has made *some* atonement for the past. Misguided young man! He might, at this moment, have been one of the proudest Englishmen in the country. There are many more, sir—Mr. Lestall—worse than he was."

"You are indeed correct, sir," replied Gasper, bowing.

"You, sir, were in the army with Mr. West?"

"No, I was travelling close to the spot where the great battle was fought. When it was over, I visited the field, and thus came upon the young man."

"Well, sir, I am sure both of us most sincerely thank you for the trouble you have taken. I am sure you will excuse my daughter."

"Old recollections have temporarily deprived her of speech. May I request you to stay here until to-morrow? Some of the roads hereabouts are dangerous for travellers."

"Dangerous?"

"Ay, robbers are about, I have heard. Within the last week or two several ruffians have been pleased to pay this quarter a visit. It is said that they come from London."

Gasper smiled.

"I do not fear robbers," he said. "I have been through too many dangers to fear such blackguards; but, as you so kindly ask me to stay, I accept with much pleasure."

So it was arranged.

The man-servant, Mr. Farmer said, was ill, and so Gasper undertook to see his horse snugly placed for the night, and the servant conducted him to the stables.

If the servant had stopped for a few moments, it is possible that she would have noticed that her master's unexpected visitor took particular care to see that saddle and bridle were quite secure upon his horse, and that he made no attempt to take off either.

Also, she might have noticed that he took the pistols from the holsters, and placed them in his pocket.

On his return to the house he found that the best of refreshments had been placed ready for him, and he did ample justice to them.

Mr. Farmer was not very talkative—that Gasper particularly noticed.

He considered it was due to the letter. It was not.

Nelly, just before she retired from the room, had said to her father:

"I wish you had not asked this man to remain. I do not like the look of him at all. Be cautious, father—be very cautious."

Mr. Farmer smiled at the time.

But when he remembered how often his daughter's warnings had been of value, he became serious.

Until nearly midnight Gasper spoke of the Battle of Blenheim, and invented many adventures in which he was the chief hero.

"You know many in the army?" asked Mr. Farmer.

"Oh, yes! a great many."

"Have you seen this daring young officer named Barrington? He is generally known as Gallant Jack."

"I have never seen him, but I have heard a great deal of him. Officers tell me that a great many of his daring deeds have no foundation."

"No foundation?"

"Nay; that they are invented by those who take an interest in him."

"In that case the Duke of Marlborough himself has much to answer for?"

"No doubt, sir; no doubt."

In a few moments more Mr. Farmer showed Gasper to his room, and then he himself retired.

But it was not to rest.

His daughter's words had made him uneasy.

When half-an-hour had passed he left his room and proceeded to Gasper's. There was no key in the lock, and, as the lamp was burning, he could see into the room.

He saw that Gasper was sound asleep—of that he had no doubt whatever, for he watched him for several minutes.

Satisfied that, in this case at any rate, his daughter was wrong, he returned to his room and retired.

Gasper, of course, had purposely left the light burning, for he had some idea that Nelly did not like his appearance, and for that reason he had retired early.

He, however, slipped into bed with nearly all his clothes on.

And he remained in one position until he heard a distant church clock strike the hour of one.

Then he got up, put on his boots, cloak, and hat, placed a belt about his waist, and thrust his pistols into it.

Blowing out the light, he opened the door, and cautiously descended the stairs, pausing every now and then to listen.

All was profoundly still.

Reaching the hall the villain quickly made his way into Mr. Farmer's study, and there he struck a light.

Looking about he found one of the servants' lanterns.

It furnished him with sufficient light to see what he was about.

The first thing he did was to open the drawers in the secretaire.

He was amply rewarded for his trouble; for in one of them he found a roll of bank notes and a bag of gold.

These he swiftly transferred to his pockets.

Next he turned his attention to a large iron safe.

That, however, was locked, and he at once saw that all attempts to open it would be fruitless.

A cabinet he managed to open with the fire-irons.

He saw nothing but books, and, with a curse, he closed the broken door.

If he had but known!

What a fortune was in that cabinet!

For Mr. Farmer was eccentric to some extent, and one of his habits was to place bank notes for very large amounts between the leaves of a book.

One of the volumes in the cabinet contained bank notes to an enormous amount.

They were awaiting Mr. Farmer's convenience to transfer them to his London bank.

Finding nothing else which he could conveniently carry away, Gasper blew out the light, and opened the window, which looked out into the yard adjoining the stables.

He was just about to leap out when he was suddenly grasped by the collar, and drawn back.

By the light of the moon he was enabled to see the face of the person who had thus stolen into the room, and seized him.

It was Miss Nelly Farmer.

She had heard several strange noises, and had finally decided to decend.

"Thief!" she said, "what are you doing here?"

"Doing?" replied Gasper, with a fiendish grin. "What do you *think* I am doing?"

"Laying your hand on what is not yours."

"By the Lord you are correct. And I thought I should be able to do so without having to strike a blow. I find I am wrong, and therefore I am sorry for *you!*"

So saying the murderous hound wrenched himself free from Miss Farmer's grasp, and ere she could draw back, he dealt her a fearful blow full in the face.

"'PRESENT!' EXCLAIMED THE VINDICTIVE CAPTAIN."

No. 10.

The poor girl dropped like a stone, and Gasper turning, darted through the window.

To reach the stables was the work of one minute ; to bring his horse out and mount him, the work of another only.

Getting into the road, he put his horse to the gallop, and soon left the house far behind him.

"By Heavens!" he exclaimed, "a wondrous good night's work, and I reckon I have spoiled her good looks. She must have suspected me all along, and yet I thought I had the appearance of a quiet, innoffensive gentleman.

Not the faintest idea had he as to whither the road led. But what did it matter ?

The principal thing was to put as long a distance as possible between himself and the house.

. Reaching the end of the road—which was of great length—he arrived at a well-wooded open space.

It was Ditton Common.

Before he had gone far across it, he saw what at first looked like the glitter of glass ; but when the moon shone out clearly, he quickly saw that it was water.

"The Thames," he chuckled. "Good—good! I shall no doubt get a ferry over if I am prepared to pay handsomely!"

With a light heart he went onward, and soon was in the centre of the common. Here he found a broad, well-kept road, with huge chestnut trees on either side. Feeling certain that this led to the river, he pushed on.

He had nearly reached the end, when suddenly a horseman appeared before him, and he was rapidly followed by another and another.

Verily it seemed as if they had dropped from the clouds.

Each was mounted on a powerful horse, and masked.

For the first time Gasper recalled Mr. Farmer's words.

He remembered he had laughed at the idea of being intercepted by robbers.

But he did not laugh now.

"Stop, my friend," said the first man ; "you are travelling too fast."

"Out of my path, fool !" cried Gasper, plunging his spurs in the horse's sides.

The animal reared, and then darted forward.

At the same instant Gasper fired at the leader of the three men.

The ball, however, went wide of the mark.

Before he could draw his other pistol, he was pounced upon, torn from his saddle, and flung violently to the ground.

"Be careful what you do," said the leader, "or we shall treat *you* to a couple of leaden pills."

Gasper started.

The voice, though it appeared muffled, seemed familiar to him.

The three men dismounted, and one took a lantern from beneath his cloak, and held it over the fallen man.

"By all the fiends in Hades !" muttered the leader, "it is Gasper Grimsby. Idiotic *fool* that I was not to have plunged a bayonet into him ere I left the battle-field. But no matter ; he will not know me."

Aloud he said :

"Lift him up."

Gasper was dragged to his feet, and sore enough he felt.

Another order Caleb gave, and which Gasper did not understand, and the two men seized his hands, and pinioned them behind his back.

He was then searched, and every article he was possessed of was taken from him.

The stolen property thus rapidly changed hands.

"You are the best man we have met for many a long day," said Caleb, "and we thank you for coming this way."

"Cowards !" hissed Gasper, boiling over with rage.

"As you will. We are not at all particular."

"Now that you have taken all I was possessed of, do you intend to free my hands ?"

"Do you particularly desire it ?"

No reply.

"We will untie your hands if you will promise to give us no trouble."

Still no reply.

"Well," continued Corder to his companions, "we will not be too hard on him ; we will unfasten his hands, but not before we have rendered him incapable of making a fool of himself."

Thereupon he took Gasper's other pistol, picked up the discharged weapon, and handed them to his companions.

Then, drawing Gasper's sword from its sheath, he broke off the blade at the hilt, and threw the pieces away ; then he cut the cord.

At once Gasper was upon him.

"Villain !" he yelled. "I will at least see the face of the man who robs me !"

Caleb tried to wrench himself free, but before he could do so Gasper snatched the mask from his face.

No cry left Gasper's lips.

He stood speechless.

He was like a man turned to stone.

When he recovered from his astonishment Caleb and his companions had mounted, and were riding away.

He heard something besides the tramp of horses' hoofs.

That was Caleb's loud, mocking laugh.

"Caleb Corder!" muttered Caleb, "*here* above all places in the world? This, then, is is what he has turned. And I am stripped of every penny!"

"But I know that Caleb Corder is in London, or near it. That information is worth much. But by Heaven I have paid dearly for it. Mr. Farmer said that it was supposed they came from London.

"There is no *doubt* about it. Yes, it is in the heart of London that I must look for Caleb Corder. Let him wait! I will have a fearful revenge. I have money in the bank, and with that I can do much. Curse him!—Curse him!

"I am without arms and without money. I may again be attacked and my horse taken from me. Then, in the event of old Farmer putting anyone on my track, I should certainly be caught."

We may add that he was not again intercepted, and that he reached Piccadilly just as morning dawned.

CHAPTER LV.

OF THE MANNER IN WHICH GALLANT JACK GETS POSSESSION OF THE WILL, AND HOW HE AGAIN LOSES IT.

OUR hero and his friends were once more in London.

At first they stayed at a popular hostelry near St. James's Park, and which was called "The Guards' Rest."

Then they were speedily joined by Mrs. Barrington.

Her joy at once again folding her beloved daughter to her heart can be imagined, and delighted beyond expression was she to find her so beautiful a girl.

As Brian O'Flinn said :

"She's as handsome as the lakes o' Killarney, me bhoys—only more so, and no blarney!"

But Mrs. Barrington—comparatively young —had by no means lost her beauty.

That Lydia saw with much astonishment; for she remembered the trials and privations through which she had passed.

And there was a certain gentleman who was present at the reunion who took particular notice of Mrs. Barrington's appearance.

That was Count Victor Montsorel.

After a day or two Jack hired a house close to the hostelry, and thither went all our friends.

Soon they were joined by the Lady Flora Greville, and she remained with them for many hours.

Jack did not monopolise her all the time.

She had frequent conversations with Mrs. Barrington and her daughter.

The reader guesses that that conversation was in reference to her marriage with Jack.

On the evening of the third day Ned Rattles, who had been, as he said, "looking about the streets," returned to the house.

He was, no doubt, excited, but he tried hard to conceal it.

He found Jack in conversation with his brother, but, after many frantic—(and furious)—motions, he managed to convey to him the intelligence that he desired to speak to him.

Jack soon joined him.

"Jack," said Ned, "I've got some news for you."

"News? Good or bad?"

"Oh, good! You see I was walking along the Strand when I came full butt against an old friend of ours, Corporal Armstrong. You remember him?"

"Quite well."

"Well, of course, considering that this was the first time we had met since the great battle, we decided to drink each other's healths."

"Naturally."

"So we went into that large hostelry called the Lion—or the Red Lion—I forget which——"

"The Red Lion—the back faces the river?"

"That's the place."

"It is evident that you and Armstrong are totally unacquainted with the place, or you would never have crossed the threshold."

"Do you know it?"

"I have heard a very great deal of it. It is the resort of thieves, and, some say, assassins. But go on."

"To tell the truth, as soon as we entered the place I thought there was something about it which was not exactly right.

"I noticed several skulking blackguards about. We ordered a bottle of wine and seated ourselves in a little nook where there is just room enough for two.

"Of course we got talking of the battle, and of the many poor fellows we knew who had been left beneath the soil of France, and we didn't take much notice of what was going on around."

"But, suddenly, a voice fell upon my ears which I fancied I knew very well. I looked sideways, and you might have knocked me down with a feather when I saw beside me, Caleb Corder."

"Never!"

"It is a fact, I assure you. Oh, don't fear,

I looked at him a good many times in order to satisfy myself."

"This is news indeed."

"Ay, my boy. But you never saw such an alteration in all your life. My opinion is that he is preparing himself for the rope. Do you understand what I mean?"

"That he has taken to a very risky business?"

"Right."

"So you really think so?"

"I should like to wager fifty guineas to one. You should see the way he is dressed. Lord! it made me laugh I can tell you. He has the appearance of a swaggering, brutal Alsatian."

"I heard him ask if certain persons were there, and the way he spoke to the host convinced me that he had some power over the man.

"Certain it is the host replied to him as if he were afraid of him."

"Is that all?" asked Jack, thoughtfully.

"No," smiled Ned, "by no means. I heard the host address him as Captain Swift."

"Captain?"

"Ay, and tell him if he went to his own room—his *own room* mark you—he would send up the persons required as they came in."

"Good. The news you have brought me, Ned, is of the very *greatest* importance. You may depend upon it, that Caleb Corder will know were Gasper Grimsby is."

Ned nodded.

"Yes," he said, "that is more than likely. But do you think he will *tell* you?"

"I will force him to."

"Well, you may try him, of course."

"I will go to-night."

"He may not be there. I should wait a little so as to be certain of a meeting."

"I will chance it. But I must go disguised."

"And I will accompany you."

"No, no. I insist upon going alone."

Ned stared.

"Well," he said, "if you insist, of course I have nothing further to say. But let me warn you to go armed."

"Do not fear as to that. But let me see—how can I disguise myself?"

"Don't disguise *yourself*—let someone else do that. There are plenty of costumiers about. You speak French like a Frenchman, and you can also imitate his actions—antics Brian calls them; so why not go disguised as a Frenchman?"

"You forget that Caleb Corder is well aware of the fact that I speak the French language like a native. He may suspect."

"You are right. I have no doubt he is well aware of the fact that you and all of us are in London."

"Yes; and so is Gasper Grimsby, if he is really in this country. I'll tell you what: I will go disguised as a Dutch skipper. I can imitate him very well."

"So you can; many's the hearty laugh Brian and I have had over it. Well, so that's decided; go as a Dutch skipper, and good luck attend you. You will, at least, let me accompany you to the costumier's?"

"Certainly."

Jack stayed in the house until ten, when he said that he and Ned were going out for a short time.

They went direct to the well-known costumiers near Leicester-fields, and, in less than half-an-hour, Jack was completely transformed.

Ned declared, with a laugh, that neither his mother nor the Lady Flora would be able to recognise him.

And there was much truth in this.

Even the costumier was astonished; and when Jack began to speak in the Dutchman's peculiar broken English, he laughed till the tears ran down his face.

Bidding Ned return to the house and make some excuse for him, Jack went to the Red Lion, in the Strand, and close against what is now the Adelphi.

It was only a two-storied building with carved wooden balconies beneath each window.

But its length was tremendous, for the back ran close against the river—so close indeed that a man, at high tide, could easily have leapt into the Thames.

Of this hostelry Jack had heard a great deal, but this was the first time he had entered it.

The host, John Poole, at once placed himself before him.

Here was a Dutch skipper—was it not possible that he had a few kegs of smuggled spirits to dispose of?

"How may I serve you?" asked the host.

"I want nothing to drink," replied Jack, in broken English; but you can serve me another way. And here is a piece of your own money to open your eyes and shut your mouth."

The host pocketed the money with a wink and a grin, which was intended to convey the intimation that he understood anything if paid.

"No doubt," he whispered. "You have a few choice articles to land? If so, Mynheer, the back of this house is the very place for it. The river touches it."

"Eh? Good! Then I shall know where to take the boat to the next time I have a few little things to dispose of. No doubt I can drive a bargain with you."

"I am the very man, and never object to purchase from one to a hundred kegs. But your business now?"

"Is with one of your friends," whispered Jack. "I have a commission for him from a gentleman. It will be a fine thing for him."

"Ah! His name?"

"Captain Swift."

"He is here. At least, I think so. I will soon tell you."

As he spoke he stepped back a few paces, and having glanced round to see that none but the Dutch skipper and himself were present, he took hold of the short hand of what appeared to be an old-fashioned clock.

At once a sound as of an iron chain running rapidly through a ring was heard.

After a pause of a few seconds both hands of the "clock" went round and round like lightning.

"Ay," said the host, "he has not gone out."

"Could you not tell that without this clock-work arrangement?"

"Nay," smiled the host; "for, you see, circumstances sometimes compel the captain to go out the back way. Pass through that little door, ascend the stairs, and you will reach the room."

Jack did as directed, and he made as much noise as he went up the stairs as was possible.

When he reached the landing a voice called out—

"Enter."

Jack pushed open a door opposite him, and entered a small room.

At the table was seated four men, and, despite his get up, he at once recognised Caleb Corder as one.

"A nice looking bully he is," thought Jack. "It is evident that Ned is not far wrong. I should like to thrash him within an inch of his life."

Caleb Corder surveyed him closely for a few seconds.

Then he said:

"Well, my man, what seek you?"

"Captain Swift."

"Good. He is here."

"Where?"

"Here. I am Captain Swift."

"Ha! Good—very good."

So broad was the Dutch accent that it was with some difficulty that Caleb Corder understood.

"Your business?" demanded Caleb.

The supposed Dutchman looked around the room and then at the three men.

Caleb understood.

The Dutchman desired to speak to him alone.

"Go below, my men," he said to the three, and in tones intended to be imposing; "but remain within call."

The three men left the room and descended the stairs.

Corder then rose and secured the door.

"Now you may speak," he said, "without fear of being overheard. From your manner I take it that you have some important business with me."

"Exactly."

"You have, perhaps, been commissioned to seek me out?"

"Ay."

"Speak freely, then, and be assured that I am paying the greatest attention. I am always open to undertake any important job if well paid, with a fair part in advance; and I have plenty to help me. If you, or those in whose pay you are, wish to remove an obnoxious person, leave it to me."

And he resumed his seat with the air of a king.

Jack could scarcely keep his hands off him. He drew nearer the table, and said, in low tones:

"First, have you seen anything of Jack Barrington lately?"

"What?"

Caleb was naturally astonished.

"Jack Barrington."

"No! What the——"

"Well"—and here Jack resumed his natural tones—"he stands before you."

And he removed part of his disguise.

Like lightning Caleb started up and laid his hand upon a heavy horse-pistol which lay on the table.

Jack, however, was too quick for him. He sprang forward and dealt Caleb such a stunning blow in the chest that he fell back doubled up for a moment.

"Cry out for assistance," said Jack, drawing forth a pistol, "and may fortune for ever desert me if I don't drop you dead at my feet! So you call yourself Captain Swift, eh? On my soul you look a pretty captain!"

"Listen to me," said Caleb. "Did I but raise my voice, you would be surrounded, and your life not worth a moment's purchase. You will understand that I am now a person of vast importance."

"In your *own* estimation, no doubt. But do not fancy that you can terrify me. A man who has fought in the thick of many a fierce battle does not care a snap of the fingers for a lot of lawless ruffians.

"Listen carefully to what I say, Caleb Corder, and do not attempt to touch that pistol again.

"Also don't attempt to touch that sword. I am here to demand from you the address of Gasper Grimsby."

"From me?"

"From you."

"Well, on my soul, you certainly ask something. How, in the fiend's name, should I know the address of Gasper Grimsby?"

"You are his partner in crime."

"No; you make a mistake. I am not his partner in anything; or if any partnership, as you call it, ever existed, then it was long ago dissolved. But by Satan! a sudden thought strikes me. What do you want of Gasper Grimsby? Do you seek a certain document?"

"I do—my grandfather's will."

"What would you be prepared to pay for that?"

"Why do you ask the question?"

"Because I can, if I think proper, produce it."

"You can?"

"Ay."

"When?"

"This moment."

"Then do so; quick; produce it."

"But to what shall I be entitled?"

"To a ball through your black heart!"

Caleb, with difficulty, forced a faint smile.

"I'm sure you don't mean that?" he said.

"I do mean it. But from what I can see, Caleb Corder, the rope will fall to your lot."

"The will is in my possession, and, if you will give me a reasonable amount, it shall be yours. I see by the terms of the document that you are entitled to a large fortune; consequently a few hundred pounds would be a small amount to you."

Jack considered.

What should he offer him?

"I will pay you the sum of one hundred pounds," he said.

"One hundred only? That is not sufficient."

"If you do not accept that amount I will set the law in motion."

"Suppose I agree to take the hundred, would you swear that you will give no information concerning me?"

"Of course," replied Jack, contemptuously; "but I warn you that if ever your villainy should bring you across my path, it is likely enough that death, or the law, will overtake you."

"Here is the will," said Caleb, as he placed his hand in his breast, took out the document, and flung it upon the table.

Jack seized upon it, hastily examined it, and put it in his pocket.

Then, opening his purse, he took out the gold pieces, and placed them on the table.

"Of course," he said, "I am not in the habit of carrying a large amount of money with me; but here are ten pounds, and you shall have the remainder by this time to-morrow. Will that arrangement suit you?"

"It must."

"Now tell me—how did you get possession of the will?"

"I would rather not say."

"I will not press you. Now, Caleb Corder, let me caution you. Be careful, or the law will have you."

"I've got my eyes open."

"You will not tell me, then, where Gasper Grimsby is to be found?"

"I know nothing of him."

"Is he in England?"

"He is in London."

Jack appeared as if about to say something else, but suddenly turning, he abruptly left the room, and, in another minute, the house. So lost in thought was he that he did not notice the many men about the place. Not the slightest idea had he that he was followed.

But he was, and we shall now see how that occurred.

* * * *

Gasper Grimsby again put up at the hostelry —or hotel, as they were then beginning to be called—and for a considerable time remained quiet.

Then deciding that it would be better to go about London in disguise, he placed himself in the hands of a man skilled in that sort of thing, and with excellent results.

"Now," he considered, "if I should run against Jack Barrington, he will not know me, nor will any of his clever friends, curse them! But the first step is to find Caleb Corder. How am I to set about it? I verily believe he is in London. Let me think. Ha! I have it. I will visit the houses beside the river."

Accordingly, just about a couple of hours before Jack set out, Gasper set off to commence his task.

"It may take days," he thought, "or weeks, but when I find him I will send a couple of balls through him as sure as my name is what it is."

He commenced at Westminster, and visited

hostelry after hostelry which he well knew were frequented by the lowest of the low.

However, he obtained no information.

In putting questions, of course, he had to use the greatest care, for the slightest error would have caused the finger of suspicion to be pointed at him.

At last he reached a small hostelry bearing the singular title of the "Three Black Cats."

He remembered it well, for he had been in it many a time.

"There used to be an ostler here," thought Gasper, "of the name of Settle. If he is here now he might give me some information."

He ordered a small bottle of wine, and, to his joy, it was served by the very man he was thinking of.

A frightful, dissipated ruffian he looked, too.

"Well, Settle," said Gasper, "how fares it?"

"What? Fares what?"

"Well—business."

"Ask the host—he knows."

"How is—but here take a drink. Is the wine good?"

"Good? of course. It always *is* when a man pays a good price. It don't fall to the likes o' me to get such stuff as this. Here's your health, whoever you are. You seem to know me; but hanged if I can remember you."

"I don't suppose you can. But I remember you well. A certain number of years ago I was with you—or near you—and a few men who placed a weighty box between——"

With a sharp cry the man started back, holding up his hand.

"Hush!" he said, in low, hoarse tones, "hush! Don't mention that for your life."

"I won't," grinned Gasper; "but you need have no fear for me. I know how to keep a secret."

"That's more than those who assisted me at that job could."

"What of them?'

"Gone."

"Gone? Where to?"

The man made a downward movement with his thumb.

"Ah, dead—I see."

"Yes, but before they were put underground they went up in the *air*. You know what I mean. And that was all because they could not keep their infernal mouths closed. Ah, there's been nothing like that hereabouts for years.

"No one seems to have any pluck now," the wretch added, after a pause; "but they *do*

say that this young buck who calls himself Captain Swift has plenty of it."

"Oh! Who's he?"

"Lord knows. He *calls* himself Captain Swift; but I don't fancy that is his real name."

"I may have met him. Describe him."

Settle did so; and it was an exact description of Caleb Corder as he had seen him at Thames Ditton.

"I'll tell you what," whispered Gasper; "that is the very man I am seeking. I can give him an excellent task. Where can I find him?"

"He stays at the Red Lion; but you won't get to see him very easily. They won't let everybody pass into the house."

"No? Well, look you, you can pass easily enough?"

"Me? Oh, yes, *rather*," grinned the man.

"Well, if you can pass me so that I can have an interview with Captain Swift, without being observed, I will give you five guineas."

The ostler was astounded.

"Five guineas for that paltry task! You don't mean it?" he said.

"Mean it, certainly. Look, here is the money; and you can see from that that my business with Captain Swift is most important. Why, I've been inquiring for him for days."

"Ah, he's not well known yet. Not long established, you see. Well, I'll take you to the Red Lion at once. You can go by the front or the back, just which you like."

"Perhaps it will be as well to enter by the back, eh?"

"In that case we must go by boat. So drink up, and come along."

Gasper at once finished the wine, rose, and followed the ostler.

He was all excitement now, but he tried hard to conceal it.

The ostler took him to the back of the hostelry, and down a short lane.

At the bottom was a flight of stone steps which led to the river, now very dark and silent.

"There's a boat here," said Settle; "but mind how you come, for the steps are slippery."

Both were soon in the boat, which was large enough to hold a dozen people; and the ostler, by means of a long boat-hook, began to propel it towards the back of the Red Lion.

It was reached in a few minutes.

"There," said the ostler, "you see that ladder? Well, that is fastened to the balcony. If you ascend it and push open the window you will be in one of the rooms. Pass right through, and you will be into the passage, and the first door on the right is the room where

Captain Swift stays. "I'll go with you if you like, and——"

"No—no; that is not necessary."

"Shall I remain here, or will you go out by the front?"

"By the front."

"So, well; up you go."

Gasper ascended the ladder, and was soon on the balcony.

It was in a very dangerous condition.

Gasper noted that with much alarm, for it shook beneath his weight.

Pushing open the window, he passed on through the room, and entered the passage which, like the room, was very dark.

He had not taken half-a-dozen steps when the three men who had been with Caleb left the room and descended the stairs.

As soon as the door was closed Gasper crept to it, and he distinctly heard all that was said.

There, by simply applying his eye to a crack in the partitioning, he saw both Jack and Caleb.

"Ho! ho!" he chuckled, "five guineas has indeed put me in luck's way! Jack Barrington here! By Heaven! this is far more than I expected!"

To every word that was uttered he listened, and as soon as Jack left the room he followed.

"For the present," he muttered, "I must leave Caleb Corder. Now that I well know where to drop upon him, I can deal with him when I think fit. What I now require is the will—and Jack Barrington's life—if I can take it without fear of discovery."

Jack proceeded thoughtfully along the Strand, and turned up a narrow lane, which was a short cut towards St. James's.

A more dark, dismal, and neglected spot could not have been found in London; nor a filthier, for it was nothing but mud; while right and left, close to the stumpy hedges, were foul ditches.

Gasper considered this an opportunity which was on no account to be lost.

No doubt not a soul was anywhere near, and so to assassinate Jack Barrington was the easiest thing in the world.

Jack had reached the middle of the lane when Gasper drew a pistol and stopped.

At this moment our hero was about fifty feet off.

Taking steady aim, Gasper fired.

Scarcely had the echoes of the report died away, and before the smoke could clear off, hasty footsteps were heard.

Gasper drew back.

But it was too late.

He was seized with a grip of iron by Jack, who, uninjured by the shot, had hurried back.

As he seized Gasper his disguise fell to the ground.

Despite the darkness Jack recognised him.

"By Heaven!" he cried, "Gasper Grimsby!"

Gasper replied not.

He was frantically trying to release himself.

"You coward!" said Jack; "murderous hound! So it is thus we meet again, eh?"

"I will not lose my hold on you, Gasper Grimsby. Surrender, villain! so that I may let the law deal with you!"

The struggle became a fearful one.

Gasper strained every nerve to release himself, so that he might draw another pistol.

But Jack prevented him.

Again and again Jack dealt him fearful blows in the face, until at last the wretch was nearly blinded with blood.

And again and again both paused to recover their breath.

Jack was too exhausted to speak now.

Nothing could be heard but the harsh, heavy breathing of the two.

No one disturbed the fight; the shot had attracted no attention.

Gasper would have used the butt of his heavy pistol; but Jack had compelled him to drop it.

But, after all, Gasper was to get the best of the struggle.

He managed, by the exertion of all his strength, to get Jack's back to the hedge.

Then, with a sudden and powerful push, he shot him into the ditch, which, in this case, was left full of black, stinking mud.

As Jack dropped he dealt him a blow which caused him to release his hold.

Jack now tried to scramble out of the ditch.

But Gasper hastily drew his other pistol.

"At last, Jack Barrington," he hissed, "I have you at my mercy! Die, you hound!—die!"

He pulled the trigger, but no report followed He was about to raise it again when the sound of horses' hoofs fell upon his ears.

Stopping, he dealt Jack two or three tremendous blows on the head just as he was in the act of drawing himself, by means of the hedge, out of the ditch.

Gallant Jack sank down, while again Gasper raised the trigger.

But it was useless.

In the act of hitting Jack with the butt-end the flint had become displaced. Stooping down he tore open our hero's clothes.

In his breast he found the will.

But this was not all.

He rifled his pockets of everything they contained, taking letters as well as gold.

"No one will find him here," he chuckled, "and he will die, as safe as that I shall live to be a wealthy man."

Nearer and nearer came the tramp of a horse.

Gasper hastily took Jack's pistols and hurried up the lane.

But a sudden thought struck him, and he darted through a gap in the hedge.

"A horse is the very thing I require," he muttered.

In a few moments horse and rider came into view.

The latter had the appearance of a countryman.

Whether he was that or not, Gasper did not care to ascertain.

When the horseman came opposite to him, he raised a pistol and deliberately fired.

Without a cry the rider fell with a crash from his horse, which immediately came to a standstill.

Gasper ran out and looked at the man.

"Ay," he muttered, "a common country clodhopper; but he is not dead. He will recover his senses perhaps in an hour or so, if not—pah! what do I care?"

Springing into the saddle he urged on the horse, and was soon a few miles from the lane.

CHAPTER LVI.

GASPER'S VISIT TO LADY FLORA—OF HOW HE FANCIES HE HAS SECURED A SPLENDID PRIZE, AND HOW HE FINDS HIMSELF COMPLETELY FOILED.

GASPER did not draw rein until he reached Hammersmith, a place with which years before he was somewhat familiar, and which was then but a tiny, and not over picturesque village.

Entering a small street, he paused before a house with a sign indicating that it was a barber's.

Over the front was the name "John Fisher," and the notification, "Barber and Stable-keeper."

Like every other house in the street, it was just closed.

Gasper stood up in the stirrups, and knocked upon the fanlight.

It was heard, and at once answered,

A night-capped head was popped from the window.

"Well, sir," said a voice, "what do you want?"

"I want you to find accommodation for my horse."

"To be sure—with pleasure. Have you been here before?"

"Often."

"Then you are aware that after ten my terms are double; but that includes a shave if you desire it?"

"I'll pay whatever you ask if you come quickly; and if you save me the trouble of going to a hostelry, why, I will pay you well for that."

"I understand. You want a bed?"

"Exactly."

"No doubt I can suit you."

He was quickly at the street door. His wife was behind him, and she said that Gasper could have her son's bed for a night, or a few nights, if he so desired, but that their rule was prepayment.

Gasper paid the amount in advance, and was then conducted upstairs, where he was shown into a small but clean room.

"Did he require any refreshment?" the woman asked.

"None," Gasper answered, "except a quantity of spirits."

This was soon forthcoming; for, in the days of which we write, barbers could supply a customer with wines or spirits, although it was against the law.

"Now, then, to examine what I have become possessed of," muttered Gasper, as he locked the door.

Seating himself at the table, he placed the articles upon it.

Of money there was little, and Gasper paid scarcely any attention to it.

But he minutely examined the letters.

There were four.

Two were from officers in the army, one was from Lady Flora, and one was written by Gallant Jack himself.

"Here, indeed, is information which I may turn to account," he considered. "Here is Lady Flora's present address—'Marley Manor, Hampton Court.' Marley Manor? Surely that is Sir George Marley's house. Ay, of course it must be. I see. She is staying there. Good—good!"

Jack's letter was to a friend, and was quite an ordinary one.

But it was of the highest importance to Gasper.

That was evident from the smile of satisfaction which rested upon his face.

He was forming a plan, and he soon decided how to act.

"Now, here it is," he muttered, as he tossed off a glass of spirits. "This Lady Flora—to whom he would have been married had I permitted him to live—is a person absolutely rolling in wealth.

"That much I *do* know. Now, why should I not possess myself of some of it? I fancy that I could manage it easily enough. I used to be an excellent hand at imitating another's handwriting, and Jack Barrington's is not difficult."

Pens, ink, and paper chanced to be on the table, and he began to imitate Jack's handwriting.

No. It was by no means difficult.

Jack's was rather a schoolboyish hand, for the reader will remember that he was on the battle-field when others of his age were at school, which would have been the case had his father been spared.

In but a few minutes Gasper had imitated several of the words in Jack's letter to perfection.

So satisfied was he that he rubbed his hands, and chuckled with glee.

Searching the room, he found a few sheets of paper stored in a cupboard, and also some wax.

Again seating himself, he wrote the draft of a letter to Lady Flora.

And then he began to commit the forgery. The first nor the second attempt satisfied him, but the third did.

The whole of the letter was a remarkably good imitation of Gallant Jack's writing. There might have been an error or two, but Lady Flora would not notice it.

The letter was as follows :—

"MY BELOVED FLORA,—

"Business of the very greatest importance compels me to at once proceed to Greenwich. Would it be too much to ask you to join me there to-morrow evening?

"I should have no secrets from you now, and therefore I will at once tell you that I am in difficulty regarding money matters. It is absolutely necessary that the sum of two thousand pounds be placed in my hands by to-morrow night, and I would rather come to you for the amount than go elsewhere.

"I shall be staying at Beech House, the residence of Captain Poole, whose wife and daughters will receive you with open arms.

"Ever yours till death,
"JACK.

"The bearer of this has my complete instructions."

"I flatter myself that this is simply first-class!" muttered Gasper, as he neatly folded the forgery and sealed it up. "And now for bed. In the morning I will perfect my plans. But let me see—how can she travel? Coach? No, that will not do. I

have it! The river. But I must get some-one to assist me. Let me think. Ha! I have it! The man Settle, at the Black Cats."

* * * *

A fine mansion was that in the possession of Sir George Marley, a very o'd and valued friend of the Duke of Marlborough.

Marley Manor was considered to be one of the finest mansions in or near Hampton Court.

There it was that the Lady Flora, for a few days, was staying with Lady Marley, for Sir George was at Brussels.

Lady Flora was very, very happy, and the reader knows why.

The evening following Gasper's visit to Hammersmith, Lady Flora and her hostess were in the great drawing-room conversing of the former's approaching marriage when a servant entered.

"A man—a soldier," she said, "has brought this letter to you, my lady;" and she handed a letter to Lady Flora.

"Ha!" cried Flora, as she tore it open, "it is from dear Jack!"

Before a minute had passed she sank into a seat.

"What is it?" cried lady Marley, alarmed at Flora's paleness.

"Jack is in some trouble—read this."

Lady Marley did as desired.

"Trouble, as you say," she said, "but it is of little account. That appears evident."

"Pray advise me."

"To be sure. I should hasten to him with all speed."

"But I cannot procure the money in so short a time."

"Do not let that trouble you," smiled Lady Marley, "what amount have you?"

"About five hundred pounds in notes."

"I will hand you the remainder. I will go and get it."

Flora struck the bell and directed one of the servants to show the man in.

He quickly presented himself.

He was attired as a private soldier; but his dress was none of the smartest, nor was his heavy beard and moustache in anything like a trim condition.

It is scarcely necessary for us to say that this private soldier was none other than Gasper Grimsby.

"You have come straight from Mr. Barrington?"

"Straight as an arrow from the gallant captain, lady."

"What then, are you? His servant?"

"I have not that honour, my lady. No, I am Captain Poole's servant."

"Did you come by road?"

"No, lady, by river. It is the quickest; and a boat, unlike a horse, requires no rest."

"I trust the men with you——"

"There is but one man, my lady. You see, we take it in turns to row."

"I see. Well, I hope the man is like yourself, to be trusted, for I am about to take with me a large sum of money."

"I can assure your ladyship that the man is as honest as the day."

"Do you wait here while I attire myself. I will send you refreshments. But as to your boat—is it safe?"

"Perfectly."

"You see it is very dark. I would rather have gone by road."

"Do not fear for a moment, lady. The boat is a roomy one, and cushions are placed for your convenience; while, fore and aft, lanterns are placed. You see, my lady, I suggested to the captain that he should delay the boat until the morning, but he would not hear of it."

Lady Flora left the room.

But, instead of going upstairs, she darted to the back, stole among the shrubs, and looked through the curtains in the room.

It was a happy thought.

What did she see?

She saw the "private" grin, rub his hands, turn to the mirror, survey himself for a moment, and then, taking off beard and moustache, wipe his face.

The operation lasted a moment only, but, by means of the mirror, Lady Flora saw his face, and the description of Gasper Grimsby, furnished her by Jack, at once rose up in her mind.

"I suspected something was wrong," gasped Flora, as she crept into the house, "but I had no idea that the wretch who has sworn to take Jack's life would himself enter the house in which I was.

"The villain! What am I to do? Oh, Heaven guide me! for now, indeed, do I require it.

"Yes, it is Gasper Grimsby! My God! What can have happened to Jack? I must endeavour to learn; but, if I am not careful, all will be lost. I must retain my coolness."

Lady Marley, she knew, was in the library, and thither she hastily proceeded, after telling the servant to supply the soldier with refreshments.

They remained closeted together for some few minutes.

In less than a quarter of an hour Flora, attired for the journey, re-entered the drawing-room, where she found the "private" at attention.

She was not slow to notice that he immediately fixed his eyes upon the bag she carried.

"I am ready," said Flora, with great composure, "pray lead the way."

Gasper led the way with alacrity, and Flora, with Lady Marley at her side, followed him closely to the edge of the river.

Settle, the ostler, stood in the stern, boathook in hand, and he assisted Flora to take her seat in the bow, which had been furnished with a couple of cushions.

Lady Marley, of course, knew all, but as she bade good-bye to Flora, she retained her composure, though she would rather have lost half her fortune than that Flora should have stepped into the boat.

She had strongly advised Flora not to go.

But it was of no use.

"I will see to what extent the wretch will go," she said; "besides, it is important that I should learn if anything has happened to Jack."

Lady Marley returned to her house, and a quarter of an hour afterwards she was startled by the loud rattle of horses' hoofs.

She, as well as the servants, hurried to the door.

Two horsemen hurriedly rode up to them.

"Lady Flora?" asked one.

"She has left on a journey."

"With Jack?—I mean Colonel Barrington, madam?"

"No; but who are you?"

The question was asked with the greatest eagerness.

"My name, madam, is Ned Rattles, and my friend here is Brian O'Flynn. We are firm friends of Mr. Barrington."

"I have heard of you," replied Lady Marley, hastily; "and you could not have arrived here at a better time. Dismount quickly, gentlemen, and take your pistols from the holsters."

Ned and Brian were astonished at these words, more especially as they proceeded from the lips of a lady.

Nevertheless they were off their horses like lightning.

"For the love of Heaven, me lady," said Brian," tell me this—will yez—where is Jack Barrington?"

"Alas! I am unable to inform you."

"Ah! thin, there's no mistake about it. Ned, d'ye see? Some accident happened to him in the Strand, or after he left it. Bad cess to the Red Lion and the spalpeens inside it! If they've injured Jack, it's a bad day's work they've done—that's all!"

Lady Marley took them aside, and rapidly explained all that had occurred.

"Gasper Grimsby!" gasped both. "It seems impossible."

Lady Flora told me that she was certain she had made no mistake."

"And yet she ventured in the boat?"

"Yes, in defiance of my advice."

"Be the soul of St. Patrick!" exclaimed Brian, "she's a brave leddy. But look you, madam—yer honour—I mean me leddy—have you a boat?"

"I have; and I was about to suggest that you follow Lady Flora."

"We will wid all the playsure in loife; an' if we can get near enough to Gasper Grimsby——"

"We'll fling him in the Thames," interrupted Ned.

"Thrue! and by Bannigan's ghost, I'll see that he don't come up again. Oh, the dirty thafe o' the world!"

"Follow me," said her ladyship. My husband's boat is at the bottom of the garden. Can you row?"

"We are by no means professional scullers," said Ned, "but I'll warrant we shall be able to get her through the water."

The boat was quickly reached.

It lay beside some stone steps at the bottom of the garden.

"It is very light, as you see," said Lady Marley, "and you will soon overtake Lady Flora. Enter the boat, gentlemen, and may fortune go with you.

"The same to yez," said Brian, seizing the boat-hook and pushing off. "Sure, you're a jewel, like another lady I know. Catch hold of the sculls, Ned, me honey, and pull like the divil!"

Meanwhile Lady Flora had remained seated in the bows of the vessel.

Not once had she stirred.

Again and again Gasper cast glances at her, and each time she appeared to be lost in thought.

But no one could be more keenly on the alert than Lady Flora.

Would Gasper go right on to Greenwich, she wondered.

Settle, who had the oars, was wondering too.

Gasper never offered to relieve him at the oars, and he was becoming tired.

No wonder.

The boat, the same used in conveying Gasper to the Red Lion, was an enormous vessel, and required all his strength.

The fact was that Gasper was keeping his eyes open for a suitable spot to land.

He discovered it at last.

It was a neglected boat-yard, about eight miles from Hampton.

"Hold," he said to Settle; "draw in here, for the lady must require refreshments."

"No; I require nothing," said Flora.

"Well, we do, my lady."

"But how are you to obtain refreshments in that apparently-deserted spot?"

"Oh, we shall find a place, my lady."

"Go, then. I will await you here."

"We would rather not leave you here alone. You see thieves may be about."

"I do not fear them. I would rather remain here."

Gasper bit his lips with vexation.

He had expected she would be too frightened to remain.

"It is of no use," he thought. I must take the other course."

As soon as the boat touched the shore Gasper landed.

Settle was quickly beside him; and as he fastened the rope to a pile, he whispered:

"All is dark and silent here. No one can know what we do. Let us go up the lane, and as soon as we return I will pounce upon her. While I hold her you can gag her. Then it will remain with you what will follow."

Gasper understood what this meant.

"Good" he said. "We will do as you say."

Thereupon they proceeded up the narrow lane which adjoined the yard.

In a few moments they returned.

Settle, who had made up his mind to earn the money promised him without further delay, was the first to enter the boat.

Pretending to pick up the boat-book he suddenly pounced upon Flora.

Our heroine had not bargained for this. She was taken entirely unawares.

Nevertheless she struggled fiercely to release herself.

With all the power of which she was capable she would have shrieked for assistance, but Settle held his filthy hand over her mouth.

Gasper had seized a piece of cloth with which to gag her when he chanced to look up.

He saw a boat being rapidly propelled through the water by one man, while another was standing in the stern.

Without pausing an instant he seized the bag, sprang from the boat, and ran like the wind up the yard.

Not for a single instant did he think of his companion.

"Every man for himself," he chuckled, "I have the money, and he loses his share."

Meantime Lady Flora had continued to

struggle, and, in a few moments, she was successful in throwing Settle off.

He stooped, seized the boat-hook, and swung it over his head.

Lady Flora raised her right hand.

There was a brilliant flash and a loud report, and Settle dropped like a log in the boat.

"Bravo !" cried a voice with a strong Irish accent, "you've dropped him as nately as can be—the spalpeen. And if yez hadn't, *we* should."

As these words were uttered a boat shot up, and, with a cry of joy and thankfulness, Lady Flora recognised Brian and Ned.

Then, bursting into tears, she said :

"I was compelled to fire. Oh, it is dreadful—dreadful !"

"Dreadful is it ?" said Brian, as he leapt into the big boat. "Well, upon me sowl ! I think it's rale beautiful. If you hadn't been quick he would have hit yez with his murtherous boat-hook—bad cess to him for a coward !"

"Don't cry, me leddy, for it's like knives into me to hear a woman cry."

"You have only done what was quite right," said Ned, who was examining Settle, " but you've not killed him. See, he is recovering already. You have broken his arm—that is all."

"It's a pity it wasn't his dirthy neck," said Brian, "but you see the principal in this bit of villainy is gone. Shall we lape out of the boat, Ned, and be afther him ?"

"No, no ; we know nothing of this place, and no doubt he does, Besides, we must not leave Lady Flora."

"Ah, well ! we'll have the wretch before long. Here," he added to Settle, who was looking around him in a dazed fashion, "get up, you greasy-looking bla'guard, an' tell us where's the scoundrel gone."

Settle shook his head.

"Don't know," he said ; "he deserted me He must have seen you coming. I didn't."

"Or you would have followed him, no doubt? How much did you get for this job ? "

"Nothing."

"Nothing !" said Ned. "Whom do you think you are talking to? '

"Don't know ; but I repeat I got nothing."

"And you'd answer nothing, you surly brute, if you could help it. But we will take care that you answer whatever questions we may put to you. If you don't, well, we'll get the law to assist us."

"I'd loike to question him wid a big blackthorn," said Brian.

"I say again that I got nothing," said Settle. "He promised me a hundred guineas, but he has taken the bag containing all the money."

"Be Jabers !" said Brian, "I niver thought of that."

"Do not let that trouble you." said Lady Flora ; I will explain all directly.

"I think we had better explain first," said Ned, "and you will then understand how we came to follow you.'

Thereupon, assisted by Brian, he gave the explanation.

"Poor Jack !" cried Lady Flora, again bursting into tears, "something terrible must have happened to him."

"Don't take on so, me leddy," implored Brian ; "let us hope for the best. Depend upon it, we shall leave no stone unturned to find out what *has* happened."

"Since he has deserted me," said Settle, "I am ready to give what information I can if I am paid for it."

"Paid for it, is it ?" said Brian ; "what will yez ax next ? "

Lady Flora saw that the opportunity was not to be lost.

"Promise anything," she whispered to Ned.

"What is your name ? " asked Ned.

The man hesitated.

"Take your time," continued Ned. "Only let me caution you against telling lies. If we consider that the information you give us is worth payment, you shall be *well* paid. But if, after paying you, we find that you have been telling lies—look out."

"My name is Settle."

"Settle is it ?" said Brain. "Well, it's a wonder we didn't settle you here. What do you do when yez *work* for a livin' ? "

"I am an ostler."

"Go on," said Ned. "What do you know of your companion ? "

"Nothing—not even his name."

He then told them of how he had taken Gasper to the Red Lion, whereat Ned uttered a prolonged whistle.

"Gasper Grimsby must have met Jack there," he said ; "and by some means penetrated his disguise."

"Ah, be me sowl !" said Brian, "it was a pity he went there at all widout us."

"He said he was going to interview Captain Swift," said Settle.

"It is all a mystery at present," said Ned, with a sigh ; "but we will at once commence to penetrate it. Our inquires must begin at the Red Lion."

After a few words with Lady Flora he said to Settle :

"Your information may, to some extent, prove valuable, so here is five guineas for you. Where do you live?"

"At the Three Black Cats, not far from the Red Lion."

Brian now—with much reluctance—bound up Settle's arm.

Then, when Ned had assisted Flora into their boat, he said:

"Go to the hostelry at which you are employed, and take my advice—drop your present style of getting a few extra guineas"

"Or the hangman will settle you," added Brian.

"I can't return to the hostelry," replied Settle, in sullen tones.

"Why?"

"How can I row with a broken arm?"

"Well, stay where you are, bad cess to yez!" said Brian.

"Let us land at Westminster," said Ned.

"Wid all me heart, me honey, and the quicker we get there the better."

Within an hour Flora was with Mrs. Barrington.

* * * *

Gasper Grimsby quickly made his way out of the disused boat-yard, but he had more than one narrow escape of falling through the rotten wood or stonework.

Once clear of the yard, he increased his speed, and soon found himself on the open highway.

He passed one or two persons, but though he would have given a guinea to know exactly where he was, he did not ask a question.

It might be dangerous, he considered. On, on, on he went, but though his fingers itched, he made no attempt to feast his eyes on the money in the bag.

At last he reached a small tavern, and after repeated knocking, was successful in arousing the host, who descended and admitted him.

"I will remain until the morning if you have a bedroom," he said, "if not, I will borrow a horse and push on."

"Oh, I have a bedroom, master," replied the host.

"Then show me to it, and afterwards bring me a small bottle of brandy."

The host complied, and so Gasper, in less than a couple of minutes, found himself installed in a small bedroom.

"I don't like the look of him," muttered the host, as he proceeded to get the spirit, "and so I'll book him for the night. It was not so very long ago that a man after his stamp put up at the Glass Bottle. In the morning it was found that he had vanished, while poor old Dick Randle, the host, was found murdered, and every blessed shilling had been stolen.

"Ha! Dick should have had my arrangement. He would soon have known whether anyone was on the move. I don't believe in locking a guest's door, nor in fastening it in any way, but I believe in a man protecting himself."

Having taken up the spirits and ascertained that his guest required nothing else, he closed the door.

Then, opening a small cupboard beside it, he took out a large, cup-shaped bell.

This he placed over the door, and connected it with a little, but powerful spring hammer.

On the door being opened the hammer would ring out a furious alarm.

It was an ingenious arrangement, and could not fail to be effective.

"Safe!" chuckled Gasper as he swallowed, with much gusto, a glass of spirits. "Safe! and possessed of all the money! Ha! ha! Gasper Grimsby, you are a clever man, and ought to roll in wealth. Perhaps I shall. I will see what can be done in the matter of the will directly. Lawyers don't move without money, and, fortunately, I am possessed of plenty. Now for it! Ha! the bag is locked! No matter, I can easily open it."

He took out a knife and made a large gash in the top.

Then he turned it upside down, and there dropped upon the table——

A shower of gold?

Nothing of the sort.

The first thing to fall out was—a stone!

Gasper dropped the bag and drew back astounded.

Then, again seizing it, he plunged his hand in and pulled out the rest of the articles.

Two more stones, four pieces of iron—evidently the feet of a coal stand—and a slip of paper.

Upon that these words had been hastily traced:

"I have recognised you! You are Gasper Grimsby! An examination of the contents of this bag will prove to you that you are not so clever as she who put them in."

Clenching his hands, Gasper started back, cursing in the most awful manner.

Truly he had been foiled most completely.

And by a woman!

It was terrible to think of.

Finally, the wretch, crushed, and in abject despair, threw himself into a chair and buried his face in his hands.

He never attempted to enter the bed.

In that position he remained until the grey

dawn struggled through the partly-closed shutters.

Then he opened the door, and was startled by the loud clamour above it.

He at once noted the arrangement, and remembered that it was not there when he entered the room.

"It is a warning to me, as well as to those within the house," he thought, "for it proves that even this man regarded me with suspicion. I must be careful—very careful."

He told the host that he desired to borrow a horse.

The host replied that he was possessed of one only, and he could have that providing he deposited the value.

That Gasper was not prepared to do.

He had but very little money with him now.

So he was compelled to depart on foot, and he decided to make his way to Hammersmith.

For some distance he went along the road like a drunken man.

"If I had her here!" he muttered fiercely, "I would strangle her!"

Of course he meant Lady Flora.

"But no matter," he continued, "I will yet be even with her. I will not rest until I have had my revenge. I will kill her as surely as I killed Jack Barrington!"

As surely as he killed Jack Barrington!

He was mistaken.

The reader will now see that Gallant Jack was very far from being killed.

CHAPTER LVII.

HOW, AND BY WHOM GALLANT JACK WAS RESCUED. THE PROCLAMATION AND THE JOYOUS RE-UNION.

THE man Gasper had dropped from his horse, of which he took possession, lay upon the ground without moving for some time.

Then something curious occurred.

The man moved his head from side to side, and opened his eyes.

But, instead of a groan, a laugh left his lips.

Presently he slowly raised himself and looked round.

"No one about," he muttered, "good. Now I'll get up. Well, on my soul, it was lucky I thought of attiring myself in a countryman's garb. If I had not, that thief—and no doubt he is one of the thieves common to London—would have possessed himself of the savings of years. If I'd a couple of pistols, though—eh? What's that?"

He got upon his feet and listened.

A groan fell upon his ears.

"Phew!" he whistled, "something is amiss hereabouts. Confound the darkness!"

Again the groan was heard.

"Hillo!" cried the man, "who calls?"

There was, of course, no answer; but the groan was repeated.

"Yes," muttered the man, "I can't be mistaken. I know a groan too well for that. The Lord knows I've heard enough of 'em in my time. Some one is in distress, and if I can help 'em I'll do so."

Thereupon he began to pace the road from left to right.

The groans recommenced, and, guided by them, the man presently reached the filthy ditch into which Gallant Jack had fallen.

"Well, may a French bullet never find a way through my coat!" he muttered, "there is a man here."

Quickly producing flint and steel, he struck a light and held it over the ditch.

"A man, yes," he continued, "and here goes to pull him out."

Seizing Jack by the shoulders, and exerting all his strength, he was presently successful in pulling him on the path.

He was covered in mud from head to foot.

As a matter of fact, he had narrowly escaped suffocation.

If the ditch had been another foot or so in depth he must have sunk right down.

Of the mud the countryman took not the least notice.

"May have had a drop too much," he thought, as he again struck a light, "and tumbled into the ditch. Well that one's an uncommon bad bed for a man. So here's——"

He paused as he held the light over Jack's face, stared, and then uttered a cry of horror.

No wonder.

Our hero's face and head was completely smothered in blood.

This, with the mud, almost hid his face from sight.

"God's love on us all!" muttered the man, "Murder has been done, or somrthing near it, for he didn't get this falling into the ditch."

Without hesitation he lifted up his smock and wiped Jack's face.

And then a mighty cry left his lips.

He started to his feet with a face that had suddenly turned deathly pale.

"Heaven and earth," he cried, "it is Jack Barrington! Yes, yes; it is indeed Jack—poor Jack—poor Jack! Who can have done this?"

Then, suddenly remembering that he had a flask of spirits in his pocket, he drew it forth and held it to Jack's lips.

Whether he swallowed any or not, he could

"THERE WAS A LOUD REPORT AND SETTLE DROPPED LIKE A LOG IN THE BOAT."

not tell on account of the darkness, for his little light had gone out.

"What shall I do? What shall I do?" the countryman murmured in broken tones. "I cannot carry him myself. Shall I run to some hostelry? No, no, I will see what effect my voice has."

Rising, he shouted with all his power:

"Murder! murder! murder!"

Echo only answered him.

"He will die if he is left here," thought the man, as great tears stole slowly down his bronzed cheeks.

Again he cried:

"Murder! Help!"

A voice besides the echo answered him this time.

It was a man's voice, but what it said he could not tell.

Nevertheless it encouraged him to shout again.

Again he was answered, and this time the voice was much nearer.

"For God's sake, help!"

"Ay, ay!" was now the clear answer, "in half a minute."

Presently the hedge on the opposite side was pushed aside, and a man came through. He was a rough-looking fellow, and attired like an agricultural labourer.

"What is it?" he asked.

"A man has been nearly murdered, my friend," was the reply. "I chanced to come upon him in the ditch. When I pulled him out, lo, I saw that he was an old friend of mine. If he is not at once attended to, he will certainly die, for he has been most brutally knocked about. If you will assist me to carry him somewhere, I will pay you well."

"Assist you? That I will. But I don't require payment for doing a good action. I may want help myself one of these days."

"Most true."

"But where shall we carry him?"

"To a doctor's."

"The nearest is a long way off. I'll tell you what—we'll carry him to my cottage across the fields yonder. If we could get through the hedge, we should soon be there. It's not much of a place, to be sure; but my wife——"

"God love you, friend!" interrupted the countryman, "a barn would serve him. Come, we'll soon move part of the hedge."

The pair set to work, but it was some little time before they could move sufficient of the deeply-rooted hawthorn hedge to permit of their carrying Jack through.

It was done at last, however, and the labourer, saying that he had better go first as he knew every inch of the ground, took Jack's legs, while the countryman took his head.

Thus across several fields—dangerous to the stranger—they passed, and at last a small white cottage was reached.

A light burning within showed that all had not retired.

"Hillo, Mary," shouted the labourer, "open the door!"

The words were scarcely uttered when the door was opened by a stout, healthy-looking, middle-aged woman.

She was quickly informed of what had taken place.

"Poor man!" she said, in truly sympathetic tones; "bring him in, Tom, and lay him on the bed here."

As she said this, she hastily threw a large piece of cloth on the white bed.

"Mary," said the labourer, "do you run for Doctor North. He is just the man for a case like this; and, while you are gone, we'll get him into bed. Poor fellow! he don't show the least sign of coming to. He has indeed been fearfully ill-used. Many a man would have died."

"Ha!" said the countryman, "he is used to wounds."

"What is he, then? A soldier?"

"Aye, one of the bravest who ever lived. You may have heard of him."

"It's more than likely. And no one can take more interest in the army than I do, for, before I took to farming, I was a soldier myself."

"You were! Then give us your fist."

The pair shook hands.

"This gentleman's name," said the countryman, "is John Barrington; his rank, a colonel—and he is generally known as Gallant Jack."

"Heard of him?" cried the labourer, "I should think I have! And that is gallant Jack? I am astounded!"

"No doubt. But now let us undress him and put him to bed."

First Jack's head was bathed and bandaged and his face washed.

Then, with the greatest care, he was undressed and placed in bed.

"I see how it is," said the countryman, "for some reason he has been disguised. Poor Jack!"

"Excuse me," said the labourer, "it strikes me that *you* are disguised."

"True, my friend," was the reply.

"You are not a countryman?"

"No; I know more of the sword, the bayonet, and grape-shot than the plough."

"Might I inquire what rank yours is?"

"To be sure. I am a sergeant, and my name is Crank."

Yes, it was indeed our old friend Sergeant Crank who had found Jack.

In another quarter of an hour Mary returned followed by the doctor—a tall, elderly, grave-looking man, whose eyes seemed to take in everything at a glance.

"Sir," burst out the sergeant, "pardon me, but I entreat of you give him every attention —use your best skill ; and among others the Duke of Marlborough will thank you."

The doctor opened wide his eyes.

"The Duke," he said. "What possible connection can he have with this person?"

"Why, sir, that is gallant Jack !"

"Never?"

"It is, sir—I swear it !"

"You shall explain directly. In the meantime I assure you he shall have my best attention. But let me add that, even if he were the poorest man in the army, he should still have my best attention."

"God bless your honour! I am sure of it."

The doctor, his instrument and medicine case beside him, was at the bedside at least half an hour, while Sergeant Crank, the labourer, and his wife watched.

It is hardly necessary to hint at the sergeant's state of mind during the doctor's examination.

Science and skill were at length successful, for, with a deep sigh, Jack opened his eyes.

A great cry of thankfulness and joy left the sergeant's lips.

"Rest, and total absence of anxiety, is what he will require for at least a week," said the doctor.

"He must not be removed from here?"

"On no account for a week. If he is removed I shall not be answerable for the consequences."

Sergeant Crank looked anxiously at the labourer and his wife.

They understood him.

"Do not fear," said the former; "he shall not be disturbed on our account. That is our son's bed, and he will not be home for at least a fortnight."

"Where am I?" asked Jack.

"In a place of safety, my friend," said the doctor.

"A few words, doctor !" whispered Crank, pleadingly.

The doctor nodded, saying :

"Be careful you do not excite him."

Sergeant Crank threw himself at the bedside.

"Jack," he said. "Jack, do you know me?"

A bright light shone in Jack's eyes.

"My dear old friend, Sergeant Crank," he said.

"Good !" muttered the doctor ; "it is an excellent sign."

"Yes," cried Crank ; "it is indeed your old friend. Oh, Jack, that I should see you like this !"

"Where is the villain?"

"Who?"

"Gasper Grimsby."

"What !" gasped Crank. "Do you mean to tell me that this was *his* work?"

"It was."

"Good God !"

"No doubt he thought he had killed me. You did not see anything of him?"

"See anything ! I wish to Heaven I had."

"Where is the will?"

"What will?"

"That I had in my pocket."

"We found nothing at all in your pockets."

"I see. He must have found out that I had the will, and so followed me. Doctor—*are* you a doctor?"

"I am, my friend, and entirely at your service."

"Will you answer me one question?"

"Assuredly."

"Shall I recover?"

"You will if my instructions are properly carried out."

"Then God help Gasper Grimsby !"

"I would I had the wretch here," muttered the sergeant ; "I'd strangle him as sure as I'm alive."

Jack, in a remarkably clear manner, now told of his visit to the Red Lion, and how he became possessed of the will.

"Well, then," said Crank, "it is certain that I must have been not far off at the time, and that it was Gasper Grimsby who fired at me."

And he told of the incident concerning the horse.

"Yes," said the doctor, "you may depend that the man who attacked this gentleman was the one who fired at you. He must, indeed, be a villain."

"Ay," said Crank, "you are right, doctor. If you knew all, you would call him something worse than that."

"But, when I come to think of it, it is most remarkable how I came to go down that lane. I was on my way to Kennington, and asked two men the nearest way to the ferry.

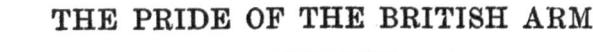

"One directed me one way, and another by the lane. That way I decided to go."

"Are you a countryman?"

"No, sir. The fact is, I have received my discharge from the army, and was about to visit my relatives.

"For two reasons I disguised myself.

"One was because, sewn in my jacket beneath this smock, I have the savings of many years.

"The other was that I was determined to surprise my relatives."

"I understand, my friend. Verily, it seems as if the Hand of Providence directed you down that lane."

"It does, indeed."

"If you are in no hurry to proceed to Kennington, I should recommend you to stay here."

"Bless you, sir! I am in no hurry. Even if I was, it would not matter. I would not leave Gallant Jack on any account."

"This gentleman is the officer so frequently and highly spoken of by the Duke of Marlborough in his dispatches?"

"The very same, sir. It's hard that a man who has been through battle after battle, and escaped the enemy's cannon-balls, should be smitten by a scoundrel in one of the common lanes of London."

The sergeant's voice was very tremulous as he said this.

"You are right," said the doctor, patting him on the shoulder, "and your emotion does you great credit."

"Lord bless your honour! I brought him up from a youngster. I have the feelings of a father towards him."

"Cheer up, sergeant," said Jack, trying to smile. "You hear what the doctor says. I shall recover."

Then he added to the labourer:

"What is your name, my good man?"

"Tom Stratton, sir," said the labourer, touching his head in military style.

"Ha! have you been in the army?"

"Ay, sir; I was in the army eight years; but it's ten years ago since I left."

"While I remain beneath your roof be assured that you shall be well paid. What is the hour?"

"Two has struck."

"When the morning advances I shall require you to go to my friends. They will be terribly anxious about me."

"I warn you against excitement," said the doctor.

"I promise you that I will guard myself," replied Jack.

"I will revisit you in a few hours, and I shall then be able to judge whether you are in a fit condition to receive visitors."

And the doctor departed wondering whether it was not his duty to at once inform the authorities of the outrage which had taken place, as he put it, "under the very nose of Whitehall."

Within six hours the doctor paid his next visit.

He found Sergeant Crank almost in despair. Jack was terribly ill.

At five o'clock he had lapsed into unconsciousness, while every now and then a few words, muttered in low tones, left his parched lips.

The doctor became very grave.

"This is indeed most serious," he said, as he gravely examined our hero. "Unless I am very much mistaken brain fever will supervene."

Sergeant Crank made no reply.

He was too much overcome.

Sinking into a seat, he buried his face in his hands.

"Did he mention his friend's address?" asked the doctor, after a long and painful pause.

"No, sir. I was anxious to get it, but remembering what you said, I refrained from bothering him."

"You did quite right. Nothing was found in his clothes?"

"Nothing whatever, your honour."

"Well, we must wait. In the meantime I advise you not to leave him."

"Not a moment, sir—not a moment."

Six days passed, and terribly anxious days they were to poor Sergeant Crank, who watched our hero like a mother would her child.

He forgot all about himself—all about his relatives.

It was of Jack, and Jack only that he thought.

The kind-hearted labourer and his wife, too, neglected all else to wait upon him.

The man tried to find out Jack's friends, but it was a failure.

He went to the War Office.

Yes, they said there it was known that Colonel Barrington's friends were in London, but their exact whereabouts was not in their books.

Had the labourer been Sergeant Crank, and had he walked to the Strand, he would certainly have run against two of our hero's friends, and, of course, have recognised them.

We mean Ned Rattles and Brian O'Flynn.

For six days and nights Jack was afflicted

with brain fever; but, the doctor said, fortunately it was in a mild form.

Then consciousness returned to him, and the doctor, who had been most faithful in his duty, announced that he was out of danger.

Sergeant Crank stole outside and fairly danced with joy.

On the same evening Tom Stratton, the labourer, still in quest of Jack's friends, strolled into a hostelry on the opposite side of St. Martin's Fields.

He called for a mug of home-brewed ale, and seated himself on one of the barrels placed for seats.

One customer was there, and he appeared to be asking the landlord some favour. .

The host granted it, and the customer, a tall, thin, grave-looking man, took a large piece of paper from his pocket, a hammer, and some nails.

Then, proceeding to a door exactly opposite the private entrance, he commenced to nail the paper to it.

Stratton took little notice of him, for he had much to think of.

But suddenly he started up.

What was that name on the bill?

Could he believe his eyes?

Yes, there was no mistake about it.

In big letters were the words:

"GALLANT JACK."

His excitement was naturally intense; but, controlling himself, he read the bill, which had evidently just been written.

It was as follows:

"TO THE GENERAL PUBLIC,—

"Whereas John, or Jack, Barrington, well known in the army and to most of the public as 'Gallant Jack' has been missing for the past six or seven days from his house at St. James's. It is supposed that he has met with some accident, and has been carried to an infirmary or elsewhere.

"This is to give notice that the sum of

"FIVE HUNDRED POUNDS

will be paid to anyone who may furnish the information which shall be the means of restoring the above-named to his heart-broken mother and friends."

Then followed Jack's description, and it was remarkably accurate; so were the clothes in which he was last seen.

Two loving hands had written this.

Lady Flora and Ned Rattles.

The bill thus concluded:

"Information to be given at Laurel House, St. James's; at the War Office, or at any of the Watch Houses."

Rapidly Stratton read this.

Then, turning, without a word he dashed out of the hostelry.

"Mad!" muttered the host, who watched him in astonishment. "And he has actually left his ale behind. I say," he added to the man nailing up the bill, "that bill looks serious."

"Aye, you are right."

"How long have the bills been out?"

"Since yesterday. We are putting them up at every hostelry."

"I hope the poor fellow will be found."

"I trust so. He is a brave man."

"Perhaps he has enemies, eh?"

"I can't say; but favourites generally have."

"Well, if anyone has done him an injury I hope they will be found and well punished."

"You may depend on that."

Meanwhile Stratton set off at a run to St. James's.

Not once did he pause.

He knew Laurel House when it had been in the occupation of a former tenant.

As he darted up to the front he nearly fell into the arms of Brian O'Flynn, who had just opened the door, intending to set out to make more inquiries.

"Hillo!" he said, "Be the powers it's making a ram of your head, you are! What has happened?"

"Gallant Jack."

"Gallant Jack? Speak — what do you mean?"

"I know where he is."

"You do? God Almighty be thanked! He is alive? Tell me that, or it's likely that I'll drop down on the step here!"

"Yes; he is alive, but very ill."

"Give me your hand, me bhoy, will yez?" said Bryan, with tears in his eyes.

He shook hands with Stratton, and then darted into the sitting-room where all our friends, including the Lady Flora, were seated, silent and sad.

"Rejoice all of yez!" almost shrieked Brian, "Jack is found! He is alive—he is. Ah, be me sowl, it's excited I am, but I can't help it. Here, look, is the man that's brought us the news."

Of course there was a great rush towards Stratton as he entered the room.

Those present appeared to have suddenly gone mad with joy.

Stratton rapidly explained all.

And he added:

"When I left this evening there was a great improvement. By this time it is likely that he has recovered consciousness."

"Let us go to him at once," said Lady Flora.

"Yes," said Ned, "we will all go. We can remain outside the cottage until the doctor gives us permission to enter. Lady Flora, you are to be sincerely congratulated. The idea of the bills originated with you, and they have been entirely successful."

"And this good man," said Lady Flora, down whose beautiful face tears of joy were streaming, "is entitled to the reward of five hundred pounds, and it shall be quickly paid to him."

"He is also entitled to the thanks of all of us," said Brian, "and, be St. Patrick! he has them wid three times three. Give us a shake iv your fist me bhoy."

"To think, Ned, that we should tramp and tramp along that Strand and go into the Red Lion—bad scran to it—again and again, and yet learn nothing. We must have passed this man time after time."

"That is certain."

"But you havn't told us the name of the gentleman who picked him out of the ditch," said Brian.

"Upon my word, I was so excited that I quite forgot it. It is Segeant Crank."

"Sergeant Crank!" cried Brian. "Well, upon me sowl, this is the most remarkable evening I iver passed in all my born days! You see, my good man, I'm complately charged wid joy. Gives us your fist, will yez?"

"Sergeant Crank!" said Ned, "of all men Sergeant Crank passes through that lane on that night. It seems too extraordinary for belief!"

"Let us go," murmured Mrs. Barrington, "let us go. I can bear the suspense no longer."

"Nor I," said Lydia.

In but a few more moments the whole party set off for the cottage.

They found the door closed.

All around was very silent, but suddenly they heard a low voice.

It proceeded from the cottage.

Lady Flora, who chanced to be nearest the door, instantaneously recognised it.

"It is Jack's voice!" she cried aloud.

At once the door was opened.

The doctor stood upon the threshold.

"Ah!" he said to Stratton, "so you have found the friends of Gallant Jack at last?"

"Well, they have come at the right time. All danger is over, and the finest medicine he can take now will be the loving words of those nearest and dearest to him."

As they entered, Sergeant Crank drew back.

He, like Brian, was fully "charged with joy."

Of course he remained "in the shadow" for some little time.

Brian was the first to leave the bedside, and his welcome to Sergeant Crank was something to be remembered.

Stratton and his wife declared that they had never seen such a warm-hearted Irishman in all their lives.

Explanations were given on both sides, and they lasted until the small hours of the morning.

Jack was astounded at the manner in which Gasper had endeavoured to extract money from Lady Flora, but, in defiance of his weakness, he could not help laughing heartily at the way Lady Flora had foiled him.

"Get well quick, Jack," said Ned, "and we will trap clever Gasper Grimsby. Don't fear, we shall get possession of the will again."

"I doubt it."

"What makes you say so?"

"My opinion is that he will destroy it."

"That will be of little importance," said Lady Flora, "for your mother can prove that she is next-of-kin. Besides, even if you did not get a penny of fortune, I have plenty for both of us.

"Let not money trouble you, dear Jack; for your mother's sake—for all our sakes get well."

CHAPTER LVIII.
IN WHICH IT IS SEEN THAT TWO VILLAINS HAVE THE SAME IDEAS.

A WEEK after the joyous re-union in the cottage and we now return to Gasper Grimsby.

He still remained at Hammersmith, and, for a long while, had been inactive.

He had passed the principal part of his time in forming plans with respect to the will and Flora.

Again and again he swore that, if he could get the chance, he would most certainly kill her for the trick she had played him. But he discarded nearly all the plans with respect to Flora, for he well knew that she would now be on her guard.

But he at least decided how to act with reference to the will.

So one evening he told the barber to saddle his horse, for he was going on a long journey, and probably would not return for some few days.

From Hammersmith he rode to Islington.

This was a tremendous distance, and the greater part of the roads were bad for travelling, for, if there was one thing which the authorities neglected in the days of which we write, it was the public highways.

They took the money of the ratepayers, as they do in these days—*sometimes* (!)—but treated with scornful contempt any application for road repairs.

If any person did not like the appearance of the foot or roadway before his or her house, he or she could repair it, and welcome.

A very nice idea, truly !

Gasper found this journey one of the longest and in every respect the worst he had ever undertaken.

The horse he rode frequently came to an abrupt halt, and refused to go on again until his sides had been lacerated with the spurs.

The real fact of it was that he was old and worn out.

No wonder Sergeant Crank—from whom the reader will remember the horse was taken—devoted not a thought to his loss.

Then again the journey seemed to make Gasper fearfully thirsty.

At any rate, he stopped at a large number of hostelries.

It was close on the hour of midnight when he reached Islington, and stopped at that exceedingly pretty hostelry called the Clock House, from the fact that its spire contained a handsome clock, which had been made in France, and presented to the host by one of the Myddletons.

It was here that he determined to make certain inquiries.

So he ordered a bottle of the best wine, and asked the host to join him.

This was not the custom of the host ; but, as it was near closing time and he was going to bed, he consented.

"The fact of it is," said Gasper, "I am a total stranger hereabouts, and I want to make some inquiries."

"Perhaps I may be of some service," said the host.

"So I thought. I heard that you were the leading host for miles around."

The host seemed pleased.

He little knew that he was seated opposite a man who was one of the most barefaced liars in the kingdom.

"You see," said Gasper, "an old friend of mine lives hereabouts. For many years she was housekeeper to Mr. John Stanmore."

"What ! Mrs. Marchmont ? "

"Ay."

"Poor lady ! "

"You don't mean to say that anything has happened to her ? " cried Gasper, in pretended alarm."

"She is in very bad health. She never recovered from the shock of her master's death."

"Ah ! I remember. Unfortunate man ! he was murdered ? "

"Yes, by a thief. If he had remained but a little while longer ! "

"He would have been caught, no doubt ? "

"Certain ; for, as soon as he escaped, Jack Barrington—he who is known as Gallant Jack—came in. He was paying his grandfather a visit."

"But Mrs. Marchmont. She is still in the old house, of course ? "

"Lord bless you—no. The house has been closed ever since the murder."

"Closed, eh ? "

"Yes. Mrs. Marchmont is living somewhere near, but I forget the place.

"But you will be able to ascertain from Lawyer Pearson, who lives about a couple of hundred yards away from the house on the left.

"You can't mistake the lawyer's house, for there's a small horse-pond with a brick well beside it."

"The, lawyer, I suppose, was a great friend of Mr. Stanmore ? "

"He was his *only* friend, I've heard say. At any rate I know this, he has the keys of the house. He has also the management of the whole of the murdered man's affairs, but he has not been able to move in the matter at present."

"How is that ? "

"Oh, he has been very ill."

"Well, I should say that if the house continues closed, everything will go to rack and ruin."

"I can't say, I'm sure ; but if there are rats about they may do a lot of damage. You see you can't keep the vermin out if you can keep stray thieves."

"Not many thieves hereabouts, though, I expect ? "

The face of the host became grave.

"There never *used* to be," he said ; but, during the past week or so a daring fellow has made his appearance on the outskirts—principally at Highgate, they say."

"What, a robber ? "

"Ay, and one of the biggest rogues unhung. They call him Captain Swift ; but, why, how you jump ! "

"By Heavens ! that is the name of the rogue who robbed me only a short time ago. So he is about here, is he ? "

"Not exactly about here, but not very far away. However, he has not been seen for two or three days, so let us hope the scoundrel has permanently transferred his presence elsewhere. Of course, you heard about the Chief Justice?"

"No. The fact is I have been ill, and have been compelled to remain in the country for some time."

"Ah, well, news travels slowly from London."

"Did he fall into the hands of this Captain Swift?"

"Listen; a reward is out for the arrest of this fellow—whom I should much like to see hanged and quartered; and one night, about nine days ago, he was suddenly pounced upon at an hostelry, which he had the impudence to enter as one of the biggest swells of the West.

"A clever officer happened to be there, and at once arrested him. Captain Swift, as he calls himself, at once drew his sword, but the officer called out for assistance in the King's name, and assistance was rendered.

"The scoundrel, by directions of Chief Justice Wendle, who signed the proclamation for his arrest, was placed in the Fleet and heavily ironed.

"On the very next morning all London was ringing with the news of what had happened at the prison.

"Swift's companions had broken into the place, overpowered the sleepy officials, filed the prisoner's irons, and taken him away.

"Now for the sequel.

"The next night Chief Justice Wendle was returning home in his coach when he was stopped by no less a person than this Swift.

"He was forced to beg Swift's pardon, and then he was taken to a ditch close by, thrown into it, pulled out again, and returned to his coach. A nice state of affairs, eh?

"But he will be caught directly, sir, and they will take precious good care that he don't get away again. And now, sir, I must bid you a good night."

"A good night to you," replied Gasper, as he left the hostelry, and remounted his horse.

The first thing he did as he proceeded was to see to his pistols.

"He may be in this neighbourhood for all I know," he muttered.

But he did not meet with a soul.

Passing Camden House, lying back in its grounds in total darkness, he quickly reached the lawyer's house.

"The house belonging to John Stanmore has been closed since his death," he mused, "and the lawyer has possession of the keys.

"Now, since it is evident, in consequence of the lawyer's illness, nothing has been disturbed, it is more than likely that great wealth remains in the house. I must gain admission to it.

"On that I am determined. The will is in my possession, and, through it, it is more than likely that the keys will be handed over to me.

"But if I cannot get possession of them by fair means, then I must by *foul.*

"Now, something of the very greatest importance has struck me.

"Caleb Corder—curse him!—must have read every word of the document, and therefore he knows that John Stanmore lived at Camden House.

"Is it not more than likely that he has thought of this while in the neighbourhood?

"I should say so. Nay, it is more than likely that he has attempted to gain *admission.*"

Dismounting, he knocked upon the lawyer's door.

In a few moments it was answered by a short, thin man, clad in black.

It was Lawyer Pearson.

Anyone could tell at a glance that he was seriously ill.

"Your business, sir?" he asked, in a voice which could scarcely be heard.

"I have called to speak to you on a matter of great importance, and——"

"If it is a matter in which the services of a lawyer are required, you had better go to someone else, for the state of my health will not allow me to practice."

"I am sorry to hear it. I have come a long distance to see you. The matter concerns the will of the late John Stanmore."

"Indeed! From whom, then, do you come?"

"John Barrington—the grandson. In proof of which I produce the will."

The lawyer was evidently startled, nay astounded.

"I understood that John Barrington failed to get possession of the will," he said.

"He obtained it at last; and here, as you see, is the document."

"Well, enter; I shall be pleased to listen to what you have to say."

Gasper chuckled inwardly.

So far, at any rate, he was successful.

Having tied up his horse—the poor wretch seemed fit to drop—he followed the lawyer into his room.

"I wonder," he thought, "how many servants he has? I must find that out."

"Perhaps, before we commence," said the

lawyer, "you would like some little refreshment ? "

"A little wine, that is all.   But pray do not disturb yourself. I will ring the bell for you."

"It would be useless," said Pearson. "No one, I am sorry to say, is in the house besides me. My housekeeper was taken very ill yesterday, and, as there was no one here to do anything for her, she was compelled to go to her daughter's ; but to-morrow a woman is coming to take her place. Here, sir," he added, opening a cupboard, "is wine. Help yourself."

Taking the will, lawyer Pearson opened it out, and looked at it.

"Yes," he said, " this the original document. It was undoubtedly stolen by the man who murdered John Stanmore, and after all it gets into the hands of John Barrington. Can you tell me in what way he recovered it ? "

"I cannot.   He did not tell me.'

"No doubt you are a bosom friend of his."

"I am proud to say, sir, that I *am*."

"May I ask your name ? "

"Colonel Howell - Evison," replied the scoundrel with all the coolness in the world.

He had taken the name of a highly respected officer.

"What are Mr. Barrington's instructions ? "

"That I was to search Camden House for a certain document."

"Document?   Did he not mention its nature ? "

"Nay.   It was, he said, marked with a—er—his grandfather's initials."

The lawyer again looked at the will, and appeared to be profoundly interested in a certain passage.

Really, however, he was thinking ; and thus his thoughts ran :

"Something is wrong here. I don't believe for one moment that Mr. Barrington would give any such instructions. A document with his father's initials? It is absolutely impossible. Evidently this man made up the lie on the spur of the moment. I must indeed be careful.

"Good God ! I may even be speaking to the very man who murdered John Stanmore ! "

Placing the will down, he said :

"Of course you have written instructions from Mr. Barrington ? "

"Only verbal."

"But did he not send a letter to me ? "

This important matter Gasper had entirely overlooked.

Had he thought of it, of course he would again have forged Jack's handwriting.

In that case, completely deceived, the lawyer would probably have given him the keys.

"No," he replied, " he did not think a letter was necessary."

"Business is business, my friend. I am a lawyer of many years standing, and know the value of being cautious."

"Then, sir, I have had my journey for nothing ? "

"Not at all.   You will tell Mr. Barrington that I am delighted he has recovered the will, and that I will be pleased to see him and take his instructions at at any time he chooses to honour me with a visit. But you must also tell him that it is against all legal rules to——"

"The fact is, sir," interrupted Gasper, rising, "I am to tell him that you refuse to allow me to go over the house ? "

"Until I have his written authority," added the lawer, firmly.

By getting up and walking to the door he desired to intimate that the interview had come to a conclusion.

Gasper's face had turned purple with rage. He at once followed the old man as he tottered to the door.

Suddenly he raised his heavy riding-whip and dealt the lawyer a blow on the back of the head.

With a wild, heartrending scream the unfortunate old man placed his hands to his head and tottered back.

Then he ran forward as if to ascend the stairs.

But Gasper sprang behind him and dealt him another fearful blow.

The lawyer, instead of ascending the stairs, reeled to the left, swayed to and fro for a moment, and then fell from the top of the kitchen stairs to the bottom.

Gasper crept to the street door, opened it, and looked out.

No one was near.

Reclosing the door, he descended the stairs and examined the lawyer.

Only one look was necessary.

The poor old man—who for months had been at the very edge of the grave—was dead.

Gasper at once hastened to the room, and, with feverish haste, examined the deedboxes placed round the shelves.

But he did not see one bearing the name of John Stanmore.

Cabinet doors, cupboard doors, and the drawers of the table he wrenched open, and examined the contents, which he scattered in every direction.

But he found no keys.

Indeed he saw nothing having the faintest reference to John Stanmore and his property.

In such a fearful rage was he that it seemed as if he would destroy everything within his reach.

He went upstairs.

But he found the rooms poorly furnished and no sign of deed boxes or papers.

Gasper stood confounded in one of the rooms.

"Am I again to be foiled?" he muttered. "Have I had all this trouble for nothing? Where can he——but I have not searched his clothes."

Down again he went, and, brutally pulling the body of the lawyer on to the landing, searched it.

He was successful.

In one of the pockets he found a bunch of keys bearing a bone label on which was written: "Camden House."

"Good, good!" he chuckled. "Entrance to the house is mine!"

But he did not leave the body until he had searched every pocket the clothes contained.

A purse containing several little things, and a ring with three keys upon it was all he found.

Blowing out the light he left the house, and tried if either of the keys fitted the front door.

Yes; one fitted, and he locked the door and threw the keys into the horsepond.

"Now for Camden House and its contents!" he muttered; "but first I will transfer the pistols from the holsters to my belt.

"Soh! now I am ready for anything. If there is—ah! curse it! I have left the will behind me! And now I have thrown the keys away. Fool that I am!

"But never mind. I know where it is when I want it. The woman the lawyer spoke of will come to-morrow, and, finding it closed, will, no doubt, depart. Lawyers never pay much, and so they don't get persons to devote much attention to them."

He found the gate leading to the front of Camden House locked.

On examining it, however, he found that it was old and rusty.

So he threw himself against it again and again.

Without result.

Rusty and old though it was, it was too strong for him.

After a little consideration he took his horse some ten feet from the gate, and then suddenly backed him.

The horse's weight at once broke the lock, and the gate flew open.

This trick might seem ingenious to the reader; but it is not original.

Gasper had seen it done in France by the British soldiers many a time.

He now led the horse through, and closed the gate.

But, before we give the result of his visit, we must turn to another of our characters—namely, Caleb Corder, alias "Captain Swift," and it will be seen that Gasper was not the only one who was thinking of Camden House.

While Gasper was in conversation with the lawyer he so foully murdered, three men were amusing themselves at a hostelry not six hundred yards away.

Each was well, if not elaborately, attired, and they were apparently provided with plenty of money; for three or four little piles of gold were upon the table, while they drank the best wines the house afforded.

One of these individuals—whom the host mistook for "lords out for amusement"—was Caleb Corder.

The one on his left—a tall, gaunt-looking man of about forty—was called Rathley; while the other, who was about Caleb's age, height, and build, was known as Leath.

Though a reward was out for "Captain Swift," he was sitting in this hostelry without any attempt at disguise.

But he was wonderfully altered.

Drink and sleepless nights had wrought a wondrous change.

His eyes were sunken, his face was ghastly pale, and though he continually laughed aloud he was by no means at ease.

His laugh was most cruelly forced; but whether his companions noticed it or not we cannot say.

The two men with Caleb were his picked companions—men with whom he chose to enjoy himself.

For two long hours the three had been playing at cards, but at last Caleb threw down his hand, and, sweeping his pile of money into his pocket, declared that he had played enough, and would smoke.

Thereupon he drew from his cloak a curiously-shaped pipe, filled it, and proceeded to smoke.

His companions imitated his action.

"Now, captain," said Rathley, "we are just in proper trim to hear about this house. Do you really think that it contains anything of value?"

"Think? I am *certain* of it. Why, man alive, didn't I tell you that one of the wealthiest men in London lived there?"

"You did. But I know a house where a

wealthy man lived, and it is now occupied by a horse-slaughterer."

Of this Caleb took no notice.

"It was," he continued, "occupied by one John Stanmore. He was murdered in the house, and since then it has been closed."

"What?" said Leath, "have none of the things been removed?"

"Nothing whatever has been touched."

"How strange," said Rathley.

"Not strange at all when you come to consider that no one as yet has come forward to claim it. But at first, like you, I was surprised when I was told that nothing had been disturbed. I was determined to satisfy myself ; so one day I got into the grounds, stole round to the back, and managed to climb a large tree which stands close to one of the windows.

"I saw right into one of the rooms, and it was completely furnished."

"But did you see anything of value?"

"Not in *that* room. The valuables would be in the rooms which were used by John Stanmore. But, if you are not willing to assist me, don't trouble yourselves about——"

"Wait, captain," interrupted Leith ; "I, for one, am ready to assist you at *once*. There are many more risky things than assisting to see what a deserted house contains."

"I also am ready," said Rathley ; "and since this is such a dark night, with the wind rising—just hark to it !—we should make the attempt now."

"Come, then," said Corder, "and let it be well understood that each will take a fair share. Pick up that lantern, and put it under your cloak ; it may be useful."

The three descended the stairs, and were met by the host.

"Horses, gentlemen?" he inquired.

"Not yet. We shall return presently," said Caleb.

The three, wrapping their cloaks about their persons, made their way to Camden House, but not in the direction taken by Gasper.

They reached the house by the back way. The consequence of this was that they missed Gasper's horse in the grounds.

Gasper had placed him behind a lot of tall shrubs ; but had the three men entered by the front no doubt their attention would have been called to the animal, for, having no grass, he was nibbling the shrubs.

Caleb was the last to vault over the fence, and in doing so he caught his foot in a large flower pot, which fell with a crash into a glass-covered box.

Had the three looked up at the house at that moment they would have seen a light suddenly appear and vanish.

That light was carried by Gasper.

He found not the least difficulty in opening the front door.

Having carefully closed it, he struck a light, and descended to the kitchen.

Here he found a lantern and an axe, and, provided with these, he visited first the rooms on the ground floor.

Each was very handsomely furnished, though now the furniture was covered with a thick layer of dust.

He noted that the sideboards contained many an article of value, and that from the walls hung many a pictorial gem which was worth a lot of money.

But the principal article which attracted his attention was a splendid oak cabinet.

He tried the keys, but did not find one to fit.

It struck him that the lock was only an imitation one, and that there was a secret spring somewhere.

He searched for it, but failed to find it.

"No matter," he muttered, " the axe will open the doors. But I will visit the other rooms first."

In the opposite room was a pretty lady's secretaire.

On the top, in a small neat hand, were these words :

"My daughter Ruth's. God bless her, and forgive me."

For a few seconds Gasper stood looking at the article, then he tried the keys, but failing to open it he deliberately split the lid with a blow of the axe, and then tore it off.

What did he see ?

First, there was an exceedingly well-painted portrait of Ruth Stanmore—Jack's mother.

It had been painted some two years before her marriage with Edward Barrington.

Gasper recognised the likeness, and throwing it upon the ground with a curse, he ground it with his heel.

Next he came upon several letters.

They were in Ruth's handwriting, and were piteous appeals to her hard-hearted father to recognise and welcome her dear husband.

Beneath these were various little things which Ruth had been fond of when at home.

All had been treasured by the old man when he saw what a huge mistake he had made, and that he had driven from him the one who would have comforted him, and made his declining years happy indeed.

All these articles Gasper hurled to the floor.

Suddenly he darted upon an article at the bottom of the secretaire.

It was a large jewel case.

In an instant he had it open, and a wild yell of joy left his lips as he saw that it was full of diamond ornaments.

There was a superb necklace, a brooch, a tiara, bracelets, and rings.

The total value would, perhaps, be two or three thousand pounds.

In a corner, on a little bit of card, were these words :

"My wife's. She left them for Ruth, and, please God, I shall live to see her wear them. —JOHN STANMORE."

"Indeed!" chuckled the wretch, as he placed the case inside his coat. "I took care that you did not live to see her wear them."

Nothing else of great value was in the room, and so he ascended.

He had just unlocked and entered one of the chambers when he was startled by a loud crash of glass.

Instantly he concealed the lantern beneath his cloak, and turned to leave the room.

But, returning, he peered through the window.

"Three men," he muttered. "Three! By Satan's own, I will swear that Caleb Corder is one of them! If that is so, he has had the same ideas as I have. If they see my horse they will be on their guard.

"Now, what am I to do?" I have a horse. They have not. Well, if Caleb Corder is one of the three, I will risk all to slay him. But it is possible that I may kill the whole *three* of them. Now, where can I hide? They will certainly search every room.

"I have it. The cabinet below."

Darting downstairs, axe in hand, he saw that the shutters were so secured that no light could be visible from without.

Then, going to the cabinet, he raised the axe.

But he did not strike.

He remembered that sound travels, and that it was likely the first blow would be heard by those without, and who were now, no doubt, close to the house.

He picked up one of the fireirons, which was pointed, and set to work.

He was successful, for in a few seconds he had one of the doors open.

Replacing the fireiron, he concealed the lantern—all alight as it was—picked up the axe, and got into the cabinet, closing the door after him.

There was ventilation, it is true, but very little of it, and he felt that in but a few minutes.

"After all," he thought, "it may not be Caleb Corder. At any rate, they are not ordinary thieves.

"By means of the lantern they carried I saw that each was well-dressed and that they were armed with swords. Of course, they may not be coming anywhere near the house."

But, in less than five more minutes, he found that they were making an attempt to enter the house.

Yes, Caleb and his companions were first of all trying some false keys.

But they had no effect.

The locks on the doors of Camden House were by no means of a common order.

"Let us get a big beam," said Leith, "and burst the door in."

"No, no ; not so fast my friend," said Caleb. "Look, this is the tree from the branches of which, as I told you, I saw into the room. Now, do you take this heavy stick, ascend the tree, and smash the glass and the framework."

"Good!" said Rathley, "that is the idea! But I know a little about climbing trees, so I will ascend, eh ?"

Leith was very glad to get out of it.

"Ay," he said ; "do."

Rathley, assisted by Caleb and Leith, was quickly among the branches, and, reaching the window, he smashed glass and framework with a dozen heavy blows.

Caleb then handed him the lantern.

"Come to the front at once !" he said.

Rathley clambered on to the window-sill, and with considerable difficulty managed to drop on to the landing.

Another few minutes, and the door was open.

"We have pitched upon a nice thing, I fancy," said Rathley. "I have already seen some valuable property."

"Of course," said Caleb, "there is far more than we can carry away. But don't fear, we can come again."

By this time they had entered one of the rooms, and it chanced to be the one in which stood the secretaire.

"Hillo !" exclaimed Caleb. "What is the meaning of this ?"

"It looks as if someone has been here before us," said Leith.

"This secretaire has evidently been broken open," said Rathley. "Look at the things on the floor, and this little picture !"

"What you say *may* be right," said Caleb, looking around ; "but I don't fancy it is ; but let us go into the opposite room."

That they found in a far worse condition.

"By the fiends !" thought Caleb, "it seems to me as if someone has had the very same idea as me. If so, who can it have been but Gasper Grimsby ?"

Aloud he said :

"We will make a close inspection of the whole place first. It seems as if someone has amused himself or herself ; but the valuables, as you see, have been left."

"Caleb Corder it is !" mutter Gasper, "if I don't leave him dead here my name is not what it is !"

Little did Caleb dream, as he looked at the cabinet, that a loaded pistol was so close to him.

But, though he looked, he made no attempt to open the door.

"Come upstairs," he said.

The three ascended and looked about them.

Though they were now satisfied that some-one who had no business to had paid the house a visit, it never struck them that anyone was *then* within it.

"The rooms here have not been disturbed," said Caleb. "Observe the number of articles about which can be turned into money."

"Look here," said Rathley, who had opened a cupboard, and taken out a box. "I wonder what is in here ?"

"We'll see," said Caleb taking and shaking it ; "it sounds like money. What can we open it with ? Do you go below, Rathley, and bring up something—say the fireirons. Here, light this taper."

With a lighted taper in his hand, Rathley descended, and selected a fireiron, the very one with which Gasper had opened the cabinet.

He was about to leave the room, when he chanced to look at the cabinet.

Wondering whether the doors were open, he crossed to it, took hold of the handle, and pulled.

At once the door came open.

The next instant Rathley fell dead before it.

Gasper had brought down his axe with all his power full upon his head, splitting his skull in twain.

He fell a mangled heap to the floor.

"What was that ?" asked Caleb, starting at the sound of the heavy thud, "hang me if I don't believe that Rathley has fallen down the stairs. Here, take the lantern and see."

Leith rapidly descended and called Rathley by name,

Getting no answer, he entered the room, holding the lantern before him.

It served to guide Gasper in the aim he took.

Leith had not taken three steps before there was a sharp report, and, with a loud cry, he dropped.

Gasper now, drawing his other pistol, seized the lantern and rushed up the stairs.

"I have him at last," he chuckled ; "he cannot escape."

Caleb did not wait to ascertain what had happened.

He had heard the shot and the cry, and then it at once flashed across him that someone besides themselves was in the house.

With the speed of lightning he rushed into the opposite room, by the window of which Rathley had entered, clambered on to the sill and to the tree, and then dropped.

As he touched the ground Gasper fired again.

But his aim was wrong this time, and, before he could withdraw his head, he narrowly escaped a shot fired by Caleb.

He was about to spring from the window when he remembered that his pistols were not now loaded.

"I'll have you yet, Caleb Corder !" he yelled. "I'll track you down !"

"So, then, it is you, Gasper Grimsby !" cried Caleb, sheltering himself behind the tree. "I would I had known you were in the house, I would have fired it, and seen that you did not get out. The next time I come across you I will not only take what you have about you, but your life ! As it is, I will give information that thieves are within the house."

What reply Gasper made he did not pause to ascertain.

He took to his heels, and was off like the wind.

Gasper paid no heed to his threat to give information, but, considering it likely that he might have more of his companions not far off, he thought it advisable to decamp at once.

The diamonds in the jewel-case would well repay him for his visit.

Five minutes more and he left the house, mounted his horse, and rode off, taking the road towards the city.

CHAPTER LIX.

THE COUNT'S TERRIBLE STORY—HOW HE, GALLANT JACK, AND OUR OTHER FRIENDS MAKE A JOURNEY TO BURNHAM, AND OF THE RESULT.

GALLANT JACK, thanks to the doctor's skill and the unceasing attention of his friends, had entirely recovered, and matters were progressing favourably at Laurel House, with the exception of one matter, which our friends—but more especially Mrs. Barrington—were arding as serious.

This was that Count Victor de Montsorel had been missing for three or four days.

It was a most extraordinary thing, for the Count, on all occasions, even if he were about to be absent only a few hours, mentioned the matter.

Since his residence with them it had become known that he had much business to attend to in England.

He, however, scarcely referred to it, and not once to a matter which, Mrs. Barrington considered, tended to greatly depress his spirits.

She noticed that he often became abstracted, and started when spoken to.

Several times, it seemed to her, as if the Count was about to reveal something, for he had seated himself beside her; but, with a deep sigh, he had always risen.

Jack was thinking about instituting a search for him, when, one evening, the Count reappeared.

Very gratified was he at the way he was warmly welcomed.

"We were about to search for you, Count," said Jack.

"You would not have found me, my friends," replied the Count, smiling sadly. "I have been many miles from here."

"May we ask to what part of the country?"

"To Burnham."

"One of the prettiest parts of England, Count," said Sergeant Crank, who had not yet returned to his relatives, though he had sent them several letters to say he was "on the road."

"It is, no doubt," replied the Count; "but I was in no mood to make notes of the scenery. My errand was a sad one," he sighed.

For some time no one spoke.

But at last Jack said:

"Count, if in anything you undertake you should require our services, command us."

"You are very kind indeed," replied the Count warmly. "I thank you sincerely, and I will tell you that have I returned here in haste to ask for the assistance of Ned and Brian."

"I am your man," said Ned.

"Be St. Patrick," cried Brian, "it's the same I am."

"For some time," continued the Count, I have been going to tell you a story, but I have refrained because I was well aware of the fact that you had already too much to think of.

"But I will tell it you now.

"Twelve years ago, just after the death of my dear father, my sister and I commenced to travel—for previously, on account of my father's death, we had been unable to.

"I was then twenty-four, and my sister—who was one of the most beautiful girls in France—eighteen.

"We were both anxious to see something of the world; but there was another reason why we desired to quit France for a long time, and that was because my sister was—as I may call it—pursued by one Pierre Carnot, who, in defiance of the fact that my sister treated his attentions with scorn and loathing, and that I had publicly horsewhipped him, sought her again and again.

"Before we left France we placed our affairs in the hands of a lawyer of the name of Lascelles—Monsieur Jean Lascelles who, at that time had one of the finest practices in the country, and who was reputed to be a man of the highest honour.

"We travelled abroad for two years, and at last we came to England. We travelled from place to place, and, finally, found ourselves at Cornwall, where, I remembered, an old friend of my father's had lived.

"But we found that he had been dead many months, and so we were compelled to put up at an hostelry, and a very fine house it was, the top commanding a magnificent view of the sea.

"We remained there for some few days, amusing ourselves with riding and sailing; but my sister becoming slightly indisposed I had to take my outdoor pleasures by myself.

"One afternoon I went out on foot, and the weather being beautifully fine, I wandered further than I had intended—in fact, I found that I had walked several miles.

"Well, I entered an inn, partook of some refreshments, and borrowed a horse. By the time I had mounted, and set off towards home, darkness had set in.

"Being unacquainted with the country, I had to inquire my way of several persons, and that caused extra delay.

"But, at last, to my great joy, I found that I was nearing the hostelry.

"I was passing a great belt of rocks, which was distant some few hundred yards from the hostelry, when I heard a piercing shriek.

"At once I drew rein and listened.

"Again and again was the shriek repeated, and each time it was decidedly nearer to me.

"I directed the horse in the direction of the sounds, and I came upon a number of men. But, owing to the darkness, I could not make out what they were doing.

"But suddenly the moon shone out, and I

saw that they were carrying the figure of a female.

"No sooner had I made this out than the shrieks were renewed. Dismounting, I rushed forward, and shouted to the men to hold.

"Imagine my horror and despair when a voice cried out, 'Victor, Victor—my brother—save me! save me!'

"It was my sister. Ay, it was indeed she, and I was unarmed. *Mon Dieu!* My blood turned cold at the very thought of it. But, recovering myself somewhat, I dashed in

"But the fight had exhausted me. I stumbled over one of the stones, and fell with a crash. When I got up I saw that the man had placed my sister in the boat, and that he was running the vessel off.

"He succeeded, and, springing in, pushed her further off with the boathook.

"Of course, I made certain that he was one of a number of men hired for the purpose, and I offered him a huge reward, and swore that I would not prosecute him or any of his companions if he would restore to me my dear sister.

"I SAW MY SISTER—APPARENTLY UNCONSCIOUS—IN THE ARMS OF A MAN ABOUT TO ENTER A BOAT."

among the men, and struck at them right and left with my stick.

"The sudden attack caused the men to pause. But it was only for a moment.

"Three or four men pounced upon me, dealt me heavy blows with their fists and the butt of a pistol, and tore my clothes nearly to ribbons.

"Nevertheless I continued the fight, and, at last, cleared a path. Down it I rushed, for I saw my sister—apparently unconscious—in the arms of a man who was just about to enter a boat.

"Imagine my feelings when the man replied:

"'No, no, count. She is mine at last, and I shall see that she leaves me not. Fare you well. This is the last you will see of your sister!'

"I at once recognised the voice of the speaker. It was Pierre Carnot himself!"

Fearfully agitated, the count paused, and again, for some little time, there was silence.

Brian was the first to break it.

"Bedad!" he cried, "I should like to have been behind Moosoo Carrot. I'd have broken

"YOU WILL COME WITH ME," SAID JACK, "OR I WILL PUT A BALL THROUGH YOUR BODY."

No. 12.

every bone in his carcase, or I'm no Irishman."

"The villain had evidently been watching you for some time," said Jack.

"Not the least doubt of it. Such a shock was it when I found that my sister was really in the power of this fiend, that I fell unconscious.

"When I recovered, everything was dark and silent. Not a soul was to be seen. My horse had vanished, and I found that I had been robbed of everything I had about me.

"I returned to the hostelry, where I found the host and all his people talking of us, and wondering what had become of my sister. From them I quickly learned how Carnot had got hold of my sister. He had sent a sailor to say that I had met with an accident a couple of miles away. My sister believed it, for my long absence seemed to point to it. Unwell as she was, she left with the sailor, and, as I have told you, she was carried off by Carnot, who had heavily bribed a number of smugglers to assist him.

"From that night I never saw my sister again until——"

Here again the Count paused, and seemed unable to continue.

At last, however, he said, in low, hoarse tones:

"Until I saw her in one of the lowest parts of London—dead!"

"Dead!" gasped all present.

"Ay; she had poisoned herself. Just before her death she placed a sum of money in the hands of a man who had a little pity for her, and a letter for me.

"This man solemnly swore that he would endeavour to find me, and eventually, by the merest accident, he succeeded.

"When he told me where my sister had been confined by the inhuman monster, Carnot, I hastened there; but too late. My sister was dead!

"I had her decently buried, and waited for days for Carnot, but he never came. Here," he added, as he took a faded letter from his pocket-book, "is the letter my poor sister wrote:

"MY DARLING BROTHER:

"When will this letter find you? Ah! when? When the grave has closed over me for months or years?

"Victor, I am about to die. You know why; do you not, dear brother? You well know that I cannot again look into your face.

"Oh! why did I not die when my father died?

"I cannot, will not, tell you of my fearful sufferings since I was forced from you by the double-dyed scoundrel Carnot.

"It is sufficient to say that he has continually treated me with the greatest brutality. I have been under lock and key in this house ever since.

"But why is it that I should speak of myself? Victor, I have a terrible revelation to make.

"Carnot has been in league with the lawyer, Jean Lascelles, and he told me that between them they have realised all your property. I do not think there can be any doubt about this, for Carnot showed me many deeds which I know should be in the hands of Lascelles.

"Ah! how the last words of the wretch —he has not long left me—continue to ring in my ears. What are they? I will tell you, brother. He said: '*So you see that I have kept my word. I swore to ruin both of you, and I have done so.*'

"Oh! Victor, by your love for me, swear before high Heaven that you will track this atrocious ruffian down and that you will punish him!

"Adieu! dear brother; may God guard you and pardon your heart-broken sister,

"MARIE."

"On my knees beside her corpse I swore to find Carnot and kill him! Then I saw my sister properly buried and hastened to France.

"I found that what my sister had written was but too true. Lascelles and Carnot had worked hand in hand and had disposed of all my deeds and securities, having forged my authority.

"But it appeared that they had quarrelled over the spoil. A duel was the result, and Lascelles was shot through the heart.

"Carnot consequently came in for the whole of the money. But I was by no means ruined, for a banker in Paris held what was really a small fortune.

"I set to work to find Carnot, but it was a total failure. I spent money right and left, but it was of no use. I could get no trace of him at all. Then I joined the army, in which, as you know, I remained until recently

"Four days ago while seated outside a hostelry in the Oxford-road, a horseman rode up, and instantaneously I recognised him. It was Carnot?

"At once I leapt to my feet. Carnot saw and recognised me, and putting spurs to his horse fled like the wind. And yet I thought I was so altered that the wretch would not recognise me.

"I mounted my horse and gave chase, but

missed him. However, I did not despair. I made inquiries here and there, and finally tracked him to Burnham."

"Are you sure he is there now?" asked Jack.

"As certain as that you are here. He passes as an Englishman, and I must admit that he speaks English better than myself——"

"Bedad!" interrupted Brian, "then he must speak it like a native."

"He does; and that fact enables him to complete the deception."

"What does he call himself?"

"Mr. Thomas Silverlock. He is the owner of the largest mansion in Burnham—Silverlock Manor—and frequently, I was told, gives the grandest entertainments. But I was informed that he keeps six men servants, and these are all Frenchmen. From what I could make out, they are something *more* than mere servants. They are a sort of bodyguard."

"Pardon me, Count," said Brian; "why didn't you gain admittance to the house—get an audience wid the black-hearted villain, and blow his brains out?"

The Count shook his head.

"No," he said, "it must be a duel between us."

"A duel is it? Faith, I'd see him hanged first. What, you, a rale gintleman, foight a duel with a bla'guard loike that?"

"It must be so. It is the custom of our country."

"Well, thin, it's a bad custom intoirely; at least it is in a case like this. Don't you think so, Jack?"

"Upon my word I do. Such a cold-blooded, brutal hound, deserves to be hanging at the end of a rope."

"With the poor lady's letter pinned to his breast—bad cess to him!"

"Count," said Jack, "I am inclined to fancy that what you think as to the servants being a sort of bodyguard is correct. And you may rely upon it that, having seen you, he will be more than ever prepared for anything. Now, I propose that I and Sergeant Crank, as well as Ned and Brian, accompany you."

The sergeant rubbed his hands with glee.

A chance of taking part in an adventure was to him like bread and meat to a starving man.

"Most sincerely do I thank you," said Count Victor; "but I am thinking of lady Flora, of Mrs. Barrington——"

"Jack must please himself so far as I am concerned," interrupted Flora. "If I speak candidly, I should say that I should be pleased indeed to know that he had taken part in an enterprise which ended in the punishment of so monstrous a villain as you have described."

"Flora speaks for me," said Mrs. Barrington, warmly; "but I agree with my Jack when he says that the man ought to hang at the end of a rope."

"What does the sergeant say?" asked Ned.

"Say?" replied Crank, "Lord bless you! I wouldn't miss such a treat for any amount!"

"Nor I," said Brian.

"Well, let us set about drawing up the necessary plans," said Jack, "for a short time we must endeavour to forget Gasper Grimsby and Caleb Corder. But, as soon as ever this job is over, we will return to them."

Early on the following evening, the party of five set out on horseback, each being thoroughly well armed.

Count Victor de Montsorel was the last to leave the house.

He sought Mrs. Barrington, took her by the hand, and gravely led her into the library.

"Ruth," he said tenderly, "as you are aware, I am about to endeavour to force this man to fight a duel. It may be that I may fall——"

"Oh, Victor," murmured Mrs. Barrington, "do not say that. Through you God will surely punish that man."

"I trust so. But, in the event of my falling, Jack will place in your hands a letter and certain documents by which you will become entitled to all I die possessed of. Nay, do not weep. Listen, Ruth. Should I return and ask you to become my wife, will you consent?"

"Yes, Victor, yes; and, by my devotion, I will try to blot from your memory the fearful past."

The Count took her in his arms, and kissed her again and again.

"Good bye," he said, "and may God bless you! You will pray for my safety."

"All of us will, with all our hearts."

Another minute and he was in the saddle.

"Now for Burnham," said Brian, "and for this black-hearted thafe o' the world, and the loikes of him. Be me sowl I'd loike to *Burnham* all!"

* * * *

The information which the Count had received in reference to Pierre Carnot was corect.

At Burnham and the surrounding neighbourhood he was known as "Princely Silverlock," on account of the profuse way in which he spent money.

"Easy come, easy go!"

His entertainments were something to be remembered, for no expense whatever was spared.

The poorer classes bowed down to and almost worshipped him ; while the rich were always glad to partake of his hospitality and to compliment him on his "superb tastes."

These never troubled themselves as to the manner in which "Mr. Silverlock" obtained his money.

But, like everybody, he had enemies, and these were not slow to hint that it was possible the money was not honestly come by, and that, some day, things might come to a sudden stop.

"Silverlock Manor" was decidedly the finest mansion in Burnham, as it was also the largest.

So large was it that only a part was used, many of the rooms being permanently closed.

Mr. Silverlock purchased it of a man who had to make himself scarce in the country as quickly as possible, and therefore no doubt he obtained it for half its real value.

He engaged four English female servants, but his men servants, to the number of six, he obtained from France, and at first they caused a great deal of comment, for they were more like troopers than servants, and were always sullen, and by no means inclined to be communicative.

But the female servants could have added more.

They could have said that Silverlock, to some extent, appeared afraid of them.

On the same night that our friends left London for Burnham, Mr. Silverlock was making his final arrangements for the entertainment of a score of gentlemen whom he had invited to a card-party.

On occasions like these, of course, gentlemen only were present.

Invitations had been sent out some days previously, or it is more than likely that they would not have been sent at all.

For, for the first time in many years, a black cloud hung over Mr. Silverlock's (or Pierre Carnot's) head.

He had fully believed that Count Victor de Montsorel had died years before.

He had caused the strictest inquiries to be made in France again and again ; he had even inquired, through others, of the banker in Paris whom he knew transacted business for the Count.

But without result.

The banker's reply was that nothing had been seen of the Count for years, and that the money at his credit had not been claimed.

It was, therefore, but natural that he should arrive at the conclusion that the Count was dead.

He thought it quite possible that he had met with some accident abroad, and had been buried without his name becoming known.

He never thought that it was possible the count had instructed his bankers to say that he was dead.

Pierre Carnot's cunning face wore a moody expression as he sat before the gilded table in his private room.

He was not thinking of the pleasures of a card-party.

Other thoughts were uppermost in his mind, and the chief was, would it not be better to at once leave the country ?

At last he roused himself, and finished writing a few words to each of those invited, to the effect that the party would, without fail, take place on the following evening.

"They are my friends," he muttered, " with but one exception, and he, I am well aware, is a most estimable person. I long to make his acquaintance."

He placed his hand upon the bell, and one of the female servants appeared.

"Tell Jean Croix I want him," said Carnot, without looking up.

In a few moments a tall, thin, middle-aged Frenchman entered the room.

This man, among other things, had the "honour" of being, to some extent, Carnot's adviser.

He had come of a good family, and had received an excellent education—considering the times.

But, like his companions, he had sunk lower and lower in the social scale, and, finally, was glad to seize upon anything which would put a few pieces in his pocket.

It was this very man who, under pretence of being an old servant, had made inquiries respecting the Count.

He had two great faults.

Primo—A great affection for drink, and he cared not a straw what it was so that it had no connection with water.

Secundo—An uncontrollable propensity to pry into his master's secrets.

And he had discovered many, and, as he considered, very valuable ones ; but he was wise enough to keep his mouth shut.

"Jean," said Carnot, " are you perfectly sober ?"

"*Oui*—as sober as Monsieur the Judge."

"In that case take these notes."

"Now ?"

"At once."

"The night is dark ?"

"Take a lantern with you," sneered Carnot.

"Have I to go far?"

"The directions are upon each note."

Jean slowly picked them up, one after the other, and examined them.

"Three or four miles altogether," he said.

"You can do it in an hour on horseback."

"What, must I not stop for refreshments?"

"Take them with you. But be off—be off. Yet wait. You have a note addressed to Mr. Hillson, at Crome House. Do you know it?"

"Aye, I know the house. But I know not the gentleman."

"Neither do I. I have not seen him yet."

"He is the rich gunsmith, monsieur."

"I am aware of that. You will obtain an answer from him."

"*Oui*—yes, monsieur. Anything else?"

"Keep yourself sober."

With a grunt Jean left the room, and, in half an hour, the house.

The first house at which he had to call was distant half a mile away.

But, before he proceeded to it, he bore to the left, and called at an hostelry, where he partook of a small bottle of wine.

Not the faintest idea had he that he had been followed.

But he had, and the one who had followed him was Ned Rattles.

All our friends had put up at this very hostelry.

Ned at once ran upstairs, and when Jean rode away again he was this time followed by Jack.

Jean, was just about to cross a small common when Jack rushed forward and seized the horse's bridle.

Jean, who was quite unarmed, uttered a shrill cry of alarm.

"All right, my friend," said Jack, in French, "I will not harm you if——"

"Ha!" cried Jean—"a Frenchman."

"By no means. I am an Englishman. You speak English?"

"I do."

"Good. Then we will converse in that language."

"What do you mean by stopping my horse like that?" demanded Jean, who had partially recovered himself.

"I want you to come with me."

"*Diable!* Where to?"

"The hostelry you have just left."

"No, no; I cannot. Business——"

"Hang your business! You will come with me, I say. If you refuse I will put a ball through your body."

And Jean heard the click of a trigger.

This caused him to go nearly mad with fear.

"I return with you, monsieur. *Ma foi!* I desire not to die yet."

Jack, therefore led the horse to the hostelry, and assisted Jean to dismount. Then he led him upstairs.

"If this is one of the so-called body-guard," thought Jack, "they are a very brave lot of men."

In a few seconds Jean found himself in the presence of the Count, Ned, Brian, the sergeant and the host.

"Yes," said the latter, "that is Jean Croix. Mr. Silverlock's principal servant."

"Most true," said Jean, looking around him in astonishment. "I have that honour."

"Oh, it's an honour is it?" muttered Brian.

When the host had departed Jack said:

"Listen to me, my friend. Where would you rather be—in France or in England?"

"Oh, monsieur, if I had the chance I would prefer *ia belle* France, for there I have friends, while here—pah! I make none."

"Why?"

"I am not allowed."

"I understand. Now, if you had the opportunity of earning five thousand francs would you seize it?"

Jean opened wide his eyes and mouth, but made no reply.

The mention of—to him—so vast a sum had taken his breath away.

"The fact of it is," continued Jack, with great calmness but firmness, "as the principal servant of Mr. Silverlock, alias Pierre Carnot——"

"Ha!" interrupted Jean, opening his eyes still wider, "how know you that?"

"No matter; we do know it. You see few things escape English officers."

"Officers? Are you officers?"

"Ay."

"Of justice?"

"Certainly—of *justice*."

There was no falsehood about this. They were officers, and endeavouring to see justice done.

Jack continued:

"I was about to say that, as the principal servant of Monsieur Carnot, you, no doubt, know a great deal of his private business."

Jean nodded.

"Well," continued Jack, "we will pay you for revealing what you know. Look, here is a purse containing one thousand francs."

Jean, tremblingly picked it up.

He seemed about to lay it down again, when Jack said:

"Come, pocket it!"

Jean hesitated; but it was only for one moment.

The next he had pocketed it.

"We are not hitting it off so well together lately," he thought.

"Now," said Jack, "you are in your master's confidence ? "

"To a great extent—yes."

"What have you learned within the past few days ? "

"He has told me but little ; but I am aware that he is frightened, monsieur—he fears, he trembles, he is appre—— what do you call it, monsieur ? "

"Apprehensive ? "

"Ah, *oui*—yes."

"What of ? "

"That he will be pounced upon by a man whom he thought was dead."

"Do you know the name of the man ? "

"I do. It is Monsieur le Comte Victor de Montsorel."

"Good," said Jack, turning and pointing to the Count. "Behold him ! That is Monsieur le Comte ! "

"*Pardieu !* You cannot mean it ? "

The Count produced and handed the astounded Jean a paper.

Jean opened it and read it.

It was a letter "to all whom it may concern" from the bankers in Paris, proving that the holder was the Count.

"Years ago ! " said Jean, returning the paper with a low bow. "I made inquiries respecting the Count at that very bank, and they told me he was dead."

"Certainly," replied the Count ; "they had my instructions to that effect."

"Are you aware of the reason that Pierre Carnot is afraid of the Count ? " asked Jack.

"*Non ;* but I am aware that he has had part of his fortune.

"And has squandered it, I suppose ? "

"Not at all, monsieur. With the money he possessed himself of he gambled in Paris, in Geneva, and in London. He was successful, and trebled the amount."

"And you, knowing that he swindled the Count out of a fortune, took a share of it ? " asked Jack, quietly.

"I ? Never ! "

"You received certain amounts of it in wages. What is that but taking it ? "

"I was not supposed to know."

"But you *did* know ; and the law of this country is that a man who knowingly takes a share in the proceeds of a robbery is a partner in the crime or an accessory after it."

Jean turned deadly pale.

"And the punishment ? " he whispered.

"Death ! "

"*Mon Dieu*—I should be shot until I was dead."

"No, you would be hanged. But, if you will assist us, nothing shall happen to you ; and you shall get clear away to France with another four thousand francs in your pocket."

"I agree."

"He is a man on whom an impression can be made," whispered Jack to the Count. "Give him an outline of Carnot's crime."

The Count did so, and it produced a marked effect on Jean.

Whatever the man's shortcomings, there was not the slightest doubt that the Count's recital horrified him.

The story, too, made many things clear to him.

"Monsieur le Comte," he said, "I will declare to you that I will do whatever you may so direct."

He meant, of course, that he would be prepared to obey him.

"Good," said the Count ; I believe you."

"Messieurs," said Jean, "I do assure you that I have done many things in my lifetime that I would like not mentioned ; but as to injure a girl so that she takes her life—*sacré*, never ! "

"Where were you bound when I stopped you ? " asked Jack.

Jean told him, and produced the notes, which the friends closely examined.

"I see," continued Jack ; these gentlemen are your master's friends ? "

"All but one, and that one he has not yet seen. But he has often heard of him. He is a great man in London. This is the note—Mr. Hillson, Crome House."

"What is he ? "

"Gunsmith to the Court."

"You are sure your master has never seen him ? "

"Certain. He spoke of it just before I set out."

"I have it ! " cried Jack," an excellent idea has struck me. Listen : I will take the note to Mr. Hillson myself and will explain all. I will get him to allow me to impersonate him, and, by that means, I shall at once obtain admission to the house."

"Good ! Most excellent," cried the Count.

"And you, my friend," continued Jack to Jean, "will give your five comrades some refreshments in one of the rooms below, and, at the proper time, lock them in."

"Bedad ! " cried Brian, who felt inclined to dance with glee. It's a good gineral you'd make, Jack."

"Now come, Monsieur Jean," continued Jack," "do you proceed direct to Crome House. I will follow. When we reach the house, do you leave me and deliver your other notes. Then return to your master, explain your delay by saying that your horse threw you, and utter not another word. You understand this?"

"*Oui;* perfectly. Monsieur speaks like a book. Perhaps monsieur might like to tell me his name?"

"I'll tell you, me honey," said Brian, "it's Gallant Jack. Have you ever heard of him before?"

"Times out of plenty—*oui.* I bow to Monsieur le Gallant Jack."

Jack supplied him with a tumbler of excellent wine, and then accompanied him to the road, down which they were soon travelling; though, for fear that they might be seen, Jack kept at a considerable distance behind.

*   *   *   *

On the following evening, at the hour of ten, every gentleman but one had arrived.

That one was Mr. Hillson.

"Mr. Silverlock" was disappointed, and he looked it.

He thought it would be a fine thing to introduce Mr. Hillson to his friends.

But at half-past ten, Mr. Hillson was announced, and there was a rush to meet him.

But it was not the wealthy gunsmith and inventor who walked into the room.

It was our hero.

"Gentlemen," he said, "as the hour is so late, I will, without delay, inform you that you are all mistaken. I am *not* Mr. Hillson, though, in order to gain admittance here, it was necessary that I should be so announced."

A bomb with its ominous hiss falling at the feet of Mr. Silverlock could not have startled him more.

"*Not* Mr. Hillson?" he gasped, speaking in faultless English. "Then who are you?"

"The bearer of a challenge to you to fight a duel to the death."

The gentleman present drew back in astonishment.

"Was the speaker mad?" some asked themselves.

"A challenge?" said Carnot. From whom?"

"From Count Victor de Montsorel."

Carnot, instantaneously turning ghastly pale, staggered back.

But, remembering that the eyes of his his friends were upon him, he struggled frantically to control himself.

He even tried to force a smile; but that was a dismal failure.

"Gentlemen,' he said, "this is the first time I have heard the name of such a person."

"It is a lie?" said Jack slowly. "You are well aware that he is your countryman, and the brother of the poor girl who, through your persecution, destroyed herself.

"Gentlemen, this man is not an Englishman, he is a Frenchman, and his real name is Pierre Carnot."

"Jean? Jean!" yelled Carnot, "the men the men—a madman is in the house!"

Jean appeared, but not the men.

They had been locked in a room below, and their yells and hammerings to be released were now plainly heard.

"Jean Croix," said Jack, "you have heard what I said?"

"Yes, monsieur."

"Am I correct—or am I simply standing here telling a parcel of falsehoods?"

"Monsieur speaks the truth."

"Wretch!" shrieked Carnot, drawing a dagger, and dashing towards Jean, "Am I, then, indebted to you for this?"

But Jack checked him.

Seizing him by the collar, he hurled him aside.

The eighteen or nineteen gentlemen present, of course, desired to be enlightened, and Jack told them the whole of the shameful story.

"Many Englishman," he concluded, when they had found the man who had been guilty of so monstrous a crime, would instantly have slain him. But the Count desires him to fight."

"And if he refuses?" asked one present.

Jack threw back his cloak, and took out a long, stout rope.

"If he refuses," he said, "I and my friends will string him up to the highest tree hereabouts."

"And, by Heavens!" cried a dozen voices, he deserves it.

Everyone saw, from Carnot's appearance, that he was as guilty as ever man could be.

The sight of the rope made him tremble violently.

Several gentlemen turned, as if about to depart.

But Jack stopped them.

"I beg of you to wait," he said, "and see fair play. The Count and three of my friends are at this moment in the grounds at the back of this house."

"May I ask who addresses us?" asked one of the guests.

"My name, sir, is John Barrington—Colonel Barrington."

"What!" cried another, "Gallant Jack?"

"I am so called," replied Jack.

"We are delighted to make your acquaintance, and regret that it is under such very melancholy circumstances. I am sure none of us will object to stay and see that there is fair play."

The others at once expressed their willingness, and turned to Carnot.

He had been considering what he should do.

He decided to fight, for he felt certain that, if he refused, the rope would be his portion.

He therefore announced his intention to fight.

"Listen, then," said Jack, "in a duel it is uncertain who will fall; for sometimes the cleverest man becomes the victim. Now it may be that the Count may fall.

"In that case you will be allowed to leave the country unmolested. On the other hand *you* may fall, and so I propose that, ere you go out you write, declaring that all the property you die possessed of is to go to the Count. Two or three of the gentlemen here present will, I am sure, witness it."

"No!" thundered Carnot; though I now admit I *am* Pierre Carnot, and that I received the Count's property, I will sign no paper."

"Enough," said Jack; what you have said is quite sufficient. These gentlemen will be prepared to prove your statement."

Too late Carnot saw this.

The whole party now moved to the grounds.

Carnot was in the centre, but Jack took good care to keep beside him.

In the grounds, in the centre of a clump of tall, graceful oaks, was the Count, Ned, Brian, and the sergeant—the latter having charge of two cases of pistols, which had been sent by no less a person than Mr. Hillson, the gunsmith.

The moon being at the full they were enabled to see pretty well what they were about.

One thing too was certain, they would not be interrupted.

Carnot for an instant looked at the Count, but it was *only* for an instant, for the Count's stern, piercing eyes caused him to shudder.

One of the gentlemen now asked in what way the duel was to be fought.

Before answering, Jack asked Carnot which he would prefer—swords or pistols—and he selected the latter.

The boxes containing the pistols were accordingly placed before him by Sergeant Crank, who invited him to select which he chose.

The selection having been made, Jack said:

"This is how I propose that the duel be fought: The combatants will be placed back to back. They will then walk forty paces—then fire!"

This arrangement was agreed to, and the two men were placed together.

At a signal from the sergeant each took forty paces.

Then the sergeant, in the stentorian tones which had rang out on many a terrible battle plain, cried:

"Fire!"

Swiftly the two men turned, and the weapons were discharged simultaneously.

At once the Count dropped his pistol and staggered back.

But he did not fall.

Brian in an instant was beside him.

It was soon seen what had happened.

A ball had struck the Count in the right hand.

It was impossible for him to fire again with the same hand.

"No matter, gentlemen," he said, "I will fire with the left."

Carnot was exultant.

He was uninjured, and considered it certain that the Count had no chance at all with his left hand.

To tell the truth, he was not the only one who thought so.

"By all the powers!" whispered Brian to Ned, who seemed rooted to the ground, "if the Count falls, I'll make him foight *me*, the dhirty spalpeen!"

Again they were placed back to back, and Carnot had the impudence to whisper:

"Don't you wish you had not sought me out, Count?"

The Count made no reply.

He was thinking of but one thing—that was his sister!

Again they walked the required number of paces, and again the sergeant cried out:

"Fire!"

As before, the weapons were fired simultaneously.

And, as we may say, exactly at the same instant one wild, piercing cry rang out.

Then followed a loud thud.

Carnot had fallen!

A great rush was made to him, but Jack was the first to reach his side.

"The wretch has met with his deserts," he said; "he is dead! See—the ball has entered his heart!"

Such was the case.

"Considering the black crime of which he was guilty," said one of the gentlemen, "his death has been far too easy."

"True," said Jack; "but the Count has kept his word. Gentlemen, on behalf of the

Count, I thank you for your attendance, and I am sure I may rely upon you to prove the words that villain uttered."

Those present declared that they would be most happy to do so, and they crowded round and congratulated the Count, who, by this time had had his wound attended to by the sergeant.

It was not a serious one, the ball having broken one of the small bones.

"What is to be done now, Jack," asked Brian.

"Well," answered Jack; "what we shall do now is this—we shall take possession of Carnot's house, and turn the men out with the exception of Jean. As to you, Brian, will you undertake a journey alone?"

"Bedad I will, wid all my heart."

"Go, then, to the hostelry. Mount the best horse, and ride to London with the news that all is well!"

"I will—I will. Shall I set off at once?"

"Yes, at once."

Brian was off like a shot.

Carnot's body was carried to Silverlock Manor, and placed in one of the lower rooms. Then the men servants, with the exception of Jean, were dismissed with a sum of money and the manor was closed.

The Count, with the assistance of Gallant Jack and our other friends, had indeed carried out his vow.

CHAPTER LX.

SETH SAUNDER'S PLAN—HOW THE TRAP WAS SET FOR CALEB—HOW HE BACKED INTO IT, AND WHAT FOLLOWED.

GASPER GRIMSBY had retured to Hammersmith, where he considered it convenient to remain for a little while.

There it was that the news reached him that Gallant Jack had been discovered, and that a reward was offered for the arrest of "one Gasper Grimsby," who had attempted to murder him.

Gasper's whole thoughts were now directed to Caleb Corder.

It is not too much to say that, if he could have laid hands upon him, he would willingly have parted with all the money he possessed. The diamonds he had not attempted to dispose of.

He resolved to retain them until he could dispose of them to advantage.

"If I can but put Caleb Corder out of the way," he thought, "I can devote all my time to Barrington. By Heaven! I will take care that I do not leave him next time until I am perfectly *certain* that he is dead.

"Plan after plan have I thought of with regard to Corder—curse the hound !—and have been compelled to reject them. And why?

"The principal reason is simply because I have no one to assist me. He, it seems, can command plenty of assistance, and no doubt he is, at this very moment, planning to get hold of *me*.

"Now, I wonder whether I could rely upon the man this barber recommends? Why not? I will try him. A few gold pieces will probably dazzle him. I will have an interview with him at once."

Downstairs he went to the barber.

"I will see the man you spoke of," he said ; "when can I do so?"

"Within a few minutes. And if you have any difficult job to undertake, you can depend upon Seth Saunders."

"What does he pay you for the recommendation?"

"Pay me? Nothing. He would not take anything from *me*."

"No? Why not?"

"I am not *high* enough."

"I see. Where does the man lodge? because I will find him out."

"Lodge? Bless you, he does not lodge anywhere. He has his *own* house."

This startled Gasper.

He had thought the man part of the scum of Hammersmith.

"He will not do," he thought.

"Yes," continued the barber, "he has his own house. That was saved from the wreck?'

"The wreck? What wreck?"

"Why, you see, Seth Saunders was, at one time, a lawyer."

Gasper stared, while the barber smiled at his astonishment.

"Yes," he continued, "it is a fact, I assure you. He was a lawyer, but he had a knack of converting to his own use other people's property; just as you might do, and——"

"What?" interrupted Gasper, "do you dare to insinuate that I am a thief?"

"I always keep my mouth shut."

"Well, on this occasion you opened it with a vengeance."

"To speak the truth only."

"That I am a thief?"

"Well, *the placards say so*," said the barber.

Gasper's jaw fell at these words.

"I don't understand," he said.

"You are aware that a reward is offered for one Gasper Grimsby, alias Captain Gravelotte, and that the placards contain a description to which you answer in every particular?"

Gasper's answer was to slip five gold pieces into the man's ready hand.

"More," he said, "if you keep silent."

"Ay, you may trust me, sir," grinned the barber. "But as to Seth Saunders. He laid his hands on too much, you see, and the law put its heel down upon him and nearly crushed him.

"It took away from him all the property he had acquired except the house I speak of—that being overlooked—and his name was for ever erased from the roll of attorneys.

"*Now*, what was he to do?—for he had no wife with a fortune. He remained for some time in his house, like a snail in his shell, but hunger, and a desire for activity, compelled him to creep out, and look about him.

"He quickly found clients, and from them obtained large sums of money."

"For doing what?"

"Doing? Lor' bless you—ask yourself. Seth is not at all particular. And if ever there was a man to plot and plan, and tell a barefaced lie without a blink—it is Seth Saunders."

"Your recommendation is first class. I think he is the very man for me. How old is he?"

"About fifty, I should think."

"Well, just take me to his house."

Accordingly the pair set out, and soon they reached the house occupied by Seth Saunders, and a very good one it was too, though it was a terribly old-fashioned one.

The door was answered by an elderly woman who, recognising the barber, admitted both without question.

The barber, who, by his unhesitating movements, appeared to be well acquainted with the house, led the way upstairs.

Halting on the first landing he called out: "Seth!"

An opposite door was opened, and a remarkably tall, lank individual, with a fearfully long face, and equally long hair, and who wore an enormous pair of spectacles, appeared.

"Hillo?" he said, "oh, it's you, eh?"

"Ay," replied the barber, "brought a gentleman that has business for you."

"Good. Pray enter, sir."

"I will go," said the barber, "two is company and three is not."

Seth Saunders nodded and grinned (it *was* a grin!) and, entering the room, closed the door.

The grin was on his peculiar face as he turned to Gasper.

But then, lo! it instantaneously vanished.

"Excuse my curiosity," said Seth, "or I should say my stare of amazement; but the fact is that you answer so well to a recently-issued placard, that I am bound to look surprised. But now to business, What can I do for you?"

"I am informed that you are the very man to keep a secret!"

"Correct."

"Of whatever nature."

"Precisely."

"And if I told you that I am the Gasper Grimsby described——"

"I should reply that I knew it. But do not fear, I shall not betray you. Now tell me the whole of your business—reserve nothing, and if I can assist you I will."

For over two hours the two men sat concocting a plot which would have the effect of completely crushing Caleb Corder.

Seth was decidedly ingenious in working out a plot, and it was a moral certainty that Caleb Corder would walk blindfold into it.

A house was to be hired in the neighbourhood of the Strand, and Caleb lured into it.

On the following evening, Seth sent a man of the name of Newman—a cunning rascal like his employer—to Caleb, and he did not leave him until Caleb—for the sum of one hundred pounds—(which was paid down) and a thousand in prospect—agreed to assist Newman's master in putting away the individual who was obnoxious.

* * * *

On the following afternoon Jack was with the Count, who was arranging his affairs, and in consequence of the wound he had received, could not write; so Jack, with his usual good nature, consented to act *pro tem.* as his secretary.

The ladies were upstairs, while the Sergeant was in the kitchen, where he was amusing himself with "chaffing" Mistress Morrell, a very pretty young widow who had been appointed housekeeper, and a very fine spread of some delicacies of the season.

A very fine occupation for the Sergeant this! It suited him "down to the ground."

Well, he deserved ease and enjoyment now, if any man did.

Suddenly Brian and Ned entered the library, both of them apologising for the interruption.

Both were excited; that Jack could at once see.

"Jack," said Brian, "we've seen the spalpeen!"

"Who? Caleb?"

"No, bedad—Gasper Grimsby."

"Never!"

"A fact, me honey. As large as life we saw him go into a house just off the Haymarket."

"Are you *sure* it was him?"

"Yes," said Ned, "there is no doubt about that; and, from the way he entered the house and was received by the servant, it is evident that he is residing there."

"He may *not* be, though."

"I feel certain he is."

"Did he ride up on horseback?"

"No, he was on foot. And he walked along the street as if the whole of it belonged to him, didn't he, Brian?"

"He did, bedad. I could scarcely keep my hands off him, the spalpeen. May the divil fly away wid him!"

"No, that's true enough," smiled Ned; "it was as much as I could do to keep him back."

"And you are perfectly sure that he did not see either of you?"

"Oh, perfectly!"

"Who do you say answered the door—a servant?"

"So he appeared to us."

"Man or woman?"

"A man."

"Depend upon it something is afloat," said the Count.

"Yes," said Jack thoughtfully, "there is scarcely any doubt of that."

After a pause he continued:

"What a pity it was you did not think of ascertaining to whom the house belonged."

"True," said Ned; "but the fact is we were so excited at seeing Gasper. But that can soon be remedied. Suppose I go at once and endeavour to find out?"

"Aye, do. But be careful, for Gasper Grimsby will keep his eyes open."

Ned accordingly set out, and was absent for an hour. When he returned he informed Jack that the house, which was known as "Park House," had been hired by two gentlemen, and who said they should stay perhaps a couple of weeks. The description given by one of them was beyond all doubt that of Gasper Grimsby.

"Enough," said Jack, trying hard to suppress his excitement. "Go below, Ned. Brian is there with the Sergeant. Tell both to come up at once. To-night, under cover of the darkness, we will surround the house!"

"I am sorry that my wound will prevent my lending much assistance," said the Count, "but I will be present."

*　　*　　*　　*

Caleb Corder was in high spirits on the following evening when he set off for Park House. He had simply to "put a man out of the way" to pocket another thousand. The door was opened by the man Newman, who conducted him to Seth, who awaited "Captain Swift" in a handsome room on the first floor. Seth informed Caleb that he was about to be visited by a gentleman to whom he owed the sum of twenty thousand pounds, but as he was not in a position to pay that amount he had decided to put the person out of the way. Caleb was completely deceived.

"What you will have to do," said Seth, "is simply this. You will pretend to be my secretary, and you will go into that ante-room and shut the door. But, first, you will place your weapons in this drawer, for, of course, an armed secretary would look suspicious. When you hear a knock at the street-door it will be the gentleman I expect. But, so that no mistake may be made, I will rush in and tell you. Then, when the gentleman walks in, you will go round to the table, and pretend to seat yourself. Instead of that you will draw your pistols, and shoot him dead!"

This Caleb understood.

Seth thereupon left him to get a bottle of wine. Having procured that he ascended to to the second floor.

There, armed to the teeth, was Gasper Grimsby.

"Well?" he queried.

"All is working splendidly," said Seth. "I showed him the ante-room, and he has placed, not only his pistols, but his sword in the drawer. Now it is *your* turn. I think I have done all I can."

"Exactly. Now I will descend. There is no danger of his leaving the room as I am descending?"

"No danger at all."

Gasper thereupon rapidly, but cautiously, descended the stairs.

Newman was at the street-door, which he opened.

Gasper went without, and knocked loudly upon it.

A few seconds afterwards Seth entered the room in which Caleb was.

"He is here," he whispered. "Quick!—the ante-room!"

Caleb disappeared within it, and Seth closed the door.

At once he went to the table, opened the drawer, took out the pistols and sword, and reclosed it.

In less than two minutes Gasper entered the room.

Like lightning he closed and locked the door, drew a pistol from his belt, and cocked it. In a few more seconds Caleb came out of the ante-room.

What pen could describe his appearance when his eyes fell upon Gasper's face?—a face that was perfectly fiendish in its expression.

For a moment he stood still, as if turned to stone.

Then, with a wild cry, he made a mad rush to the drawer and tore it open.

When he saw that the weapons had disappeared another wild cry left his lips, and his arms dropped to his sides.

He saw all now.

The plot which had been formed and worked out was as plain to him as the sun at noonday.

Gasper Grimsby was there to kill him; of that he was certain.

He had spent a lot of money in getting him there, it is true; but if he slew him, the greater part of it would be found on him.

Gasper, who had been watching his frantic movements with satisfaction, was the first to speak.

"It is me, Caleb Corder," he said. "Gasper Grimsby stands before you. You recognise me, don't you, eh?"

"Ay!" replied Caleb, in hoarse tones; "and do you call this a fair way of having revenge?"

"Fair? You talk of fair way? Ho! ho!"

"You are well armed, and yet you saw that my arms were taken away."

"To be sure. What? do you fancy that I would fight a duel with you? No, no! Not with a low hound like you! I could have pounced upon you elsewhere, time after time, but I refrained because I wanted to talk to you first, and not only to talk but to torture."

"Torture!" gasped Caleb.

"Ay, torture. It is not my intention to kill you at once. I will kill you inch by inch."

"Fiend!"

Gasper grinned.

"Fiend if you like," he said, "but you must admit that I am the cleverer man of the two."

"I would I had the man who lured me here in my clutches for a moment."

"No doubt. You are——but do not attempt to edge round that table. It will be of no use, for the door is locked, We are here quite alone, Caleb Corder, and no one is likely to interfere.

"Shots cannot be heard from the outside. Thus you will see how carefully everything has been planned."

Caleb made no reply to this.

Like a wild beast suddenly driven to bay he stood.

"I am a dead man," he thought. "I think I know what he means by torture. Presently he will fire; I shall fall, and then, at intervals, he will plunge the point of his sword into me. I remember him doing it once in France."

Caleb was in a fearful state.

From head to heel he was bathed in perspiration.

Again and again his wild eyes wandered to the door and the window.

Gasper, however, watched him as a cat watches a mouse.

Suddenly Caleb's eyes rested upon the fire-irons.

At once he made a dash to them, and seized the poker.

As he stooped Gasper fired, but it was very low, so that the shot should not have a fatal effect.

The shot struck Caleb in the fleshy part of the thigh, but it did not cause a serious wound.

It was enough, however, to cause him to utter a terrific yell.

Turning with the heavy poker in his hand, he seized upon the wine bottle, and with his left hand hurled it with all his force at Gasper's head.

Gasper leapt aside, and the bottle, crashing against the wall, was shattered into a hundred pieces.

Then Caleb seized the massive table, and, exercising all his strength, pushed it over.

He thought to pinion Gasper against the wall, but this was a failure.

Again Gasper fired, but this time the ball went wide of its mark.

It struck the massive mirror, splintering it in every direction, and of course rendering it valueless.

Caleb now, maddened by the pain of his wound, sprang upon Gasper and dealt him a blow across the head that staggered him.

Caleb no doubt thought that Gasper was provided with two pistols only.

But he had three, and he drew the third from his pocket, and pointed it at Caleb's legs.

He wanted to "drop him" only.

But, as he pulled the trigger, Caleb seized a chair and held it before him.

In this case the pistol missed fire, and Caleb, with a fearful oath, lifted the chair and hurled it at Gasper's head.

It struck him, and inflicted an ugly wound on the cheek.

The combatants paused.

Both were breathing heavily—both were eyeing each other like a couple of maddened wild beasts.

The beautiful room already presented a sorry spectacle.

In addition to the smashed mirror, a number of costly vases had been hurled to the ground, while the pretty carpet was dotted here and there with patches of blood which had trickled from Caleb's wound.

"It is useless, Caleb Corder," said Gasper. "I have sworn to have your life, and I will have it !"

"Don't be too sure."

"I am certain of it !" hissed Gasper, as he drew his long sword. "That poker will be of no use to you."

"You cowardly hound !"

"It is my intention to torture you, Caleb Corder. I have said so before, and I say so again."

"If I had a sword, by the foul fiend I would torture *you*."

"Would you, Caleb, eh—*would* you, you low-born hound ?"

"Low born ! What are you ?"

"A gentleman, Caleb Corder—a gentleman, I say."

"In your *own* opinion, that is all."

"I repeat—a gentleman, Caleb."

"Well, if you are, give me a chance, and let a sword be brought me."

"Ho !—ho ! Shall I leave the room, and get one for you ? No—no, Caleb, no sword for you."

Caleb made a sudden dash to the window, and brought the poker down upon it, smashing the glass and some of the framework.

He thought that this might attract attention.

But there was little fear of that, because the window of this room looked out upon the back.

Gasper advanced steadily towards him, and, approaching close enough at last, he plunged the point of his sword in his breast, taking care, however, that it was only a flesh wound.

It was sufficient to cause Caleb to utter another wild cry.

The next moment he again sprang upon Gasper, beating the sword aside with the poker.

Gasper's heel kicked against the fallen chair, and he stumbled.

Of this Caleb took advantage.

In an instant he threw the poker aside, and, seizing Gasper by the throat, pressed him backwards.

It was impossible for Gasper to save himself.

Down, with a mighty crash, he went, Caleb on top of him.

The latter tried to draw one of the pistols from Gasper's belt, intending to use the butt end.

But, instead of a pistol, his hand came in contact with a dagger.

That he at once drew from its sheath.

"Ha !" he yelled, "I have *you* now ; and I will torture *you* !"

He raised the weapon, but Gasper succeeded in seizing his arm with his left hand, the while he tried to use his sword with his right.

But it had become fixed in the chair, and in pulling it out, it broke off within a foot of the hilt.

He was thus compelled to use it daggerwise,

Again and again he inflicted terrible wounds on Caleb's body ; but, at last, Caleb contrived to free his arm, and in a few moments Gasper Grimsby was a dead man.

Caleb left the dagger buried deep in his heart.

Then he attempted to rise, but he found it impossible.

He could not move an inch.

He tried to shout, but his tongue clove to the roof of his mouth.

"Dying," he gasped, "I am dying. But he is *dead*—I have killed him. He thought to have it all his own way. If I could but get into my clutches the man who spoke to me in this room. I could not leave—leave—the place goes round—my head swims—blood floats—before—before——"

The sentence died away on his bloodless lips, and, with a heavy groan, he fell prostrate upon Gasper's body.

He was dead !

Meantime something interesting was occurring without.

While the fearful fight we have described above was in progress, Jack, Brian, Ned, the Count and the Sergeant, all thoroughly well armed, made their way to Park House.

Arrived there, which they did just after the battle in the room had terminated, the Sergeant and Brian were posted at the back, with orders to prevent anyone leaving the house.

Then Jack knocked upon the front door.

Receiving no reply he kicked at it.

This time a voice asked—

"Who is it ?"

Jack promptly replied—

"Officers of justice."

"Indeed ?" said the voice, "and what do officers of justice do here ? We do not require their services."

"What do we here ?" said Jack, "we demand the person of one Gasper Grimsby."

"Who ?"

"Gasper Grimsby ?"

"We do not know him."

"No ? Well you may know him under another name. If you——"

"Go away ! go away !"

"We will stay here until you choose to open the door. And understand this—men are posted at the back ; so it is impossible for anyone in this house to get away without being seen."

No answer was returned to this ; but, while Jack and Ned were consulting as to the advisability of attempting to burst the door open, it was thrown back.

Seth Saunders appeared.

"Who are you ? Are you the present holder of this house?" asked Jack.

"No."

"Who is, then ? "

Seth Saunders turned, for his arm had been pulled by Newman.

"Better make a clean breast of it, since they have murdered each other."

"We can't tell that both are dead."

"If they are not both dead, then I never saw a dead man in my life. Did I not mount the ladder and look through the window twice ? "

Seth hesitated a moment, and then he said :

"Well, the fact is I hired the house and gave my name ; but the one who is, or was, responsib'e is the man you are in search of."

" Was ? "

"Ay ! for he is dead now."

"Gasper Grimsby is dead ? "

"Yes ; and so is Captain Swift."

"Quick !—where are they ? "

"In a room above."

"Give me the key."

"It is not in my possession. Gasper Grimsby entered the room and closed the door after him."

"It would be better if this man told the whole story," suggested the Count ; "for it is certain there is one to tell."

"Ay," said Jack, "tell us what has occurred here ; but I warn you that if you tell us falsehoods you will suffer for it."

Seth immediately told the whole story, though he took care to hold himself blameless in the matter.

It was indeed a most disgraceful story, and shocked the listeners to no small extent.

"Come," said Jack, "let us ascend. But, first, do you, Ned, tell Brian and the sergeant."

These quickly appeared, and the whole party ascended.

In a few moments they burst open the door and entered the room.

Jack, as well as the others, drew back with a cry of horror.

For some few minutes not a word was uttered by either.

Jack was the first to speak.

"By Heavens !" he said. "Here, indeed, a fearful fight has raged. Look at the pair of villains. They have fought each other in a far more determined and terrible manner than foes on a battle-field."

"They have saved each other from the rope," said the Count.

"Thank God !" said Ned, "we can wash our hands of them for ever. But what is now to be done ? "

"But one thing—inform the authorities. First, however, we will search the bodies of both."

Ned and Brian lifted Caleb from Gasper's body, and then, plainer than ever, was seen how awful the fight had been.

Caleb's pockets contained nothing but a sum of money.

It was the remains of the amount handed him by Newman.

Several papers and letters were found upon Gasper, as well as a great deal of money.

Jack watched the search with much impatience.

"No will?" he said.

"No," replied Ned, "it does not appear to be upon him."

"Tear open his coat."

This was done, and, beneath his shirt, was found a jewel-case.

It was opened, and the glittering contents displayed.

Jack took it, and read the words which had been written by his unfortunate grandfather :—

"My wife's. She left them for Ruth, and, please God, I shall live to see her wear them.

"JOHN STANMORE."

"Where on earth could he have got these ? " cried Will.

"Depend upon it he has broken into Camden House. Fool that I was not to have thought it possible that one or the other would do so."

"Bedad, then, a man can't think of everything," said Brian, "but we will go there to-morrow, and see."

When the party descended they found that Seth and Newman had taken their departure.

"Let us return at once to Laurel House," said Jack. "I long to place these jewels in my mother's hands. It will show her, more than anything, how her father repented of his cruel conduct."

CHAPTER LXI.

ON HAPPINESS THE CURTAIN FALLS.

THE following day Jack and Ned visited Camden House, which they found in possession of the authorities.

From what the officers told them they proceeded to the lawyer's house, and the woman who had charge of it, informed them how the lawyer had been found.

On the morning after the murder she had visited the house to do some work.

Failing to be answered, she became alarmed, for she remembered how ill the old man was, and she procured assistance, when the door was burst open.

A search had been made, and among other things the will had been found on the lawyer's table.

The true story of what had taken place Jack never learned.

But he was in possession of the will once more, and he at once placed it, with instructions, in the hands of an eminent lawyer.

*   *   *   *

Now that Gasper Grimsby and Caleb Corder were dead, our friends felt that they had no enemies who wished to bar their happiness; and, accordingly, they prepared for the happiness to which they were certainly entitled.

In a month from Gasper's death Jack led Lady Flora Greville to the altar, and, at the same time, Ned Rattles was married to Jenny Heathcote.

They went straight from London to Marley Manor, Hampton Court, it being understood that the others would follow later.

They did, within a couple of weeks, when no less than three marriages took place simultaneously, and at the same church, for Brian—happy Brian!—led Lydia Barrington to the altar, and was attended by the Count and Mrs. Barrington, and by the gallant Sergeant, who had persuaded Mrs. Barrington's pretty housekeeper, Mrs. Morrell, to share his fortunes.

The whole met at Marley Court, where, for a month, they were entertained by Lady Marley.

In less than six months Mrs. Barrington and Jack proved their identity, and became entitled to John Stanmore's vast property.

So at last, after many, many adventures, many of them dangerous in the extreme, the curtain falls upon perfect peace and happiness.

Our characters each lived to a green old age, frequently visiting each other, and sometimes going over the events of the past.

Despite his great fortune, our hero did not desert the army entirely; and, wherever he went, officers and soldiers had always a warm welcome for the PRIDE OF THE BRITISH ARMY,

"GALLANT JACK."

THE END.

www.ingramcontent.com/pod-product-compliance
Lightning Source LLC
Chambersburg PA
CBHW081004280626
47160CB00017B/2838